Black Duck

JANET TAYLOR LISLE

SLEUTH
PHILOMEL

For Richard Lisle, with love.

This is a work of fiction. Names, characters, places and incidents are either the product of the author's imagination or are used fictitiously. Any resemblance to current events, locales, or to living persons is entirely coincidental.

COAST GUARDS KILL THREE SUSPECTED RUM RUNNERS

FIRE ON UNARMED SPEEDBOAT BLACK DUCK WITH LARGE CARGO OF LIQUOR

NEWPORT, DEC. 30—Three alleged rum runners were killed by machine gun fire and another man was wounded near Newport shortly before 3 o'clock Sunday morning, according to the Coast Guard. The men were in a 50-foot speedboat well-known locally as the Black Duck.

The boat, carrying a cargo of 300 cases of smuggled liquor, was stumbled on in dense fog by Coast Guard Patrol Boat 290. A burst of machine gun fire killed all three men instantly in the pilot house. A fourth crew member was shot through the hand. No arms were found on board.

"The shooting is unfortunate but clearly justified by U.S. Prohibition law forbidding the trade or consumption of liquor anywhere in the United States," a Coast Guard spokesman said in a statement to reporters last night. "These rogue smugglers threaten our communities and must be stopped."

Other details were not available as authorities kept them guarded.

The Interview

A RUMRUNNER HAD LIVED IN TOWN, ONE OF the notorious outlaws who smuggled liquor during the days of Prohibition, that was the rumor. David Peterson heard he might still be around.

Where?

No one knew exactly. It was all so long ago.

Well, who was he?

This was equally vague. Someone said to ask at the general store across from the church.

It would be a miracle if the man was still alive, David thought. He'd be over eighty. If he were anywhere, he'd probably be in a nursing home by now.

But it turned out he wasn't. He still lived in town. Ruben Hart was his name.

The number listed in the telephone book doesn't answer. There is an address, though. David has his mother drop him off at the end of the driveway. It's June. School is over. He tells her not to wait.

The house is gray shingle, hidden behind a mass of bushes that have grown up in front of the windows. David isn't surprised. It's what happens with old people's homes. Plantings meant to be low hedges or decorative bushes sprout up. Over time, if no one pays attention, they get out of control. David's family is in the landscaping business and he knows about the power of vegetation. He's seen whole trees growing through the floor of a porch, and climbing vines with their fingers in the attic. Left to its own devices, nature runs amok.

David knocks on the front door. After a long pause, an old fellow in a baggy gray sweater opens up. David tells him straight out why he's come: he's looking for a story to get in the local paper.

They won't hire me, but the editor says if I come up with a good story, he'll print it. I want to be a reporter, he announces, all in one breath.

Is that so? the man says. His face has the rumpled look of a well-used paper bag, all lines and creases. But his eyes are shrewd.

I'm a senior in high school, David explains to build up his case. It's a slight exaggeration. He'll be a freshman next fall.

He receives a skeptical stare.

Then the man, who is in fact Ruben Hart himself, *still kicking,* as he says with a sly glint of his glasses, invites David in.

My wife's in the kitchen. We can go in the parlor.

David has never before heard anyone say that word, *parlor,* to describe a room in a house. He's read it in stories from English class, though, and knows what one is.

The chairs are formal and hard as a rock, just as you'd expect.

I suppose you're here to find out about the old days, Mr. Hart says. His voice is raspy-sounding, as if he doesn't use it much.

I am.

Must be the liquor Prohibition back in the 1920s you're interested in, rumrunners and hijackers, fast boats and dark nights.

Yes, sir!

I wasn't in it.

You weren't? David frowns. *I heard you were.*

I wasn't.

Well.

I guess that's that, Mr. Hart says. *Sorry to disappoint you.*

Did you know anyone who was? David asks.

I might've. Mr. Hart's glasses glint again.

Could you talk about them?

No.

That was the end of their first meeting.

A week later, David tries again. He's done some research this time, found a newspaper article from 1929 about the Coast Guard gunning down some unarmed rumrunners, and learned the names of beaches around there where the liquor was brought in.

The first rumrunners were local fishermen who wanted to make an extra buck for their families. They'd sneak cases of booze onshore off boats that brought the stuff down from Canada or up from the Bahamas. But there was too much money to be made, as there is in the drug trade today. Hardened criminals came in and formed gangs. People were shot up and murdered. The business turned vicious.

My wife's gone out, we can sit in the kitchen, Mr. Hart says this time.

When they settle, David has his plan of attack ready.

I don't want to bother you, but I read about some things and wondered if I could check them out with you. Nothing personal, just some facts.

Such as? The old man's eyes are wary.

Was Brown's Beach a drop for liquor? I read it was.

I guess there's no harm in agreeing to that. Everybody in town knew it.

And were there hidden storage cellars under the floor of the old barn out behind Riley's General Store? Across from the church, you know where I mean?

They're still there, as far as I know.

One other thing, David says. *There was a famous rum-running boat around here named the* Black Duck . . .

That was the end of their second meeting.

The man closes up, won't even make eye contact. He says his heart's acting funny and he's got to take a pill. Five minutes later David is heading back out the driveway. He hitches home this time rather than wait for his mother. He's touched on something, he knows it. There's a story there. How to pry it out of the old geezer?

He's still wondering a week later when, surprise of all

surprises, Mr. Hart calls him. He's managed to ferret out David's home number from among the dozens of Petersons in the telephone book.

I'll talk to you a bit. An old friend of mine is ill. You've been on my mind.

David can't see the connection between himself and some old friend, but he gets a ride over there as soon as he can. His father drives him this time, grumbling, *You're making me late. What's wrong with riding a bicycle? In my day, we went everywhere under our own steam.*

David doesn't answer. In a year and a half he'll be old enough to drive himself and won't need to put up with irritating comments like this.

Sorry about your friend being sick, he says to Mr. Hart. They're in the kitchen again. The wife has gone away to visit her brother out of state.

Took a turn for the worse the beginning of the week, Mr Hart says. *Jeddy McKenzie. He and I grew up together here. His dad used to be police chief in this town.*

He gazes speculatively at David. *Ever hear of Chief Ralph McKenzie?*

David says no.

Well, that was way back, during these Prohibition days you're so interested in. The law against liquor got passed and the government dumped it on the local cops to enforce. That was a laugh. What'd they think would happen? Afterward, Jeddy moved away, to North Carolina. I always hoped I'd see him again. We were close at one time. Had adventures.

What adventures? David asks.

Mr. Hart's eyes flick over him, as if he still has grave doubts about this interview. He goes ahead anyway.

Ever seen a dead body?

David shakes his head.

We found one washed up down on Coulter's Beach.

David knows where Coulter's Beach is. He swims off there sometimes. *Was it a rumrunner?* he asks.

Mr. Hart doesn't answer. He has watery blue eyes that wink around behind his glasses' thick lenses. It's hard to get a handle on his expression.

This was in the spring, 1929. Smuggling was in high gear. Thousands of cases of liquor coming in every month up and down this coast. Outside racketeers creeping in like worms to a carcass, smelling the money. People look back now and think those days were romantic, all high jinks and derring-do. They're mistaken.

David has brought a notepad along, expecting to jot down interesting facts. *Not romantic,* he writes at the top of the page. (What are *high jinks?*) After that, he forgets to write. Mr. Hart's raspy voice takes over the room.

So, Jeddy McKenzie and I came on this body.

ON COULTER'S BEACH

THE WIND HAD BLOWN IT IN.

A stiff sou'wester was in charge that day, shoving the waves against the shore like a big impatient hand. Jeddy's head never could keep a cap on in a blow. I remember how he walked bent over, holding his brim down with both hands. I stalked beside him, eyes on the sand.

"Clean beach," I'd say gloomily whenever we rounded a corner.

We'd been hunting for lobster pots since lunch and would have gone on till dinner if not for the interruption. Marked pots returned to their owners paid ten cents apiece. We were fourteen years old and in dire need of funds. You couldn't get a red penny out of your parents in those days. They didn't have anything to spare.

"There's got to be some! It blew like stink all night," Jeddy shouted over the wind.

"Well, it's blowing like murder right now," I cried back, without an inkling of how true this was about to become.

We rounded a spuming sand dune to a burst of noise. Down the beach, braying seagulls circled at the water's edge.

"Something's driving bait. Maybe a shark," Jeddy said. "Those gulls are getting in on the kill."

I shaded my eyes. "No, it's something else. I can see something floating in the water."

"Dead shark, then."

"Or a dead seal. Too small for a shark. Come on."

We took off at a jog, wind tearing at our clothes. When we got there, though, all we saw was a busted-up wooden crate knocking around in the waves. Nothing was inside, but we recognized its type. It was a bootleg case, a thing we'd come across before on the beach. If you were lucky, and we never were that I can recall, there'd be bottles still wedged inside—whiskey, vodka, brandy, even champagne—smuggled liquor that could bring a good price if you knew what to do with it. Jeddy and I weren't lawbreakers. We'd never even had a drink. But like a lot of folks along that coast we weren't against keeping our eyes open if there was a chance of profit in it.

"Coast Guard must have been sniffing around here last night," Jeddy said. "Looks like somebody had to dump their cargo fast."

"Maybe. Could be it's left over from a landing. They've been bringing stuff into the dock down at Tyler's Lane."

"How d'you know that?"

"Saw them," I boasted, then wished I hadn't. It was no secret that Jeddy's dad was on the lookout for rumrunners. Police Chief Ralph McKenzie was a stickler for the law.

Jeddy gave me a look. "You saw somebody landing their goods? At night?"

I shut my trap and inspected a schooner passing out to sea. I knew something Jeddy didn't.

"What were you doing at Tyler's at night?" he demanded. "It's way across town from your house. Ruben Hart! You're fibbing, right?"

"Well." I gave the crate a kick.

"I thought so! Next you're going to say it was the *Black Duck*."

"Maybe it was!"

"You're a liar, that's for sure. Nobody ever sees the *Duck*. My dad's been chasing her for years and never even come close. She's got twin airplane engines, you know. She does over thirty knots."

I glared at him. "I know."

"So did you see her or not?"

"Maybe I heard somebody talking."

"When?"

"Couple of days ago. It's dark of the moon this week. That's when they bring the stuff in."

"Who was talking?"

"I better not say. You'd have to tell your dad."

"I wouldn't. Honest."

I shrugged and gazed across the water to where the lighthouse was standing up on its rock, high and white as truth itself.

"Come on. I'd only have to tell him if he asked me direct, and why would he do that?" Jeddy said. "Did somebody see the *Black Duck* come in at Tyler's dock?"

"Listen, I don't know," I said, backing off. "I heard a rumor there was a landing, that's all. Whoever did it could've cracked some cases to pay off the shore crew that helped unload. That's one way they pay them. Everybody gets a few bottles."

"Well, you should know," Jeddy said, sulkily. "Your dad is probably in deep with the whole thing."

"He is not!" I drew up my defenses at this. "My dad would never break the law. He might not agree with it, but he wouldn't break it."

My father was Carl Hart, manager of Riley's General Store in town. He was a big man with a big personality, known for speaking his mind in a moment of heat, but there was nothing underhanded in him. He dealt fair and square no matter who you were, and often he was more than fair. Quietly, without even Mr. Riley knowing, he'd help out folks going through hard times by carrying their overdue accounts till they could pay. He wouldn't take any thanks for it, either, which is why my mother would find a couple of fresh-caught bluefish on our front porch some mornings, or a slab of smoked ham or an apple pie.

"Now, Carl, what is it you've done to deserve this?" she'd ask, raising an eyebrow.

He'd shake his head like it was nothing, and never answer.

My father was tough on me growing up. He was an old-fashioned believer in discipline and hard work, far beyond what was fair or necessary, it seemed to me. There never was much warmth or fun between us, the way some boys have with their dads, but one thing I was sure of: he was an honest man. Whatever mischief was going on along our shores at night—and you'd have had to be both blind and deaf back then not to know there was a lot—it wouldn't have anything to do with him.

Jeddy knew it, too. "Your dad wouldn't break any law," he admitted. "I was only saying that."

"I knew you didn't mean it," I said.

We almost never fought. Whatever Jeddy thought or felt, I understood and respected, and I'd step back and make allowances for it. He watched out for me the same way. I guess you could say we'd sort of woven together.

Our mothers had grown up in town and been friends themselves all the way through school. When they married our dads, they became friends, too. In the early days there was a steady stream of lendings and borrowings, emergency soups and neighborly stews between our houses, the sort of thing that goes on so easily in a small town. Then, in the middle of one winter, Jeddy's mother got sick. It turned out to be the flu that took so many that year.

Her death stunned everyone in town, but it struck the McKenzies like an iron fist. Eileen was her name, and she'd been the heart of the family, the strong one in the house. Jeddy's dad just collapsed. For a while, he didn't go anywhere or do anything.

Jeddy was seven at the time, in the first grade with

me. I remember how I'd walk over in the afternoons after school and sit on his front porch in case he wanted to come down and play. Sometimes he did and sometimes he didn't. I'd stay awhile—the place was too quiet to even think of knocking—then go off if he didn't appear. We both knew without saying it that I'd be back the next day. It was a way we'd worked out to help him get through.

Jeddy's dad had been head man on a local chicken farm, but soon he quit that and began to commute over to Portsmouth to train for police work. The state force was just starting up. It pulled him away from old connections, including my parents, and maybe that's what he wanted. Even when he was hired a year later for the job of our police chief, he kept his distance from us. He never spoke to anyone about the blow he'd suffered, but thinking back, I wonder if he wasn't still trying to depend on his wife for a strength he didn't have. Anyone visiting at the McKenzies' could've seen it. He was keeping her around, strange as that sounds.

Her coat and hat hung on a hook in the hall, as if she'd only stepped out for a moment. Her wedding china was on display in the parlor cabinet. Her sheet music sat on the piano. Her bold handwriting filled the book of recipes that lay open, more often than not, on the counter in the kitchen where Marina, Jeddy's older sister, was now in charge. She'd been a frightened nine-year-old when her mother had died. Seven years later, at sixteen, she was running the house.

It was Marina who served us supper when Jeddy asked

me to stay over evenings. It was she who washed up after, darned her father's socks, hung the laundry and took it down. She changed the beds, swept the floors, hauled in coal for the stove. With the sleeves of her school blouse rolled tight above her elbows (at this time, she was still only a high school sophomore) and one of her mother's cotton aprons wrapped double around her waist, Marina handled all the jobs a grown woman would. I couldn't get used to that, seeing a girl that age taking on what she did. Only a certain watchful gaze she leveled at the world gave a glimpse into what it must have cost her.

"I'd tell you if I knew who it was at Tyler's, really I would," I said to Jeddy that day on the beach, to make things right between us.

He nodded. "I know you would. And I wouldn't tell my dad."

"Of course not."

"It'd be just between us."

"Always has been, always will be," I announced. I couldn't meet his eyes though. I'd already broken that trust. There was something I wasn't telling him, something I couldn't.

Maybe he suspected, because he gave me a long stare. Then he let it go, didn't say any more about it. I wonder, though, when he thinks back—as I know he has done plenty of times over the years, just like me—does he remember that conversation the way I do, as the first crack in our friendship? I wish I could ask him.

What happened next that spring afternoon is something I know Jeddy remembers. I can see us standing there, two raw-boned boys beside the bootleg crate, seagulls wheeling overhead, making dives on a tidal pool up the beach from us. Almost as an afterthought we wandered toward this pool, not expecting to see anything. It came into view with no more drama than if it had been a sodden piece of driftwood lying on the sand: a naked human leg.

A DARK-RIMMED HOLE

IT'S ODD HOW A SHOCKING SIGHT CAN SHAKE your mind so you don't at first register the whole, just the small, almost comical details. Like the hand complete with fancy gold wristwatch, wedding band and neatly clipped fingernails we saw bobbing on the water's surface as we came toward the pool. Above it, swathed in a shawl of brown seaweed, a rubbery-looking shoulder peeked out, white as a girl's. Above that, a bloated face the color of slate; two sightless eyes, open. And there in his neck, what was that? I saw a small dark-rimmed hole.

The body was surrounded by floating shreds of what had once been a fancy evening suit. The feet were bare, with the same wrinkly soles anyone would get who stayed in a bathtub too long.

"Looks like he's been in the water awhile," Jeddy said. "Is it somebody?"

He meant, "Is it somebody we know."

"Don't think so," I said. "Anyhow, he was shot."

"Where?"

"In the neck. See there?"

Jeddy leaned forward to look. The hole was in the skin

just above the collarbone. "Oh," he said, and stepped back fast.

"We could check his pockets," he suggested. "See if he's got a wallet or something with his name on it."

"Go ahead," I said. "I'll hold your hat."

He took it off and gave it to me, then bent to touch the body, which rocked a bit under his hand.

"Maybe we shouldn't disturb anything."

"Maybe not," I said, as squeamish as he was.

"My dad would look if he were here."

"He'd have to."

Jeddy squared himself and went forward again. Reaching into the water, he felt the sodden sides of what remained of the dead man's pants for where the pockets would be.

"I can't feel anything."

"Try his jacket."

Jed patted down the black floating garment and shook his head. "Guess he lost everything at sea."

"Or he was frisked after they shot him," I said. "Anything in his back pockets?"

"You do it," Jeddy said. He'd had enough.

I went forward and felt around, trying not to brush up against the corpse's skin. It had a cold, blubbery feel that turned my stomach. My hands ran into something. I brought out a pipe and a sodden satchel of tobacco.

"Guess he was a smoker."

Jeddy took them for a look, then handed them back. "Are you sure that's all?"

"Yes."

"We need to tell someone."

"Your dad."

"Let's go back to my house. I can call him from there."

After this, though, action seemed beyond us. For a time we stood rooted in place, staring at the dead man, and at the pool of gray water he lay in, and at the gulls who floated on the incoming swells just offshore, watching our movements with cold yellow eyes. Death was no more to them than a ready-made meal. Neither of us had seen a drowned man before, not to mention a corpse with a bullet hole in its neck.

"I bet he was with the mob," said Jeddy, who had no clearer idea than I did at this time what that might be. "Maybe he was in on the landings at Tyler's Lane."

"Wearing an evening suit?"

"Well, maybe he's a high roller from Newport and he tried to double-cross somebody and they found out."

"Or maybe they double-crossed him."

The newspapers were full of such stories. My mother tried to keep me from reading them, but I got around her on that as I did on most things. Al Capone and his Chicago gangsters were in the headlines daily. In New York City, Lucky Luciano was fighting it out with a couple of other gangs, and from all accounts blood flowed regularly in the streets. It was thugs gunning down thugs for the most part, battling over territorial rights to extortion and payoffs.

Right up in Providence there was Danny Walsh, one of

the big-time bootleggers. He was always having people bumped off. You could tip your hat the wrong way at Danny Walsh and that was it, your number was up. To Jeddy and me, all this underworld activity seemed glamorous. We knew the cast of characters, we knew the lingo. Like a lot of kids at that time, we followed gangland murders the same way we read the comics.

This body was real.

"Whoever he is, those gulls are going after him soon as we leave," Jeddy said.

I examined the waiting flock. "You think they'd eat him?"

"Sure, why not. Gulls eat everything."

"Well, there's nothing to cover him with."

"Scare 'em off," Jeddy ordered.

For the next quarter hour, we threw stones and yelled and ran out in the water to make them fly away, which was a waste of time. Not a gull batted an eye. The whole group simply paddled sedately out of reach, then turned to stare at us again. Jeddy flung his cap on the ground. His temper could flare up quicker than mine.

"Stupid birds!"

"The only thing is to get somebody back here fast as we can."

"All right. Let's go."

We began to run down the beach, stopping to heave more threatening volleys at the gulls. Even before we reached the first bend, we could see the flock edging closer to shore, getting ready to pounce.

"Cannibals," Jeddy panted. "Wish I had a gun."

Around the end of Coulter's Point, we let loose and raced for our bikes.

The person who answered at the police station was the force's part-time bookkeeper, Mildred Cumming. She sounded sleepy when she took Jeddy's call, but she'd snapped to a moment later.

"A dead man? . . . Shot! Anybody from around here? . . . Right. I'm getting Charlie. Hold on, kiddo, don't you go anywhere."

From the stairs in Jeddy's front hall, I heard everything. The McKenzies' telephone was new to the house, a wall model tucked into a special alcove under the staircase. The town had paid to have it installed so Chief McKenzie could take calls at home. Jeddy wasn't supposed to use it, but this was an emergency.

There was a long wait while Mildred went to get Charlie Pope, deputy sergeant at the station, who was most likely across the street at Weedie's Coffee Shop, jawing and reading the papers. Normally, there wasn't much that went on day to day in a hamlet our size. People knew each other too well. With only one road into town, any suspicious character who didn't get noticed on the way in was sure to be pulled over on the way out. The whole police force amounted to only two individuals, neither of whom cared to carry a gun.

"This is me. Yeah, I heard," Charlie told Jeddy when he got came on. "It's a man, you say?"

Jeddy said it was.

"What's he wearing, could you see?"

Jeddy explained about the evening suit.

"Your dad's not here. Gone to New Bedford to see a fellow. Back in a couple of hours. I'll try to get a message to him. You boys stay where y'are. I'll be at your place soon as I can."

"We'll meet you at the beach," Jeddy said. "There's a pack of gulls down there getting at the body. We'll stand guard till you come."

This caused an explosion on the other end of the line.

"You stay put!" Charlie's voice boomed out, so loud that Jeddy jerked the receiver away from his ear. "I don't want you going down on that beach again! Now that's an order!"

Jeddy rolled his eyes and said all right. About then, the front door opposite me opened and Marina came in, her dark hair loose and streaming from the wind. A single glance at Jeddy on the phone was all she needed.

"What happened?" she asked me.

"We found a body washed up on the beach."

"A fisherman?"

"Probably not."

"What beach?"

"Coulter's."

"What were you doing down there?"

"Looking for lobster pots."

I avoided her direct gaze. With her hair blown that way and her face glowing from the cold walk home,

Marina McKenzie was almost unbearably pretty. I was at the age where it embarrassed me to find myself noticing this.

"Did you get any?" she asked.

"No," I said to the floor.

Jeddy finished his conversation with Charlie and put the telephone receiver cautiously back on its hook.

"We're to wait," he informed me. To his sister he said, "Charlie Pope's coming."

Marina wrinkled her nose. "That weasel, why him?"

"Dad's in New Bedford. They're calling him."

"Is it anybody from around here?"

"We don't think so. He's all dressed up and has a gold wristwatch. A bunch of seagulls were on him. We shooed them off."

"Maybe he fell off the New York boat," Marina said.

"He was shot," Jeddy said. He followed his sister down the hall and into the kitchen. "There's a bullet hole in his neck."

Behind on the stairs, I waited for what Marina would have to say about this, but nothing came. That was like her. She was a careful person who tended to keep her thoughts to herself. Not that she was shy. She knew how to speak up when she wanted, even to her own father, the chief of police. She just wasn't a gabber like some girls her age. It was another thing I'd noticed about her.

I heard the sound of a cupboard door opening and closing. She was starting supper, as she did every afternoon at about this time. I knew that house, felt easy there, more comfortable than in my own. At home my father loomed large in my sight, and whatever was talked about, whatever was thought, seemed to revolve around him. Often it had to do with the store, where I worked most afternoons, though never hard enough to please him. He'd set a standard of performance that was beyond me, or so it seemed to me then, and though he never expressed it, I was aware of an undercurrent of disappointment in his dealings with me. It was as if he knew me better than I knew myself, and had detected some weakness at my center. Against this flaw, whatever it was, I was in a constant state of struggle.

At the McKenzies', the pressure lifted. The family was just this side of poor. Chief McKenzie drew a good deal less salary than what my father made managing the store, and there were few luxuries. The only bathroom was downstairs off the kitchen. There was no hot water. Upstairs, the rooms were still without electricity—Jeddy and I went to bed by candlelight when I stayed over. Everywhere the furnishings were cheap and old.

None of this mattered to me. I'd come to love the dim light and dusty corners, the worn armchairs and drab curtains. Nothing was ever moved or changed. Marina had barely enough time to keep up with daily tasks, and none at all for the mail-order frills and home improvements my mother was so fond of. Then again, even if there had been time, and money, change was not something those who lived in that house would have wanted.

On the wall opposite the stairs where I sat that afternoon was an old photograph of Jeddy's mother. It was a
formal studio portrait that had been painted with a wash
of color to give her face a more lifelike appearance. Mrs.
McKenzie had had dark hair and serious eyes like Marina.
She held her head the same upright way her daughter
did, and a wrinkle on her forehead was identical to one
that rose on Marina's forehead in thoughtful moments.

I'd come across Chief McKenzie staring at this portrait of his wife more than a few times, and I could guess
why. She had a gaze that gave you strength. That day on
the stairs, I remember how Eileen McKenzie's eyes
seemed suddenly to lock onto mine, as if she'd recognized
me and was asking me to stay; as if she'd accepted me as
a member of her family. I knew it was silly, but I smiled
and nodded back.

"I'm frying chicken for supper," Marina's voice said
from the kitchen.

"Can we have potato salad?" Jeddy's voice asked.

"If you peel," Marina replied severely.

"Can Ruben stay? It's Saturday."

"If he wants. Tell him he can use the telephone to call
his mother. But he has to peel, too."

"Ruben!" Jeddy called. "Want to stay for supper?
Marina's frying chicken."

I got up and went in the kitchen.

"What are you grinning about?" Marina asked me, her
mother's stern eyes on my face.

"I don't know, nothing."

"You've just found a body on the beach and now you're grinning like a hyena and you don't know why?"

"Nope," I said, grinning wider than ever.

Something about the dopey way I said this must have struck her funny, because she turned her head to hide a smile.

"Ruben Hart, have you no respect for the dead?" she said, trying for a prudish tone. It was no use; she started to laugh.

"Marina!" Jeddy exclaimed.

"I'm sorry!" she cried, and put a hand over her mouth. "I don't know why it's so funny. It's Ruben's fault for getting me going."

She sent me an accusing look and turned back to the chicken. But a second later she began to laugh again. Soon, she was shaking with laughter.

Jeddy and I eyed each other in alarm. We'd never seen her like this. Jeddy scowled, and I would have, too, except that suddenly I found this breakdown to be wonderful beyond words. All the strictness had gone out of Marina's face, which collapsed and turned pink no matter how she tried to stop it.

"Don't look at me!" she gasped, wiping her eyes. "A person has the right to laugh in her own kitchen!"

Jeddy and I stood before her, solemn as two owls, though there must've been the twitch of a grin on my face.

I never did find out what set Marina off that day, but

it changed the way I thought about her. She was still far ahead of me, an older girl who could make me blush just by meeting my eyes. But I'd caught sight of another person living inside, someone wilder and freer, less bound by the rules around her than she allowed others to see. That was something back then to recognize in a girl, and it filled me with excitement. I couldn't have begun to explain why.

THE DISAPPEARANCE

SUPPER WAS LAID OUT, READY TO BE COOKED, when Charlie Pope finally arrived at the house three hours later. By then, it was after six. Jeddy and I were in a fume.

"He'll be eaten up!"

"What took you so long?"

"Hold your horses, we'll get there soon enough. Mildred got through to your dad," Charlie said to Jeddy. "He's on his way."

Marina threw on a coat and followed us out the door.

"Well, if it isn't the Queen of Sheba. Out for a bit of fun?" I heard Charlie say to her in a sarcastic voice.

"I'll come if I want."

"Course you will, honey. You always do what you want, don't you?"

Marina brushed past him and we went out to Charlie's car for the drive to the beach. I saw how careful she was to keep her distance from him. She sat in the backseat with me, arms folded across her chest. Something was wrong between Charlie and Marina. Jeddy didn't notice, but I did.

The sun was low in the west when we arrived at the

beach. The strong winds of that afternoon were dying. The air smelled of seaweed. We walked single file down the sandy path toward the shore. Jeddy, in the lead, slowed and lifted his head.

"What's that noise?"

We all cocked an ear. Through the crash and roll of waves came a high, droning buzz. It grew louder as we marched over a rise in the dunes. Jeddy pointed across the bay.

"It's an airplane!"

I looked and saw a tiny gray form floating above the Newport peninsula. Airplanes weren't an everyday sight at that time. We all stopped to watch.

"Probably some tycoon coming in from New York," Charlie said. "I read in the papers how they've built a landing field over there. Come and go like thieves in the night."

He walked ahead, suddenly impatient. "Let's get moving. I haven't got all day."

We set off again, and it wasn't long before Jeddy and I were squinting along the beach, expecting to see the pack of gulls hard at work at the water's edge. The closer we got, the more we couldn't see one bird.

"That's strange," I said. "Gulls never give up."

When we came up on the place, the reason was clear. The shallow pool where the body had lain was empty.

Jeddy stared in disbelief. "It was here!"

"It was," I agreed.

Charlie glanced up the beach, then out to sea. The

dead man could not have floated away. The tide was too low, still going out, in fact.

"The flock of gulls was there," Jeddy said, pointing. "They were coming after him when we left."

"Must've been hungry," Charlie said, flashing a grin at Marina. She turned her head away. To Jeddy, he said, "You're sure this was the place?"

"Yes, sir. It was here!"

"Lying just where, would you say?"

"In this little pool of water. Half in, half out."

"A man, you said, and he was all dressed up?"

Jeddy explained again about the torn evening suit, the watch, the wedding band and the seaweed.

"He had bare feet," I added. "His face was kind of mushed in."

"Well, there's no sign of him now. No sign of anything," Charlie said, sounding oddly satisfied. "If somebody came and dragged him off, there'd be marks, wouldn't you think? There's not even any footprints."

We all looked. The beach was smooth, except for the tracks we'd just made coming across the sand. Woven in among them were our first tracks, Jeddy's and mine. No one else had been on that stretch of shore for the last eight hours.

"They might have come in by sea," I ventured.

Charlie shook his head. "In here? Naw. It's too shallow for a boat."

That was true. The shelf of the beach extended way out into the water.

"Well, listen. There's something else," Jeddy said. He sounded desperate. "There was an empty wooden case that was washed in with the body. A bootlegger's case. That's gone, too."

Charlie's expression changed at this.

"You think this guy was a rumrunner?"

"I don't know. I'm just saying . . ."

"How could you tell he was shot?" Charlie wanted to know.

"We saw a hole in his neck, at the bottom," Jeddy said.

"Yeah, but was there any blood?"

Jed shook his head. "It must've all washed away."

"Any sign of bruising?"

"I didn't see any."

"This hole was from a bullet, you say?"

"Yes, sir."

"And how did you make that out?"

"Well, I don't know. It just seemed that it was."

"There's a lot of things that 'seem,' " Charlie said, glancing over at Marina again.

"I know, but this body—"

"Especially with things like bodies," Charlie snapped at Jeddy. "There's a lot you can't tell from just looking at them. I mean, there are officers whose job it is to say what happened and how it was done and when and where and so forth." He stopped and gave Jeddy and me a look.

"The thing is, I wouldn't be spreading the rumor of somebody that's shot washing up here," he said. "Since we don't even know for sure that he was shot."

Jeddy said, "Oh."

"In fact, if you can keep the news down about this body at all, it would be best."

"It would?"

"And you, too, Marina. Keep it under your bonnet."

"My *what*?" she lashed out. "And who says? You?"

"Your *dad* and me," Charlie answered. "We're going to be reporting this supposed body to the proper authorities, and they're going to be reporting to those above them, and it won't do any good to have rumors flying about."

"Supposed body!" Jeddy exclaimed. "What does that mean?"

"It means just what it means."

"There wasn't anything 'supposed' about this body!" Jeddy said. I saw he was losing his temper. There wasn't much good that could come from that.

"When you find out, will you let us know who it was?" I asked Charlie.

"I might," he answered. "And then again, we may never know exactly."

"Exactly what?"

"What happened."

Marina laughed out loud. "I can see this investigation is off to a good start," she said.

Charlie glanced at her angrily, turned his back and walked off.

"So, is that it?" I called after him.

"It is," he spat over his shoulder. "Whew! Seaweed stinks to high heaven around here."

There was nothing more to be done. Charlie was determined to drop the case. Even Jeddy's father, who came a few minutes later, gave us a stern look, as if he was displeased that such a thing as a body should have turned up and been found by anyone, let alone his own son. Now that it had conveniently disappeared, he seemed in no mood to discuss it further.

"I stopped by the house and saw that supper's ready to be cooked," he said to Marina. "Shouldn't you be back there getting to it?"

She spun on her heel without answering and strode away. Charlie and Chief McKenzie went off down the beach for a private chat while Jeddy and I waited. Ten minutes later, the four of us set out after her for home.

Jeddy swung into step with his father. Whatever happened, Jeddy never stayed mad at his dad for long. You could see how he revered the man by the way he walked beside him, matching his stride.

"Hey, Dad, Ruben is coming, too," he said. "Marina said it was all right."

"Coming to what?" Chief McKenzie glanced down at him.

"Supper," Jeddy said. "He called his mother. It's all set."

"Well, he can't. Not tonight, whatever Marina said."

"But why?"

The chief shook his head. "Because I say so."

"But Marina invited him! And it's Saturday night."

Chief McKenzie glared. "I don't care what night it is,

I've had enough fuss and furor for one day!" he thundered. We all looked at him in astonishment.

"What are you staring at?" he shouted. "Marina's not the head of this house, whatever she may think. Take a rain check, Ruben, all right? Tell your folks I'm sorry. We'll see you another time."

"Yes, sir. All right," I said, and that was that. No one spoke another word the whole way down the beach, or in the chief's car going back to the McKenzies'. I picked up my bike and scooted for home like a dog in disgrace.

Marina was already back by that time. She'd taken the walking path across the Point that cut between the roads. I saw the white of her apron through the kitchen window as I pedaled by. At the last minute, she looked out and gave me a wave.

That made me feel better. Marina always was a great one for bucking a person up. She could keep her head in murky weather, too, which was a good thing because, with the arrival of that body, murk is what was heading for us. Jeddy and I couldn't see it yet, but the fog was out there, sifting and swirling, already beginning to close in around the McKenzies' house.

The Interview

THE OLD MAN HAS BEEN TALKING FOR almost an hour when he goes suddenly quiet. (David writes the phrase *swirling fog* down on his notepad, to remind himself where they've left off.)

They sit in silence for a while, Mr. Hart with his eyes closed. Way, way back is where he is, *lost in the folds of time.* David read that somewhere. He didn't really understand what it meant then; now he gets it. Mr. Hart has vanished over the horizon. He's back with his pal Jeddy in 1929. Maybe he knew this was going to happen. Maybe it's why he called up David and decided to talk, as a way of getting there, of revisiting the scene now that Jeddy is so sick. There's some knot in their past that's bothering him.

David has more pressing interests. *So, who was the man on the beach?* he wants to ask. *What's Charlie Pope covering up?* But he can see that the old guy's out of gas. Anyway, it's almost dinnertime and David is due home himself. His mother has a fit if everyone's not there to sit down at 6:30 sharp.

Should I come back tomorrow?

Mr. Hart grunts, eyes still shut.

I'd like to come back tomorrow, David says. *You didn't even get to any smuggling yet, or to the* Black Duck. *I guess you know that the crew on that boat was shot. They wouldn't stop and the Coast Guard opened fire with a machine gun. I read an old newspaper story about it.*

Behind his glasses, Mr. Hart's eyes blink open.

Leave that alone, he rumbles. His eyes close again. David makes his way quietly out of the house, uncertain whether he'll be allowed back.

But the next day when he knocks at a little past noon, Mr. Hart's front door flies open and the old man appears at once.

I've been waiting all morning. Thought you'd chickened out!

David grins. *Sorry, I had to wait for someone to drive me.*

How old did you say you were?

Seventeen?

You seem younger. Mr. Hart fixes him with a spectacled stare.

David avoids his gaze. He wishes he'd never started this bit of fraudulence. It's not like him. He usually keeps things on the level. He was just so afraid he'd be turned away. He wants to get this interview, needs to write this story. He allows the lie to stand.

They sit in the kitchen again, where Mr. Hart takes off his glasses and polishes them energetically on his sweater. His eyes are clearer today, sea-colored. Out from behind their lenses, they have a bright, youthful look. For a second, David catches sight of another Ruben Hart, the boy who was Jeddy's friend, co-explorer of beaches and admirer of older sisters.

Where were we?

Swirling fog, David says. *It's closing in on the McKenzies' house.*

He's brought his notebook again and is determined to make a better attempt at writing things down. His dad is on his case about getting a summer job. He's pressuring David to work in the garden shop that's part of the family landscaping business. So far, David has refused, not an easy stand to take.

Well, don't expect any more handouts from me! his father raged. *It's about time you started supporting your own lifestyle.*

What lifestyle? David had protested. *How can I have a lifestyle when I live at home?*

You know what. Movies, magazines, computer games. All that stuff you buy at the mall. Books.

Books! You mean, for high school next fall? His parents had always paid for those.

They'll cost me a fortune. You could help out if you had a paying job.

I'm trying to get a job with a newspaper, David had explained. *That's what I'm working on. I'm researching a story.*

It hadn't gone over. He had nothing to show for it. His dad is a hands-on guy who measures industry by what he can see: gardens plowed, hedges pruned, lawns seeded. Another reason for the notebook. If David can produce evidence that he's not wasting time, that he has good intentions, his father might cut him some slack. He might realize that David has a plan for his life, even if it doesn't include Peterson's Landscaping and Garden Design.

Who was the dead man in the evening suit, did you ever find out? David asks Mr. Hart now, to get him back on track.

Not right away. There was a clue, though, right under my nose. Something I'd overlooked.

What? David says, ballpoint poised and ready.

MUZZLED

I'D FORGOTTEN THE DEAD MAN'S PIPE.

That night, after supper, I took my jacket upstairs to my room and felt something in the pocket. There was the pipe. I'd stuffed it in without thinking. The leather pouch was there, too, one of the simple foldover packs so many men carried in that day. I turned it around in my hands and opened it. The leaf inside was still damp, alive with scent. An odd feeling swept me that I was out of bounds, prying into something that was not my business. Though that was absurd. The dead man on the beach would never know what I'd taken.

I'd told my father about the body the minute he'd come home from Riley's store that evening. He'd quietly told my mother, and she, in whispers, had informed her sister, my aunt Grace, who lived with us and worked at the post office. Silence seemed to be the way my story was to be treated until Aunt Grace broke ranks, as she often did. She was unmarried, younger than my mother, and known for stating her opinions whatever company she was in. It was not how a woman should conduct herself, my mother believed, and she was always frowning at her and trying to quiet her down.

"So it's come to this, murder on our own shores," Aunt Grace blurted out as the four of us sat eating a late supper that night.

"Who said anything about murder?" asked my father. "A man washed up, that's all we know for sure."

"A man with a bullet hole in his neck, Ruben says. It was just a matter of time," Aunt Grace went on. "And now they've taken to stealing bodies to hide their crimes."

"Come along, Grace. There's no evidence of that," my father said. "It'll be investigated, I'm sure."

"It's the liquor that's causing this! There's no enforcement of our laws."

My mother looked disapproving. "The trouble is that the Coast Guard can't keep up. Our local police have no support. There's too much smuggling going on."

"They could keep up if they wanted," Aunt Grace shot back. "They're in league with it, most of them, making a bundle for themselves under the table."

"Hush, dear," my mother said.

"Well, they are! Just no one wants to say it. What's become of this country? It's all commerce and greed."

"We'll discuss this later, at a more appropriate time," my mother said with arched brows. She meant, "a time when Ruben is not here to listen."

"In case you forgot, I'm the one who found this body!" I protested.

"Ruben, please. We've heard enough about bodies. The subject is now closed," my mother declared with finality.

As if that weren't muzzle enough, my father took me aside after supper to back up Charlie Pope's warning.

"There's no good to be had in stirring up rumors. You and Jed keep a clamp on your mouths and we'll all be the better for it."

"But who would go and take that body? And why didn't Chief McKenzie want to do anything about it?"

"He does want to. And he will, so keep what you saw to yourself. I mean it, Ruben, this is not our affair. Don't go worrying your mother by bringing it up again."

Alone in my room, I closed the pouch with an angry snap and put it down. I picked up the pipe.

It was made of good wood, smooth and glossy, though seawater had mottled it in places. The stem had a fashionable dip with a nice lip. Riley's sold pipes, though none so fine as this one. I ran my finger over the bowl and remembered the expensive wristwatch on the dead man's floating hand. Whoever the man was, he'd had style and the money to support it.

Downstairs, a door slammed. I heard rapid steps leaving the house and looked out in time to see my father getting into the store truck parked in the yard. He often borrowed it for transportation. That evening he was taking it back. There was the whir of the starter, and the distinctive cough of the engine. The headlights came on, bright as twin suns in the dark. The night was moonless again, and perfectly clear. It was just as it had been two nights before, when the only illumination had come from a dusty froth of stars high overhead.

Back at my desk, I stowed the pipe and pouch in a drawer and sat staring out into space. A picture of shadowy forms moving silently up a beach came into my mind.

Tyler's Lane.

I'd been there, of course, despite what I'd let Jeddy think. I hadn't planned to be, never would have been under ordinary circumstances. My mother liked to keep me home at night, as much for companionship as anything. My dad so often worked late at the store. Aunt Grace had a social life of her own. I was the only child at home. My older brother had moved away to take a job in Providence. My sister had married young and gone to live in Vermont. It's the lot of the youngest to be clung to and fussed over. Except that night, I got lucky. Old Mrs. LeWitt went on the rampage for her medicine.

BLACK DUCK

"FOR GOD'S SAKE, CAN'T SHE WAIT UNTIL morning?" I heard my father bellow in the front hall. It was past ten o'clock. My parents had already gone to bed. He was downstairs in his pajamas. Dr. Washburn was at the door.

She couldn't wait, the doctor said. She'd sent word by his office. Her nerves would fray to pieces if she didn't get her tonic.

"Hell's bells!" my father shouted. Mrs. LeWitt lived far out on the Point. Her prescription had come in late to Riley's store from Providence that afternoon. Dad had brought it home with him and forgotten all about it.

"Carl!" My mother hushed him over the hall rail upstairs.

"Somebody must go tonight," Dr. Washburn insisted. "I'd take it myself, but Mrs. Clancy's come into labor. I'm late there already. Just stopped here on my way."

I was hanging out the door of my room, ready with a solution I thought my mother would never agree to, when:

"Send Ruben," I heard her tell my father. "He's wide

awake. He can ride his bicycle down there and be back in no time. It's a beautiful night. He'll come to no harm."

"Ruben!" my father yelled up in desperation. "Would you mind making a trip to the Point at this hour?"

I was out in a flash looking over the rail. I said I wouldn't mind. No, I wouldn't mind at all.

It was the sort of spring night that makes you want to leap like a wild animal. Outside, barreling down the Point road through the crisp salt air, a furious energy rose in my bones. I wanted to ride on forever. I'd been cooped up for years, or so it seemed, following directions and doing what was right, living up to expectations that were somebody else's. You can only take orders for so long, I decided, then you've got to break free and make your own rules.

The more I thought about this, and about where I was headed at present in life, which was working for my father at the store until the end of time, the faster I pedaled. I was in a state of high mutiny by the time I got out to Mrs. LeWitt's. It took an act of pure will to put on a delivery boy's polite smile as I came up on her cabin.

I needn't have bothered.

Mrs. LeWitt, in a terrifying flannel nightdress and hair net, was in a far worse mood.

"Well, it's about time!" she shrieked. "Thought you'd never get here!" She snatched the package out of my hand and shut the door so fast she nearly took off my nose.

I laughed bleakly at myself and set off for home, going slower. The bulb in my bicycle lamp had burned out. I pedaled nearly blind at first. Then my eyes began to adjust. Pale fields floated toward me out of the blackness. Stone walls hulked and spun past. Stealthy, scuttling creatures crossed in front of me, shadows come and gone. About midway home, I glanced toward the bay rising to view on my left and there, with my new night vision, caught sight of something I might otherwise have missed.

Tiny lights were winking out on the water. Red, then white. Red, white.

I knew what they were. A boat was on its way up the east passage, sending out a code. After a bit, the lights went dark and I couldn't see anything.

I coasted to a halt to listen. A chorus of spring peepers rose from a nearby marsh. Then, as the wind shifted a bit, I heard clearly, coming up over the fields, the dull, repetitive thud-thud-thud of powerful engines driving through water. The boat's lights flashed on again. It was signaling its position every minute or so. I couldn't see, but suspected that someone on land was signaling back. In those days, houses on shore were few and far between and there was little to give direction to a boat traveling without lights under cover of dark.

I watched until I was sure where the craft was going to put in, then leapt on my bike. A few minutes later, I turned down Tyler's Lane, pedaling for all I was worth. Jeddy and I often came down this road to fish, or in our endless quest for lost pots. There was a rumor about town that the rocky beach at the end was a favored drop for smugglers. The Coast Guard must have heard this, too, because it wasn't unusual to see a patrol boat bobbing off-shore during the day, binoculars trained on the decrepit wooden dock that ran out from the beach. Now, on this perfect moonless night, I hoped the rumors were true. I wanted more than anything to see a bootleg landing close up.

I was riding down the middle of the road, where it was less chewed up, when headlights flashed in back of me. The sound of shifting gears sent me over to one side and, seconds later, a car bore down. I swerved and rode full speed into a field of tall grass, flung myself off the bike and lay still. The outline of a huge Packard raced past, going headlong for the beach. I stayed low, breathing hard, and a good thing, too, because after a minute another machine went by, a fancy touring car of some kind, followed closely by what looked like a Pierce-Arrow. I raised up for a second look and saw the big, arrogant taillights flash red. All three vehicles were out-of-towners. No one I knew owned wheels of this caliber. Peering over the grass, I saw other lights down on the beach.

The time had come to ditch my bicycle. I wheeled it to the field's edge, laid it down in some weeds and began to walk toward the water, using a low hedge along the road for cover. The closer I went, the more I could see that those three cars weren't by any means the all of it. The beach was boiling with activity. There must have been twelve or fifteen cars parked here and there, as well as trucks, a couple of delivery vehicles, even a horse van. On the beach itself, shadowy forms of men milled around in light cast by a row of headlights. They were the shore crew, silent for the most part, looking often out to sea.

Soon, the sound of a boat's engines could be heard and the wallowing form of a craft appeared out of the dark, slowly approaching the shore. I dropped to my knees and crawled up behind a pile of rocks at the far edge of the beach. What I saw next nearly stopped my heart.

Mr. Riley, owner of Riley's General Store, was standing not twenty yards away, staring intently at the incoming boat. He wore a fisherman's cap pulled low over his eyes instead of the snappy fedora he sported on visits to the store. But his double-chinned profile showed up clear in the glare of headlights. Though he was short, far shorter than my father, his meaty chest gave him the hunched look of a bulldog. More than once I'd had the impression that my father played a careful hand around the guy.

A shout came from one of the men onshore. Mr. Riley walked down to the water's edge. He was wearing city shoes and stood fastidiously out of range of the waves. The speedboat, painted an anonymous gray, sat low in the water, obviously carrying a load. It approached the dock at a fair clip, waiting until the last moment before turning and killing its engines. The craft drifted neatly wharfside and lines were tossed toward the old dock's pilings. An eager crew of men rushed out along the dock's length. With the hull pulled snug, unloading began.

Wooden cases from the boat's hold were lifted and passed along a chain of human hands down the dock and up the beach to the back of a waiting vehicle. The work went swiftly and largely without sound, except for grunts and occasional bursts of laughter when a heavy crate slipped or caused someone to lose his footing. Through the gloom, I picked out some men I knew from town. Henry Crocker, a local farmer, was there, along with Reg Blankenship, who raised hogs up the river. There was Horace White, a mechanic in the gas station at Four Corners, and Tony Rabera, a handyman and gardener for summer folk who needed upkeep on their vacation houses.

In all, some twenty men labored to bring the cases up the shore. As each vehicle was filled, it drove off into the night and another truck or van or a fancy roadster backed up to the feed line. Like a silent film, the action played in front of me: the frantic movement of the shore crew, the flicker of headlights coming and going.

The hour when my mother would have expected me home had now come and gone. I knew I should leave, but I could not. A quarter hour went by, then another. Finally, with more than half a hold of cargo still on board, an ocean swell came in that caused the gray-hulled boat to roll and crash against the dock. Work halted while boat lines were untied and cast off. With a roar of engines, the skipper began the process of moving the speedster around to the other side of the dock, where it could be in the lee and more protected from the surge.

All this took time, and at last I saw no way but that I must go. I crawled backward from my rock hiding place until I came to the edge of a field and could slide into its bushy shadow.

From there, I felt safe enough to gaze back once more at the activity on the water. The rumrunner craft was in the process of approaching the dock again. The wheelman was a young man, dark and dashing as a pirate, it seemed to me. He revved the powerful engines, idled them and, with an expert hand, allowed the boat to drift into position. As it swung around into the dazzle of headlights, I caught sight for the first time of the ship's name, painted along the starboard bow.

Black Duck.

A second later, the boat swung away. The dark captain brought the bow into the wind, revved up once more and cut his engines. Across the suddenly peaceful water I heard him give out a full-throated laugh of satisfaction. Then the chain of men on the dock began to reform for another round of unloading. With all eyes turned toward the water, I chose this moment to sneak away up the dark lane.

1

THE SECRET

MY MOTHER WAS AT THE DOOR WHEN I CAME in, but I was ready for her. I told her my bicycle lamp had burned out, that I'd been forced to walk a good part of the way home. Somehow, she believed me and I escaped to my room, where I lay awake, in a haze of disbelief. The *Black Duck*. At Tyler's dock!

She was half phantom, known all over Narragansett Bay for her daring runs and yet rarely glimpsed by ordinary folk. Her skipper was too smart and her crew too skilled. She'd eluded the Coast Guard and the Feds for years, and made a laughingstock of local police who tried to track her movements.

Cornered against some dark beach, the *Duck* gunned her big engines and roared to freedom, leaving pursuers to wallow in her wake. If, by some fluke, she was caught carrying goods and ordered to halt for inspection, a dense cloud of engine smoke would erupt from her exhaust pipes and she'd speed away behind it into one of the hundreds of coastal inlets known to the crew.

They were local men from local families with a need to make ends meet during hard times, different altogether from the big-city syndicates that were beginning to bully their way into the business at that time. Many folks quietly cheered them on around their supper tables, proud that one of their own could outsmart both the government and the gangsters. At Riley's store, I'd listened in on more than a few back-aisle conversations.

"Heard the *Duck* was up to Fogland last night, making a drop," I'd hear a fisherman say, shaking his head in what should have been disapproval but sounded more like supressed glee.

"That so?" a friend would reply, and several other men would suddenly materialize and gather round to hear the story.

"Yup. The Coast Guard picked up a tip that she was bringing in a load of hot Canadian whiskey from an outside rig. They'd staked out three cutters up there waiting for her, and guess what?"

"She got away!"

"She did. Dumped her goods in the bay and got clean away. Led 'em on a wild-goose chase up the east passage."

"Oh, Lord, I wish I'd seen it."

"You could'a heard it if you was up there onshore. The C.G. had a spotlight on her and was firing across her stern. They ordered her to stop, but it didn't do no good. She turned on the juice and disappeared."

"She does nearly forty, y'know."

"I heard she's got a steel-plated hull."

"Her skipper's out of Westport, somebody said. Making money hand over fist."

"He's out of Harveston, I know it for a fact. And he's not just in it for himself, they say. He gives from his profits to local families in need."

"Is that so?"

"I heard it was."

"Somebody you know?"

"Me? No. I don't know who it is."

Nobody knew who her skipper was. Or nobody would own up to knowing. And now I'd seen him. I'd watched him at work in all his swagger and bravado. My first thought, tearing home on my bike that night, was that I couldn't wait to tell Jeddy.

Only later in my room, thinking back to the men onshore, men I knew and respected and who knew and trusted me, I began to have second thoughts. Jeddy was my friend, but there was so much at stake. Not least, there was my own father, the manager of Riley's store. I wasn't sure what Mr. Riley was doing on that beach, but I thought it best for my dad if no one heard his boss was there. Chief McKenzie was breathing fire to put a stop to the *Duck*. Jeddy might swear he'd never tell him, he might truly believe we could keep a secret between us, but he loved his dad and stood up for him, and I knew how easy it would be to make a slip.

Newport Daily Journal, December 31, 1929

BLACK DUCK TRIPLE SLAYING UNAVOIDABLE, OFFICIAL DECLARES

FAIR WARNING TO HALT WAS GIVEN

NEWPORT, DEC. 31—The Coast Guard cutter that fired on the Black Duck last Sunday, killing three men, gave a clear signal for the vessel to stop and surrender according to D. W. Hingle, commander of the Newport Coast Guard Station. The patrol boat opened fire with a machine gun after the Black Duck veered and attempted to flee.

"The loss of life is sad but was unavoidable," Hingle said in a statement last night. "The laws of the United States must be maintained. The smugglers defied the government officers and took their punishment. They have no one to blame but themselves."

The Liberal Civic League has asked for further investigation, and questions of negligent homicide have been raised by state residents who charge the Coast Guard with being "out of control" in their pursuit of smugglers.

"This was murder, pure and simple," said Henry Borges, of the League. "The crew was unarmed. Bullet holes are stitched down the side of the pilot house. There is no evidence that any 'fair warning' signal was given."

The dead are Alfred Biggs and William A. Brady of Harveston, R.I., and Bernardo Rosario of New Bedford, Mass. The sole survivor, Richard Delucca, also of Harveston, is in Newport Hospital, being treated for a gunshot wound to the hand.

The Interview

![wavy lines decoration]

IT'S AMAZING THE COAST GUARD EVER caught up with anybody back then, David Peterson says to Mr. Hart. *The smugglers could run circles around them in their souped-up fishing boats. It must've been frustrating.*

It was, Mr. Hart agrees.

They're in the kitchen for another round, the third day of their interview, which is taking on a life of its own. David didn't even need to knock when he arrived this morning. Mr. Hart's door was wide open.

I read that the Coast Guard was supposed to give fair warning to suspected rum-running boats before they could shoot, David says. *Blow a horn or shoot off a warning gun. They had to catch the crew with smuggled liquor on board or they couldn't arrest them. I guess that's why the bootleggers were always dumping stuff overboard.*

Mr. Hart gazes at him thoughtfully, as if he's taking his measure. *You sound like you've been doing some research.*

I went to the library after we finished here yesterday. Found another old newspaper article, David says.

He doesn't reveal that he's been reading up on the *Black Duck* shooting in particular, which he's begun to realize was a big deal back when it happened. People were outraged. They wanted the Coast Guard investigated for murder. The case never went anywhere, though. Two weeks after the event, the Coast Guard was cleared by a federal grand jury of all wrongdoing.

None of this can David discuss with Mr. Hart. The ground rules for this interview have been established, though nothing has been stated outright. They are: Don't Ask and You May Be Told. The old man is especially wary of questions that attempt to connect him personally to the *Black Duck*.

Don't believe everything you read in the papers, he says now. *There's usually a world of difference between what's reported and what probably went on. Behind every story there's another story.*

David nods. He's aware that people often don't agree with how the news is reported. His father cancelled his subscription to the *Providence Journal* after reading an editorial about toxic weed-killers that sent him into a rage.

I'm not paying another cent for this birdbrained newspaper! he'd yelled. *Next they'll be calling for a ban on mousetraps!*

Whatever happened to the *Black Duck* out there in the fog, the "murk" as Mr. Hart calls it, has been further eclipsed by the passage of time. Most people from that day have died. There's no way of getting back there for a clear view.

Or is there?

You remind me of Jeddy somehow, Mr. Hart says suddenly, his blue eyes taking on a more friendly gleam. *It's easy to talk to you. Jeddy and I could be together all day and never be tired of it. Like this.*

Thank you, David says. He's begun to feel warmth for the old man in return. His manner is brusque, but he is honest and direct, and has an offbeat sense of humor that David really enjoys. Ruben Hart would have made a great friend if only he'd been born seventy years later.

You know, we don't always intend to do what we do, Mr. Hart announces suddenly.

Such as?

I didn't mean to get into what I did, and I know Jeddy didn't, either. He had a good heart. It was the times.

David nods, but he's lost. Whatever Mr. Hart is talking about—some betrayal is what it sounds like—must come up later in the story.

The old man sighs, leans back in his chair and by mistake knocks into a cardboard milk container on the counter behind him. David leaps and rescues it before it goes over.

Whoa! That was close. Shouldn't this be in the fridge?

The counter is crowded with other things, too. Greasy plates, unwashed glasses, a stack of sticky pots and pans. It looks like the wife is still away. Mr. Hart has been cooking for himself and not bothering to wash up.

When's your wife coming back?

When she can.

You must be missing her.

I'm doing all right.

Where'd she go?

North Carolina.

You didn't want to?

Mr. Hart shakes his head. *Wasn't invited. I never am when she visits down there.*

Well, go on. So the Black Duck *came in at Tyler's. What happened next?*

What happened was that Jeddy and I couldn't leave well enough alone. We were curious, you know, where that body might've gone.

Of course, David says. *Who wouldn't be?*

ABSENT FROM SCHOOL

I WASN'T THE ONLY ONE TO TAKE HEAT FROM my dad after we found the body on Coulter's Point.

The next day, Chief McKenzie lowered the boom on Jeddy so hard that it looked as if he'd never have another afternoon off in his life, not for lobster-pot hunting or anything else.

"I've got to get a job," he told me when we met on Monday for our walk into town to the school. "My dad said I've got too much free time on my hands and it's leading to trouble."

"What trouble? That we found that stiff?"

"No. I don't know if it's even about that. He said I'm too old to be hanging around on beaches. If I want to make money, I should get a real job."

"How about working at the store with me?" I said. "I could ask my father if Mr. Riley would hire you. You wouldn't make that much, but we could do it together."

Jeddy shook his head. "Dad already signed me up to start next week at Fancher's chicken farm. I'll be mucking and plucking and watering the flocks."

"You won't make anything there!"

"I know."

"Isn't that where your dad worked one time?"

Jeddy said it was. "That's how he got me the job."

We walked along in gloomy silence. Chicken-farm work was dirty and smelly. There seemed to be nothing more to say in the face of such a blow. Jeddy's fate looked sealed even worse than mine. I felt so bad for him that I almost let loose and told him about the *Black Duck*, if only to cheer him up. But we were passing the police station across from Weedie's just then and a knot came in my throat and I kept quiet.

We were almost to school when I thought of something else I could bring up.

"So, about that body, what do you guess happened to it?"

"I don't guess, I know. It got took," Jeddy said. He was still sore about the whole thing, I could see.

"Well, I know that, but the question is, why?"

"My dad told me not to talk about it."

"Oh, come on," I said. "My dad told me that, too. But we've got to talk about it. That's the most interesting part, that they told us not to talk about it."

"My dad said we could get in hot water by sticking our noses in," Jeddy said. "I think it's big-time mobsters fighting with each other."

I nodded. "Could be. The thing I keep wondering about is *how* the body got took. No way you could get a boat in at low tide. And there was no mark on the beach. It's like it somehow got lifted."

"Lifted?" Jeddy said. "You mean like lifted up?"

"Yes."

Jeddy frowned. "I don't see how."

"You don't?" I already knew where this was leading.

"Well . . ." He gazed at me. I could almost see the flash go off in his brain. He was remembering the far-off drone of a motor across the bay, the glimmer of silver wings in the sky.

"That plane we saw!"

"Right. If it had pontoons, it could've landed out in the water. Those seaplanes draw less water than most boats."

"But it was windy that day. They're no good in the wind."

"The wind went down, remember? It was almost calm by the time we got back there. A plane could've coasted in pretty close. Somebody could've got off and grabbed the body and gone right back up. Wouldn't have taken more'n a few minutes."

"Might've been the Coast Guard," Jeddy said. "They've got seaplanes."

"The Coast Guard doesn't go around stealing bodies. If they pick up a body, you hear about it."

"I guess it was somebody else, then. The only thing is, how would they have known where the body was? We were the only ones that knew about it. That plane would've needed somebody to tip 'em off where to land."

"I guess somebody *did* tip 'em off."

Jeddy paused and looked over at me. "Charlie's got a radio in the station," he said.

I nodded. "Remember how he took an ice age to get to your house?"

"And he didn't want us going back on the beach."

"Your dad wasn't too happy we were there, either," I reminded him.

That brought us to a standstill. Neither one of us wanted to make a guess as to what it might mean. I waited to see which way Jeddy was going to jump, whether he'd do what his dad wanted and shut up, or stick with me.

"Well, I think it's unfair," he said, at last. "We found that body and we should be able to know what happened to it. They can't treat us that way, keeping us out of everything."

"You're right!" I said. I pounded him on the back.

"If a plane came in there, it was in broad daylight. Somebody must've seen it or heard it," Jeddy went on. "Who lives down around that beach?"

"Nobody. It's too far out. Except there's old one-eye, Tom Morrison. He's got a shack on the salt marsh behind the dunes."

"That crackpot. I heard he eats raccoons."

"I heard he's got a raft and poles around all night hunting blue crabs," I said. "How about if we go down and pay him a visit?"

"Good idea."

"Soon," I said.

"Yeah, I'm for it."

"Before he forgets. He's that old."

"All right with me."

At this point, we entered the school. And we were proceeding with the most dutiful intentions across the front foyer toward our classroom when the earsplitting clang of the day's opening bell burst over our heads. This was a brand-new electrical device, hooked up that fall to replace the principal's old hand bell, and we nearly jumped out of our skins. But then, as we were recovering, we looked around and noticed something.

Absolutely no one was in sight.

The front hall was empty. So were the corridors. All the students and the teachers were inside their rooms, and the principal had gone back into her office.

"We're late!" Jeddy whispered ecstatically.

"Too late!" I crowed with delight.

A crafty look came into Jeddy's eye. "I'm beginning to wonder if we were ever here," he whispered.

I shook my head solemnly. "I didn't see us."

Without another word, we turned and ran back out the school door, and I remember how the early spring sun beamed down our backs as we hightailed it in glory across the fields toward the shore.

TOM MORRISON

WHAT JEDDY AND I KNEW ABOUT ONE-EYED Tom was what everyone in town knew: that as a young man he'd been a good fisherman. He'd had a boat and a crew and the kind of rugged strength it takes to pull a living from the sea.

But the sea has a way of breaking down even the best. One gusty afternoon, a wave swept Tom's first mate overboard, and he sank and disappeared before Tom could reach him. A few years later, a storm came up and smashed Tom's boat into the rocks, and he had no money to replace her. Then he went to work as crew for others, but a boat hook caught in his eye one day and tore his face so badly that he had to quit working.

After that, according to the story, his moods turned foul. The word went around that he brought bad luck on board a boat, and even when his face healed, no one wanted to hire him. Then his wife left him for another man, and he was forced to sell his house. And so he had retreated, alone, far out on the Point, to a shack that had once housed hens by the side of a salt pond.

From then on, he'd kept away from humanity and rarely come into town. Jeddy and I had caught sight of his gaunt figure in the distance during our treks around Coulter's Point. Neither one of us had spoken to him, though, or dared to follow the sandy footpath that led back to his shack, as we were doing now.

Tom was nowhere in sight when we arrived. We skulked around a bit. The whole place was in a shambles, overgrown with weeds and pond brush, scattered with old tins, rusty tools, broken bottles and the like. The house was actually a pair of coops nailed together, and badly so, for one side had taken to leaning far over on the other, which was itself listing at a dangerous angle. It looked to us as if a hurricane had been through, and perhaps if you thought of what life had served up to poor Tom, you could say he'd weathered more than one.

If he was still around.

A half hour later, we were about to give up and head back toward the beach when the crunch of footsteps came from the bushes. An elderly dog staggered into the yard, followed by an old man carrying a long-handled net bristling with crabs. He halted and looked us over with one rheumy eye. The other was a whitened disk in its socket.

"Hello, Tom!" I managed to call out.

This brought a second suspicious glare. Jeddy weighed in with, "We're here to ask you something, if it's not too much trouble."

Under its gray bush of beard, Tom Morrison's chin made a chewing motion, as if he were mulling this over.

Then he walked toward the house, urging his moth-eaten mutt along. He propped his net against the stoop, where the crabs rattled their claws and scrabbled together, still very much alive.

"It's no trouble of me!" he called at us. "It's trouble of you t'come all the way here."

He sat down against the chicken coop door and pried off his boots. Gruff as he was, we could see he was curious about why we were there. He was throwing us half-glances and muttering to himself. After a bit, he motioned us across the yard to sit down near him on a mound of clam shells.

"This here's Viola," he said, in a somewhat more friendly tone. The dog thumped her tail.

She was about the most beaten-down dog I'd ever seen, and so stiff-jointed, she had to circle around four or five times before her old legs would agree to let her down on the ground. But she had a gentle face and a sweet way about her. When she'd settled, Tom reached out and stroked her with a wide, rough hand.

"Hello, Viola," Jeddy said, leaning forward to give her a pat. She thumped her tail again. Then we got down to business.

"What we want to know," I began, "is if a seaplane came in here a few days back. Not here, I mean, but off the beach out there. It would've had pontoons and made a good amount of noise, and we wondered if you saw it."

Tom stared at me out of his good eye. I was trying my best not to look at his bad eye, which had no pupil and bulged from his head like a peeled egg. Most people would've put a patch over something like that out of plain good manners. Tom was way past worrying about such things, I could see.

"Why we're asking is, we found a dead body there a couple of days ago," Jeddy continued, probably thinking it might help to give the whole story. "And when we left to report it, somebody stole it. And there were no signs of where it went, and no one's talking about it. We think that's fishy."

Tom stared at him. He still didn't trust us and was holding back on an answer. Something else had already answered for him, though. A fancy gold watch was around his wrist. Jeddy and I both saw it. When Tom saw us looking, he raised his arm to make a proud show of the thing.

"We sure would appreciate anything you could tell us," I said. "It was midafternoon when we were there. A bunch of seagulls was making a racket over the body."

"Doing more than making a racket," Tom replied, gazing fondly at the watch. "Having quite a banquet for themselves. Quite a banquet!" He glanced up, amused by his own words.

"But then, somebody must've come. Flown in is what we guess," I pressed him. "We came back later, about suppertime, and nothing was there. No gulls and no body."

"And no empty liquor crate," Jeddy put in. "It'd been there, washed up with the body."

Tom stared at us. "Well, I got that," he said. "After you left. There it is. Might be of use one day."

We looked where he was pointing. The crate was lying cocked up against an overturned skiff across the yard.

"So you saw us," Jeddy said.

Tom grinned. "How d'ya like my new watch?" he asked, holding up his arm again.

"We like it," I said. "It was on the dead man, right?"

"He don't care," Tom said. "He got no use for it now. Anyways, I left him his wedding ring."

"We won't tell," Jeddy said. "We just want to know about the seaplane. Did you recognize the guys in it?"

"Naw. I don't know 'em. Somebody'd been keeping a watch on these beaches, though. Been a big speedboat nosing up and down the coast all week, like it was looking for something. Then in comes the plane."

"Was it the Coast Guard?" I asked.

"Nope. Nobody I ever saw. Tough guys." He paused and sucked in his breath before uttering his next remark. You could see it was distasteful to him, something he didn't want to dwell on.

"They got machine guns," he said. "When they come off the plane there's two of 'em, and they wade ashore holding the guns over their heads. One takes and shoots the dead man. Rat-a-tat-tat. Shoots him dead again. Then they laugh. They drag him out through the waves back to the airplane, and take off."

"Where'd they go?" Jed said.

Tom shrugged. "I stayed hid. I was glad I took time to cover my tracks."

"They never saw you watching?"

Tom shook his head grimly. "They're shooting dead men, so I see they're not particular to what gets shot. Me and Viola, we stayed hid."

School being in session until 2:00 P.M., it seemed best to keep a low profile until that hour. After our talk with Tom, Jeddy and I stuck around in the yard and played with Viola, who still could fetch a stick, though it took her a while to get it back to you. Meanwhile, the old man disappeared inside his shack to heat up a pot of water to cook the blue crabs he'd caught. That was how he ate, never mind what time it was. Schedules the rest of us followed, like breakfast, lunch and dinner, night and day, had lost their pull on him. He was living free of all rules, even the most basic.

I was watching him like a hawk, I've got to say. I'd been under a heavy regime of right and wrong, good ways and bad ways, ever since I could remember, and to see one-eyed Tom out from under, cracking blue crabs at ten o'clock in the morning and falling asleep without even getting up from the table, was a sort of revelation to me.

About noon, with Tom snoring in his chair, Jeddy and I went back to the beach and lay around out of the wind in the dunes. Unless you're a seagull, there's nothing comfortable about an open beach on the Rhode Island coast in May. Keeping our heads down, we ate our school lunches. Afterward, for sport, we crawled around looking for terns' eggs in the dune grass. It was too early in the season for turtles to be laying.

"Well, that's the end of it, I guess," Jeddy said as we rested after these activities. We were back on the subject of the dead man. "The guy was in deep with some bad characters and got shot. My dad is right, it was rumrunners and we probably don't want to know any more about it."

"Makes you wonder, though," I said. "Why were they looking for a guy that was already dead? Then they shoot him again, like they can't stand his guts."

"Maybe it wasn't them who shot him in the first place," Jeddy said. "Maybe it was somebody else and they needed to prove to themselves that the guy was dead. He was probably double-crossing everybody."

"He was a high roller, that's for sure. He must've been hauling in the dough to afford a watch like that. That pipe and tobacco pouch, they're both quality, too."

There was a pause in the conversation while we looked over the dunes at a fishing rig that was chugging along offshore. It passed the beach and went on up the coast.

"Well, you know what Marina thinks," Jeddy said.

"What?"

"She thinks Charlie Pope's gone in with a big bootleg gang. He's been acting like he's some kind of hotshot."

"She doesn't like Charlie. She put him in his place, too. Marina knows how to do that."

"She doesn't like Charlie for a good reason," Jeddy said. "Don't tell anybody, but he tried some funny stuff on her."

"What do you mean?"

"She was walking home from the bus after school one day, and he pulls up in his car and says for her to get in, Dad wants to talk to her. So she gets in, and he starts driving to Harveston. When she asks him what's going on, he says 'nothing,' he just wanted to get to know her better."

"That's crazy. He's ten years older than her."

"I know. So she says to take her home. He says he will, but he has an important errand up the road, and will she just sit tight until it's done? Police business, he says. So, she says all right, and when they get to Harveston, he goes into some place by the train station, and comes out ten minutes later with a couple of guys in suits who shake his hand and drive off in a fancy car.

"When he got back in the car, Marina asked who they were. He told her not to worry about it, they're old friends. He was showing her how important he was, I guess. Then, on the way home, he starts up with her again and pulls into a field off the main road."

"That scum. What's gotten into him?" I was getting furious listening to this. "What'd Marina do?"

"She got out and started walking."

"He didn't touch her, did he?"

"He tried, but she got out too fast. She went back to the main road and walked, and he was driving along beside her, begging her to get in, that he wouldn't do anything, but she didn't trust him and kept walking. Then Emma Pierce came along in the Harveston taxi, and Marina flagged her down and got away. She came home okay."

"She told you all this?"

"She didn't want to. She would've kept it a secret like she does everything. But I saw her getting out of Emma's taxi up the road from the Commons. She was afraid I'd tell Dad about seeing her, and that he'd ask her about it. I had to swear not to say anything. Dad would go through the roof if he knew what Charlie did."

"I wish she'd tell him. Charlie'd get fired!"

"That's what I said, but Marina said, 'Don't tell,' because Dad is funny about stuff like that and he might blame her."

"Blame her! He wouldn't." All this was giving me a new view of what it meant to be a girl with a pretty face.

"He might. He gets mad if he sees anybody looking at her the wrong way. Last summer, when Elton White came over and sat on the porch without even asking, Dad said it was Marina's fault, that she was leading him on."

"Marina wouldn't do that!"

"I know. He wouldn't listen to her, though. He told her he'd have his eye on her from then on."

At this point, we were interrupted by the sound of a motor out on the water, and we peered up over the dune again. A high-powered rig was coming in to the beach. We flattened out and watched.

THE KILLERS RETURN

THE BOAT WAS A DOUBLE-ENGINE SKIFF BUILT for speed, we could see that right away. Three men were on board, including the wheelman, who was a good skipper because he knew how to bring the skiff in close to a rock that stuck out from the beach, and turn her so his two passengers could jump off. The tide was low and nobody got wet. We watched, hardly breathing, as the two walked down the rock to the beach. We were hardly breathing because they were carrying machine guns.

"Oh, Lord, it's them back again," Jeddy whispered. "What're they up to?"

"Looks to me like they're going to see Tom," I said.

That was it, all right. They passed close by our hiding place in the dunes and walked in toward his shack on the marsh. One was a big guy in overalls and suspenders, and a broad-brimmed hat. The other wore a fisherman's cap and was smaller but sharper-looking. From the ugly set of their mugs, we knew they meant business. We sat tight after they went by. A couple of minutes later, we heard yelling and a yelp from Viola. I couldn't lay low anymore.

"I'm going to go see what's up."

"I will, too," Jeddy said.

We crept toward the pond, staying off old Tom's path. We hadn't gone very far when we heard a machine gun go off, one short blast, then one longer one.

Jed dropped down and wrapped his arms around his head. "Oh, no, no," he moaned. "They've gone and shot Tom."

I was scared, too, and I crouched down beside him but with my eye on the road. Pretty soon I saw the two thugs come hustling back toward the beach, their guns across their shoulders. Out on the water, the wheelman must've been watching for them, because the speedboat was already moving toward shore to pick them up. The two went out on the rock the way they'd come, and the skiff hovered alongside it and they jumped on board. Then the wheelman buttoned her up and roared off, passing outside West Island. It looked to me as if they were headed to Newport.

As soon as the boat was far enough away so they wouldn't spot us, Jeddy and I got up and ran like madmen to Tom's shack. We expected to find him sprawled in the yard, but there he was! We couldn't believe our eyes. Old Tom was all right, and he was sitting outside his door, bent over a little but still very much alive.

We yelled and jumped for joy. "Tom! We thought you were killed! Oh, Tom! You're all right! Who were those guys? What did they want?"

He didn't answer and he didn't look up. We couldn't figure out what was wrong.

When we came a little closer I saw he had Viola in his arms. A sick feeling came into me and my knees got weak. I stopped running and let Jeddy go ahead. Tom had his face in Viola's fur. He was holding her and rocking her back and forth in a sort of agony. Jeddy got down and put his hand on Viola's neck and it came away red.

Tom was talking to her when I came up. "Old dog, oh, old dog. Don't you mind, don't you mind," he was saying. He kept rocking her, as if it would bring her comfort. There wasn't anything that would've done that, though. Her eyes were open but the light had gone out of them.

Jeddy turned to me with a terrible face.

"They shot her," he said. "They've gone and killed Viola."

It was quite a while before we could gather ourselves enough to think of what to do next. I felt numb all over and Jeddy was just as bad, I could see. One glance at Tom Morrison was enough to break your heart. He wouldn't let go of Viola, kept rocking her and whispering into her ear. When a half hour had passed and he was still at it, we began to worry that this was the final catastrophe in his life that would drive him over the edge forever.

"C'mon, Tom. Let's get up," I said. "You've got to tell us what happened."

"I believe I'll just sit here with her awhile longer," he answered in a quavering voice.

So we sat on with him, and in the end I saw it was a wise thing to do. Viola was killed in a most sudden and horrible way. She was dead as dead could be, but all around us nature was carrying on. The southwest wind began to drop, as it often will on a spring afternoon. The seaweed smell of the beach drifted in on it, along with the familiar cries of gulls. The sun went in and out of clouds, progressing toward the horizon. Gradually, Jeddy and I began to feel steadier, as if the sea and sky and birds and whatever else was out there were wrapping themselves around old Tom's place, just as he was wrapped around Viola, and telling us "don't you mind, don't you mind."

Tom must've felt some peace come into him, too, because at last he put Viola down and got to his feet. He went out back of his shack and came back with a couple of shovels. He handed one to Jeddy.

"She'll need a resting place," he said. "The sooner the better."

He showed us a shady corner of the yard where Viola liked to lie on hot afternoons, and we took turns digging. When the hole was deep enough to take her, Tom carried Viola across to it, and put her in just as she was, and covered her up after one last look.

"Take her to the good place. She were the best of dogs," he said, nodding up at the sky, as if to give God the go-ahead.

Then we bowed our heads to say a prayer for her in our thoughts, though by this time I wasn't in a very prayerful mood. I was over my shock and getting angrier by the minute. The only thing I could think was that I was going to catch up with the two bums who'd killed Viola and make them pay for it. But first I had to find out from Tom why they'd come.

"They was looking for something," he said.

It was getting on toward late afternoon by the time he came around to giving us this information. Jeddy and I had been pressing him to tell us what happened, and he kept putting us off. The thugs had been in his shack and torn it apart on the inside. His chair and table were overturned, the bed mattress was on the floor, the stove pipe was pulled out of the wall. We helped him put things to rights, swept up some broken dishes and pounded out a dent in his big boiling pot. He owned very little and it didn't take us long. How any man could get by with so few possessions, I don't know.

Afterward, we told him we had to go. Marina would be expecting Jeddy home. I should've been at the store long ago for my afternoon job. I knew I'd have to tell my dad some story about being kept after school, which was going to take some doing since I hadn't been back to the place all day. Jeddy asked Tom one more time what those tough guys had wanted. Finally he answered: "They was looking for something."

"For what?"

Tom held up his arm. The dead man's gold watch was gone.

"Grabbed it right off me," he said. "But that weren't it."

"They wanted something else?"

"The big one kept yelling: 'Where's his wallet? We know you took it.' I told 'em over and over there wasn't no wallet. I didn't take nothing else. He got real mad, went in my shack and kicked stuff around. Finally the little one stuck his head in and stopped him.

" 'C'mon, Ernie, he ain't got the ticket. Let's get outta here.' So the big one comes out. But Viola was standing there and he tripped over her. That made him mad again and he up and shot her."

I couldn't believe it. "But why?"

"There's no why to it. He tripped, that's all. Wasn't Viola's fault. She was just standing there." Tom shook his head helplessly. "He up and shot her, and then they took off. Whatever that ticket is, I don't know. I didn't take nothing else. Only the watch. They could've had it back without grabbing, too. Just ask, that's all. They didn't have to . . ."

He was overwhelmed and mopped his eyes. "I never thought somebody could do a thing like that," he went on in a ragged voice. "Kill an old dog because you trip over her. I just never thought it."

"We're going to report it," Jeddy said. "Don't you worry, my dad is going to know about this."

Tom nodded. You could see he didn't care one way or the other. What was done was done, as far as he was concerned. Viola was killed and that was the end of the story. All the way walking home that afternoon, I felt bad for him. I was also afraid of what would happen when Jeddy's father found out how we skipped school that day.

"Do you have to say anything yet?" I asked Jeddy. "Tom doesn't care. Maybe we should keep today to ourselves."

"Nope, I'm telling him," Jeddy said, determined as he could be. "I've got to. It's police business, two guys coming in, roughing up old Tom and shooting his dog. It's my responsibility to tell."

"Well, take me out of it," I said. "You can say you were down on Coulter's by yourself."

Jeddy shook his head. "I'm telling the whole truth about both of us," he said.

"Why, when there's no use in it?" I was getting hot under the collar.

"Because it's right. It'd be a lie any other way."

"It'll be all right for you maybe, but for me, it won't be," I told him. "My dad is going to take it out on me. He's a stickler for stuff like this. It's not just school. I should've been at the store all this time. The store is *my* responsibility."

"Well, I'm sorry about that, but I can't help it," Jeddy said. "This is police business."

"I didn't know you were working for the police," I yelled at him.

"I didn't know you were such a liar," he yelled back.

After that, we were too mad to talk any more. We walked up the road staring straight ahead, and if thoughts could freeze air, there'd have been a big block of ice between us.

As soon as I could, I veered off and took a shortcut across the fields toward my house. I didn't know what I'd say to my father that night. Then, as it turned out, I didn't have to say anything because he'd been in Worcester all day picking up supplies, and nobody missed me at the store. They must've thought I went with him.

Also, by pure luck, I met Mary Marquez, who was in my class, on my way back and she gave me the assignments for the next day. I got home and did my schoolwork first thing, which impressed my mother. So, for the time being anyhow, everything came out all right for me.

Only, late that night, I woke up and thought about Tom Morrison in his shack behind the dunes. I thought how he must be missing Viola. Here was a man who'd had big dreams once, but who'd been beaten down to the point where he wasn't asking for anything anymore. All he wanted was just one old dog and a shack by a pond. Then look what happens.

Life wasn't being fair to Tom, that's what I decided. It kept taking things away from him. He was trying to live it the best he could and, over and over, it kept taking things away.

The Interview

THE OLD MAN STOPS, LEANS FORWARD, BURIES his face in his hands.

That's enough for today.

David looks down at his notepad and discovers that, once again, he's forgotten to write anything on it.

Life not fair, he scrawls hastily while he can still remember. *Tom Morrison. Blue crabs. Thug stumbles over dog (Viola). Shoots it.*

He shakes his head at himself. He'll have to improve if he's going to be a professional journalist. Maybe he should learn shorthand or buy a tape recorder. Newpapers have started checking their reporters' research notes. They want to be sure they're getting the truth. Some phony articles have been uncovered recently, written by reporters who made things up.

I thought you said you and Jeddy never fought, David says, nitpicking. At least he can go after the old man's contradictions.

We never did, Mr. Hart answers. *Till that day.* He turns away in his chair, making it clear that he doesn't want to talk anymore. David plunges ahead anyway, a little meanly.

This time, I think you were wrong. Jeddy was right. He had to tell his father the whole truth. His dad was the police chief. A crime had been committed.

That's backseat driving. If you knew my father, you wouldn't have told, either.

David nods. Knowing his own father is quite enough to see the point of this argument.

Also, you don't know the whole story about Ralph McKenzie yet, Mr. Hart adds.

I can bet he was under some pressure to go along with things, David says. *Especially if it's like you say, that small-town cops didn't make much salary in those days. It sounds like the McKenzie family could've used the money.*

I guess you could put it down to that.

Why, was there something else?

Mr. Hart doesn't answer; the shop's closed for today.

Is it okay if I come again tomorrow? David asks. *I hope I'm not taking too much of your time. There's more here than I expected.*

My time? I've got more of that than I know what to do with.

Well, is there anything I could bring back for you? From the store, I mean? David noticed there wasn't much in the refrigerator when he put the milk in, just some kind of white soup in a plastic container. A guy that age shouldn't be living alone.

Is someone helping you with shopping? he asks.

Mr. Hart's eyes brush over him. *Someone helping me, did you say?*

Yes. It looks like you could use a hand around here, with your wife away.

The old man raises an eyebrow. *From you?* he asks, and laughs. *So, are you driving now? I mean, aside from giving out free advice to old fools like me.*

Well . . . no. Actually not yet.

A senior in high school and you can't drive a car?

Well, ah . . .

In fact, you're not in high school yet, are you? You'll be a freshman in the fall. You're in no position to interview anybody about anything. You've never even had a job that wasn't handed you by your family.

That's true, David admits, his face getting hot. *How'd you find out?*

I've got my sources. I may look slow, but I can still get around.

Sorry, David says. *That was stupid of me. I guess I stepped out of bounds.*

You did.

I'm sorry I lied about high school, too. I was afraid you wouldn't talk to me if you knew my real age.

Figured that, Mr. Hart says. *I don't mean to needle you. I'd guess you have some of the same problems I used to have as a kid. Your dad's got a big landscaping business, I hear.*

He does.

You're supposed to work there for nothing?

Well, almost nothing. He gives me a little. It's kind of taken for granted that I'll be going in with him.

And you want to get away from what's expected. You want to break ground on your own.

David nods. *My idea is to go for journalism. I'd like to write.*

Well, I admire that, Mr. Hart says. *Everybody should have a chance to start fresh, take possession of what's truly his. You know, I never did that. Professionally, that is.*

Why not?

The Depression came on and jobs dried up. I stayed here and took over managing Riley's store from my father. Jeddy made it out of this town, but I didn't. Seems kind of funny to me now.

Did Jeddy leave because of something his father did? Chief McKenzie, I mean, David asks.

I may get to that, Mr. Hart says. He waits a minute, then adds: *And then again, I may not. I haven't decided.*

You said you didn't start fresh professionally. But you had something else going?

I did, yes.

Which is the reason you stuck around here?

Yes, I'd say so. I've been lucky in other quarters.

Which are?

Ruben Hart gazes at him a long moment. Then, in the maddening way he has of ignoring direct questions that cut too close, he changes the subject.

If you still want to do something for me, there is one favor I could ask, he tells David.

Okay. Shoot.

There's a pair of hedge clippers out in the garage, hang-

ing high up on a hook. If you could get 'em down for me, I'd be obliged. I'd like to do some pruning around this place before the wife gets back. I was noticing this morning as you came in, it's a jungle outside the front windows.

Sure, David says. *No problem at all.* He goes to look for them.

The question about Chief McKenzie nags at him, though. Later, as he's driving home with his mother, he asks her: *Did you ever hear of a police chief in this town named Ralph McKenzie? He would've been here in the 1920s.*

She shakes her head. *Too long ago for me. There might be a record of him at the town hall.*

The next morning, on their way to Mr. Hart's, David has his mother stop by. He checks with the clerk, but finds no reference to anyone named McKenzie. There's nothing mysterious about this, however. The records on police chiefs only go back to 1930.

COCKFIGHTERS

WHATEVER JEDDY TOLD HIS FATHER ABOUT the gunmen on Coulter's Point, it didn't come to anything. As far as I could see, nobody heard about it. Chief McKenzie never went down to investigate. I know he didn't because I began keeping an eye on Tom Morrison after that.

Jeddy and I weren't on speaking terms, and even if we had been, he was working at Fancher's chicken farm and I was working at the store and there was no time for us to be together. It got to be a habit of mine that if I had an afternoon off, usually on weekends, I'd go see Tom. I'd bring him a newspaper and a pound of coffee or a loaf of store bread, something to give me a reason for the visit. We wouldn't do much, just sit around and shoot the breeze, but I got to like him and I believe he liked me.

He never complained about anything, not the weather or his lost eye or any of the bad luck that had befallen him. If you started him telling stories about his fishing days, he could be very entertaining. I asked him if he didn't want to get another dog to keep him company, and he shook his head. He said any dog that wanted to come find him, he'd take it in, the way he had Viola. Otherwise, he wasn't looking for one at this late date.

"How did Viola come to you?" I asked.

"Swam in," Tom said, his good eye brightening. He loved to talk about her. "She were a long-distance swimmer in her day. What I believe is, she come over from Newport."

"Swam over? Impossible! She'd have to go five miles or more."

"That's what I believe she did. The reason I say so, I have a friend with a boat who came across a dog swimming off Land's End over there. He didn't think nothing of it till he came to visit me one day. And he says: 'I swear if that isn't the dog I saw swimming.' I already knew she was good in the water, so I didn't doubt it. She'd swim alongside my raft while I was out crabbing, be in the water for a couple of hours and never get tired. This was a while back when she was a younger dog, of course."

After a story like this, he'd get quiet. His beard would go into the chewing motion that meant he was working something through. He wasn't a man easy in his own skin. He had days of darkness and bad humor, though he did his best not to show it. He told me once that his battles in life were as much against himself as any other demon. "Weather and women included," he added, with a wink.

He was a character, all right, and fascinating to me for his determination to follow his own path and take orders from no one, lonely as that was.

As the days passed, I wondered why Chief McKenzie wouldn't show more interest in what had happened to him, if in fact Jeddy had told his father, which I didn't doubt. But I let it ride. Tom wasn't complaining and, at that time, there was so much going on of a cloak-and-dagger nature around the area that two goons with machine guns probably didn't amount to much. Chief McKenzie soon had his hands full in another direction anyway.

A couple of gaming men arrived from Massachusetts and began running cockfights out in the woods. This was a matter of putting two long-taloned roosters together in a ring and watching to see which one would tear the other apart. It was a grisly amusement that tended to attract bad types. Soon roughnecks from all over were showing up to bet on the cocks. They were drinking and carousing and getting into fights themselves. Chief McKenzie wasn't about to tolerate that kind of behavior. One night, he and Charlie went out and broke up the party. They ended by arresting a good number of outsiders.

There was a small jail in town connected to the town hall that mostly went unoccupied. All the week after Viola got killed and all the week after that, it was full of spitting, cursing, riffraff cockfighters waiting for their court dates to come up in Providence. The judges had gotten behind with all the smuggling cases that were coming in and a backlog had developed.

People in town went by to get a look at the outsiders, then they'd saunter over and buy a soda at Riley's store and talk about it. I was hauling stock like a mule there every afternoon, building up some capital in case my father ever heard about the day I took off. One afternoon, Marina dropped by to get a few groceries and she came out back to talk to me.

"I hear you and Jed aren't getting along," she said. It'd been over two weeks by then.

I just nodded. I felt sore enough about our falling-out that I didn't want to talk about it, and anyhow, the way she looked was taking its usual toll on me. She had her dark hair pulled straight back in a ponytail that went halfway down her back. This was to show she meant business, I guess, but a few strands she didn't know about had come loose and were bouncing around on her neck. I was trying not to look at them. I could see how a guy like Charlie Pope might go after her, crazy as that was. In my eyes, and maybe in his eyes, too, Marina was a natural: beautiful without trying and without caring about it, either. That was a mistake, of course. I still had a lot to learn about girls. The truth was, she just hadn't yet met the person who would make her care.

Strangely enough, Charlie Pope was what Marina had come to speak to me about.

"Has he been over here bothering you?" she asked.

I shook my head.

"Well, he's been at Jed."

"About what?"

"The dead man you found. He thinks you and Jeddy might've taken something off the body."

"Like what?"

"A wallet."

My heart took a leap. It put Charlie in the same ring with Tom Morrison's gunmen. All of a sudden, Charlie Pope didn't seem like some small-town cop taking a few dollars to look the other way. He seemed a lot worse.

"There wasn't anything on him," I told Marina. "No wallet or ID. Only thing was a pipe and a tobacco pouch." I didn't mention the gold wristwatch. That would've brought up Tom Morrison, and I couldn't see the use of it. "What's Charlie looking for, anyhow?"

"He won't say." Marina gave me one of her extra-sharp glances and lowered her voice. "Listen, Ruben. Charlie's into some rotten business. You watch out for him, all right?"

"Does your dad know?" I asked. "Can't he do something about it?"

"He has to be careful, too. Charlie's got connections."

"What connections? Can't your dad report it?"

"He's doing what he can. You just keep an eye on yourself. And get straightened out with Jed," she added, more lightly. "It's not the same without you hanging around all the time. Anyway, you've got supper coming."

I knew she was talking about how Chief McKenzie had dis-invited me the afternoon we found the body. I'd been missing their house a lot. It felt good to know one person at least was missing me.

"Thanks!"

She flashed me that fine smile of hers and went back up front to do her shopping.

After that, I couldn't stop grinning. All the next hour, I was putting on the steam and working twice as hard as usual out of pure happiness. Mr. Riley was there on one of his visits from Boston, and he must've noticed. He pulled me aside when Dad was out of the store.

"You're getting to be a big, strong fellow."

"Yes, sir," I said, proud to be complimented but also suspicious of what he wanted.

"I could use a fellow like you. Would you be interested in taking on a job tonight?"

After seeing him on the beach at Tyler's, I had an idea already of what it might be, so I hedged. "I'd better check with my dad," I told him. "He might not want me out riding around like that."

"I believe I could fix it with him," Mr. Riley said. "If I did, what would you say to this?" He handed me a ten-dollar bill. It bowled me over.

"Well, I guess I could do a job if my dad says so."

"That's all right then," Mr. Riley said. "Your pop's a good man. Finest manager a man could have. You be down at Brown's Cove tonight at nine o'clock and there'll be another ten dollars for you. And a bit of an adventure, as well."

He gave me a wink and walked off.

I wanted to go down to Brown's, no doubt about that, but I also wanted to be sure it was all right with my father. It seemed odd to me that he'd agree, since as far as I knew, he'd kept himself clear of the rum-running business. When he came back in the store, I asked if I could speak to him. He said not right then.

Later, I tried to ask him again, but he put me off. It was a busy afternoon, with kegs of molasses and sacks of flour coming in, and egg deliveries from a couple of farms. I didn't get to speak to him in private until just before I was leaving to go home to supper.

"Tell your ma I'll be late tonight," Dad said. "You two go on and eat. I'll be home for a bite about nine."

I said I'd tell her. "There's something else," I said.

He'd been about to walk off, now he wheeled around on me. He knew what I was going to say. Later, I found out he'd been twice to talk it out with Mr. Riley, and that was why he kept putting me off.

"All right! You do what's been asked of you," he snapped, before I could even open my mouth. He was angry. "It'll be just this once."

My chin dropped a little. I didn't like the way he was agreeing to it, like he was being forced to.

"I won't do it if you say not to," I told him.

"I'm saying do what's been asked and keep it to yourself," my father repeated, as if he couldn't bring himself to mention what it was. "I'll deal with your ma when I get back."

"So, I should just ride my bike down to Brown's after supper and—"

Dad cut me off right there. "How many times do I have to say it? Now, get on home!"

I went. I had a bad feeling about what might have gone on between Dad and Mr. Riley, but it didn't last long. Twenty dollars was a small fortune to a kid in those days. The money wasn't the only thing, either. I'd known other boys, mostly older than me, who'd been hired onto shore gangs. You'd never want to ask them about it, and they wouldn't be stupid enough to boast, but there was an unspoken awe and mystery that surrounded them and left a big impression on the rest of us. Now I was to be one of those chosen few. Whatever my father might think, that was something I wouldn't mind.

What he told my mother about where I went that night, I never asked. I know that when I got back from the job, long after midnight, there was a plate of cookies set out in the kitchen, and a note from her telling me to pour myself some milk. Otherwise, my mother never said a word to me and I never said anything to her. I'd come home safe and eaten the cookies and that was all she had to know. Which was a good thing because if she ever had found out what went on that night, she'd never have trusted my father to let me go anywhere again.

THE JOB AT BROWN'S

IT WAS DAMP OUT. DARK AND MUDDY ON THE road. A spring rainstorm had been through during the day and not much had dried off when I left for Brown's Cove that evening. I pedaled slowly. The wind was blowing into my face, which led me to thoughts of Jeddy and his cap that would never stay on. Seeing Marina that afternoon had made me homesick for him, if you can be homesick for a person. We hadn't said two words in as many weeks and had taken to walking to school by different routes so as not to run into each other.

I was ready for a change.

It wasn't Jeddy's fault his dad was who he was. When I thought about it, I could even admire how Jeddy was sticking to his guns, backing up his father in a difficult time. I knew I'd do the same for my father if it came to that.

I made up my mind to speak to Jeddy as soon as I could. We'd work it out. He'd agree not to ask me what was going on along the beaches. I'd agree not to let anything slip that he'd have to report as "police business." We'd been friends for so long, it didn't seem as if it'd be that hard.

Brown's Cove was a good three miles out of town. Before long, I knew I wasn't the only one headed there. Five or six vehicles rushed by me in the dark, driving without headlights. One of them was Mr. Riley's fancy red Lincoln. I knew it well. He parked out front of the store whenever he came down from Boston. I'd replaced the bulb in my bicycle lamp and had the beam cocked way up to spot out potholes ahead. I think Mr. Riley recognized me as he went by because an arm came out and waved just before the Lincoln disappeared into the dark. I liked that, being recognized by Mr. Riley. He was giving me a lot more scope than my own father, trusting me to do a big-time job.

I'd never been on the beach at Brown's, though I'd passed it going upriver on the Fall River boat a couple of times. It was a natural cove sheltered by a dip in the coast, a good place for a hidden landing. When I rode up, about twenty men were already there and a bunch of skiffs were pulled up on the beach, oars set and ready. The place was lit up bright as day with oil lanterns planted on the beach and car headlights shining across the sand. When I looked across the water, I was astonished to see a freighter looming like a gigantic cliff just outside the blaze of lights. It was in the process of dropping anchor. I soon found out that she was the *Lucy M.*, a Canadian vessel that usually moored outside the twelve-mile U.S. territorial limit off the coast to avoid arrest.

The way the Prohibition law was written, the Coast

Guard couldn't touch an outside rig, since it was in international waters. So ships from Canada and the West Indies, Europe and Great Britain would lie off there, sell their liquor cargos and unload them onto rum-running speedboats like the *Black Duck* to carry into shore. Sometimes as many as ten or fifteen ocean-going vessels would be moored at sea, waiting to make contact with the right runner. "Rum Row," these groups of ships were called. You couldn't see them from land, but you knew they were out there lying in wait over the horizon. It gave you an eerie feeling, as if some pirate ship from the last century was ghosting around our coast.

I couldn't believe the *Lucy M.*'s captain would be so bold as to bring her into Brown's, where any Coast Guard cutter in the area could breeze up and put the pinch on her. Nobody at Brown's seemed worried about it, though, and unloading operations soon commenced.

The skiffs on shore rowed out and took on burlap bags, which was how the liquor was cased this time, then rowed in and were unloaded by the shore gang. I was assigned to a gang of eight men that handed the bags up the beach to waiting vehicles. It was a smoothly run operation, two gangs working at once, and a bunch of skiffs rowing out and back so that just as one skiff was unloaded and took off for more cargo, another would land, stuffed to the gunnels. We worked our tails off for an hour, took a short break, then started again. The men on my gang were all good fellows, some of whom I knew from town. They weren't used to having someone as young as me on the job, and I took a lot of kidding, but I didn't care. I was happy to be there, making my twenty bucks.

Along about midnight, someone came running onto the beach, shouting: "Feds! Feds!" Right behind him came a car. It slammed on the brakes and men in dark suits jumped out with pistols. They were Prohibition agents. After them, two state patrol cars drove in, and a bunch of uniformed police officers ran onto the beach, some of whom were carrying guns, too.

It all happened so fast that I stood there, frozen to the ground. Tino, a guy I'd been working with, grabbed my arm.

"Hey, kid, hoof it!"

I took off after him. We dove behind a sand dune, then split up and crawled off into the beach grass. After about five minutes, I heard footsteps come up close to where I was lying flat out in the grass. I held my breath and the feet went away over a nearby dune. I never knew if it was the police, the Feds, or one of the shore crew scouting for a buddy. I was too scared to look.

Later, loud voices sounded from down on the beach. I crawled to the top of my dune and took a peek to see what was happening. The car lights were still blazing, and I saw Mr. Riley in a circle of police officers. Charlie Pope was there, and so was Jeddy's dad in his leather vest with his badge shining out. Mr. Riley was mad as a wet hen. His face was bright red and he was yelling.

"I bought protection!" he shouted. "I paid you for it. What're you doing here, messing up my landing?"

Chief McKenzie said something I couldn't hear that made Mr. Riley even more furious.

"Who're you working for? The big boys?" he shouted. "What'd they pay you to do this? It's my drop. I paid for it!"

Meanwhile, two men in suits who must have been Federal agents came up. They took hold of Mr. Riley on either side and snapped handcuffs on him. He tried to shake the guys off, but didn't get anywhere. They started walking him to a car. He kept glancing over his shoulder at the *Lucy M.* out in the cove. She was pulling up anchor.

"Where're you taking my cargo?" Mr. Riley yelled. He kept on yelling until they put him in the car. The last I saw of him was his fancy shoes, the ones he never liked to get wet, disappearing as they closed the car door on him.

The police had rounded up a few other members of the shore gang, handcuffed them and put them in cars. But after the Feds left with Mr. Riley, Chief McKenzie gave an order to let everyone out of the patrol cars. He and Charlie undid all the handcuffs and let everyone go.

It was beyond me what had happened. The chief drove off, followed by a caravan of vehicles, leaving the beach in darkness except for one oil lamp somebody had forgotten. Out in the cove, the *Lucy M.* was under way, heading off into Narragansett Bay. She was heavy in the water, still carrying a lot of cargo. We'd only unloaded her about halfway. I couldn't figure out where the Coast Guard was, and why no one was coming to stop her. She went out onto the bay and steamed down the coast, lights full on, as if she were the most law-abiding ship in the world.

I lay quiet for a few more minutes, then got up and found my bike in the dark. I was about to take off for the long ride home when Tino strolled up.

"Hey there, kid. I've got a vehicle in a field at the top of the lane. If you want to walk up with me, I'll give you a lift home."

"Can you take my bicycle?" I asked.

"Sure can." He was a nice guy, a dockworker who'd come all the way over from New Bedford to do this job. I'd heard him talking to the other shore workers earlier. We set off, me wheeling my bike.

"Some night, right? That's how it goes sometimes," he said.

"Does this mean we don't get paid?" I asked.

"Afraid so."

I shook my head. "I don't get it. The Federal agents arrested Mr. Riley, but then the police let everybody else go?"

"Sure they did. That was part of the deal." Tino gave a laugh. He was an old hand at rum-running, and knew the game.

"What deal?" I asked.

"The deal to put this guy Riley out of business, I guess. The way I see it, Riley thought he'd paid the Feds and the cops enough to look the other way for this landing. But somebody got to them and paid 'em a little more to take an interest."

"How'd you figure that?"

"Just from what I heard on the beach. Riley was yelling his head off at that cop."

I looked at Tino. The cop he was talking about was Chief McKenzie. I couldn't see him taking a payoff to double-cross Mr. Riley. They knew each other from town.

"The police must've gotten a tip about this landing tonight," I said. "That's why they were here. I guess they let the crew off because they were local guys."

Tino laughed merrily at this. "The police got a tip, all right, just not from who you might think. Riley's an independent operator in this area. It's no secret he's made a bundle running his own show. My bet is, somebody bigger wants to take him over."

"Who?" I asked.

"Y'don't want to ask that," Tino said. "Y'don't want to know. But if I was to make a guess, I'd say it's an outfit up in Boston. Big boys, like Riley was yelling. I hear they're on the move."

"You mean a gang?" I asked. "Like the Mafia?"

Tino gave me a look. "You didn't hear it from me."

"What'll happen to Mr. Riley?"

"He'll pay a fine and maybe sit in jail a couple of months. Nothing much. He's lucky. If it's the Boston guns he's up against, they're tough eggs. They could've knocked him off like Tony Mordello."

"Who's Tony Mordello?"

"You never heard of him? He was working the New Bedford area up where I come from. I bet this guy Riley knew who he was."

"Well, what happened to him?"

"He was running a big operation in champagne and Canadian whiskey, making money hand over fist. He'd been at it awhile, had fancy cars, a big house, furs for his wife. We were all working for him, doing real good for ourselves. Then the show falls apart. From what I hear, he got a visit from a couple of guys who wanted a piece of the action, and he told them to shove it. I guess he didn't count on who they were. One night about a month ago, Tony disappeared."

"Is he dead?"

"Nobody knows and nobody wants to ask. He went to a poker game in his evening suit and never came home. Now his operation is being run by couple of smart guys they call the College Boys, out of Boston. It's a real syndicate. They've got their own muscle."

I kept quiet after that. It was pretty clear to me who the dead man on Coulter's Beach must have been.

I told Tino where I lived. When we came to the end of my driveway, he helped me unload my bike.

"Don't know if I'll see you again," he said. "I'll probably be sticking closer to home now. It's getting too chancy on these out-of-town jobs."

I nodded and thanked him for the ride.

"Watch out for yourself, kid," he said, and drove off into the dark. Looking after him, I realized I'd never even told him my name.

Five minutes later, I was reading my mother's note and eating her cookies in the kitchen. I thought I'd handled everything fine until I went to pour myself a glass of milk and it splashed all over the table. I looked down at my hand. It was shaking like a branch in a storm.

THE BREAKUP

I SAW JEDDY ON THE WAY TO SCHOOL THE next morning. He had his cap on backward, which is what he did when he was having trouble with something. I knew him so well, I could almost tell what the trouble was. If he looked mad, it had to do with Marina or something that happened at school. If he was walking slow and looking sort of defeated, it was his dad. Jeddy was walking slow.

I came up on him and got into step.

"How's things?" I said.

He didn't answer.

I thought a little and said: "Guess what? Mr. Riley got arrested last night."

"How come?" Jeddy asked, without looking at me.

"I don't know. My dad got a call this morning. Mr. Riley's up in the Fall River jail." I was lying to Jeddy, but what I said was true. A man had come knocking at our door at 6:00 A.M. A half hour later, my father was on his way up to Fall River in our Ford.

"My dad said he's been running rum," Jeddy volunteered.

"Who has?"

"Mr. Riley."

"When did he say that?"

"A while back. My dad's had his eye on him."

"How come you didn't tell me?" I asked him. I was happy to hear the chief had been watching Mr. Riley. It put him on the right side of the law, which, after last night, I hadn't been sure of. Still, I thought Jeddy should've let me know since Mr. Riley was my father's boss.

"It was police business," Jeddy said, glancing over at me. I knew he was starting up on the argument we'd had. I didn't want to do that anymore.

"How about riding down to see Tom Morrison on Saturday?" I said. "I've been back a few times. We could go crabbing on his raft."

"Can't," Jeddy said, not looking.

"Why not?"

"I'm working at the farm on Saturday."

"How about Sunday," I said.

"I'm working on Sunday, too."

"Not all day."

"Yes I am," Jeddy said.

I gave him a hard stare. When he finally looked back at me, I said, "You don't want to be friends anymore?"

He gave a kind of defeated shrug, as if it was out of his hands.

"We don't need to talk about anything. We could just . . . you know."

He knew what I meant.

"My dad said I don't have time," he told me. His eyes slid away. I could tell that wasn't what his father had said.

"What's going on, Jed? Is it my dad? Does the chief think he's in with Mr. Riley?" It occurred to me that Chief McKenzie might believe that. My dad worked for Riley, after all.

Jeddy shook his head. "I just don't have time," he repeated.

"Because if he does, he's wrong. Come on, you know my dad's not in on it. He never would be." I stopped walking and looked over. "I might be, but never him."

I was dropping a clue, hoping Jeddy would ask me what I meant. In our good days, he would have. It was part of how close we were that we could read each other's minds. *You might be in on it?* Jeddy would've said. *What's this "might be"?* It would've given me an excuse to tell him where I'd been the night before. I was dying to be asked. I wanted to tell him about the *Black Duck*.

Jeddy didn't look at me. He kept on walking. That scared me. It seemed as if a terrible new wall was going up between us and nothing I said or did could stop it.

For a moment, I thought I'd tell him anyway. I came so close. When I think back now, I know that's what I should have done. If I'd kept to our rule of no secrets and told Jeddy what had happened at Brown's, how I'd seen his dad and all, it might've brought us together again. We could've compared notes and talked through what was happening. That might've given us a larger frame to put around things, a frame that took in a few fog banks and murky nights, not just the sharp daylight of right and wrong, which was the kind of childish picture we'd been living in up to then.

We were entering new territory, Jeddy and I, only we didn't realize it. The world was about to get tougher on us, more complicated, and there we were fighting with each other instead of sticking together as we'd sworn to do.

We came up on the school. I glanced over at him. He was looking kind of sick. I had a pretty clear idea by then what the trouble was between him and his father, and it made me angry. Chief McKenzie had no right to give orders like that. Whatever side of the rum-running business he was on—and I honestly didn't know what to think right then—he had no right to cut Jeddy away from a friend like me. Why he would do it, I couldn't understand. He knew me and he knew my dad about as well as anybody could. All I could think was, it must be a mistake.

"Listen, it's all right," I told Jeddy. "You can steer clear of me if it's easier for you. Your dad will see the truth sometime, then we'll get back together. Anyway, we'll always be friends, right? Nothing can stop that."

Jeddy didn't answer. His head was turned away and I could see from how his jaw was set that he was holding himself in. He wanted to say something, but he couldn't.

We walked along in silence for a couple more minutes. At last, he gave the tiniest nod, as if he was saying good-bye, and lit out up the road. I stopped and waited till he was inside the school before going on myself. It seemed the right thing to do to give him some room.

THE SQUEEZE

MY FATHER CAME BACK TO THE STORE FROM Fall River late that afternoon. He'd been there all day trying to get Mr. Riley out of jail, but the judge was a hard-nose and wouldn't set bail.

Right off the bat, Dad called a meeting of store employees to put the record straight.

He explained how Mr. Riley had been busted in a raid on Brown's Cove, which everyone already knew from the gossip flying around town. He said Mr. Riley would have to sit in a cell for a few days until things got worked out, and that a lawyer was on the case and he'd have his day in court. In the meantime, Riley's General Store was to go ahead with its usual business.

"Nothing has changed," Dad told us. "This store is not involved with Mr. Riley's arrest. Neither is anyone who works here. Smuggling is not part of our business, and that," he went on, sending a warning look around the stockroom where we were all gathered, "is how things will continue to be as long as I am in charge."

It was a good speech, I've got to say. For the first time, I understood why my father had been so careful not to voice an opinion, one way or the other, about rum-running. It was his responsibility to keep Riley's General Store open and on the right side of the law. Our community depended on Riley's, and he was going to see that it was well served.

I couldn't help noticing, though, that while he was giving the eye to Bink Mosher, the butcher, and Fanny DeSousa, the cashier, and even to the new stock boy, John Appleby, he never once glanced at me. This was deceitfulness of a sort, for all the time he was talking about no one being involved, he knew I'd been there on Brown's with Mr. Riley. He knew he himself had given me permission to be there.

It opened my eyes to watch my father walking the fringes of dishonesty that afternoon, though I could appreciate why he did. It was to protect the store and to give me cover, and certainly to spare my mother the worry of knowing where I'd been.

Something else began to bother me. My father didn't level with me privately, either. All the rest of that day, I waited for him to take me aside and talk to me about Brown's. I badly needed to hear his views on Mr. Riley's arrest. Was it good or bad? I wanted to tell him about Chief McKenzie being on the beach, about the charges Mr. Riley had made against him and how everyone else had been let go afterward. Was Tino right? Had Mr. Riley been set up?

Gradually, it dawned on me: Dad was never going to speak to me. He didn't want to know about my night on the beach. He even avoided being alone with me, as if he was afraid I'd embarrass him by bringing it up. If I'd been older, I might have understood. The less said the better was his old-fashioned way of dealing with a situation that had gotten out of hand, that was scaring him, maybe, because Mr. Riley had gone to jail.

As it was, I was hurt by his silence, which I turned on myself. I knew I was far from perfect, a disappointment to him as a person and a son. Now I believed I'd sunk so low that he couldn't bear even my company anymore. Cast off in this new, frightening way, I stayed out of his sight as much as I could. And that was too bad, because right then was when I could have used his help.

Charlie Pope caught up with me late one afternoon as I walked home from the store. He pulled his car over to the side of the road ahead of me and waited until I came up. Then he opened the door and stepped in front of me.

"Howdy, Ruben," he said, eyes sharp on my face.

I said hello.

"Wanted to speak to you about one small thing."

I looked at him. Ever since Jeddy had told me what he'd tried with Marina, I'd thought he was a snake. Now, just like one, his tongue flicked out over his lips, leaving a thin film of spit.

"Y'know that body you and Jed found a few weeks back?"

I nodded.

"You might be interested to hear it's been identified."

"So you found it again?"

"Never was lost. Turns out the Coast Guard spotted it from the air just after you left. Went in there in a seaplane and picked it up before we got there."

That was a lie. I kept quiet.

"He was a New Bedford man, drowned off his boat while he was sport fishing," Charlie went on. "One of those sad accidents. People don't know the power of the sea. They get a hold of some fancy boat and think they've bought the keys to heaven. Go off by themselves. Don't take precautions."

I didn't say anything. He went on.

"The fellow was a well-known businessman over there, owned a couple of restaurants. Made quite a bundle for himself. I hear his wife's in a bad state. Two little kids. You can imagine how it'd be. She believes he had some papers on him from a deal he was negotiating. It wasn't in his wallet. That turned up on the boat. Actually, one slip of paper is what they're looking for. You didn't by any chance see something like that when you found the body?"

"What kind of paper?" I said.

"I dunno, receipt-sized. Y'know, they're trying to clean up his affairs, get the estate straightened out. She is, I mean. His wife. That piece of paper would be helpful."

"Did you look in his pockets?" I asked sarcastically.

Charlie's lips twitched. He glanced down at his feet. When he glanced back up, his eyes had turned mean.

"We looked in his pockets. Yes sir, we certainly did. What I want to know, kid, is if *you* looked in his pockets."

"I didn't," I answered. I gazed directly at him. It was a bold-faced lie.

"And you didn't take anything else off that body?"

"No. I didn't even touch it. Neither of us did."

I added this to protect Jeddy. I hoped to God he'd said the same thing.

"I find that hard to believe," Charlie said. "Two kids and a body alone on a beach. First thing you'd do is search him." He was really putting the squeeze on.

"Not us," I declared. We stared at each other.

"He'd been in the water awhile," I said. "Could be this piece of paper dissolved. Or washed away."

"That'd be a shame," Charlie snapped. He got back in his car and put his head out the window. "Listen up, Ruben, you better be telling the truth. This isn't some game of hide-and-seek we're playing."

I didn't turn a hair. "Who's we?" I shot back. "You and Chief McKenzie? Or are you in this by yourself?"

He licked his lips again. "You're a smarty. I'd watch my back if I was you," he said, and drove off.

When I got home, I went up to my room first thing and closed the door behind me. I opened my desk drawer and searched around in the rear of it. The pipe and tobacco pouch were there, pushed into a corner. I brought them out into the light, feeling again the strangeness of having them in my possession. It was like holding a little piece of the dead man's life, a very personal piece that only those closest to him would have been familiar with. His wife, for instance.

Now that Charlie had told me about her, I could imagine her. She must have watched the man open his pouch and fill his pipe after dinner on many nights. What was his name again? Tony something. His young children would have caught the scent of tobacco smoke traveling up the stairs to their bedrooms. They would have gone to sleep with a peaceful image of their father in their minds. Their father, the rumrunner. Would they ever know the real story of how he'd died?

I opened the pouch to sniff the leaf myself, and with its tang in my nostrils came a sudden thought. I pushed my fingers down into the tobacco and poked around. In a second, I brushed against something, and going deeper, I pulled out a slim paper scroll. It looked like a cigarette to me, a fancy one with a fine gray-green design, somewhat misshapen from being in salt water for so long. A bit odd, yes, but a man might store a cigarette he wished to smoke later in his tobacco pouch.

It was only as I stared at this object that a faint sense of recognition arrived in my head. I put the pouch aside and began trying to unroll the thing. Seawater had stiffened it and collapsed the ends. I managed at last to spread it flat on my desk, and there, in a flash, the exotic greenish design turned commonplace. Before me lay one half of a fifty-dollar bill.

THE BILL

I LOOKED IMMEDIATELY FOR THE SECOND half. Nothing else was in the pouch. The bill had been neatly torn in half, but why anyone would do such a thing to perfectly good money was beyond me. Fifty dollars was way too much to waste that way. I wondered if it might be counterfeit, or, a longer shot, was carrying a message of some kind. After dinner, I borrowed my mother's magnifying glass from the table in the front parlor where she used it to read the newspaper.

Under the bright beam of my desk lamp, the grainy image of General Ulysses S. Grant became a series of uninteresting swirls, revealing nothing. His stern face ended at the left ear, where the bill had been torn. On the bill's back, the grand U.S. Capitol building in Washington, D.C., was sheared off down the middle. Nothing unusual there, either. I'd heard that counterfeit bills lacked the tiny red and blue threads that run almost invisibly through the background of real money. This bill had red and blue threads galore. It was real.

I gave up in disgust. Half a fifty-dollar bill was about as useless as an old bottle cap. Worse than useless, I decided, because it made you think of what you might have bought if you'd only had the rest.

If Jeddy and I had been talking, I would've showed my discovery to him and we could've had a good time making up theories about it. Instead, I tucked it between the pages of my geometry book that night, and over the next couple of weeks mostly forget about it. From time to time, it would slip out when I did my assignments. I'd reexamine it—the half was now a flattened square—and slide it back between the pages.

One day at school, I was stashing my books in my locker, getting ready to go to lunch, when I heard a voice in back of me say:

"Here, Ruben, you dropped something."

I turned around to find Jeddy holding out the piece of bill. He'd been standing back, waiting for me to finish loading my things so he could get to his locker, which still was, as it always had been, right next to mine.

"It slipped out of your book."

"Thanks." I took the bill from his hand. He watched me put it back in the book with a comical look on his face, as if to say, "Saving up to buy something with that?" I knew he was wondering about it.

"I found it in the dead man's tobacco pouch, all rolled up," I explained in a low voice. "I thought it was a cigarette."

"Too bad it wasn't," he said. "Might've been good for a smoke at least."

I laughed and so did he. We'd put in some time with

a pack of Lucky Strikes behind the McKenzies' garage not long before our breakup. For a minute we stood grinning at each other, remembering. I thought maybe that was an opening, but Jeddy turned and walked off and never said another word. My heart fell. I saw nothing had changed. He was sticking by his dad, true blue, to the end.

Mr. Riley's court date came up about midway through May. Chief McKenzie sent Charlie Pope to testify and Riley was convicted by a federal judge in Providence of "possessing and transporting liquor." He was sentenced to eight months in jail. At the store, the staff shook their heads over it.

"He got the book thrown at him," Bink Mosher said.

"You can bet there's some shenanigans behind it," Fanny DeSousa agreed. "I tell you what, I don't trust anybody anymore."

A lot of people in town were angry. Other folks who'd been brought in by the Feds under similar circumstances had gotten off with a fine. The jail sentence was unfair, most believed. There was a general suspicion that money had changed hands to put him behind bars. I even heard my father tell my mother and Aunt Grace that he'd gotten a bum rap.

"The whole thing stinks to high heaven," he said. "Somebody was out to get him, and they did. There's judges getting paid to—"

"Didn't I say so?" Aunt Grace interrupted. "Every which way you turn, somebody's asking for a payoff."

"Surely not here in town," my mother said. "Ralph McKenzie's an honest man."

They were all in the kitchen. I was listening from the top of the back stairs leading down, and I waited to hear what my father would say to this. There came a clank of dishes—they were washing up from supper—then the sound of the sink emptying.

"Carl, what've you got against him?" my mother said finally, with more impatience than she usually allowed in her voice. "We all used to be such good friends. I know Ralph's changed some since Eileen died, but who can blame him? He loved her so. I can't see why you look that way whenever I bring up his name."

There was no answer. I heard a squeak from the back door as it opened. A minute later, our old Ford was revving up and on its way out the driveway.

The Interview

I WENT BY RILEY'S STORE AFTER WE FINISHED here yesterday. You're right, there are old storage cellars still under the barn out back, David tells Mr. Hart on a hot afternoon in what has now become the month of July.

They're not the only ones, by any means, Mr. Hart answers. *You take a close look at some of the older farmhouses down near the water, you'll find trapdoors, false ceilings, closets in unlikely places. Everybody was hiding the stuff, both for selling and drinking.*

They're sitting outside in Mr. Hart's front yard, on plastic lawn chairs under a tree. David helped carry the chairs from the decrepit garage teetering on its last legs in back of the house, the same place he found Mr. Hart's moldy, calcified clippers.

It must be a law of nature, David thinks, that when folks get old, everything around them ages too: their bathrooms and kitchens, their rugs and chairs, their cars, their clothes, their pets, their books, their eyeglasses.

Just try and buy an old person anything new, though, a garden cart that actually works or a rake to replace the one with half the prongs broken off. They'll protest. They don't want it. David sees it all the time at Peterson's Garden Shop. (Despite what his dad says, he's already put in a good amount of time there over the years.) The old stuff is like family to them. You wouldn't throw out your wife just because she's lost a few teeth.

Mr. Hart goes on:

There's a house up in Harveston where a pipe runs from the beach all the way up to a big holding tank under the garage. They'd pump Canadian whiskey by the gallon up there and repackage it for delivery—you know, siphon it into olive oil tins or gasoline drums, anything to fool the Feds if they were stopped on the road.

Creative thinking, David jokes.

You wouldn't believe how creative you can get when it comes to making money outside the law.

I thought you said you weren't involved.

Like I told you, I had friends in the business. Close friends.

Well, I guess none of them has come into this story, yet, David says, slyly. *Unless you're about to get close to Charlie Pope or Mr. Riley.*

I'm not.

So there was somebody else?

A big important somebody, that's right.

Well?

Keep your cap on, you're about to meet 'em.

TOM MORRISON'S VISITOR

ONE SATURDAY AFTERNOON I WAS PEDALING toward the harbor with a package of stuff for Tom Morrison when I came up on Marina bent over her bicycle along the side of the road.

"What's the matter?" I called out. When she pointed, I saw that her front tire was flat. It had picked up some kind of steel tack and the air was already all but gone out of it.

"Where'd this come from?" I said when I got over to her. I tried to pull the thing out, but it was stuck in too deep to get leverage on.

"Look," she said, "they're all over the place here."

A great mass of tacks was lying along the roadside, and also on the other side of the road.

"I guess somebody knocked over a nail keg," was the best I could come up with.

"Oh, it's the rumrunners," Marina said, shaking her head. "They let loose with these out the back of their trucks if the cops get too close. My dad's always coming home with flat tires. Now what am I going to do?"

"Where were you going?" I asked.

"I was thinking of buying some fresh clams down at the docks, for chowder tonight. And taking a ride on a nice June day. I guess I'm headed back home, like it or not."

There was a long silence after this while she leaned down and poked at the tire again, and I looked on, thinking about possible solutions to the problem that I would never dare to mention to Marina. She had on a blue sweater and a red bandana over her dark hair, which tumbled halfway down her back. I could've stood there all day looking at her, and very well might have if she hadn't decided she'd waited long enough for me to come to my senses.

"You wouldn't give me a ride down there, would you, Ruben?" she said, standing up. "I mean, unless you're in a hurry, making a delivery for the store. I wouldn't dream of holding you up."

Something was wrong with me and I didn't know what. A year or two before, the idea of riding Marina to the harbor wouldn't have made me think twice. She would've climbed on board and we'd have been off in a minute. Now I felt as if I'd been hit over the head with a ton of bricks and received some serious brain damage.

"It isn't," I said.

"Isn't what?" Marina asked.

"A delivery. I mean it is, but . . ."

"Oh, well, in that case . . ."

"No, really . . ."

"Definitely not. You're on a job, I see that now."

"No!"

"Well, you've got a package."

"I know, but . . ."

"Ruben, no. You don't have time."

"Yes, I . . ."

"I'm just going to walk back and . . ."

"No, Marina. I can do it!" I was in a frantic state by this time.

"I've gotten you in a fizz by asking you to do something you can't," Marina said. She had that serious wrinkle between her eyes that always finished me.

"No!"

It was several minutes more before we worked things out, and she finally did sit herself down on my handlebars. This was such a nerve-racking pleasure that I couldn't think of one thing to say. She tried out a comment now and then, otherwise we rode in silence.

"Where were you going, actually?" she asked me at last.

When I said it was just to Coulter's Point to see Tom Morrison and bring him some coffee grinds, she insisted we stop by on the way back, after she'd bought the clams.

"Tom Morrison," she said. "Is he still down there in that chicken coop? I haven't thought about him in years."

"He's still there," I said. "Jeddy and I went to visit him a while ago, and I've been going by since. He's a grand old fellow. Do you really want to come? I might stay a few minutes."

Marina said she'd be more than pleased. It would give her a look at the beach, which she hadn't seen lately. So down we went, and we were quite a load on the bicycle with the addition of a couple of bushels of clams in a burlap sack and Marina laughing and balancing them on her knees.

"I'd offer you supper for all this trouble, but I guess you and Jeddy haven't patched up yet," she said. "What's the matter, anyhow?"

I didn't want to say that the real stumbling block was her own dad, so I shaded things a little.

"Jeddy wants to report everything to the police," I told her. "What I think is, you've got to pick and choose."

"Well, I'm not getting in the middle of that one." She laughed. She thought a minute and added, "You know, it's hard when your father works in law enforcement. It's like a spotlight is shining on you and you've got to do everything by the book, whether you think it's fair or not. Otherwise you'll be going against him, out in public, for everyone to see. Give Jeddy some time. He'll find a way back."

"You think he will?" I felt a little hope spring up in me.

She smiled and nodded. "You've always been friends. You can't just stop."

By this time, we were near where the dirt road to Coulter's ended and the dunes began. As we rounded a final bend, I saw that Tom Morrison had a visitor. A rowing dory was pulled up on the shore near the path that went in to his shack.

We dumped my bike. Marina put her sack of clams in a tidal pool between the rocks to keep them fresh, and we walked in through the dunes. I was jumpy about who we'd run into and kept a sharp eye out as we came up on Tom's junk-strewn yard.

One thing I wasn't expecting was a big white dog I'd never seen before that came charging toward us, barking like fury. While we were backing away, trying to talk some sense into the beast, the door of Tom's house flew open and out came Billy Brady, an older kid I knew. He'd lived in town until his family had moved to Harveston a couple of years before. Marina knew him, too. He'd graduated from the regional high school the year before.

"Sadie!" he shouted. "Hey, Sadie, stop that!"

This was to the dog, who looked to me like a white Labrador, an unusual sight around our parts. Anything purebred was. This being farm country, dogs mostly roamed free and far afield, where they met up with other dogs out of reach of human interference. All kinds of combinations of mutt would result, to the general improvement of the species, some would argue.

"Billy Brady, is this your pup?" Marina yelled over the racket.

"She is. Gives off a good alarm, doesn't she?" he bellowed back.

He strode forward to capture Sadie and drag her away from us. He was a good-looking fellow with a rowdy head of black hair who'd filled out a lot since I'd last seen him. Behind him came Tom Morrison, grinning from ear to ear. I didn't know if it was Billy or his dog that was responsible, but Tom looked the happiest I'd seen him since Viola.

Turned out it was both, and maybe Marina, too, because Tom hadn't set eye recently on a "female biped," as he was shortly to tell her. When Sadie quieted down, we made introductions, which weren't really necessary because we all knew each other, only from different walks of life. I asked Billy how he'd come to be there.

"Just keeping up with this coot," he said, jabbing a thumb in Tom's direction. "I get by every once in a while."

"Every once in a long while, you mean," Tom teased him. "Been more'n a year, hasn't it?"

Billy said it had, and he had plans to do better in the future. "My dad worked for Tom on his fishing schooner in the old days, till it got wrecked. They had some high times together from what I hear."

"We did," Tom said. "Otis Brady were one of the best. Could spot a school of blues a half mile off."

"Did your dad pass on?" I asked Billy.

"Last summer," he said. "Didn't you know?"

"What happened?"

"Well, I guess you could say he ran into some lead. The Coast Guard aimed too high."

Tom Morrison's face darkened when he heard this. "I didn't know he'd got shot," he said. "I heard it was a boat explosion that brought him down."

"That's the story the Coast Guard's been telling," Billy said, a bitter tone in his voice. "I believe different. There was an explosion, all right, but it came after, when the boat went up on the rocks. My father was shot dead at the wheel. With a machine gun."

"Was he smuggling?" Marina asked.

"Who wants to know?" Billy fired back. He knew full well who Marina's dad was.

She fixed him with her straight-in-the-eye look and said, "Billy, you know I don't work for the police."

"How do I know when you live in the same house as them?"

"Because I just told you!" she exclaimed. "You can judge me how you want."

He gazed back at her for a moment, then dropped his eyes. She'd outstared him the way she did anyone she came up against. Somehow, in the midst of his defeat, Billy Brady must've decided to trust her, because he went on to answer her question.

"My father had a couple of hundred cases on board, most of which went to the bottom when she blew up," he said. "The Coast Guard came back and fished out what was left the next day, and took it away for themselves. What I believe is, it was a setup."

"You mean the Coast Guard shot your dad for his load?" I couldn't believe that.

"Not for the liquor. The Guard was after him, all right. But some of those officers are out of control. They've started taking the law into their own hands. There's a big Boston gang that's trying to muscle in around here, and what I believe is, they ratted on my dad to one of these maniac officers, tipped him off to my dad's run that night, hoping he'd go in and shoot up the boat. Which he did.

Officer Roger Campbell, if you want to know his name. He says he didn't intend to hit anybody. Swears he was just giving 'fair warning' to stop. But everybody knows you don't fire warning shots with a machine gun into a ship's pilot house."

"Is that what happened?" Marina asked.

"It is," Billy said. "That's according to all three men who were my dad's crew that night. Somehow, those warning shots went astray. I won't say any more."

Tom looked grim. "Whether it's from the Coast Guard or the gangsters, we're losing some good men to the rum business," he said. "And good dogs, too."

Billy nodded and turned to me. "I heard about what happened to Viola. That's one reason I'm here, to see if I can get an idea of who it was that shot her."

"Who's Viola?" Marina asked. Tom brightened up at this and invited her over to see Viola's grave in the corner, where he proceeded to launch into the old dog's remarkable aquatic history. Meanwhile, Billy and I had a short talk.

"Tom says you and Jeddy McKenzie were on the beach the day the thugs dropped in," he said. "What'd they look like, if you don't mind my asking. I've got friends in the business, local guys, you know, who might've come across them."

I told him about the big mug in the wide-brimmed hat and his little narrow-eyed friend, about the machine guns they carried on their shoulders, and the speedboat with the real professional skipper at the wheel.

"They were looking for something they thought Tom had taken off a dead body that washed up. When they didn't find it, they shot Viola."

"The old buzzard didn't tell me about any dead body," Billy said. He glanced over fondly to where Tom was carrying on, at great length, to Marina. I saw his eye linger on her, too. "Any idea what they were after?"

"Tom said they kept talking about a ticket of some kind."

Billy's head jerked around. "A ticket?"

"That's right. He didn't know what they meant."

Billy gave me a slow smile. "A ticket! Well, that's their game then. Mystery solved."

"What d'you mean? What is it?"

"A ticket's what the boys call a document that proves you've got a paid contract for a shipment of liquor. Usually means a big shipment, one that's arriving on a freighter. There's a bunch of renegade operators out to hijack the cargo on these vessels whenever they can by pretending they're runners for the buyer onshore. A ticket solves the problem. The runner gives it to the freighter's captain to prove he's the right guy. The man who was shot must've been carrying one. Who was it? Somebody from around here?"

"We never knew for sure because the body disappeared right after Jeddy and I reported it. We were the ones who found it. Chief McKenzie didn't do much to follow up, but somebody told me later it might've been a man from New Bedford." I was playing my cards close to my chest.

Billy gave me a glance. "Tony Mordello."

I nodded. "That was the guy."

"So that's where Tony ended up. He was a big operator, too." Billy shook his head.

"Did you know him?"

"By reputation. No more'n that. The rumor is that the College Boys of Boston took him out. They wanted in on some of Tony's action and he wouldn't go along with them. I guess they didn't know about this other deal he'd done until after their hoodlums dumped him. Too late, they hear he's carrying this ticket. They send out a couple of thugs to look for his body."

I didn't say anything. It was making me nervous that Billy Brady knew so much about Tony Mordello and the College Boys.

He cleared his throat and stepped up closer to me. "Now listen, Ruben. There wasn't one of those documents on him, was there? When you and Jeddy found him, I mean. Nothing that would fit the description of a ticket? It could be a piece of paper, like a sales receipt, signed and dated. But a simpler thing they use is a dollar bill torn in half."

My heart skipped a beat.

"He didn't have one," I said, quickly.

Billy gave me a sharp look. "You're sure?"

I nodded.

"You could get yourself in trouble holding one of those things," Billy said.

I kept my mouth shut. A gleam was in his eye that I didn't trust.

Marina came back over with Tom then, and told me we should think about getting along if she was ever going to be home in time to cook up the clams she'd bought for supper.

"Clams!" Billy glanced at her. "You wouldn't be making clam chowder, would you?"

"Thought I might," Marina said, tossing her hair back from her face.

"How about some corn bread and a bit of bacon to go with it?"

"Could be done." She gave him one of her appraising glances, which he met straight this time with the flash of a smile.

After that, she wasn't in such a rush to get going and we stood awhile longer shooting the breeze. Sadie leaned up against first Billy and then Tom, asking for attention, which she got plenty of from both.

"Where'd you find this sweet lady?" Tom asked, ruffling her ears. He'd taken a shine to her.

"She was given me by a fellow in Harveston," Billy said, "for a good turn I did him. She's purebred white Labrador."

"I was thinking she's something special," Tom said. "Can she swim?"

"Like a fish," Billy said. "She'll go off the high-diving rock down at Walter's Point if you give her a good reason."

Marina laughed at that. "What's a good reason?" she asked.

"How about clam chowder for supper with corn bread and a ration of bacon on the side?" Billy said, giving her a wicked grin. They all broke up laughing, but I didn't. I could see Billy Brady had taken an interest in Marina and, worse, that she didn't mind.

Later, on our ride back down the main road toward home, I tried to make some bright conversation, but Marina wouldn't bite. She was mulling over something, gazing at the fields we passed with an absent expression. I'd seen her in these quiet spells before and knew better than to interrupt. We came to her bike and she insisted on getting off and walking the rest of the way by herself.

"I could take the clams and drop them at your house," I offered. "How are you going to carry them and wheel that busted bike at the same time?"

She told me no, she'd had enough free transportation for one afternoon. Then she warmed up again and thanked me for the favor I'd done carrying her to the harbor.

I said I was jealous of Jeddy for getting to have her clam chowder that night. Of all the things Marina cooked for us over the years, that was my number-one favorite.

"Don't worry, there'll be plenty of other times," she said. Then she paused, and I could see she was trying to decide whether to speak about something else.

"Ruben Hart, you'll keep quiet about where we went this afternoon, won't you?" she said at last.

I said I would.

"My father wouldn't like to hear that I've been down at Tom Morrison's talking with the likes of Billy Brady. His family's been in the rum-running business since it began."

"They might be thinking twice about staying in that business since Billy's dad was shot," I said.

Marina shook her head. "They're not, I'm afraid. Or Billy hasn't, anyway."

"What d'you mean? Is he smuggling now?"

"More than that." She leaned closer to me. "Can you keep a secret? Tom Morrison let it slip when we were talking back there. Billy's skippering liquor runs on the *Black Duck*. He was there asking Tom if they could use his place for storage."

KNUCKLING UNDER

THE MINUTE I GOT HOME FROM TOM Morrison's that afternoon, I took that torn-in-half fifty-dollar bill out of my geometry book, rolled it up the way it had been and hid it back inside Tony Mordello's tobacco pouch. Then I stuffed the tobacco pouch under my mattress and sat down on top.

A picture of the *Black Duck* coming in at Tyler's Beach rose into my mind. I had no doubt now who the dark, laughing man at the pilot's wheel had been. Billy Brady was carrying on his family tradition. The cocky skipper whose crew outran the Coast Guard night after night, who threw up ingenious smoke screens and vanished like Robin Hood into their mists, was from Harveston, right up the road. Part of me was breathless that he was somebody I knew.

But another part lay low and cautious. There'd been something a little too pushy about Billy's interest in Tony Mordello's ticket. I hadn't liked how he'd pressed me about it, and now that I'd lied about having it, I didn't want to go back. The best thing for me, I decided, was to pretend I'd never opened that tobacco pouch.

And that was what I did. As the weeks went by, the danger seemed to pass. The pouch stayed where it was, squashed under my mattress, a strange souvenir I couldn't quite bring myself to throw away. No one else bothered me about the rolled-up bill, and whatever Tony Mordello's secret deal had been, I supposed it was as dead as he was. His fabulous shipment had ended up in somebody else's hands and it wasn't up to me to worry about whose they were.

Even as one problem seemed to clear up for me, though, another was developing for our family.

With Mr. Riley in jail, my father became responsible for more than just the day-to-day operations of the store. Goods ordered from Boston, such as tobacco and dress fabric, hardware items and a line of footwear carried by the store, now fell under his supervision. He spent more time on the telephone and longer hours over the account books. He was rarely home for supper, even on weekends.

It got so bad that my mother started bringing his evening meal to the store, determined he'd have it hot and on time. Often, she'd stay if he needed help with shelving or pricing. I spent these evenings at home. I wasn't expected to work overtime no matter what was happening at the store. It was a given in our family that my schoolwork was more important, that I'd be following in my father's footsteps soon enough, learning the business of running a store, which, in our town back then, was about as important and well-paying a job as could be found.

Being manager of Riley's store was to be a gift my father would pass on to me, and up until that spring of 1929, there seemed no reason that he wouldn't be able to. His position seemed rock solid. He was well-liked and trusted, a beacon of honesty in the community. For the most part, Mr. Riley had seen the benefit to his store of honoring this reputation, and allowed my father to maintain a buffer of ignorance about the bootlegging operations going on behind the scenes. Occasionally, the buffer was breached, as when Mr. Riley had asked me to work at Brown's and my father had felt pressure to agree, but this was the exception.

Now, with Mr. Riley absent from the store, the breach widened and the shady world of his rum-running operations began to encroach directly on my father's pristine territory. For though Mr. Riley had been arrested, his "import business," as I heard him call it more than once, continued apace. From the number of out-of-town vehicles with Massachusetts plates that began to park in front of the store, it was easy to figure that Boston's College Boys had succeeded in muscling their way in and taking charge of rum-running operations in our area.

The first thing that happened was that my father discovered a large storage "hide" for liquor on the store premises. It was dug into the floor of the barn behind the store's main building, and had probably been there a couple of years. In the past, the place had been kept padlocked, off-limits to store personnel, and if my father ever wondered what was under there, he never acknowledged it. That

June, as Mr. Riley cooled his heels in jail, my dad received a visit from a pair a husky strangers who presented him with a key to the hide and told him to make himself available on certain nights.

This, to his credit, Dad refused to do, and Mr. Riley, from his jail cell, found another man not connected to the store to do the job. Just knowing about the hide, though, confused and outraged my father. No longer could he ignore the fact that liquor was coming and going from store property. One evening, he poured himself out to my mother in the kitchen while I listened from my post at the top of the back stairs.

"Turn a blind eye to it, Carl," my mother advised. "Pretend it doesn't exist and go about your own business."

"But it does exist! It's right there under the floor."

"I know, but it doesn't concern you."

"It didn't concern me as long as I didn't know about it. Now I know, and it concerns me," my father said. His voice rose to a pitch I hadn't heard before.

"The store's the important thing," my mother told him. "You don't want to get involved in these outside activities. Mr. Riley knows how you feel. He's always seen to it you're kept out of things."

"Riley's not there to draw the line anymore," my father said. "I have bums coming in that you wouldn't believe, pressuring me to open up more storage space. I tell 'em, 'No! I won't do it!' Then I get word from Riley to let 'em have the shed, let 'em borrow the delivery van for Friday night. I know what it's for, but what can I do? It's his store, not mine. I'm afraid he'll find somebody else to run the place if I don't knuckle under."

"Oh, come, he wouldn't fire you!" my mother exclaimed.

"Wouldn't he, now, if he saw I wasn't going along? He must make ten times on smuggling what I clear in legal sales in a month. It's money, not law, that speaks loudest to him."

My mother was silent. I think she'd caught sight at last of the corner my father was in. I know I saw it. Our family was on the line, our whole way of life.

My mother spoke again, a dark voice of warning.

"Whatever you do, keep Ruben out of it."

"I'm trying, let me tell you."

"Carl, you keep him out. Trying's not good enough."

Once again, my father left the kitchen without answering. He retreated into the parlor to read the newspaper while I tiptoed back to my room.

Listening down the back stairs was something I'd done since I was small, a way of cutting through the false front of calm my parents so often laid over their real views and worries. This time, I wished I hadn't done it. I was shocked to hear my father talk about "knuckling under" to a slickster like Mr. Riley. It seemed unfair that a man of my dad's worth should be forced to go against his moral conscience in order to keep his job. That wasn't something that should be asked of anyone, I thought, and I was amazed that my mother would advise such a thing.

That night, I couldn't sleep for thinking of my father's

problems. Along about midnight, I got up, dressed and went outside to walk around. It was a windless evening, clear, with a bright moon hanging in the sky. I went up to the main road, crossed over and in a short time found myself coming up on the McKenzies' house, which I hadn't been near in some time.

Late as it was, a light shone from the kitchen. That gave me an idea. I slipped into their yard and crept close to one of the windows, thinking I'd have a little fun spying if it was Jeddy doing his schoolwork or Marina up over some sewing.

A warm glow rose from the room. The sight of the familiar wood counters, of Mrs. McKenzie's china cabinet and the black stove in the corner, gave my heart a wrench. I wished more than anything to be back inside those friendly walls. If Jeddy had been there, I'd have gone in in a minute to talk to him. I was longing for our old selves, sick of having to look the other way and pretend not to care whenever we passed in the hall at school.

There was a person in the kitchen, but it wasn't Jeddy. Chief McKenzie sat at the supper table, working by the light of a small table lamp. He'd taken off the leather vest he wore in his official police capacity, and rolled up the sleeves of his shirt. I took a moment to figure out what he was doing. Knowing what I did about the scrimping that went on in that house, it was about the last thing in the world I'd ever have expected: he was counting money.

There was a lot of it, stacks of bills piled up neat as you please. The chief was working over them slowly and methodically, the way he did everything he put his mind to, from police files to household accounts. No one would ever accuse Ralph McKenzie of neglecting his duties, whatever else they had against him. He didn't like error or failure, and kept strict control to avoid it.

I watched him lick his finger, count out a number of bills, take up a pencil and make an entry in a book. He tucked the bills into a white envelope, sealed it, wrote a name on the front. He put the envelope aside, and started over again, counting more bills, recording them. I was too far away to read what he was writing on the envelopes, but I could guess: they were names.

I knew about payrolls. My father paid the store staff weekly using identical white envelopes. Chief McKenzie was doing the same, except that the amount of money at his elbow was far more than my father had ever handled. It took my breath away to see that much cash in one place, as if somebody had robbed a bank.

For a quarter of an hour I watched him through the window. Then a hound dog that lived on a farm down the road came rambling up on the yard and caught sight of me. I guess he took me for a burglar, because he started to woof. The chief jumped up from the table and came across to the window to look out. I ducked around the corner of the house, the dog at my heels, yammering away.

In another minute, I heard the back door slam, and knew Chief McKenzie was outside. That scared the devil out of me. I took off into some brush. He heard me running and came round the house after me.

"Hey, who is that? What're you doing here?"

There was no stopping me then. I was running flat out, going through hedges, jumping stone walls, kicking at the dog, who was excited by all the action and stayed right up with me, nipping at my shins. I crossed over the main road and went down into a swamp on the other side whose terrain I knew. The dog didn't like that—it was a bog known for snakes—and quit following me after a few minutes. Even then, I didn't stop. I went crashing through pools of muck, up banks covered with ferns, down again into ooze that came over my ankles until I floundered through to the higher ground of the field behind our house.

There, I paused. And listened. Far in back of me, I heard that hound dog baying its head off. I was still in a panic, breathing hard and half expecting Chief McKenzie to come rearing up out of the swamp after me. I ran across the field and crouched down behind our old pump house, where I could keep an eye out in case anyone came across the field to our yard.

Finally the dog quieted down. The night grew peaceful again. My shoes were black with mud. I took them off and sneaked inside, went up to my room and lay down on my bed in my clothes. They were wet, but I didn't care. I was burning up from the run home and couldn't seem to cool down. I lay there sweating, wondering if the chief had recognized me in the dark and, if he had, what he'd do about it.

That night seemed to last forever.

I heard my dad get up, go in the bathroom and head

back to bed. I heard a couple of doves outside my window fluttering their wings and cooing under the eaves where they'd built a nest. Around about 4:00 A.M. the cocks on a farm down near the river began to crow, and still I wasn't asleep. My eyes were wide open. I was out there looking through the McKenzies' window, into that kitchen where I'd eaten so many meals. Jeddy was upstairs asleep in his room, his baseball cap hung on the back of the door. Marina was across the hall in her own bed, dreaming whatever mysterious things girls dream. There were probably ten perfectly legal reasons why Police Chief Ralph McKenzie would be up late counting out stacks of money at his supper table. I just couldn't right then think of what they might be.

HOME IMPROVEMENTS

A WEEK LATER, SCHOOL CLOSED AND THE summer began. The days grew hot, the beaches filled up with rich city folk who had summer houses along the coast.

I began working full-time at the store. Jeddy kept on at Fancher's chicken farm, though I know for a fact he was only part-time because I'd watch him go into the police station across from Weedie's some mornings. He was starting a sort of unofficial apprenticeship, following in his father's footsteps just as he'd told me he planned to. Some mornings I'd hang around outside Riley's to catch his eye as he walked by.

"Hi, Jeddy," I'd say.

"How's it going?" he'd ask me back. That was it. If I tried for anything more, he'd pick up his pace and scoot away. I didn't push it. I remembered what Marina said about him having to work things out. It seemed sad to me that he'd be protecting the honor of his dad's position when Chief McKenzie wasn't exactly living up to that honor himself.

I was wary of the man now, afraid he might have seen

me running away that night and have it in for me. He never said a word, but something about his manner, how his eyes brushed over me when he came in the store for his morning newspaper, gave me warning. "Don't get in my way," that look seemed to say. And I didn't. I ducked back behind the shelves, kept out of his sight. I didn't tell anyone what I'd seen him doing in his kitchen. It wasn't my business, I decided, and anyway, my nose wasn't so clean in that department, either.

From continued espionage on the back stairs, I began to be aware that my own father was dealing regularly, both face-to-face and on the telephone, with racketeers from the Boston gang, under orders from Mr. Riley. The secret room beneath the storage building out back was in constant use. Many mornings, I saw fresh tire marks running across the back lot. Anyone could have noticed. They were heavy marks, the kind a laden truck might leave.

One afternoon, John Appleby slid past me. "Hey, Rube. You want a job tonight?" he whispered.

"What job?"

"There's a boat coming in up at Fogland Point. They're paying twenty bucks a head to unload her."

It surprised me that he'd be involved. He was a year behind me at school and still had the baby face of a ten-year-old.

Thanks but no thanks, I told him. I figured one thing my dad didn't need on top of all his own trouble was me getting caught down on some beach.

"Too bad," John said. "It's going to be fun. A bunch of

us are going down. I guess your stomach couldn't handle it."

"My stomach doesn't have anything to do with it."

"That's right, it's your dad, isn't it? He has you on a short leash, keeping you penned up and pretty for better things."

"Who says?"

"Everybody."

"Like who?"

"Jeddy McKenzie," he said, smirking.

I didn't believe him.

"Jeddy would never say that," I told him, and walked off. John and I had never seen eye to eye. I was given better jobs at the store and had a higher position since I'd been there longer. My impression was he thought I didn't amount to much and had only been hired because of my father.

John Appleby wasn't the only person to offer me shore work that summer. I could've been out a couple of evenings a week if I'd wanted. I began to hear about boys even younger than John who were making twenty or thirty bucks a job. Sometimes their folks would be in on it with them, sometimes they wouldn't be. Even when they weren't, it was obvious they knew what was going on. Parents were closing their eyes to it because the money was so good. You could hardly blame them; many in our town were in low-paying work like farming or fishing and that kind of money was helping them get through.

"It's like picking dollars off a tree," I heard a lobsterman say in the store. "Whether you like it or not, money's growing up there. If you don't put your hand out, somebody else will."

As July turned to August and August crept toward September, the rum-running traffic on our shores went into high gear. At night, I'd hear the hum of tires going over the road accompanied by the barely detectable drone of a muffled engine. Dark vessels slipped along the coast making for beaches that exploded with light and action for a few hours, then went back to being abandoned coves in the morning.

The *Black Duck* was in the news. Aunt Grace saw the article in the morning paper.

"Outfoxed the Coast Guard again," she said in a gleeful whisper over breakfast. My mother, off in the kitchen at that moment, had banned the subject from our table. It pained her, she said, to think of such goings-on. What I thought more likely was that it pained my father to hear about something he wished he weren't part of. That morning, as on nearly every other, he'd already left for the store.

"What happened?" I whispered back.

Aunt Grace leaned foward to show me the story. Two nights before, the *Duck* had been spotted by a Coast Guard cutter going up the West Passage. Ordered to halt and be searched, she'd sped off, leading the Guard on yet another merry chase. It ended with the cutter beached on a tidal sandbar along a barren stretch of coast. The eight guardsmen on board had been forced to swim ashore, swallow their pride and flag down help along the road.

"I bet that about killed them," I said.

"It did!" Aunt Grace laughed. "They're mad as hornets. Listen to this." Bending closer, she read in a low voice:

"*Speaking after the incident, Captain Roger Campbell, officer in charge of the beached Coast Guard cutter, told the* Journal, '*The* Black Duck *is a coastal scourge in this area that must be stopped. Our government will not tolerate brazen lawbreaking of this kind. Someday someone is going to open fire on that boat.*'"

"I've heard of that guy Campbell before," I said. "Isn't he the one who fired on Billy Brady's father?"

Aunt Grace wasn't aware of that, though she'd heard the Brady family was in the rum-running business. I didn't tell her about Billy's connection to the *Black Duck*. He'd probably been on board during the chase, maybe even at the wheel. His wicked grin flashed into my mind, and I imagined the enjoyment he must have had leading Captain Roger Campbell and his crew up onto that sandbar.

My mother came in from the kitchen then, and we closed up the newspaper and began a discussion about whether the Chicago Cubs would get in the World Series against the Philadelphia A's that fall. Aunt Grace was a maniac about baseball, a terrible know-it-all who kept up with all the players and could reel off statistics faster than a ticker tape. Nobody in town could outdo her.

"You'll never find a husband at this rate," my mother

would scold. "You want to build up a man's ego, not squash it down under a pile of facts he should know better than you."

"I can't help it if they're all dumb as doornails," Aunt Grace would fire back, just to irritate my mother even more.

As that summer wore on, it seemed that smugglers were everywhere. You couldn't fish down at the harbor in the evenings for fear of running into liquor landings. Families told their children to stay off the beaches at night lest they stumble on men with guns. Meanwhile, all anybody had to do to buy a bottle was head down to a certain fish hut at the town dock at a certain time of day. And this was small potatoes compared to other sales going on.

The rich summer folks were buying their stuff by the caseload, through their own private bootleggers. That summer of 1929, they entertained like never before, serving cocktails and wine, champagne and brandy on the wide front porches of their elegant seaside homes. Late, late into the night, you'd hear wild dance music coming across the fields from the shore. I got a job bartending at a couple of those parties, learned to make whiskey sours and rum tonics, and how to ice a martini glass. It was an easy way to earn a buck. I would've liked to keep at it, but September arrived. The season came to an end. The summer people went back to Providence or Boston or New York. School started again, and in October the stock market crashed. Huge fortunes went down the drain; jobs began drying up. Nobody felt like celebrating anymore.

That didn't stop people from wanting liquor, though. The smuggling went on. Oh, how it went on. As to who in our town was involved, about the only thing that could be said for sure was a lot of folks were suddenly making home improvements.

I wasn't the only one who noticed that a new roof went on the McKenzie house in early November. Or who heard Fanny DeSousa boasting about her fancy electric stove. John Appleby's parents built a whole barn. Other families were quietly affording indoor bathrooms, new porches, secondhand automobiles.

The Harts were right in there with the best of them, I've got to say. We installed heat in our second-floor bedrooms. My mother went to Providence and bought herself a fox-fur stole. She wore it into Riley's store the next day, looking about as silly as a peacock in a chicken house.

"For pity's sake, keep it at home, can't you?" my father shouted at her when he came back that night. She burst into tears and ran upstairs.

I felt sorry for her. She'd always wanted a stole. Now that they had the money to buy it, she couldn't understand why my father was so angry.

I knew why.

"They're paying me to keep my mouth shut. That's how I make my living now, by shutting up," I heard him tell Aunt Grace later that same night.

"Oh, Carl, you mustn't say that. Don't be so hard on yourself."

"I'm not being hard on myself. If I don't say it, who will?"

"What else can you do? Everyone's in the same boat."

"I could stand up and put a stop to it. I could tell them all to go to hell."

"Tell who?" Aunt Grace asked. "Mr. Riley, you mean? He's no more in charge than the King of Siam!"

That was true enough. While Mr. Riley continued to send orders from his prison cell, the Boston College Boys had long ago taken over the reins of his operation, and many others along the coast. Not only courtroom judges were in these gangsters' pockets. Their influence now extended into the offices of a good number of Rhode Island legislators, as my father well knew. Aunt Grace was right. There was no one to appeal to, and even if there had been, who but a lunatic would blow the whistle on a game that was making so much money for everyone, at every level?

The stakes were about to go higher, though. Unbeknownst to my father and all but a few in our town, a larger and more powerful gang of players was already poised on the horizon, ready to strike.

A NEW WIND

THE FIRST I KNEW ABOUT THE NEW YORK mobsters coming into our area was about a week before Thanksgiving. A stranger with a flashy tan fedora cocked over his forehead came in the store and bought a pack of cigarettes. Then he sat on the public bench just down from our front door to smoke them. Anybody who came by, he struck up a conversation.

"Name's Stanley Culp, and that's a fine old cemetery you've got there behind the church," he'd remark.

Or: "You mean there's a police station in this sweet little town? Can't imagine what ever goes wrong here!"

Or: "What, that place there's the post office? Not much bigger than a postage stamp, is it? Haw, haw!"

He'd raise his hat to the pretty farm wives driving in for supplies. "Morning, ma'am, fine-looking boy you've got there. Nice weather we're having. Yes, I'm from New York City, you guessed right."

The reason people were guessing right about his origins was his car, which was a fancy twin-six engine Packard sedan with New York plates. He didn't let on what his business was, but soon enough people began to understand. He was there for the special purpose of making friends.

He gave fifteen dollars to the Bishop's Fund at St. Mary's and an equal amount to the collection plate at the Congregational Church on Sunday morning. He tucked a dime into the pocket of any child who came past his bench, which picked up business at the store's candy counter a good bit.

When Abner Wilcox, whose wife, Marie, had just died after fifty years of marriage, wobbled up on his cane, Stanley Culp bought him a chocolate bar and talked to him for a solid hour. That was an act of unusual kindness. Though everyone in town was suspicious, we all had to admit that Mr. Culp was doing good.

"And asking nothing in return. *So far*," Mildred Cumming whispered when she came in for a soda pop one afternoon. She'd been keeping her eye on him from the police station.

"Charlie's having kittens wondering who he is," she added. "I've never seen him in such a state."

"What's the chief say?" Dr. Washburn asked her. He'd come by for a hunk of store cheese and some pipe tobacco.

"Chief McKenzie's been out of town all week. Far as I know, he doesn't know anything about it."

"Where'd he go?"

"Took Jeddy up hunting to Vermont for the Thanksgiving holiday. Said he needed a break."

"I can believe that," the doctor replied. "From what I hear, he and Charlie've been spending more time going at each other than after these infernal bootleggers."

Relations between Chief McKenzie and his deputy had gone sour over the summer. They rarely covered cases together anymore, and had been seen arguing in public. Charlie's manner, never specially pleasant on even his best days, was now continuously surly, while the chief went about with a new smugness, as if he'd received some promotion that Charlie didn't qualify for. And perhaps he had. I was still keeping a wary eye on the chief, and one thing I'd noticed was that Mr. Culp's Packard wasn't the only vehicle with New York plates showing up regularly in town. More than a few afternoons, there was another car, a racy black sedan, parked in plain view in front of the police station.

About an hour after Mildred left with her soda, Charlie himself came over. He stood outside the store and started a conversation with Mr. Culp that was soon audible all the way back into the stockroom, where John Appleby and I were stacking crates. We went up front to see what was happening.

"As official law-enforcement deputy of the town, I'm ordering you to vacate these premises!" Charlie was yelling when we got there.

"Oh, come along," Mr. Culp said, giving him a friendly grin. "I've been having a grand time meeting these folks." He gestured toward Dr. Washburn and the small crowd of us who'd come out of the store. Fanny DeSousa was there, and Aunt Grace, too, over from the post office. "Can't see no reason to leave now."

"I know why you're here. You can't frighten me!" Charlie bellowed, sounding scared down to his under-wear.

"Frighten you?" said Mr. Culp, looking up lazily. He knew who Charlie was the same way he knew everything about our town. A week of sitting on that bench had ac-complished a lot more than just us getting to know him. "Why would I want to frighten you? If I was to want any-thing, it'd be to say this: if you can't beat 'em, join 'em. That's my message to you."

Charlie brayed out a laugh. "So, you think you're going to join up with us? Hah, that's a good one. You can't barge into a town like this."

Mr. Culp smiled. "No, no, you misunderstand. I'm not doing nothing like barging in. I'm telling you, real nice, it's time to take a powder."

Charlie practically expired with fury over this. "Take a powder! Meaning what?"

Mr. Culp removed his flashy hat and set it down on the bench beside him. "What'd you say your name was?"

"My name is Deputy Sargeant Charles Pope!"

"Yes, Deputy Pope, meaning this. About now, if I was you, I'd be heading on back to that run-down caboose of a police station. I'd put my feet up on the desk and take a good long snooze."

Charlie let out a snort and shook his head.

"Let me put it even more clearly," Mr. Culp went on. "There's a change coming, a new wind in this town. If you try to stop it, why, my guess is it'll blow you down."

All of this was said in a mild tone, as if Mr. Culp was sorry to be speaking these words but saw no way around it. What he meant was only vaguely understood by most of us looking on, but Charlie knew. His eyes bulged and his tongue came out for its snaky flick over his lips.

"You won't get away with this," he snarled. "Chief McKenzie's due back tomorrow. He won't tolerate it!"

Mr. Culp smiled. "Oh, I don't think the chief'll mind too much. Ralph and I have come to an understanding about matters of this kind. Now, go on along before somebody has to take you."

To our amazement, Charlie did. He turned and walked away toward the police station on legs stiff with rage. Stanley Culp watched him. When Charlie had disappeared, he took out his pack of cigarettes and offered them around to the men, passing over John and me and Fanny DeSousa and Aunt Grace. It was still considered improper in our parts for ladies to smoke in public, and like us, they wouldn't have expected to.

"Fine cold weather we're having," Mr. Culp said when he'd seen to it that everybody was lit up. "I hear autumn's the choice season on this coast. Better than spring, they say. Clearer, bluer, beautiful sunrises and sunsets. You never want to leave a place like this in the fall, am I right?"

There was something about the tone of this question that caused us all to nod quickly. Mr. Culp smiled. He put his hat back on, winked at me and launched into one of his New York jokes. It wasn't that funny, but beside me John Appleby gave a big laugh. When I went inside, he stayed to shoot the breeze with Mr. Culp. He was still there a half hour later when my father noticed and ordered him back to work.

The Monday after Thanksgiving, Marina came to find me in an outbuilding behind the store where I was working my afternoon shift.

It was the first I'd seen of her since mid-October. She'd been going out of town that fall, staying with some high school friends in Harveston over the weekends, commuting to school from up there and coming home to catch up on housework during the midweek days. I'd heard she and her father were at odds over it. He wanted her home, taking care of him and Jeddy, the way she had been doing since her mother died. I no longer knew the inside workings of their family, but the word was she'd stood up to him and declared independence. Which she'd won, it appeared. Recently, and not without a lot of grumbling, the chief had started hiring old Mrs. Smithers to come in part-time to cook.

Harveston was where Marina had spent all of the Thanksgiving holiday while Jeddy and the chief were in Vermont. Now they were back and she'd come home, in a blaze of new glamour, I thought. She'd been to Boston and bought a smart wool coat, deep green with a leather collar, high style to my countrified eyes.

She hadn't come by to impress me, though, or to show me any special interest at all. What she wanted was to give me a lecture. Her subject was Mr. Culp.

"Don't you know who he is? He's with the New York mobsters. They're trying to break in around here. You should tell your dad to run him off," she announced, before I'd hardly had time to say hello. That set me on edge.

"My dad said he's sitting on a public bench and it's none of our business," I answered. "Anyway, the guy's giving out cash and people are coming in here and spending it, so we don't mind."

"You should be protecting folks, not setting them up," Marina replied. "The man is looking for a fix, that's plain as day."

"A fix!" I said. "Who does he want to fix?" I'd never heard her talk this way. She seemed to have acquired a whole new vocabulary since we'd last conversed.

"Your dad, for one. He wants him on his side when the shooting starts."

"If there's going to be shooting, why don't you tell your own dad? He's the one with the badge."

I turned to walk off.

"Ruben, wait." Marina caught my arm. "My father won't do anything and neither will yours. They're both in it up to their necks."

"That's a lie!" I told her. "Speak for your own family, not mine." I was offended that she'd lump my father in with hers, when anyone could see there was no comparison.

Marina gave me the kind of glance you give a five-year-old who thinks the moon is made of green cheese.

"There's something else," she said. She lowered her voice. "Remember how those Boston gangsters came in and killed Tom Morrison's dog last spring?"

I glared at her. "Of course I remember."

"They were looking for the ticket to a big liquor shipment."

"I know that, and it's long past," I said. "That shipment must've come in months ago."

"It didn't," Marina whispered. "It's still coming. And the word going around is, the ticket's still good. Over three thousand cases, signed, sealed and paid for. The big syndicates have got wind of it and they're looking to horn in. That's one reason you've got a New York mobster sitting outside your store. Ruben, listen to me: Billy Brady wants to see you."

Suddenly I saw where all this talk of "fixing" and "setting folks up" and "mobsters" was coming from.

"So you're in touch with Billy?"

"We talk now and then."

"That's right, he lives in Harveston." I put two and two together. "Lucky thing you have friends up there."

"Yes, it is. So what?"

From her tone, I suspected there was a lot more going on between her and Billy than she was telling. That galled me. I didn't have a leg to stand on with Marina, but the idea that Billy Brady was moving in on her touched a nerve. All those years eating supper in the McKenzies' kitchen had mounted up in my mind to a form of possession, I guess.

"Billy'll be down at Tom Morrison's late this afternoon," Marina said. "He'll come in by boat. Will you go to see him?"

"I will not! All he wants is to get his own hands on that shipment. He's after money, same as everyone else."

"That's not true," Marina said. "You don't know him. People in Harveston say he's been helping families out from what he makes. That's why his crew's got the good name it has."

"Well, I wish he'd stay away from Tom Morrison," I shot back. "He'll get him in trouble hanging around there all the time. It's not fair to drag an old guy like that into anything to do with the *Black Duck*."

Before I'd even finished saying those words, Marina was reaching to cover my mouth.

"Shh-shh! Not so loud."

I tore her hand off me. "There's nobody around here."

"There's always somebody around everywhere," she whispered. "You just don't notice. And Ruben, they're watching you specially."

"Nobody's paying any attention to me, that's one of my problems." I sent her a furious look.

"They are. It's why Billy wants to see you. There's a new rumor that you've got it. The ticket, I mean, the thing you and Jeddy found."

I'd already guessed that was where this discussion was headed, and it scared me. I wasn't about to show that to Marina, though.

"Who says I have it, Charlie Pope?" I asked, stonewalling the best I could. "Look, I've said it a hundred times, all there was on the guy was his pipe and—"

Marina slapped her hand over my mouth again, and this time I let it stay there. From behind us came a soft squeak. We looked around. The trapdoor in the floor across the room had risen up a little. After a moment of silence, John Appleby came up the ladder out of the old root cellar, a storage area no longer in use since part of it had caved in during the winter.

"John, what're you doing down there?" I demanded.

"Just getting some potatoes," he said. He held up a bag.

"Potatoes are in the side shed now. There's nothing in that place."

"Yes, there is," John Appleby said. "There's potatoes."

He slid by us with a smug look.

"See what I mean?" Marina whispered after he'd gone. "You should be careful what you say."

"John Appleby's not a spy. He's a kid with a big chip on his shoulder is all."

Marina shook her head at me. "Will you go and meet Billy?" she asked again.

"No!" I told her. "Even if I wanted to, I couldn't. My dad won't let me off for anything anymore. We're all working like dogs here to keep up. You tell Billy Brady you delivered the message. Someone is watching me. Well, I'm real glad to hear it!"

I stormed off, and this time Marina let me go. When I looked back, she'd disappeared up front.

I stayed away from that part of the store for the next hour and didn't see her again. Toward the end of the afternoon, though, I opened the trapdoor of the old cellar and looked in. It was black as pitch inside, so I got a book of matches and went down the ladder. All it took was one strike to see that there wasn't a single bag of potatoes in the whole place.

Newport Daily Journal, January 1, 1930

BLACK DUCK SURVIVOR CHARGES COAST GUARD GAVE NO WARNING BEFORE OPENING FIRE

"IT WAS A SETUP," NAVIGATOR SAYS

NEWPORT, JAN. 1—The Coast Guard cutter that intercepted the Black Duck in fog early last Sunday morning gave no warning before unleashing deadly machine gun fire, according to Richard Delucca, the Duck's navigator and sole survivor. Delucca's three shipmates were killed in the barrage, the most violent incident to date along these shores.

"There was dense fog out there and we came up on the cutter so quick that we thought we'd run into it," said Delucca, 24, speaking to reporters for the first time from his bed at Newport Hospital.

"We didn't know it was a government vessel. They gave us no warning shot and no signal to stop. They started firing that machine gun and kept firing. I believe it was a setup. Somebody tipped them off that we'd be coming. Everybody knew Campbell was out to get the Black Duck," Delucca said, referring to Officer Roger Campbell, skipper of C.G. Patrol Boat 290, who gave the order to shoot.

Delucca lost his thumb in the incident. He has been charged with smuggling illegal liquor.

His account was denied by a Coast Guard spokesman. "They were trying to escape. These unfortunate killings resulted from an honest effort to enforce the law," he said.

The Interview

YOU STILL HAD THAT FIFTY-DOLLAR BILL, *didn't you?* David Peterson asks when Ruben Hart lumbers back from the kitchen, carrying two glasses of lemonade. Outside, a summer rain is cascading down on the yard. They've taken shelter in the dark parlor. The room is hot, even with the windows open.

Don't expect much. It's store-bought, Mr. Hart says, handing over the lemonade. *If my wife were here, we'd be having the real thing.*

That's okay, David says. *I like store-bought.* The truth is, he's never had any other kind.

Did you still have that tobacco pouch under your mattress? David asks again.

Of course.

With the half a fifty rolled up inside?

Would you throw something like that away?

No. One thing I don't understand. Why did Tony Mordello's freighter take so long to show up? Was it lost at sea or something?

For six months? No.

So?

It was always scheduled for a December delivery. That's how Tony Mordello had set it up. He wanted his shipment in time for the holiday season, when he knew he could sell it at a good price. He was buying low and selling high, good business practice.

And then he was shot with the ticket on him, David says.

Hidden in his tobacco pouch, that's right.

How does that work, using a torn bill as a ticket? I still don't get it.

Easy. The captain of the freighter Tony hired to bring his liquor down here has the other half. They did the deal face-to-face up in Canada. Then, when Tony's runners go out to get the shipment in their speedboats, they have Tony's bill and match it with the captain's. Everybody knows they're dealing with the right outfit.

Pretty cool, David says. *It's like a signed contract.*

Mr. Hart smiles grimly. *It's better. There are no names written down, and bills can be folded small. They stand up longer, too—in seawater, for instance. Tony Mordello ran a smart operation. If the College Boys hadn't murdered him, he'd have made a second fortune off the huge cargo coming in on this freighter. His wife could've bought herself another diamond necklace and Cadillacs for the kids.*

So now the Boston College Boys were after you?

Not only them. The New York mob, too. At least, that's what Billy Brady had sent Marina to tell me. I didn't believe him, though, knucklehead that I was.

But how would they have known you even had that fifty?
You'd kept it secret all that time.

One person knew.

Who?

Mr. Hart gets up painfully from his chair. Wet weather
raises havoc with his joints.

Let me show you something. He shuffles over to one of
the formal, white-doilied parlor tables and fumbles
around amid the framed photographs, bending low, trying
to find the right one in the parlor's gloom. Whatever
pruning Mr. Hart has managed so far with his medieval
clippers hasn't improved visibility in here. David, who's
had more gardening experience via Peterson's Landscaping than he likes to admit, offered to lend a hand but
was turned down. *Help* is a not a word in the old man's
dictionary.

Finally Mr. Hart selects a small photo in a silver frame
and walks back across the room. He holds it out to David:
a black-and-white snapshot of a skinny kid wearing a baseball cap and standing beside a bicycle.

Who do you think that is?

I don't know.

Guess.

Jeddy McKenzie? David says.

You're right. Mr. Hart nods solemnly. *My old friend
Jeddy. He'd seen me with the bill in front of my locker.*

But . . . did he tell?

I believe he did. He told the chief.

How could he? He was setting you up.

He was. In the name of police business, that's what he was doing.

He must've thought his dad would step in, somehow. He wouldn't have done it on purpose, would he?

That's a good question. I don't know the answer. Maybe I don't want to know.

THE MUFFLED ENGINE

I WAS IN A BLACK MOOD WHEN I LEFT THE store that afternoon, angry at Marina and sore from unloading stock all day. If I'd been smart, I would have headed straight back to my house and stayed put. But my mother was there, as she always was, ready and waiting to ask how my day had gone.

"Going home, kid?" Stanley Culp gave me the eye as I slouched by.

"Why would I want to go there?"

"So, you're off for a ride? Well, take care of yourself."

I wheeled my bike into the street and pedaled away, feeling his shrewd gaze on my back.

If there was, as there was later said to be, an old Ford station wagon with Massachusetts plates keeping watch on the store from an alley across the road, I paid no attention.

I didn't care, either, that Charlie Pope, hustling away from the police station on some errand, shot me a cool glance over his shoulder and picked up speed.

Chief McKenzie, standing in the station door, was either just coming in or about to leave. His heavy profile faded back out of sight as I passed. Perhaps he was making a note of the direction I was taking, perhaps not. I couldn't be bothered to pick up on such details.

I remember that Ann Kempton, the local seamstress, waved at me from her backyard as she took in laundry from the line.

A group of younger boys was in the field beyond the school whacking a baseball around and whooping it up. They'd been in the store buying sodas earlier, where they'd been warned to keep their voices down and wait their turn at the counter. I knew every one of them by name, such is the closeness of a small town, and now, hearing the crack of the ball on the bat, and their shouts, a darker feeling swept over me.

I was trapped in this place. While Marina visited Harveston and Boston, meeting up with the world, I hauled pickle barrels in Riley's back room, where not even my father looked in on me anymore. He'd given up trying to make me into something he could like.

I laughed cynically, a Stanley Culp kind of laugh. I'd take a ride, all right. I'd go missing for a while. Supper could wait on me for once. Let them wonder where I was.

And so I set out toward the back country, down a road I'd seldom biked which wound away from the sea, past rocky farmland and shrub-clogged forests. The November daylight began to fade and still I went on, furiously at times, suddenly in a rage that even one-eyed Tom Morrison was no longer specially mine. He was Billy

Brady's friend, and Billy's father's before that. The free life he led came out of weakness and retreat, not anything strong he could pass on to me. He was as likely as anyone to bend before the wind.

And what a wind. I imagined Billy now, coming in by boat to the beach, striding up the path to Tom's shack. Billy Brady, tall and broad-shouldered, his white Labrador loping at his side; Billy, with all the glory of the *Black Duck* blazing out, and his easy, joking manner that charmed everyone.

Deep in these thoughts, I rode on through the darkening landscape. Over an hour passed before I thought of going back. My legs had begun to ache. The sun was down by then, and the road dim. An eerie silence rose on all sides and I was suddenly aware that I was far, far out in the country. I was turning to head home when the sound of tires came from the bend ahead. I flicked on my bicycle lamp and drew to the side.

The vehicle, driving without headlights, rode toward me with a ghostly quiet. As it passed, I recognized the whir of a muffled engine and glanced back over my shoulder. It was a Ford coupe, one taillight out.

The vehicle braked, stopped and began to reverse direction. A moment later the car came up in back of me and I squeezed over a second time to let it by. But it hung back and, little by little, moved up closer until I felt the heat of the motor on my legs.

"Come ahead!" I yelled, gesturing for the driver to go

past. He would not. When I looked back to see what the trouble was, a face pushed up close to the windshield and broke into a toothy grin.

Fear spiked through me. Even so, I couldn't believe that anyone could mean me harm. A game is what I thought, and for another hundred yards, I played my part by riding as far to the left-hand side as possible without going in the woods. Finally, with a roar, the big roadster pulled out to pass and I thought I'd be left in peace. But that was not to be. With stealthy calm, the vehicle moved up until the broad side windows were abreast of me. Out of the corner of one eye, I saw faces through the glass.

"Hey! Give me some room!" I called out.

There was no response, and in the next second I saw that I wasn't to be allowed even my slim edge of road. The side of the car moved closer until, with a last impatient swerve, it struck me. I lost my balance and went flying into the woods, where a darkness darker than night dropped over me.

WHERE'S THE TICKET?

THE SOUND OF VOICES DRIFTED DOWN TO me, as if through the depths of an ocean. For a while I was too far sunk to pay attention. Then, slowly, I surfaced and opened my eyes. My head felt heavy and swollen. Without even looking, I knew I was a prisoner.

The room I lay in was cold and dark, with the dank air of a cellar. Faint fingers of light crept in beneath a closed door. I tried to get up and could not. I was bound to a bed of some kind, roped down so tight the twine cut into my shins and wrists.

The voices came from above, along with other noises: chairs scraping, china clinking, the heavy tread of boots. A smell of frying meat and wood smoke wafted down. I guessed that I was lying below a kitchen and that a meal was under way. As I listened, the conversation began to piece itself together.

A man with a flat Boston twang spoke loudest and most often. He was angry about some job that had gone wrong. Cases had been lost, "scuttled" was his word. With that, I knew I was in the hands of a gang of rum-runners.

"Well, we know where we dropped 'em. They're not going anywhere," a younger voice replied.

"So why didn't you go back already?" the Boston voice said. "There's a hundred cases of Johnny Walker Red just lying out there in the harbor? Wait'll the big boys hear that!"

"How're we supposed to get 'em when it's blowing from the north?" a high, nervous voice asked. "You can't do nothing when it's blowing that way."

"The big boys don't care if it's blowing from Timbuktu! You get out tomorrow night and pull up those cases before they wash ashore. Get that guy with the fancy hook that did it for us last time. What's his name?"

"Louie," somebody said.

"Yeah, him. What'sa matter with you guys? You should'a thought of that yourself."

Everybody was quiet for a while. Then someone with a country drawl launched into a story about a new transport van he had that was painted to look exactly like a Bushway's Ice Cream truck. He was laughing about it.

"The Feds are out of the loop on this one! I've got that truck backed up to my cow barn a couple'a times a week, taking on loads for Boston, Providence, wherever. Only thing is, my neighbors next door had been watching. Last week one of 'em buttonholes me and says with a wink: 'All this Bushway's coming and going! You sure must be making a pile of money in the ice cream business.'

"I told him: 'Yeah, we got great ice cream. Comes straight from the isle of Bermuda. You ever try that flavor?'

" 'And what flavor is that?' he asks.

"I say to him: 'Hot buttered rum!' "

A heavy round of guffawing came down through the floor. Then chairs squeaked and it seemed as if the atmosphere changed. A more serious topic arose, one that must have been under discussion before I woke up, because it sort of started in the middle. I took a while to catch the drift, but when I did, my ears were burning.

"How many cases are we talking about?" a voice asked.

"Over three thousand, fancy stuff like champagne and high-priced scotch." This was the Boston accent again.

"Jeez, that's worth a bundle."

"It was scheduled to come in for Christmas. Now the big boys have got word it should be arriving just before New Year's. She's a freighter name of *Firefly*."

"She's coming from St. Pierre?"

"Canada, yeah. Packed to the gills. A private trader. She's bypassing Boston and coming straight down."

"How come?"

"Don't know. Our gang didn't set it up."

"So who did?"

"That big operator who was running around us, Tony Mordello, in New Bedford. He knew he'd make out big on it. Guess what he used for a ticket?"

"What?"

"A fifty-dollar bill ripped in half."

"Fifty bucks!"

"He had it on him when we bumped him off, but nobody knew. Then, one of his boys talked."

"So, who talked?"

"That stoolie cop Charlie Pope. He was in with Tony until he saw what happened to him. Then he decides to come over to our gang to keep the deal afloat since it's already paid for. He stays in touch with the Canadians, pretends Tony's still alive and in charge. Everything's on schedule except no one can find Tony's ticket. Charlie has his suspicions about where it went, but he can't prove it. Then the big boys get a new tip. That's why the kid's downstairs. They heard he's got the ticket stashed away somewhere."

"Where'd the tip come from?"

"Who else? The badge."

"That cop is in on everything."

"Slippery as an eel. I keep warning the big boys, don't trust him. Whoever pays him the most, he goes with. Anyway, if this kid knows where the fifty is, I'm supposed to get it outta him. Hey, Ernie, did you check on the punk lately?"

A minute later, footsteps sounded on the stairs coming down to my cellar. I took a couple of deep breaths, then a key turned in the lock and the door swung open.

My first idea was to keep my eyes shut and play dead. My head was burning up, though, and the ropes were cutting into me. When Ernie looked in, I looked back at him and asked for a drink of water.

"Harry!" he called. "He came to. What d'ya want me to do?"

"Let him alone. I'll be down."

"He's asking for water," Ernie called. "He can't have it till he talks, right?" He was a big man with a wide, fleshy face. Some greasy scrap from supper still hung on his chin.

"Get him some," came the reply.

The door closed. Ernie went back upstairs and returned with a mug, which he tipped so hard into my mouth that most of the water ran down my face.

"Here! Get your head up!" he said. Since even my neck was tied down, this was impossible. Ernie thought that was hilarious. He sat back and laughed at me.

A thin, narrow-eyed man wearing a fisherman's cap stepped into the room. I recognized him right off. Suddenly I knew who Ernie was, too. They were the gangsters with the machine guns who'd shot Tom Morrison's Viola. My blood went cold.

"Let the kid up," the thin guy said. "Nobody can drink lying down."

"Sure thing, Harry."

I was untied and allowed to sit up on the edge of the bed to drink more water. Three other gang members came down to watch. One of them was John Appleby.

"Hello, Ruben," he said, with a sneer.

If I could, I would have spit in his face. I'd figured out by then that this was the Boston gang headed up by the College Boys. Marina was right, they'd been all around me, watching and waiting. I'd been a blind fool.

As soon as I'd drunk my fill, Harry started in on me. He was the one with the Boston drawl.

"We know you picked that body on the beach. We

know *what* you picked, too, so don't bother with the funny stuff. Where's that fifty-dollar bill?"

"What bill?" I said.

"You know what. Your little friend saw it." Harry stabbed his finger into my chest. "He says you put it in a schoolbook. Where is it now?"

I kind of choked. I'd more or less forgotten Jeddy had seen me drop the bill in front of our lockers. Even worse, though, I couldn't believe he'd tell on me. My mouth got dry.

Harry moved in so his breath was on my face.

"What's your name, kid?" he asked.

From behind him, John Appleby answered for me. "Ruben Hart. His dad is manager of Riley's store."

"Now, Ruben, listen up. We don't want to hurt you. We want to get you back to your dad as soon as possible. This is just business, see? That bill is part of a deal we're doing. We've got to have it or the deal won't go through. So, where's this book? At school?"

If only that bill still was in my book at school, I would've told them. If I'd had it on me, I would've handed it over in a minute. What did I care about some freighter from Canada? The trouble was, it was in the tobacco pouch under my mattress at home, and I didn't want Harry or Ernie or any of those gangsters going anywhere near my house. My mother and Aunt Grace were there, probably by themselves.

"I don't have it anymore," I told Harry.

"C'mon, kid. We're not stupid."

"I threw it away."

"That's a good one."

"I did. How did I know anybody'd want it? You can't buy anything with half a fifty dollar bill. I kept it for a while, then I threw it away."

"Where? When?"

"At school, in the wastebasket in my classroom, about a week ago."

Harry's eyes went narrow. I could see he didn't believe me and was trying to make up his mind what to do about it. The rest of the gang stood around like vultures, watching.

"C'mon, boss, let me pop him a few times," Ernie said. "He'll talk."

Harry looked as if he was considering this when a phone started ringing upstairs.

"Get that," he ordered. John Appleby went for it. You could see he was low man on the totem pole, the same as he was at the store. After a minute, he yelled down:

"Harry! It's the badge."

"That weasel. What does he want?"

"He says to quit working on the kid. On orders from the big boys."

"What? Why?"

"The badge says he got a call from Boston. There's been a change of plans. They're sending somebody else over to talk to the kid."

Harry went into a string of terrible curses when he heard this. "Here I've done the dirty work and caught the punk, and now they're turning him over to somebody else? That doesn't make sense. Hold the phone, I'm coming up."

"He hung up already."

A grim look came over Harry's face when he heard this.

"I smell a rat. I'm calling Boston to check this. You take over with the kid," he told Ernie, and went off.

I was petrified. I knew if I was left in Ernie's hands, I'd be dead, or knocked out again at the least. Just looking at Ernie told you he lived his life on a short fuse. Any little thing could set him off. He'd shot Viola for tripping over her.

Harry must have had second thoughts, too, because halfway up the stairs he stopped and yelled back.

"Wait! Tie the kid up again. And Ernie, don't touch him. You hear me? I don't want no mark on him when I come back."

So I was tied down to the bed again. Ernie looked disappointed not to be able to work on me, but he followed orders. Since I was awake, he gagged me this time. When he finished, John Appleby, who'd been hanging around smirking, gave my bed a kick.

"How d'ya like that?" he said. "You're in trouble now and your daddy ain't here to fix it, is he?"

I tried to look daggers back at him, but he just laughed at me. Then he and Ernie closed me in and went upstairs. I was alone in the dark again, except for those little fingers of light coming under the door. I began to get scared.

For one thing, I was wondering who this cop "the badge" might be. Or rather, I wasn't wondering, I was pretty sure I knew. The air around me suddenly got colder and denser. The walls of the cellar seemed to creep in on me. I tried to wiggle my feet and hands to keep the blood flowing, but slowly the feeling went out of them. I gave up and lay still. Whatever was ahead for me, I knew I didn't have anything but a prayer to raise against it.

SEEING STARS

TIME PASSED, I COULDN'T TELL HOW MUCH. Hours, maybe. I dozed on and off. At one point, I heard a knock on the door upstairs and a lot of feet stamping around overhead. There was some talking. I couldn't make out the words.

I heard the next thing all right: a gun went off from a place that seemed right over my bed. My heart took a giant leap. Upstairs in the kitchen, someone swore and another shot let loose. I heard a body fall down, then a bunch of grunts and crashing furniture. A fight was going on. A few minutes later, it stopped, and footsteps came thudding down the stairs to my cellar. The door blasted open. A couple of brand-new characters walked in.

"Found him!" one yelled. He came over and started trying to yank me off the bed.

"He's tied down," the other guy said.

"Well, cut him loose."

The second man flicked open a jackknife and cut me free. They both started trying to drag me up the stairs.

"C'mon, kid. Walk!" they were telling me, but my legs had gone dead. I couldn't make them work. Finally, one of them hauled me over his shoulder like a sack of flour and we went up.

"Where am I going?" I asked.

"Shut up," he said.

We came to the top of the stairs and turned down a hall that led to the front door. On the way, I saw Harry and Ernie standing in the kitchen with their hands in the air. Somebody was holding a gun on them and they didn't look happy about it. John Appleby had a gun on two others. The little squealer had switched sides.

A man was lying on the floor. Whether he was shot dead or just wounded, I couldn't tell because I was traveling sort of upside down and backward. I caught a glimpse of Harry turning around to watch me as I went by.

"Who are you guys?" I heard him say to one of the boys holding the guns. "Hey, we can cut a deal. You want in on the freighter? Tell the badge we got no problem with that. We didn't know he wanted to go that way. We got no problem at all."

Nobody answered. Harry looked as if he couldn't believe what was happening. I couldn't believe it, either. I was being kidnapped again.

My head slammed into a hard edge. I saw a fountain of sparks and then a warm, wet curtain came down over my eyes. I'd been thrown into the backseat of a big roadster and now a bunch of guys were piling in after me. The engine cranked up and we started away down the road. The man sitting next to me was angry.

"Idiot! He's bleeding like crazy. Why'd you dump him like that?"

"I didn't!"

"Can you stop it?"

"Get that blanket outta the trunk."

My head was feeling strange, woozing in and woozing out. They tried sitting me up, laying me down, wrapping handkerchiefs around my head and covering me up with the blanket. Nothing would stop me. I was bleeding all over the place.

"He's going to need a docter," somebody said. "We can't deliver him this way. Take the gag off."

When they got it off me, another voice in the front seat said: "We ain't got time for no docter. Listen, kid, we didn't mean to hurt you. Can you breathe better now?"

I nodded. There was something familiar about that voice. I'd heard it before.

"Cripes, he's a mess. Farino, what were you thinking, throwing him in like that? You know he's gotta talk!"

"Well, he weighed a ton."

"What'd he hit?"

"A case of booze."

"Cripes!"

The car went very fast at times and slowed down to a crawl at others. There were a number of turns and swerves. They'd laid me down on my back on the seat, my legs stretched across two or three laps. Whenever I opened my eyes, I could see stars shining in the dark sky through the car window. I recognized a couple of constellations

Jeddy and I used to point out to each other: Orion's Belt and Scorpio. I saw the Big Dipper. After a while, we must have been driving in more or less one direction because the same constellations stayed there, inside the window frame. I'd get dizzy and close my eyes, and when I opened them, Orion would still be riding along with me. I didn't know where I was going but even in my bad state, I knew who I was going with. Somewhere along the way, I figured out who that voice in the front seat belonged to.

Stanley Culp.

I was traveling with the New York mobsters.

"Hello, Mr. Culp. It's me, Ruben Hart," I remember saying once. I was dumb enough to think he'd somehow missed this fact.

He glanced at me over a shoulder in his lazy way. "Sorry about this, kid," he said, and turned back around.

I must have passed out because the next thing I knew, I was being carried from the car and taken inside another house. The room I was put in this time was upstairs, a kind of attic. I was still bleeding, going in and out of consciousness. At some point, a man with a face that sagged like a old sack down one side came to look at me. I figured he was one of the kingpins because everyone was kowtowing to him, holding his coat and backing up to give him room. He leaned over and gave me a hard stare.

"Poor kid. You messed him up good," he said.

That was it. He left. He'd decided I was beyond talking at that moment, and he was probably right. The funny thing was, I was ready to talk if only I could have. I was scared sick. These New York gangsters struck me as real efficient professionals, the kind that don't play around with dumping bodies at sea that might wash up on shore later. If they wanted to get rid of someone, they'd know how to do it. Like Danny Walsh in Providence, there'd be nothing left behind and no one to tell why.

Later, when I found out that the man with the sagging face was probably Lucky Luciano himself, come out from New York City for the very purpose of directing operations in our area, I wasn't surprised. A face like that you don't forget. A face like that could've asked me and I would've told him: "Under the mattress, in the tobacco pouch." My mother and Aunt Grace would've had to take their chances.

After a few hours, one of the New York gang brought me up a bowl of soup and stood around while I tried to eat it.

"If I were you, I'd get better fast and talk," the guy said. He had a sort of deadpan face. There was no telling what he was thinking.

"I will," I croaked.

"They don't want you around here. They'll get rid of you."

"Thanks," I said.

"Even if you talk, they'll probably get rid of you," he went on. "It's cleaner that way. Nobody to squeal on us."

After that, I couldn't eat anymore. He took the soup bowl, tied me up and put the gag over my mouth. He turned out the lights on me the way the Boston gang had done, closed the door and went downstairs. The only window in the room had a shade pulled over it. I was alone in the dark, and this time there were no fingers of light to hang on to. I began to drift.

At times I seemed to be on a rolling sea, and at other times I lay in a dark forest, trees waving over my head. I imagined myself floating up toward a ceiling, which I expected to bump into at any moment, though I never did because it always lifted higher in the nick of time to make room for me. What I found out was, there's a point beyond which you can't bring up enough energy even to be afraid anymore. What was happening was happening, and I wasn't me but a spectator to myself, waiting and watching and, in an oddly distant way, curious to see how it would end.

Sometime later, a loud creak woke me up. I thought a piece of roof was being pried off right over my head. I waited but nothing else happened. I'd decided I'd been imagining things again when a quieter sound started, a sort of gnawing or jimmying. It came from the window in my room. I heard whispering. Someone was trying to get in.

Suddenly, the window was raised. A wave of cold air blew in from outside. The shade buckled and was pushed aside, and a leg came in over the sill. Somebody was in the room with me. A black shape stood just inside the window, looking around, trying to get its bearings. I held my breath. After everything that had happened, I didn't know if it was a friend or someone else out to get me.

At last, a voice whispered: "Ruben? Are you in here?"

"Mm-mm-mm," I said through my gag.

The dark shape came forward and stooped over me. A cigarette lighter came on in my face. In its flash, I saw Billy Brady, and he saw me.

"Gotcha!" he whispered, and squeezed my arm. "Here, hang on to to this."

He put the burning lighter into one of my hands that was tied to the bedpost, then set to work with a knife to cut through my ropes. One by one, he sliced them off. He pulled me up and unknotted the gag over my mouth. I was never so happy to see anyone in my life.

"How did you know I was here?" I said. I was groggy, still not sure if this was a dream or real life.

"Shh-shh!" Billy leaned close and said in my ear: "Don't talk now. There's a ladder set up outside the window. I'll be right behind you. Move real slow."

Slow was the only way I could move after being tied up for so long. I inched across the room, climbed out the window and went down that ladder one shivery leg at a time. It seemed an age before my foot hit the ground. Then Billy came down beside me and, hardly breathing, we went across the dark yard to the road. We were almost there when someone rushed at me from behind a bush and two arms went around my neck. A voice said, "Thank God!" in my ear.

I didn't have to look to know who it was. Marina McKenzie. When she'd finished hugging me, she started up shaking me.

"Next time listen when someone tells you to watch out," she hissed. "You could've ended up dead."

"I know," I whispered. "I think John Appleby set me up. He was playing both sides."

"That skunk. No wonder his family was getting rich. Anyhow, we've got you back, so it's all right."

There was no more time to talk. We began sneaking away down the road behind the tall, dark form of Billy Brady. He wasn't alone. Two men came up behind us carrying the ladder. Around the bend, two cars were waiting, idling with their headlights off.

Billy went over and talked to the driver of one and sent him off on some errand. Then we all piled into the other car, an old station wagon. Marina, Billy and I were in the backseat while the others sat up front with the driver.

"No talking till we get past these crooks," Billy warned. The driver nudged the accelerator and started off coasting to keep the engine quiet. We drifted past the house where the New York mobsters had held me. Not a sign of movement came from inside.

"Out cold from celebrating too hard, most likely," one of Billy's friends snickered after a minute.

"Those New York goons thought they'd pulled a double whammy on the College Boys," a second one said. "Ruben here wasn't the only thing they hijacked. While the one bunch was holding everybody at gunpoint in the kitchen, the rest of the gang was out back with a truck, helping themselves to a shedful of the College Boys' whiskey. Must be a hundred cases they brought back with them, stacked behind the house."

"There *was* a hundred cases, you mean," the first man said. "Rick, tell Billy what we did."

"Alfred and I laid claim to a few while you were springing Ruben. We've got 'em in the back with the ladder."

They all let loose and whooped at that.

"You fellas've got the stickiest rum-running fingers I ever saw!" Billy said. Turning to me, he added, "I hope you don't mind a bunch of renegade smugglers being your angels of mercy."

I grinned and said it was all right by me.

"Then I'd like to introduce you to the crew of the *Black Duck*. It's thanks to them we could pull off this stunt."

As the car picked up speed, hands started coming out to me in the dark, and though I couldn't see their faces very well, I tried to thank each one for coming to my rescue. There was Alfred Biggs, ship's mechanic, with forearms the size of tree stumps. There was Rick Delucca, Billy's partner and navigator on the *Duck*, who'd known Billy at Harveston High School and brought him in on the *Black Duck*'s operations after Billy's dad was killed. Behind the wheel was Bernardo Rosario, the *Black Duck*'s radio man, even younger than Billy, though he had a wife and two kids at home.

"How did you find me?" I asked him. "I thought I was a goner."

"You never were, Marina had you under surveillance,"

Billy answered. "In case you don't know, she's our trusty watchdog on land," he added, no doubt thinking he was paying her a compliment, much as he prized his friendship with those animals.

"Trusty watchdog!" she protested. "I certainly hope not!"

"Secret agent, then, or how about Director of Intelligence? We had a notion you were about to get snatched by those Boston foxes, Ruben, and were keeping an eye out. We would've rescued you quicker, except the New York gang beat us to it. I hadn't figured on them. We were trailing you all over."

I looked at Marina then, wondering if she had any idea of the part her father had played in my abduction. I suspected she didn't, and kept quiet on that subject. The truth is, I wasn't sure about the chief myself. He was into the racket so deep, on so many levels, it was impossible to guess what his game plan was. I could bet my safety wasn't high on his scoreboard, though.

"So, you're working for the *Black Duck* now?" I asked Marina. I knew she had a mind of her own, but that was the first I'd had an inkling she'd take it so far.

"Not at all," she said. "I'm trying to keep them out of trouble."

Everybody roared with laughter at that. ("Fat chance," Alfred Biggs told her.) I was glad we'd gone a piece down the road or the New York gang might have been woken up and come after us. The *Black Duck*'s crew was a cheerful, wisecracking bunch. As for Captain Billy Brady, whatever I'd thought of him before, I changed my mind that night. I knew he'd risked his skin for me, and asked his friends to do the same. There'd never be a way I could properly thank him, even if his motives weren't completely pure. Which they weren't, as I found out a moment later.

"Now, Ruben," Billy said, leaning toward me in the car. "Where is this ticket you've got? The word going around is it's half a fifty-dollar bill, ready to match with the captain of the *Firefly*'s. You know that boat's carrying over half a million dollars' worth of goods."

I was opening my mouth to announce exactly where it was, thinking it was the least I could do for him, when I felt a hand take mine under cover of dark.

"Ruben threw it out, didn't you?" Marina said softly, looking straight ahead.

I didn't know what was going on, so I kept quiet.

"You wouldn't toss it!" Billy said. "Come on, Ruben, you didn't do that."

"He did. He told me," Marina went on, keeping my hand deep in hers. "About a month ago, wasn't it?"

"Yes," I said.

"He didn't know what it was," Marina went on.

I nodded. "That's what I told the Boston gang, too. What good's half a fifty-dollar bill?"

"Wait a minute!" Billy yelled at Marina. "If you knew he'd tossed it, why didn't you say so? You could've let me know before we went to all this trouble to snatch him."

She locked eyes on him with that level gaze of hers.

"Billy Brady, I'm astonished. What were you intending to rescue, Ruben or the ticket?"

Billy sagged back against the seat, shaking his head.

"That beats all," he groaned. "The *Firefly*'s finally coming in after all these months and now there's no one to claim her cargo. Her captain will see there's been a misfire and probably turn tail and head to Canada. Tony Mordello would have a good laugh over that. All his liquor going back out to sea. I guess he won the last round at that poker game after all."

"I guess he did," Marina answered, giving me a knowing smile. She squeezed my hand and let it go.

I never asked Marina why she made me tell that lie, but it wasn't hard to figure out. Anyone could see that the *Firefly*'s shipment was too big and too hot for a small smuggling operation like the *Black Duck*'s. Billy Brady's interest in profit had begun to get the better of his good sense. Marina was doing exactly what she'd said, trying to keep the *Duck* out of trouble, though even then she must have known she was playing against the odds.

All the time we were driving the dark roads back to town, I'd assumed I was headed home. Not until the car took a sharp turn and began to bump over a surface that was obviously not the road into my house did I look out. There, just visible in the faint light of what was now early dawn, I saw a span of choppy ocean that could only be the water off Coulter's Point.

"Aren't you taking me home?"

The car went silent.

"Not right away," Billy said after a pause. "Your name's out and around about this ticket. We think it's best if you lay over with a friend of the family until things settle down. Your parents know you're safe. I sent word by Doc Washburn in the car back there."

"Doc Washburn! Was he in on this?"

"He was. The doc knows this town inside out. He's no rumrunner, but we call on him if we need him. Your father's been worried sick about you. I've been in touch about tonight. Our plan was, if we got you back, you'd be safer away from home. He said he'd spread a story you've gone to visit your brother in Providence. That should cover you for now."

I tried to imagine my father being worried sick about me, but couldn't bring up that picture. More likely, he'd be worrying about who he'd find on such short notice to do my work at the store.

At this point, the car slowed and rocked even more crazily over the ground, and a dog started barking.

"Sadie! Stop that racket!" Billy shouted out the window.

A second later, we came up on two chicken coops leaning together at an angle that looked as if a hurricane had been through. I knew what friend of the family he'd been talking about.

A SAFE HAVEN

TOM MORRISON WAS EXPECTING US. A LARGE oil lantern was hanging on a hook outside his door, casting a faint light across the cluttered yard. I was dead tired by this time. My head had started bleeding again and I had a hard time of it just to walk inside. I remember Marina sitting me down at Tom's table and offering me a steaming cup of her very own clam chowder. She'd made up a batch at home and brought it to leave with Tom so I'd have something she knew I liked to eat. But that morning I could hardly stay upright in the chair.

"Leave him be for now," I heard Tom say. "He's gone through the grinder. You and Billy go along. I'll look after him, don't you worry."

The next thing I knew, the room was empty, and Tom was taking off the towels that were wrapped around my head. He bathed my wound in warm water, and wrapped it again in some kind of cloth. Sadie tried to lay her head in my lap, but Tom told her to keep off me. I believe I finally ate a little, and drank a quantity of water before sleep took me out on a great dark tide. Not until evening did I open my eyes and find myself in Tom's bunk. And there he was a minute later, looking down on me as gentle as a nurse.

"Looks like the three of us is going to be shipmates for a spell," he said.

He was including Sadie in his count, and well he might. She was right there leaning over me with him, only lower down, drooling sympathetically on my face.

I pushed her snout away. "Is Sadie living with you now?"

"She's consented to have me for the time being," Tom replied, ruffling her ears so her feelings wouldn't be hurt at being shoved off. "Billy don't want her on the *Duck* no more. Says it's getting too hot out on the water, what with the shooting and double-crossing going on these days."

"Did she used to do his jobs with him?"

"Oh, Lordy, yes! She's an old smuggling hand. Get Billy to tell you about her sometime. She can smell a Coast Guard cutter around a bend. Sets up to yipping. Out on West Island, there's a drop she guards. The thieves keep away, knowing she'll tear them to shreds if they so much as put one foot ashore."

"The *Black Duck*'s got a place out on West Island?"

At this, Tom clapped his hand over his mouth. "I'm talking too much," he said. "You just forget what I said. This isn't your business and you don't want to know about it."

For once, I didn't mind that at all. I really didn't want to hear any more about smuggling or rumrunners at that moment. Tom went off to fix me a bowl of Marina's chowder, leaving Sadie and me to start getting to know each other better.

That was the beginning of what I look back on now as one of the happiest times in my life. For the next couple of weeks, I stayed with Tom and he took care of me. I was up and about in a day or so, though I had to be careful not to move too fast or my head would spin. We'd crossed into December by then and the days had a frigid edge to them, though a bright sun seemed always to be beaming down around Tom Morrison's chicken coops. Maybe it was just being out from under my old life, away from the humdrum of schoolwork and Riley's General Store, but I felt like a bird escaped from a cage.

We spliced rope and wove crab traps on the stoop the first few days. Then, though the season was drawing to a close, I went out crabbing with Tom on his raft. Sadie came, too. He was teaching her to spot crabs underwater, the job Viola'd had.

"One-eyed folks like me don't get a read on depth the way most people do," Tom explained. "The world's kind of flat to us, though you get so's you fill it out with some imagination of your own. The trouble with crabs is, there's no room to imagine 'em if you want to catch 'em. They're either there or they're not. Am I right, Sadie?"

She'd just then come out of the water after a dive off the raft, and her answer was to start shaking herself from head to tail, thoroughly dousing us with freezing pond water. It got so bad, we had to push her back in.

When we weren't on the raft, we skulked around on

the beach, looking for interesting objects that might've washed up. I told Tom about a bride's hope chest Jeddy and I had found one time full of sheets and towels and ladies' silk underthings. We were so embarrassed that we dug a hole and pushed the whole mess in before anyone could catch us with it.

Tom said that was by no means the most unusual thing. A crate of Florida oranges had washed up on his shore once, ripe and delicious. He'd eaten every one.

More darkly, he told me of a boot he found with a human foot still in it.

"Was it the mob, do you think?"

He said it might've been, though this was a few years before their kind of murderous activity was widespread.

"Could've been sharks or ocean currents or any number of things," he went on. "You never know with the sea. It's a place unto itself. There's baby seals who get parked here on this beach by their mothers. They'll be migrating down the coast, usually early in spring, and the little ones grow tired. The pup'll be here a day or two, laying over, then the mother'll come back to pick him up and they'll start off on their travels again.

"Gives you a strange feeling coming across one of those pups. They've got a human child's eyes, but how they look at you, it's unnerving. Like they're in touch with some wildness no human could ever know. They're from an undersea world that's far beyond our knowledge, with rules and reasons that have nothing to do with ours. A privilege it is to live alongside such a mystery, and have the chance once in a while of staring it in the face."

In the evenings, Tom would light his kerosene lantern and cook up some supper. There wasn't ever much doubt what it would be. I had crab in just about every way a crab can be made edible, in soup, grilled, poached, stewed, steamed, fried, baked, fricasseed and then some. Sadie ate right along with us.

After dinner, we'd sit with our feet up on the warm cast-iron stove and talk or not, whatever we felt like. There was no need to be polite or say something you didn't mean just to fill up space in the conversation. Nobody was harping on anyone to wash up or take off his boots. Nobody was watching the clock about when to go to bed. It was heaven to me, and an eye-opener, too, that Tom had found a way to live that was the right way for him, even if it wouldn't agree with what other people might think.

Never once did Tom dig into the reason why I was there, and that was good of him since I didn't want to think about the fool I'd been to get myself kidnapped. My head wound was healing and my heart was, too, I guess, because the darkness that had been in me for weeks, worrying about my father and the store and where I was headed in life, cleared off. I was whistling on my way to the woodpile—it was cold enough so the stove in Tom's shack was going by then—and ruffling Sadie's ears right along with Tom.

December moved on, and Christmas came and went without anyone bothering much about it. Tom had his own take on seasons and holidays that was completely out of time with the rest of the world. Billy's crewman Alfred Biggs came down and brought me a sweater my mother had knitted for me, and a book from Aunt Grace, and that was about all there was to it. No tree or decorations or singing or turkey dinner. What I found out was, they didn't matter to me as much as I'd thought they did. I was happy without. It occurred to me that some of Tom Morrison was beginning to rub off on me.

It wouldn't last, of course. Couldn't last. Out to sea, I'd watch laden schooners tacking upwind, or fishing sloops sneaking into coves beyond Coulter's at dusk. I'd hear a seaplane buzz over the bay and I'd know that real life was out there with its shifting fogs and confusion, ready to come in on me again given the slightest excuse.

One bright, unusually warm afternoon at the end of December, it came. I was down on the beach by myself looking for washed-up fish heads the inshore trawlers might have dumped that would do for a soup. Crabs had begun to disappear with the cold and Tom was moving on to his winter menu. From the direction of West Island, a dark speck appeared on the water. In short order it became a boat heading toward the mainland at a high rate of speed, a white plume of water rising off her stern. Right away, I knew she wasn't headed for the harbor or any other place. She was coming straight in to Coulter's. I took off back to Tom's shack to warn him.

He'd spotted her already and was out front, up on a dune, squinting against the sun. Sadie was standing tense beside him, preparing to bark her head off as usual. As I came up, Tom laid a hand on her snout and said:

"Looks like we got visitors."

"Is it . . . ?" I was afraid to say. All I was thinking about was thugs and machine guns.

"No. Not them." He cupped his hand like a spyglass around his good eye. "I believe it's a craft you don't often catch a glimpse of in the light of day."

A minute later, as we both watched, the speedster roared into Coulter's at full throttle, cut engine and turned sideways to the beach. At the helm, the dark outline of the skipper was visible in his captain's cap, working the controls. Even at that distance, I knew him.

Billy Brady was one of those fellows that stand out a long way off. As the *Black Duck* drifted softly in toward the beach, I saw a girl come up beside him in the wheelhouse, a red bandana tied over her long, brown hair.

"Marina!" Tom exclaimed. "Go meet 'em, Sadie."

He let the dog free and followed her down the path as fast as he could hobble. Last of all, I went, eager to see them, too, but sad as well, guessing this arrival meant my happy days with Tom Morrison were nearing an end.

FOG

THERE WAS JUST BILLY AND MARINA ON
board the *Duck* that warm blue day. To see them side by
side, dropping anchor, securing the line on deck, lowering
the little skiff into the water and, Billy at the oars, rowing
in to shore over the waves, was to know without a doubt
that they'd thrown in their lot together. They were laughing and fooling around like a couple of kids. Whatever
hope I'd had, if you could even call such an impossible
dream "hope," that Marina would wait for me to catch up
with her in life blew away.

It was no use being jealous or angry at Billy. He was
above and beyond anything I could be. They stepped out
of the skiff holding hands, grinning over some private joke,
barely aware of Tom and me calling out our hellos as we
came down the beach.

Then Sadie was on them, wild to see Billy after all that
time, galloping around in circles and barking so loud, nobody could hear a word. Billy brought out a ham bone
he'd saved up for her, and wrestled her for it. At last she
got it away and took off into the dunes.

"You're a nervy pair to be out on the *Duck* in broad daylight!" Tom teased them as we walked down the sandy path to his cabin. To Billy, he said, "I hear the whole United States Coast Guard is out to lay you low."

"Well, I've got nothing on board this afternoon. They'll have to be patient!" Billy kidded back.

"Nothing but Marina McKenzie, the brightest pearl in the sea," old Tom said. He grinned at her. "I hope you know you're putting yourself at risk traveling with this scurrilous pirate."

"I believe I've decided to take that risk," Marina replied. Though she said it with a smile, a darker tone was in her voice. I guessed she was under no illusion as to what she'd entered into.

"Come on in," Tom said when we came to the cabin. "Can I take it for granted that you'll both stay for supper? You'll be surprised, I'm sure, to hear we're having crab. It's the last of it, though. Ruben and I are going on to fish-head chowder tomorrow."

Billy laughed and said it would be a special pleasure to stay, due to the tricky situation they were in.

"And what's that?" Tom asked.

"Marina can't be seen with me in town," Billy answered. "Her dad's laid down the law. He's a great believer in defending a woman's honor."

"He needn't worry. I'm doing that perfectly well by myself," Marina countered, giving Billy a push.

"You are!" He laughed. "I can't make a dent."

Marina turned to me. "Billy's not taking it serious, as

you can see, but it's true about Dad. He heard about us getting together up in Harveston. That snake Charlie Pope found out and told him."

"I thought Charlie and the chief weren't getting along."

"They aren't, which is the very reason Charlie went and told. He was aiming to get back at me and Dad all in one swoop. It's worked, all right. My father's on the warpath against Billy."

"Does he know you're in with the *Duck*?" Tom Morrison asked Billy.

"If he doesn't know by now, he's blind, deaf and dumb," Billy said. "What he can do about it is another question."

This boastfulness didn't go over well with Marina. A worried wrinkle came up on her forehead and she seemed about to speak when Billy announced it was time to get on with things. He told Tom he had a plan to put before him. The two went inside the cabin for a private talk. Marina drew me back outside to give me the latest news of home.

"Everybody's fine. They're holding to their story of you being with your brother, though folks in town are beginning to wonder what's taking you so long up in Providence. The school's on your case, too. Your father told them you're taking classes up there. He said no one would know the difference once you got back. You'd catch up in a blink with all the brains you've got."

"He said that about me?" I swear it was the first compliment I'd ever had from him.

Marina nodded. "He did. He's missing you, Ruben. This whole episode's given him fits."

We sat down on Tom's stoop in the last of the afternoon sun. Out to sea, a strange fog was gathering over the waves. It appeared that the warmth of the day was having an unusual effect, for rarely did the ocean produce mist in winter.

"What's happening with Jeddy?" I asked. I'd been thinking of him a lot.

"You know, he's been wondering the same about you," Marina said. "That's something he'd like to fix."

"What is?"

"The two of you. He said he wants to get back together sometime."

"Well, how about right now? Does he know where I am? Tell him to come down for a visit."

"Oh, Ruben," she said. "If only I could. He thinks you're up in Providence, like everybody else. The way things are, it's probably better he doesn't know the truth."

"But why?" I asked. "He wouldn't tell, would he?"

Marina sighed. "I don't know. There's a lot between us we don't dare talk about."

Jeddy had quit at Fancher's, she said, but was still in and out of the police station, following his father more closely than ever.

"He knows Dad's been a partner on some pretty shady deals, but he'd rather overlook it," she said. "It doesn't fit with Jeddy's view of what he'd like to believe. I'm just as bad if it comes to that. We're both shutting our eyes. In

the beginning, Dad just did small favors for favors in return. He'd stay away from certain beaches on certain
nights, or keep the State Patrol off roads where liquor was
being trucked through. Now I think he's in deep with a
big-city gang and doesn't know how to get out."

I thought this a mild description of the chief's activities after what I'd heard and seen during that year, but I
kept my mouth shut.

"I wish my mother were here," Marina went on. "She'd
set him straight. He never speaks to Jeddy and me about
it, of course."

"Of course." I knew how that was. My heart went out
to Jeddy. I saw how he was caught in the snarl of the
liquor racket even worse than I was. If he stood by his old
rule of "police business," he'd have to turn the chief in, and
if he stood by his dad, he'd be lying to himself about what
he knew was a crime.

Beside me, Marina sighed and shook her head.
"Sometimes I stop and wonder what's right," she said.
"And there isn't any answer, so I just go along. I guess, in
the end, if you have to make a choice, you do what's best
for the people you love."

I nodded, though I wondered how Marina herself
would ever apply that rule. She had her father on one
side and Billy Brady on another, and neither of them were
on the right side of the law. I didn't know what I'd do if I
were in her shoes, so I didn't say anything. We sat silent
together watching that unseasonable fog rolling toward us
in great white billows. It was the sort of fog that, once it's

settled over the bay, hangs on till morning, giving plenty of cover to anyone who might need it.

"What's Billy got going for tonight?" I asked.

Marina glanced up. "Well, you might as well know since you'll find out soon enough. A boat's come in from Canada with a big load of holiday liquor. It's a shipment that could make up for some of what he might've had if the *Firefly* had come through. The whole crew is going out in the *Black Duck* to bring it ashore. They want to land the cases here at Coulter's, and store them overnight with Tom. If Tom'll allow that. Billy's trying to talk him into it right now."

"So Tom hasn't been in on things?"

"He doesn't like the liquor-smuggling business. It was losing Viola that turned him against it, I think. He's never gotten over the way she was killed."

"You don't go on jobs with Billy, do you?" I asked.

"I have," she admitted. "It's a wild ride, all right. Lately, there've been too many close calls. The Coast Guard's been stepping up their patrols. It's harder than it was to get a speedboat in shore. Also, the big gangs are muscling into Billy's territory. There's always danger some stool pigeon like Charlie Pope will hear about one of his jobs and rat to the Coast Guard."

"So the Coast Guard is taking bribes, too?"

"Some are and some aren't, the same as everywhere. A lot of officers are honest enough, but the *Black Duck* has slipped through their fingers once too often. They wouldn't mind a hot tip on her whereabouts, no matter who it comes from. I wish Billy'd quit, but I know he never will," she added. "The money's too good. He's making ten times what he ever did fishing."

At this point, Tom Morrison gave us a shout from inside. We'd been hearing some banging around in the kitchen and guessed he was cooking up supper while Billy talked to him. As we opened the door, he was laying out bowls and spoons on the table. We came in and sat down to a steaming crab stew.

"Tom's stubborn as an old mule," Billy told us while we ate. "He won't take any liquor back here. I'm going to have to get transportation straight off the beach."

"You're lucky you can use my beach!" Tom said. He was agitated. "I'm not in favor of losing another dog. Your dog, if it comes to that. Or having my cabin smashed to pieces. I'll be lying low tonight with Sadie and Ruben, so don't be sending any of your rummies back here."

"You narrow-minded coot!" Billy exclaimed. "Here you could make a bundle and get away from these broken-down chicken coops, and you won't lift a finger to help yourself."

"I'm lifting my finger in the direction of peace and quiet," Tom replied. "Money's no answer to what's needed in my life."

That finished the discussion. He wouldn't hear any more of Billy's plans. He was good-natured about it. Not long after, he had Marina and me laughing at some tale from his early days. Finally Billy resigned himself and joined in with us.

It grew dark and Tom lit candles. We sat for another half hour, talking and drinking coffee while Sadie snuffled around below, looking for scraps. When she gave up on that, she lay down on Billy's feet, in hopes, I suppose, that she could keep him there forever. It was what we all would've hoped for, Tom and Marina and me, if we'd known how fast the end was coming. We didn't, though. Even with all the signs pointing in one direction, we didn't want to think that way. Fair warning, they say. But you have to be ready to see it when it comes.

The Interview

~~~~~~

A TELEPHONE IS RINGING. OVER AND OVER. From some room back in the house.

Mr. Hart doesn't hear it. He's still in Tom Morrison's chicken coops, eating crab stew and dreading the future.

Want me to answer the phone?

The phone?

It's ringing.

Where?

I don't know. Where is it?

Mr. Hart looks around with a dazed expression.

Outside, rain is still coming down and they're still in the parlor, sitting on those rock-hard chairs. In darkness now. The wet weather has caused a strenuous new bout of growth in the window bushes out front. It really is time to cut them back, David thinks. He can hardly see his notepad.

He still brings the pad with him every day, believing he'll be taking notes, though he never does. Perhaps, he thinks, he's not suited for journalism, a profession requiring a bloodhound nose for the truth, wherever it lies hidden, and (apparently) an ability to write in places only a bat could navigate.

In the bedroom, Mr. Hart says about the telephone. *Can you get it for me?*

David races back and answers. At first, there's silence from the other end. Then:

Ruben? A woman's anxious voice.

He's here, David assures her. *I'm just answering for him. Wait a minute. I'll get him.*

The old man is already making his way to the phone. He mouths to David: *Must be the wife!* and slices a humorous finger across his throat.

David grins. He goes back to the parlor to give them some privacy. The small tables laden with photographs are there, evidence of Mr. Hart's long life with friends and family. While he waits, David wanders around examining them.

A head shot of a very pretty girl with laughing eyes and long, dark hair catches his attention.

There's an old wedding photo, a mass of bridesmaids and groomsmen fanned out around the happy couple. Ruben Hart and wife? The groom is too decked out in wedding finery to tell.

The next photo stops David in his tracks. It's of a fishing vessel tied alongside a pier. Three men stand on deck, gazing straight into the camera's eye. A fourth is in the wheelhouse, his face just visible through the glass. David bends closer and, despite the parlor gloom, reads the boat's name in faded letters on the bow.

Black Duck.

There it is!

He picks up the photo. The men staring out at him are young and earnest-looking, nothing like the wisecracking outlaw crew he'd imagined. They're wearing plain fisherman's overalls and heavy rubber boots. Two are solemn, and have taken off their caps in honor of the camera. The third wears a captain's hat cocked jauntily over his forehead. He's raising his hand in greeting, a teasing smile on his face, as if he knows the photographer.

None of them looks remotely like Ruben Hart, but then David wouldn't have expected him to be here. He was a kid at the time, fourteen years old. The only survivor of the *Black Duck* shooting was Richard Delucca, a man in his early twenties, according to the newspaper. There's no telling which of this crew he is, though David would bet a good amount that Billy Brady is the guy in the cocked hat.

He returns the photo to the table. It gives him an odd feeling to look into the young faces of men who will soon be dead. Their eyes announce confidently: *I have my whole life in front of me!* They have no idea of their approaching fate. Even if they'd appreciated the risk they were taking, and had "no one to blame but themselves," as the newspaper clipping said, David feels a deep regret for the waste of their lives. He wants to warn them: *Don't go. Watch out. It's not worth it!*

For the hundredth time, he wonders what happened out there in the fog. Were they machine-gunned without warning, as the most recent newspaper article he found seemed to report? Or did Rick Delucca, member of a crew caught with over 300 cases of liquor on board, a crew with a reputation for brazen escapes in the past, tell that story in self-defense? There's one person still alive who may know the answer.

In the back room, David can hear the old man winding up his conversation with Mrs. Hart.

You come home when you're ready. I'm fine here. . . . No. No. Don't you worry, I've got plenty. I'm still working on your clam chowder!

A hearty act. Reality shows up a moment later when Mr. Hart clumps back into the parlor, lowers himself onto a chair and gazes dismally at the floor.

He's gone, he announces. *Just heard it from my wife.*
Who?

Jeddy McKenzie. Died early this morning. He glances up. In the split second before he looks down again, David sees tears welling up in his sea-colored eyes. *I hope you won't mind me stopping early today. Don't have the stomach for any more.*

Of course not. So, your wife was looking after Jeddy?
She was. It's over. She'll be coming home now.
You won't be going there?
He wouldn't want me. Now you'd best go.
Can I do anything? Really, I'd like to help. I could run an errand. Whatever.

Come tomorrow, Mr. Hart says, wearily. *And bring a*

good pen to write with. You'll be hearing something that's never been told.

David leaves him sitting alone in the shadowy room, an old man haunted by a friendship broken seventy years ago. Does it have something to do with the *Black Duck* shootings? The photo of that boat and its doomed crew rises up before David again. On the spur of the moment, he decides to go by the town library one last time, in case he's missed anything. He mounts his bicycle and heads out.

The rain has slowed to a fine drizzle. David's tires slap methodically against the wet pavement. Something about the weather makes him think how Ruben Hart once rode these same roads on his bicycle. And there, in a flash, as if answering a call, the ghost of the young Ruben descends. David feels him, can almost see him, pedaling at his elbow. For a long minute, they ride together, side by side, the wind rushing past. Then it's over. The ghost departs. David pushes ahead alone. He picks up speed and races over the wet road toward the library. Time is running out. December 29, 1929, is about to arrive. Fog is rolling in across Coulter's Beach toward Tom Morrison's cabin, which means it's already thick out on the bay. All the signs, as they say, are pointing in one direction: Mr. Hart's story is coming to the end.

The Newport Daily Journal, January 2, 1930

COAST GUARD RECEIVED TIP-OFF TO BLACK DUCK'S ROUTE

LAY IN WAIT TIED TO CHANNEL BUOY, UNDER COVER OF DENSE FOG

NEWPORT, JAN. 2—The Coast Guard cutter that opened fire on the Black Duck early Sunday morning, killing three men and wounding one, was tipped off to the rum runners' route by a local police chief, according to the Coast Guard officer in charge, Capt. Roger Campbell.

An earlier report that the Coast Guard had stumbled by chance on the craft was incorrect, Campbell said.

"We got direct word from a local police chief that the Black Duck would be coming in to a beach along that coast. We knew they'd be steering for the bell buoy off West Island in that thick fog, so we tied up there to wait for them. Sure enough, they came along about three A.M."

Campbell refused to name the source for the tip. He insisted again that the rum runners were warned before his marksman opened fire with a machine gun.

Questions have been raised as to whether the victims were given adequate legal warning before they were shot down. The federal statute on the pursuit of smuggling craft requires that a shot be fired in warning before effective firing is started if a suspect fails to halt when ordered.

DECEMBER 29, 1929

WE WERE STILL SITTING AROUND TOM Morrison's table when, about 10:00 P.M., voices sounded outside the cabin.

Billy sprang up and went to open the door. Rick Delucca and Bernardo Rosario, his radio man, came in. Alfred Biggs was behind them. He'd brought his cousin Manny, from Portsmouth, along to lend a hand. Billy was surprised by that. He'd expected somebody else and gave the guy a look. He didn't like outsiders coming in on his jobs.

"Manny's okay," Alfred assured him. "I'll vouch for him personally. He's a hard worker, and you'd be doing him a good turn. His family's in need."

Billy nodded. "Well then, glad to help. We'll need an extra man out there, all right." He shook Manny's hand.

Sadie took one look at this army of strange boots coming through the door and scooted out from under the table. She retreated around the corner to Tom's sleeping quarters. Tom looked as if he would've liked to do the same. Never had there been such a crowd in his chicken coops, and never, I'm sure, had he ever wanted one. Still,

Billy was a favorite of his, and while he wouldn't shelter liquor, he'd agreed to let the *Black Duck*'s crew meet there before the job that night.

"C'mon over by the stove and let 'em have the table," he told Marina and me. We got up and sat down with our backs against the wall. Shortly, we were listening in on a discussion of logistics that must have taken place hundreds of times, for this was just another transport job in a long line of them, and nothing, including the fog, seemed specially out of the ordinary.

"I made radio contact with our vessel. She's a schooner out of St. Pierre by the name of *Mary Logan*," Bernardo Rosario began after they were all seated. "She's safely anchored and we have her position. Her captain's set to load from midnight on. He says it's pea soup out there. You can't see ten feet from your own nose."

Billy nodded at Rick Delucca. "We'll be steering by compass, heading for the bell buoys. Are the channel charts on board?"

Rick said they were there.

"All right. Now here's something else. Tom doesn't want liquor near his place. That means we'll need transport off the beach tonight as soon as we bring the hooch in. A big load like this can't lie out in the daylight."

"We need to get word to our truck drivers," Alfred Biggs said. "Somebody has to go up to Harveston right away and tell them to get down here."

"I figured that," Billy said. "Anybody want to volunteer?"

Nobody said anything. Everybody wanted to go out on the *Black Duck*. Finally Alfred spoke up. "Let Manny do it. Our vehicle's parked out there by the beach. He'd be a good one to go. He knows the roads around Harveston. Used to live there."

"Is that so?" Billy asked.

Manny shrugged. "Do I have to?" he asked his cousin. "I was hoping to be out on the boat tonight."

"You'll get your chance," Alfred said. "Just tonight, do what Billy wants. Take the car and round up the Harveston drivers. I'll give you the address where they're staying."

Manny saw there was no use arguing and slumped back in his chair. I didn't like his expression. He seemed like a whiner to me.

"We'll be down a man, the same as before, without Manny," Rick warned. "It'll take more time to load off the *Mary Logan*."

"I thought of that," Billy said. "We've got a man right here to take his place."

"And who might that be?" Alfred inquired. "Not old one-eye, I hope!"

Everybody laughed, which was mean of them. Tom put his lips together and took this rudeness without comment, but Billy wouldn't stand for it. For all his adventuring and interest in profit, Billy Brady was a loyal friend to those he cared about.

"Leave Tom out of this," he snapped at Alfred. "He sees further with his one eye than most people with their two."

"Well, who is it then?" Bernardo demanded.

What Billy said next blew the top of my head off.

"Who we've got is Ruben Hart, if he'll agree to it." Billy gazed at me, straight and serious. "Will you, Ruben? It'd be a favor you could do me after the one I did you."

Beside me, Marina sat up. "No, he won't! What a terrible idea. His father would never let him go."

"Well, that's just it," Billy said, giving me his wicked grin. "His father's not here to have a say. So I'm asking Ruben direct. Will you be a fifth man on the *Black Duck* tonight? We could use your muscle, and you'll have a night to remember, I guarantee it."

There wasn't any time to think about this amazing proposition, and even if there had been, I believe I'd have come to the same decision. It rose up through my blood on a reckless tide of defiance, the same wild feeling I'd been nursing all that year of wanting to get out and prove something to myself. Nothing I could do would hold it back.

"Yes, I'll go!" I answered. The crew laughed again because I sounded so breathless. To my left, Tom Morrison slowly shook his head, but he didn't say anything.

"Well, that's settled," Billy said. "Now it's time we went down to the beach and got aboard the *Duck*. She's gassed to the brim, ready to head for open sea. Manny will give you a lift home on his way to Harveston, Marina," he added to her. "Watch the evening newspapers tomorrow. You might catch the *Black Duck*'s name in print."

"Why would I want to do that?" Marina shot back. "It's

bad enough to have to worry about all of you. Now you're taking Ruben? He's too young and you know it!" She turned her back and wouldn't look at Billy, even when he went over to her.

"Come with me a moment," I heard him say in a low voice. When she still turned away, he took her hand and pulled her off around the corner to Tom's private sleeping quarters. I never knew what he said to her in those last minutes before we left. I heard his voice, quiet and confiding, rising and falling, and no sound at all from her. He must have told her something that came close to the right mark, though, because when they came out together, she was wiping her eyes and nodding.

"You know where she lives?" I heard Billy ask Manny while Marina went across the room to thank Tom for supper.

"Of course," Manny said. "It's Chief McKenzie's place. I've been there before."

An alarm should've gone off in Billy's head at that, and maybe a faint one did, because I saw him stop a moment and give Manny that same careful look he had in the beginning. Then Marina came back and we put on our coats. Two minutes later, we headed out Tom's door into the murk.

Looking back now, it seems that the ocean had never heaved with such a sickening roll or the fog been so glutinous as it was the night the *Black Duck* made its way out toward the schooner *Mary Logan*.

I was no seaman, but not a landlubber, either. I'd fished many times off a boat, and motored up and down the coast with friends since I was a kid. I knew West Island from sailing trips Jeddy and I had made out there for swimming and rock climbing on summer days. That evening, as we chugged out from shore, the island was invisible except for a threatening roar of surf.

We went by safely and came out on the open sea, though how Billy Brady and Rick Delucca managed to navigate at all was a mystery to me. They stood side by side in the pilot house, one at the wheel, the other lounging over the charts, bellowing cheerfully back and forth, their voices all but drowned out by the *Duck*'s big engines.

Once beyond the lighthouse, Billy turned on a new course which put the wind behind us, and we slid even faster through the blinding white mist. For over an hour we thudded along this way, until it began to seem we were trapped in an endless dream and would never see the shapes of the real world again.

At last, lights blazed in front of us and we came up on the sprawling form of the schooner *Mary Logan* anchored bow and stern to keep her in place. Billy and Rick had struck her right on the button. I saw them raise their fists and touch knuckles in a kind of boyish glee. And when I think of it now, they still were partly boys at heart, taking pleasure in battling dangers that would've made older men sweat.

It took us over an hour to load the liquor onto the *Duck*. The *Mary Logan*'s captain was a niggler, intent on keeping his decks clean and his hull buffered against the side of our boat. After he and Billy had matched tickets— in this case halved one-dollar bills did the trick—he stood aside and offered no help from his crew. I worked like the devil, and so did Billy and everyone, to bring the load on board. It was whiskey for the most part, several hundred cases at least. When we'd filled every crook and cranny on the *Duck*, we packed her little lifeboat with more cases, roped them in under canvas, and lowered the skiff astern to trail behind us.

"There's a night's worth of New Year's celebrating to be had off this!" Alfred Biggs called out with a grin.

"A week's worth, you mean!" Bernardo shouted back, bringing a laugh from everyone. We cast off. Billy revved the big engines and we began the bumpy trip back to Coulter's.

By this time, it was after 2:00 A.M. We were headed into the southwest wind now, facing the wallow of an ocean swell. My stomach started to go queasy. It wasn't improved by the closeness of the fog, which seemed to thicken as we drew nearer to land, or rather to where we thought land must be. Once again we were in a ghostly, immaterial world. Billy, who was steering by the ship's compass, cut our speed in case of miscalculation, and we went on blindly, keeping our ears tuned for the channel bells.

I was hanging out over the starboard rail, wondering if Tom Morrison's crab stew was about to make an early exit, when I heard Rick Delucca bellow.

"Dead ahead! What's that?"

We weren't doing more than about five miles an hour. The sound of a bell buoy rang out, and all at once I saw a black shape rising up through the murk not fifty feet in front of us.

In the pilot house, Billy swore. He goosed the engines to try to swerve. A second later, we all recognized what it was. A Coast Guard cutter, one of the big seventy-five-footers, was tied to the bell. We came up on it fast and passed close, our bow going just under theirs. We'd no sooner cleared than a light shone straight at us, a horn sounded and something whizzed past my head. From behind me came the crash of splintering wood. It took me a few moments to realize what was happening. I heard that machine gun rat-a-tat-tatting, but it didn't seem real.

By the time I caught on, bullets were slamming into the deck on all sides and the glass in the pilot house had shattered. Somebody screamed to take cover. I flung myself over the boat rail and hung just above the water. In the pilot house, a commotion had broken out. I looked and saw Billy go down. He fell over the wheel and Rick leapt to pull him up. Then the boat began to weave and lurch like a bronco. She'd veer one way, then another, and it was clear that no one had control of the wheel. I was trying to hang on and climb back over the rail, but after a violent swerve my hold broke. Off I came on a wave and dropped into the sea.

The sudden cold took my breath away. I clawed to get up the side again, but the boat suddenly bolted out of reach. Then the lifeboat was on top of me, hitting me on the head. I went for it like a drowning man, which I nearly was, and managed to haul myself into it and slide under the tarp. There I lay down on top of a pile of liquor cases.

Never have I been so cold in my life. I wasn't trembling so much as shimmying from head to foot, and I curled myself up for what little warmth I could get. Meanwhile, the lifeboat careened after the *Duck* on its twists and turns, and a fear began to build in me that we were pilotless. I remembered Billy describing how, after his dad was shot, his boat had plowed into the rocks and exploded. When I raised the tarp to look for the shore, an icy slap of seawater hit me in the face.

Finally, the ride quieted. From the waves' motion, I sensed that we were circling around. Someone was at the *Black Duck*'s helm, though I didn't yet know who. Then we must have come up on the Coast Guard cutter again. I heard Rick Delucca's voice shout out:

"Put up your guns! I've got wounded men aboard!"

A guardsman barked back, "You're under arrest. Bring your boat alongside!"

Rick did that. He'd no sooner touched hulls than two guards leapt onto the *Duck*'s deck and grabbed him. I was spying out from the lifeboat and saw how they dragged him onto the cutter, blood gushing from his hand. In short order, the *Duck* was lashed to the cutter's side, and my lifeboat was hauled in from where it had been bobbing to stern. I had a bad moment thinking those guards might be curious about what was under the tarp. They roped the lifeboat tight behind the *Duck*'s stern and never bothered to look. After that, I kept my head down and had only my ears to tell me what was happening.

Rick Delucca was putting up a fight. The guards were trying to take him down into the cutter's cabin. He kept pleading to stay on deck.

"My friends need help," he cried over and over. "They're hit. They're bleeding! Let me go back aboard."

They didn't allow him that liberty as far as I could tell. I don't think anyone else went over onto the *Duck*, either. An order was called out to cast off the bell, and the cutter got under way.

Later, the newspapers would report that "three rum-runners" all died instantly in the rain of bullets. I know that's not true. Someone was alive for a while. I heard moans and knocking sounds from the *Duck*'s afterdeck, though by the time we made Newport, all was quiet up there.

The guards tied their cutter up to a pier, unroped the *Duck* and cleated her to a separate piling. I heard them take Rick Delucca away. He wasn't saying much by then and, with all the blood he'd lost, was probably in shock. I know I was. I was shaking and quaking under the tarp so hard that it's a wonder nobody noticed and came to find me.

After a while, the cutter sped off and the *Black Duck* sat unattended. The cutter's captain went down the dock to call for medical help. He was Roger Campbell. I heard the crew address him several times. I wish now I could've risked taking a glance at the man I'd heard so much about, but I stayed low. Another half hour passed before the last of the guardsmen disappeared into the nearby Coast Guard station. I saw my opportunity and crept out.

It was dark, still too early in the morning for any show of sun. A bunch of Canada geese had flown into the harbor. They were huddled close to shore, honking in that sad, bleating way geese have when they're cold and wondering where their next meal is coming from. I went up on the *Black Duck*.

Three bodies were lying together on her deck where the guards had dragged them. I went over and looked down. They were on their backs, shoulder to shoulder—Billy Brady, Bernardo Rosario and Alfred Biggs. Their eyes were closed and at first they didn't seem that dead to me. They looked peaceful. It was as if they'd been stargazing, or telling stories to each other like boys on a camping trip, and had fallen asleep together looking up at the sky.

Except something was out of place. Someone had tried to put Billy's captain's hat back on his head. It was leaning crooked over one ear, a thing he never would've allowed in life. I reached out and took it off, but the spell was broken: I knew those men weren't ever going to wake up again.

After that, I didn't touch them. I stood back, holding Billy's hat against my chest. The wind was cold. Seawater slapped against the pier, sounding tired and bored, as if after all nothing much had happened. I felt sick. There should've been more fury going on, people screaming or the sea howling over who was lying there. I saw how murderously quiet death is, how even Billy Brady with all his charm and wit wasn't going to be able to talk back to it. That scared me worse than I'd ever been scared before. I got off his boat and ran down the pier.

Nobody saw me leave. I skirted the naval docks and took off down the road. The newspapers never got wind I was there that night. The Coast Guard didn't find out. Rick Delucca never let on, either, I don't know why. Maybe he was protecting me, or maybe he just forgot. He was in and out of court for the next two weeks, being arraigned and charged with violating the Prohibition laws. In the end, some deal went through, the charges were dropped and they let him go. People said he was never the same afterward.

I wasn't, either. I went home that day to my parents and Aunt Grace, and I stayed there. All the things I'd been doing before, I started up with again. They were good for me suddenly. The store was a good place to work. School was okay, and I did well there. I went on to the high school and when my father told me there wasn't enough money to go away to a four-year college, I didn't mind. I didn't want to go anyhow. I went over to a technical college that had started up in New Bedford and got a degree in business administration. Then I came right back and helped Dad run the store.

The laws banning liquor had been repealed by then. They went out in 1933 when the whole country voted against them. It had begun to sink in that the violence that came from keeping liquor out of people's hands was a lot worse than the violence of people drinking to their hearts' content.

I knew the truth of that more than I wanted to. For years afterward, Billy Brady walked into my line of vision every time I saw a speedboat tear down the bay, or I came across a fisherman on the beach with his dog.

I never told my parents or Aunt Grace I'd been out on the *Black Duck*. I never told any of my friends at school. The newspaper articles about the killings appeared, and I kept silent. When Roger Campbell and his crew were cleared of wrongdoing, people around here went crazy. They believed the government was covering up a crime. Still, I never gave my opinion about it. The funny thing was, even though I'd been there on the spot, I wasn't sure myself whether the Guard had given us fair warning.

There are times when truth becomes invisible, I think, beyond the reach even of those who believe they're closest to it. And so I've never talked about what happened, or tried to describe it to anyone all these years.

With the exception of one person.

MARINA

THE MORNING AFTER THE SHOOTING, BEFORE I went home, I stopped by the McKenzies' house.

Dawn was just breaking when I got there. I'd hitched a ride out of Newport on a milk truck heading for one of the big dairies on our side of the bay, then walked the rest of the way into town. My clothes had dried, but I knew I probably looked as bad as I felt. I stayed off the main street, hoping no one would see me.

I didn't knock. The kitchen door was open as I knew it would be. I hadn't been there for months, but everything looked the same. The kitchen table was in its place under the lightbulb, already set for breakfast. The counters were neat, and Mrs. McKenzie's china was put away carefully in its corner cupboard. I went by her portrait in the front hall and felt her eyes follow me as I turned up the stairs. I went slowly, on my toes, avoiding a creaky board I knew at the top.

Nobody was up. Chief McKenzie was snoring in his bedroom down the hall. Jeddy's door was open a crack. I peeked in and saw him buried in his blankets.

I slipped by to Marina's bedroom, went inside and

closed the door behind me. She was sound asleep, her hair tossed across the pillow. I was afraid to wake her. I wished I could keep the news I had to tell her to myself. I wished she'd never have to hear it.

After only a minute, she knew I was in the room. Sleep is porous that way. There's usually a window raised somewhere in the unconscious mind. Her eyes opened and she looked straight at me.

"Ruben? What is it?" She sat up.

"Something's happened."

"That's Billy's hat," she said.

"Yes." I still had it in my hands.

"The *Black Duck*'s in trouble?"

I nodded. "We ran into the Coast Guard."

"Billy's in jail?"

"No."

"In the hospital?"

"No."

"Well, where is he?" she asked. Then she looked at me and knew.

It was the worst thing I'd ever had to see in my life, to watch her face cave in the way it did. I couldn't think of what else to do, so I went over and sat on her bed and put my arms around her. I started to tell her what had happened. Halfway through she began to cry. When I got to the place where we came on the Coast Guard cutter tied to the bell buoy, where the machine gun went off and the *Duck* veered away, she covered her face and told me to stop.

"I can't hear any more."

So we sat together listening to the morning sounds outside the window. A rooster's plain-and-ordinary cock-a-doodle-doo. A car's motor starting up. Someone whistling a church tune out on the road.

Footsteps sounded in the hall.

"My father's up," Marina said.

"Don't let him know I'm here."

She went across to the door and turned the lock. When she came back, she asked in a whisper:

"Was it Roger Campbell's cutter tied up to the bell buoy?"

I said it was.

"He's the man who fired on Billy's dad. Everybody knows he's loose with his guns. Billy thought he was crazy, and maybe he is. He was after the *Black Duck*, ever since they led him on that wild chase up the bay onto a sandbar."

I said I remembered that.

"If he was tied up to the bell, that means he was expecting somebody."

"It seems like it," I said. "No one would be out there otherwise. The fog was too thick. You couldn't see ten feet."

"I think he was tipped off," Marina said. "Somebody knew the *Duck* would be coming that way."

"Who?" I asked.

"I don't know." Her eyes filled with tears again. "Everyone around the bay was rooting for them. They kept clear of the syndicates and they didn't carry guns. I know Billy was on the wrong side of the law, but who would want to set a man like Roger Campbell on him?"

We looked at each other and didn't know. It would be a few days before Marina read, along with the whole town, the newspaper story about a local police chief who'd called up the Coast Guard and done just that.

The Last Interview

DAVID PETERSON IS STANDING TRANSFIXED on the front porch, a pair of brand-new hedge clippers from Peterson's Garden Shop in his hands, as Mr. Hart finishes this last bit of his story.

Chief McKenzie was the tip-off man?

That's what the caller said.

I knew it! That double-crossing rat. Was it to stop Marina from seeing Billy Brady? Or because the Black Duck *was running liquor in the New York mob's territory? Or was Roger Campbell paying him for information?*

Mr. Hart shrugs. *Any one of those reasons would do. And probably would've done if Ralph McKenzie had made that call.*

Wait a minute. He didn't?

No.

But, who did?

Mr. Hart turns to look at the progress David has been making on the bushes over the front windows. *You sure are clearing a space there. I'll be sunbathing in the parlor before long.*

Who called? David asks again.

It wasn't the chief. He wasn't at home when Manny brought Marina back from Tom Morrison's that night. Jeddy McKenzie was there, though.

David stares at the old man. *Manny Biggs ratted on the* Black Duck? *His own cousin was on board.*

He was playing for more money, I guess. He knew he'd get paid for his information, probably a lot more than Billy would've paid him for rounding up the truckers in Harveston.

So Manny told Jeddy about the Black Duck's *trip out to the* Mary Logan *that night.*

I believe so. Left a message for the chief is probably what happened.

And Jeddy called the Coast Guard?

He had to. It was police business. He was stepping into his father's shoes.

How did you find this out?

Jeddy told me.

David sits down on a porch chair. *When?*

I stopped by his room on the way out of the McKenzies' house that morning. I wanted to tell him the Black Duck *had been caught. He said he'd made the call. "How could you?" I asked him. "You don't know what you did."*

"I know what I did," Jeddy said. "I was following the law."

David looks out across the lawn, which needs cutting. Out by the road, a single dead, leafless tree limb is poking through the swirl of greenery. It should be taken down before it causes harm by falling itself, he thinks. It might drop on a car coming in the driveway, or a person walking out there.

What happened then?

What happened was the chief packed up. He and Jeddy left town. Everybody wanted to get rid of Chief McKenzie by then. The Black Duck *was a hero to our folks. They all read the newspaper article and thought the chief had been the tip-off man. He covered for Jeddy, and they went down south to . . .*

North Carolina, David says.

That's right.

And Jeddy never came back.

No. I never saw him again. Marina visited every few years. After the chief died, that is. She couldn't forgive her father for what she thought he'd done to Billy Brady. She never guessed the truth. I wasn't going to tell her and Jeddy certainly wasn't, either.

You must hate him, David says to Mr. Hart. *You must hate Jeddy McKenzie's guts.*

I don't. It was all too much for him, I think. He'd believed in his father, and in police business, and in the clear divide of right and wrong. Fog wasn't something Jeddy could deal with.

Mr. Hart takes his glasses off and wipes his eyes. *The thing is, he was a good kid. Like you. He was trying to find his way, trying his best to do what was right.*

For a long moment, they sit quietly together, gazing at the yard. Then David gets up and starts in again on the bushes with the new hedge clippers.

He can't imagine how he'll ever be able to write all this down.

AN ARRIVAL

STRANGELY, EVEN AFTER THE STORY IS OVER, and he knows everything, and nothing is left to be told, David Peterson doesn't stop going by Mr. Hart's house. He rides over the next day, and the next, and the next. There's a lot to be done around the yard. David cuts and prunes, digs and snips, plants and grooms. He takes down the dead tree limb out by the road. He's good at this work and, out of sight of his father, really enjoys it. The old man is happy to have him. They talk easily back and forth.

Have you written my story down yet? Mr. Hart asks.

No, David admits.

Well, get going. I'm not going to last forever!

I don't know how to start.

At the beginning, Mr. Hart says. *At Coulter's Beach, when we found that body. I've still got Tony Mordello's to-bacco pouch, if that'll get you going.*

Is the half fifty-dollar bill still in it?

Where else?

The old man goes in his bedroom and comes out with a limp leather pouch that looks as if it's been squashed under a mattress for most of its life. Which it has, Mr. Hart acknowledges. He never found a better place.

Open it, he orders. David does, and there amid the now almost scentless crumblings of what used to be tobacco leaf, he finds the old half bill, wrinkled and pale with age, but still giving off an aura of intrigue.

You take it, Mr. Hart says. *I don't need it anymore.*

Really? The pouch, too?

It's yours. Time it passed to somebody else.

Thanks! I'll keep it safe.

I know you will.

I hitched down to Coulter's Beach the other day. Tom Morrison's shack isn't there anymore, David says.

Mr. Hart nods. He's spruced himself up this morning. His hair is slicked back. He's wearing a clean shirt. Broom in hand, he's been sweeping off the porch, all the while keeping an eager eye on the driveway. He heard from his wife last night. She's coming home today. Could arrive anytime.

Tom's chicken coops went out in the 1938 hurricane, Mr. Hart says. *Tom didn't care. He'd died and gone to the town cemetery five years before. I used to wonder how he was bearing up in such a civilized place, with all that company.*

David grins. *What happened to Sadie? After Billy was killed, I mean.*

She stayed on with Tom just as you'd expect. Became a great crabber. Marina and I went down there from time to time. Tom always cheered us up. He was one of those that carry on no matter the hardship. It showed you what was possible.

I walked around that cemetery, David says. *I found Eileen McKenzie's grave.*

Mr. Hart answers with a grunt. *That cemetery has a good part of the town in it now. At least the part I grew up with.*

I saw John Appleby's name on a stone. Is that him?

Must be. He died young. A hunting accident is what they said. I always wondered. He was the kind of stinker nobody likes having around.

Fanny DeSousa, Mildred Cumming, Charlie Pope.

Yes, they're all there. Mildred just died, lived to be ninety-six. People last a long time around here. Did you see the Hart plot in the south corner? It's where I'm headed. My father and mother are both in residence. Aunt Grace, too. She never could find anyone who knew the score better than she did.

I saw them. I couldn't find any McKenzies besides Eileen.

Nope, and you never will. Jeddy wouldn't want to come back dead any more than he did alive. I don't even know where the chief is buried.

What happened to Marina?

This question goes unanswered, and when David looks up from the bush he's attacking with the clippers, he sees Mr. Hart staring at him. His glasses give off an amused glint. *If you don't know already what happened to her, I guess I won't tell you.*

At that moment, the sound of wheels comes from the driveway and a taxi pulls up. Mr. Hart drops his broom like a hot potato. He gives his hair one last swipe, straightens his shirt and hustles down the porch steps to greet it.

She's here! he cries to David. *She's come back at last!*

AUTHOR'S NOTE

THERE ARE TIMES WHEN HISTORY SEEMS SO close, you can almost reach out and touch it.

The beaches and coastal inlets around my small Rhode Island town are unchanging places where the past can still wash in on the tide, bringing the same dark nights, sudden lights, disembodied voices and sounds of speedboat engines known to residents here during the 1920s rum-running era. My father recalls being awakened, at age eight, by a commotion on the shore below his family home. Bootleggers! Breathless, he watched from his window as their headlights danced across the sand.

Black Duck was written out of this immediate local memory, and features a notorious rumrunner craft of that name, which really did smuggle thousands of cases of liquor in to our shores during Prohibition before meeting her final fate. Manned by a crew of four from communities around Narragansett Bay, the *Black Duck* ferried goods off foreign ships from Canada, Europe and the West Indies. These boats moored along the southern New England coast outside U.S. territorial limits, beyond the legal reach of the Coast Guard. Rum Row, they came to be known, and as the decade wore on, their numbers in-

WRITERS IN TRANSITION:
Seven Americans

WRITERS IN TRANSITION:
Seven Americans

by H. WAYNE MORGAN

American Century Series

HILL AND WANG • NEW YORK

Manufactured in the United States of America
by The Colonial Press Inc., Clinton, Massachusetts

To AILEEN AND WILL HILLMAN
in constant affection

Contents

Contents

Introduction

THE ESSAYS in this volume are in a sense old-fashioned. They are not technical in nature, and are in fact not literary criticisms at all; they are most properly called "appreciations." In writing them, I have tried at all times to retain a sense of history and cultural change as well as a sense of the literature involved, for each figure has seemed to me to be important as a spokesman of cultural transition as well as an artist. One may look at works of art in many lights. I have chosen to try to capture the artist in his work, and to show the importance of his work in cultural change.

This is not a "thesis" book in the sense that a single theme or group of themes unites it. At first glance, the figures discussed seem to have little in common. The subject matter ranges from the austerity of Edith Wharton to the primitivism of Sherwood Anderson; from the formal prose of Ellen Glasgow to the loose autobiography of Thomas Wolfe; from the bittersweet fatalism of Stephen Crane to the optimism of Hart Crane.

On closer examination, however, several themes emerge from the material to unite these writers. Each in his own way and to his own degree was a spokesman of cultural transition as well as an artist. Each had a distinctive view of his role as a writer. And each invariably dealt with themes that set him in the midst of the cultural crisis that surrounded his work. Each was also in his way distinctly American, concerned with the fate of his culture and country and anxious to save the tenets which he held dear, and to forge new tools with which to meet the challenges of a changing world order and new cultural standards.

The world of the late nineteenth century, commonly called the Victorian Era, was as different from the mid-twentieth century as night is from day. One has only to examine the literary and historical sources of each period to be struck by this fact. Two generations carried America from provincial security to the dangers of international leadership. The ramifications, the stresses and strains, the responsibilities and tragedies of that transition are by no means either fully outlined or resolved even at mid-century. As in all great transitions, this was not merely a question of politics but of culture in the profoundest sense. The artists in these essays met those challenges in ways that were typical of many Americans. I have tried to discuss their reactions in an effort to highlight the effects of this cultural transition on literature.

From its inception, the American experiment rested on the assumption that rural life transcended urban life; the Jeffersonian dream of Arcadia rested on the principle that America would be free and democratic only so long as she was a rural nation, with an agricultural economy. Throughout the eighteenth and nineteenth centuries that theory had a basis in fact, for the nation was indeed an agricultural one. The changes introduced by the Civil War, however, turned the tide toward industrialization. Expansion of the frontier slowed as the twentieth century approached; the pioneer virtues of independence and cultural continuity based on contact with the land and individual labor with creative materials assumed a new importance in American literature as they declined in fact.

In the twentieth century the focus of American life has shifted from the country to the city. Inevitably that transfer registered its impact on American letters. In three quite different ways, three of the writers considered in this book wrote of that change. Willa Cather viewed the last stages of frontier life on the great plains and in the American Southwest with a feeling that transcended nostalgia and became a testament to the force of the agrarian ideal as well as a testament to her concept of artistic function and her own inherent creative drive. Ellen Glasgow lived through the passing of the old Southern ideals as industry and commerce replaced the agrarian aristocracy of her section, and focused her answer to its challenges in a call for literary tradition to preserve cultural continuity. Of her peers, she spoke most eloquently and with greatest force for a living tradition in life and letters that would avoid the intransigence of the old ways and soften the crasser aspects of the new. Sherwood Anderson, of Midwestern origin, also dealt with the passing of the agrarian world, but from the other direction, for he came in time to accept industrialization as a fact, fully conscious of its far-reaching ramifications in the social order. Alone of these three he perceived the possibilities of creative unity in the machine and its new civilization.

Similarly, the late nineteenth-century Victorians looked upon social classes as more fixed than do their grandchildren. Perhaps the most profound social change in recent American history was the end of the rule of the old society based on landed and inherited wealth, and the rise to social prominence and cultural arbitration of the new spokesmen of wealth based on industry and finance. In the course of three generations, this has brought a redistribution of wealth and political and cultural power among the masses that has changed many aspects of American life. Moreover, this struggle at the beginning of the twentieth century took on sectional as well as class aspects, as the new Westerners triumphed over their long hated and envied Eastern masters. Edith Wharton mirrored this transfer of power in her fiction. Herself of the Eastern aristocracy, she broadened her view of the struggle to make of it a great cultural and intellectual crisis. Whatever the technical faults of much of her work, she redeemed her novels by this broadened vision. She realized at least that the change she observed at first hand was more than a transfer of money and social status; it was in fact a transfer of cultural power. Dwelling in a zone between the old and the new, personally committed to much of the rebellion of the youth of her day while hating their means and dreading their inevitable triumph, Mrs. Wharton mirrored in her work the changes that overtook American society in the decades before the First World War marked the end of the old order.

The transfer of cultural power from the old landed aristocracy to the classes and groups drawing wealth from industry and finance merely marked the end of the agrarian domination that shaped American culture in the nineteenth century. The waves of industrialization which swept away this standard ushered in changes that affected every level of American experience—social, intellectual, economic, political. Sherwood Anderson and, to a lesser degree, Hart Crane, concerned themselves directly with the rise of industry and the impact of the machine on society. Willing to meet the challenge, each in his way devised a means to combat it. In the end, both accepted a new role and called for the artist to participate directly in the new experiences.

As literary innovators, Stephen Crane and Hart Crane occupy important positions. Stephen Crane attempted in his brief but penetrating works to set a new standard of insight as well as of form, and for all the slightness of his work, he remains an intriguing and important figure in the first phases of literary naturalism and realism that triumphed over Victorian sentimentality at the turn of the century. Hart Crane, writing a generation later, attempted an even more formidable task: to outline and attain a new level of consciousness as well as a new poetic form. Critics who have concentrated on his symbolism and compelling language have often failed to grasp the larger and more profound importance of his work—the realization that the last vestiges of the old cultural order were passing under the impact of new forces, and his demand for artistic vision as a means of unifying mankind through love in the midst of these chaotic changes. As yet relatively undiscovered by critics and readers, Hart Crane may well be the greatest American poet of the century, not only for the beauty of his poetry but more importantly for the compelling quality of his vision.

The classification of writers, like all artists, into categories of great or near-great is at best arbitrary; it may well be that none of the figures examined here are truly great in the sense that their work will survive centuries hence. Yet each was an accomplished artist within his limitations, and the work of each deserves treatment as art as well as reflections of a cultural milieu. Since each dealt with themes common to all men and all ages, their work has survived to be studied as testaments to personal quests and personal beliefs that are valid to all men. The deep strains of humanism, the reverence for individualism and humanity in general, and the belief in the heritage of art as an expression of imagination and creative emotion evident in the works of all these writers further helps establish them as worthy of study. Their individual and collective searches for order in the midst of chaos marks their art as the fruit of an inner quest that may help all readers in the same situation.

All of the subjects of these essays retained a distinct attitude and cultural orientation which can only be called American. However critical they were, none was so embittered as to welcome destruction of the basic tenets of American experience on which each separately and all collectively drew. Even Edith Wharton, an almost Jamesian exile in France, was fascinated by America and wrote largely of its problems. Two of these figures, Hart Crane and Thomas Wolfe, were deeply concerned with America's role as an artistic and cultural arbiter. Crane's magnificent poem *The Bridge* is a testament to his country's future and to the validity he felt would make the American experience triumphant in the end. The whole corpus of Thomas Wolfe's writing is devoted to the American experience in a manner and with a depth that sets him apart as the leading modern literary spokesman of the American experience. A deep belief in the inevitable triumph of American art forms marks all his work, and only his death prevented his becoming the spokesman for the vivid and vital tradition which he described in the immense autobiography which he left behind.

Thus, collectively these artists are significant and interesting as spokesmen of cultural transition and as representatives of many of the changes that have accompanied the twentieth century in America. Individually, each poses fascinating problems for the student of their art. It is in this light that I have written these essays, and it is in this light that I hope they will be read. I do not expect everyone to agree with my conclusions. In none of these studies have I attempted to be exhaustive. They are not biographies, and within the limits and design I have imposed they could not be critically exhaustive. I have intended only to suggest, and by treating certain important themes in the work of each artist, to stimulate interest in the writer's work rather than in literary criticism as such.

Austin, Texas   H. W. M.
June 1962

Acknowledgments

Grateful thanks are due the following firms and persons for permission to quote copyrighted material:

STEPHEN CRANE: To Alfred Knopf, Inc., for Wilson Follett (ed.), *The Work of Stephen Crane*, 12 vols. (New York, 1925); *The Collected Poems of Stephen Crane* (New York, 1930); Robert W. Stallman, (ed.) *Stephen Crane: An Omnibus* (New York, 1952); Thomas Beer, *Stephen Crane* (New York, 1923). To Syracuse University Press for Corwin K. Linson, *My Stephen Crane* (Syracuse, 1958); and Edwin Cady and Lester G. Wells (eds.), *Stephen Crane's Love Letters to Nellie Crouse* (Syracuse, 1954).

EDITH WHARTON: To Appleton-Century-Crofts, for *French Ways and Their Meaning* (New York, 1919); *The Age of Innocence* (New York, 1920); *A Backward Glance* (New York, 1934); Percy Lubbock, *Portrait of Edith Wharton* (New York, 1947). To Charles Scribner's Sons for *The Fruit of the Tree* (New York, 1907); *The House of Mirth* (New York, 1905); *The Valley of Decision* (New York, 1902); *The Custom of the Country* (New York, 1913); *The Writing of Fiction* (New York, 1925); *Ethan Frome* (New York, 1911).

ELLEN GLASGOW: To Mrs. Irita Van Doren for permission to quote from the works of Ellen Glasgow, especially the volumes published in the Old Dominion editions by Doubleday, Doran and Co. To Harcourt, Brace, and World Inc., for *The Woman Within* (New York, 1954); *A Certain Measure* (New York, 1943); *Vein of Iron* (New York, 1935); Blair Rouse (ed.), *The Letters of Ellen Glasgow* (New York, 1958).

WILLA CATHER: To Alfred A. Knopf, Inc., and to Miss Edith Lewis for E. K. Brown's *Willa Cather* (New York, 1953); Edith Lewis, *Willa Cather Living* (New York, 1953); "Nebraska: The End of the First Cycle," *The Nation*, 117 (September 5, 1923); *Not Under Forty* (New York, 1936); *On Writing* (New York, 1949); *Death Comes for the Archbishop* (New York, 1927); *One of Ours* (New York, 1922); *Lucy Gayheart* (New York, 1935); *Obscure Destinies* (New York, 1932); *The Professor's House* (New York, 1925). To Houghton Mifflin Co. for *My Antonia* (New York, 1918); *O Pioneers!* (New York, 1913); *The Song of the Lark*, rev. ed. (New York, 1937).

SHERWOOD ANDERSON: To Harold Ober and Associates for *Windy McPherson's Son* (New York, B. W. Huebsch, 1916); *Marching Men*

(New York, B. W. Huebsch, 1917); *Poor White* (New York, B. W. Huebsch, 1920); *Many Marriages* (New York, B. W. Huebsch, 1923); *Sherwood Anderson's Notebook* (New York, Liveright Publishing Co., 1926); *Perhaps Women* (New York, Liveright Publishing Co., 1931); *Beyond Desire* (New York, Liveright Publishing Co., 1932); *Sherwood Anderson's Memoirs* (New York, Harcourt-Brace and Co., 1941). To The Viking Press for *Winesburg, Ohio* (New York, Compass Books, 1960). To Little, Brown and Co., for Howard Mumford Jones and Walter B. Rideout (eds.), *The Letters of Sherwood Anderson* (Boston, 1953).

HART CRANE: To Philip Horton and to The Viking Press for Philip Horton, *Hart Crane* (New York, 1937). To Coward-McCann, Inc., for Hart Crane, "Modern Poetry," in Oliver Sayler (ed.), *Revolt in the Arts* (New York, 1929). To the Liveright Publishing Co. for *The Collected Poems of Hart Crane*, Black and Gold ed. (New York, 1933). To Brom Weber for Brom Weber (ed.), *Letters of Hart Crane 1916-1932* (New York, 1952).

THOMAS WOLFE: To Harper & Brothers for *The Web and the Rock* (New York, 1939); *You Can't Go Home Again* (New York, 1940). To Charles Scribner's Sons for *Look Homeward, Angel* (New York, 1929); *Of Time and the River* (New York, 1935); *The Story of a Novel* (New York, 1936); Elizabeth Nowell (ed.), *The Letters of Thomas Wolfe* (New York, 1956); John Skally Terry (ed.), *Thomas Wolfe's Letters to His Mother* (New York, 1944).

WRITERS IN TRANSITION:
Seven Americans

Stephen Crane: The Ironic Hero

Mystic shadow bending near me,
Who art thou?
Whence come ye?
And—tell me—is it fair
Or is the truth bitter as eaten fire?
Tell me!
Fear not that I should quaver,
For I dare—I dare.
Then, tell me!

The Black Riders (1895)

STEPHEN CRANE was everyone's ideal of what a successful writer should look like.[1] Thin, slightly ethereal, surrounded by an aura of disheveled charm, he looked out on the world with eyes that seemed to have seen a great deal, though he was never old enough to talk in terms of the wisdom that comes with age. He punctuated his conversation, when he felt like talking, with an engaging smile, at once sad and happy, that seemed to say that wisdom came with other things than age. He walked with a slight stoop, was careless of his appearance, smoked incessantly, and seemed in poor health, though his sinewy frame was in fact far more robust than it appeared. He early mastered a peculiar style of English that became his medium, with less attention to grammar than to impression, infusing it with the same sadness that flashed around his eyes and mouth. His words, like their author, made friends easily and showed the inner soul of a reporter who was essentially a poet. He traveled widely, searching for some lost horizon, reported his experiences to a wide audience, lived an exciting and colorful life, and died young at the height of his fame. He was never old, outwitting death, it seemed, by leaving behind an aura of youth, the recollections of an enigmatic personality, and a slight but influential and hauntingly beautiful body of work.

It was even so in his infancy and youth. The last and least ex-

1

pected child of an elderly minister, he was frail when born in Newark, New Jersey, on November 1, 1871. It seemed to all who saw the infant that he would die, but he survived and quickly displayed a strong will. Fond of color, puckish but well behaved, he noted the details around him with mature eyes. His older brothers adopted a protective attitude and tried to help him understand his world. His father's theology did not settle in his mind, and though he worshiped his devout mother he could not follow in her doctrinal footsteps.

Even as a child he had a way with words. A remarkable memory made his eye for color and detail an invaluable asset. He memorized long lists of formidable words and invented others when the ones at hand did not suit him. One older brother was a newspaper reporter, and Stephen knew printer's ink long before he went to school. Words were colors to him as a child, and he who would one day be famous as a word colorist and literary impressionist loved color. Red was his favorite—red mittens, red boots, red scarves. It was alive, red; it meant something to his young soul.

He once said that he was a Jerseyman of long lineage, for his ancestors dated from colonial times; some were prominent in the Revolution and the period that followed. His father's death threw him further on his mother's scant resources, for unfortunately, long lineage in his case did not carry with it easy wealth or even ample funds. But his mother did not demand strict accounting, for he was the apple of her eye, and he spent many hours and days at the seashore and riding horseback. He seemed more frail than he was, and displayed the ethereal quality that others noted later. "Stevie is like the wind in the Scripture," his mother once sighed. "He bloweth where he listeth." [2] There was much in that fond mother's remark to illustrate his whole future, for he was essentially an undisciplined artist and man. Though he wrote easily, he could not apply himself to things which did not interest him. His poorest work was that which he forced himself to do.

Emerging manhood meant study and college, and lacking personal discipline, he disliked both. He attended several colleges, but majored largely in baseball, a consuming passion which he thought toughened his mind as well as his body. He dabbled in writing as he drifted from school to school, though he did not read widely in the course of his studies. "Humanity was a much more interesting study," he remembered later. "When I ought to have been at recitations I was studying faces on the streets, and when I ought to have been studying my next day's lesson I was watching the trains roll in and out of the Central Station." [3] He did develop a taste for new literature, and appreciated Tolstoy, though admitting his dullness, admired some of Mark Twain and Hamlin Garland, and denounced the French realists of the Zola school.

He was not yet twenty when he began work for the New York *Tribune*. Surprisingly, he was a failure as a reporter. He was unwilling to stick to the bare facts or to indulge in the breathless fantasies that passed for news reporting. He did not seem to grasp the details that interested readers and editors. He saw other, deeper meanings; irony, color, intuition all flashed before his eye as he saw newsmaking scenes around him. He was miscast as a reporter, for his ability at reporting was more apparent than real. He had the pen of a writer, the soul of a poet, and the eye of a painter. Many geniuses strived for mastery in him. They would have destroyed a lesser man. Much of his genius lay in combining his talents. It was hard to say which strove harder for mastery, writer or artist, for everywhere he turned he saw color. "Steve reveled in the use of words as a painter loves his color," his close friend Corwin Linson noted. "To create unusual images with them, odd conceits, quaint similes, was as natural as to eat when meal time came. He loved to cut his phrases sharply." [4]

He could not please the newspaper editors or himself, and two years of desultory free-lance reporting followed between 1890 and 1892. It was a bad time to be in the reportorial wilderness, for New York swarmed with eager young men hoping for success in the world of words and news events. Crane stayed with friends like Linson, and pooled his resources and talents with those of other struggling artists. Many people knew him, few knew him well, none completely.

Like all times of apprenticeship and gestation, these months and years of his early twenties were basic to Crane's later art, for the impressions and ideas he gathered and amplified filtered through an emerging art that gradually clustered around a view of life.

As he tried his hand at reporting and occasional hack work, Crane realized that his ambition and inner needs called for more than routine writing. His meditations were interrupted by several intense and poignant love affairs, and his view of life sharpened under the impact of these and the growing realization that the world around him was far from well with everyone. "I do not confront [life] blithely," he wrote his friend Nellie Crouse. "I confront it with desperate resolution. There is not even much hope in my attitude. I do not even expect to do good. But I expect to make a sincere, desperate, lonely battle to remain true to my conception of my life the way it should be lived, and if this plan can accomplish anything, it shall be accomplished. It is not a fine prospect." [5] There was little posturing in this frank declaration, for Crane detested nothing quite so much as the self-pitying artist and the posing dilettante. He meant what he said; he would give his best with no illusions, and if he failed he would not be surprised.

The life he saw around him fortified this attitude. An artist must have material, and Crane rejected the standards of his age. He who would in time be classed as a social outcast and a literary innovator early turned from the sentimental fiction and middle-class morality that regulated the culture of his day. In the twilight of the 1890's, he prepared a new fire. He toured the slums, walked the Bowery late at night, invaded the gambling dens, brothels, and flophouses that constituted life for much of the populace in New York City. Occasionally he fled to the seashore to swim or visit his nieces and nephews, or to the country to ride the horses he dearly loved, but the city he often hated still fascinated him. The play of forces that defined and shaped men's destinies was much starker there; that was really what fascinated him. Perhaps in that he could find the answers to the questions that plagued him.

By 1893 he was ready to make his literary debut. He chose a properly shocking method, for *Maggie*, his first novel, which he published that year, was an explosion in a mud puddle. No trade publisher would accept it, so Crane borrowed the money to print it himself. His secret hopes that the story would lift him to immediate fame and success and rescue him from his debts and a steady diet of cheap potato salad were doomed to disappointment, for *Maggie* caused scarcely a ripple. The few copies that were sold brought little reaction; the review copies he sent out were unread; the massed remainders became his property, and he was amused when a friend used them to start a fire. The success he dreamed of did not materialize with his first novel.

And for good reason. A generation accustomed to nothing more severe than William Dean Howells' pallid realism and Mark Twain's carefully pruned satire, and which sweetly savored the sentimental and nostalgic in fiction, could scarcely be expected to welcome *Maggie*. The story was simple, and like all of Crane's work, brief. It detailed the lives of Maggie, "A Girl of the Streets," and her family. They inhabited a dank portion of the Bowery with which Crane was familiar, but their environment might have been that of any large city. They spoke a language, punctuated with many expletives, that was scarcely English. They had standards of conduct that bordered on the animal. The father and mother were drunkards who abused the children; the children's playground was a street of cursing hack drivers; their highest aspiration was the next meal; their standard of behavior was the gutter.

He laid bare on every page of *Maggie* the whole underworld of conflict and emotion which his age pretended did not exist. The slang was spelled out; the vilest scenes minutely described; no sordidness escaped his pen. In a few brief, terse chapters, he pulled the rug from under sentiment and showed all the dirt, squalor, fear, misery, and sordidness of much of life that his generation chose to gild with an artificial thing called "good taste." The very tone of the book was overwhelming, for nowhere did Crane preach, nowhere did he draw a conclusion, nowhere did he judge anyone's morals or standards. His tone was elevated, dispassionate, neither harsh nor sentimental. He told his story; the reader could judge.

How it must have shocked the few people who read the book to see descriptions of tenement life as Crane knew it to be:

Long streamers of garments fluttered from fire-escapes. In all unhandy places there were buckets, brooms, rags, and bottles. In the street infants played or fought with other infants or sat stupidly in the way of vehicles. Formidable women with uncombed hair and disordered dress, gossiped while leaning on railings, or screamed in frantic quarrels. Withered persons, in curious postures of submission to something, sat smoking pipes in obscure corners. A thousand odours of cooking foods came forth to the street.[6]

Crane knew fully what he was about. Richard Watson Gilder, editor of the elegant *Century Magazine*, read the manuscript and protested the style and subject matter. "You mean that the story's too honest?" Crane asked blandly.[7] Gilder admitted that he did; the *Century* could hardly run it. Crane inscribed a printed copy to Hamlin Garland, who had taken an interest in his work. "It is inevitable that you will be shocked by this book but continue please with all possible courage to the end," [8] he wrote.

Crane tried to show in his dispassionate and unsentimental way the tragedy of Bowery life, and in a larger sense subscribed to the belief that men were often creatures of their environment. "If one proves that theory one makes room in Heaven for all sorts of souls (notably an occasional street girl) who are not confidently expected to be there by many excellent people," [9] he wrote Garland. He tried to show evil circumstances, and while he did not subscribe to any simple theory of environmentalism, he could not shut his eyes to its influence as his fellow writers seem to have done. "He studied human nature in the gutter, and found it no worse than he thought he had reason to believe it," he wrote of Maggie's brother. "He never conceived a respect for the world because he had begun with no idols that it had smashed." [10] Yet this same Jimmie, who never perceives that he is the architect of his sister's ruin, can say breathlessly: "Deh moon looks like hell, don't it?" [11]

Maggie's environment inculcated in her a fatal weakness which, compounded by inexperience, leads to her seduction. Her little society and family, ironically, cast her out, and she turns to prostitution, which results in her suicide. The story lacked finish and was poorly developed. The characterization was often weak, but the book was powerful and in its terse reporting was devastating. It was not its message alone, but its manner that so deeply impressed the book's few readers.

Reduced to its simplest form, the environmentalism of *Maggie* was a protest against social and economic inequality. Crane viewed his own work in part as an effort to expose those inequalities and he was deeply concerned with the hunger, misery, and poverty which was the lot of much of mankind. He strongly disliked the New York police, who reciprocated the feeling. The down and out, prostitutes, beggars fascinated him and he often recklessly risked his reputation to help them. He hated injustice and inequality. He would have been happy had his work revealed or helped correct any of these ills.

But there was a quality of study and an attitude of mind in him which raised his work above that of social protest. He was not a muckraker or social critic; he was first and foremost an artist. His view of poverty, inequality, and injustice was more personal than social, more private than public. If his work was in fact a social influence, it was more incidental than intentional.

On the surface, *Maggie* was a story of environment, a story that bade fair to open new subjects for writing. But there was something in *Maggie* that many people missed; there seemed to be no heroes. The makings of heroism seemed absent at first glance, but they were there, for in Crane's mind they were in every man; only heroes used them. He once said that "I tried to make plain that the root of Bowery life is a sort of cowardice. Perhaps I mean a lack of ambition or to willingly be knocked flat and accept the licking . . . I had no other purpose in writing 'Maggie' than to show people to people as they seem to me. If that be evil, make the most of it." [12] In all the squalor and filth of the novel, in all the broken lives and hellish life, in all the layers of social disease and poverty he portrayed, he found something profound that escaped most people: men are not evil, they are weak, and they are weak because they do not respond to the opportunities to be courageous. Courage, the resistance to environment, was a cardinal virtue to him, for it was at once an expression of individualism and a transcendence of individualism. The fault of *Maggie*'s characters is their weak refusal to try to rise above their world. If the book has a hero, it is, paradoxically, Maggie herself, for she alone had the courage both to attempt to rise above her surroundings and to flaunt the spurious values of her family and circle. She became a prostitute, a thing forbidden even in her depraved household. In defying she died, but in dying thus she was heroic, for she moved beyond her world. She, like Crane, was an ironic hero.

Crane poured much labor and thought into *Maggie*, and for all its faults it was a good beginning. Howells recognized Crane's talent and the force of his writing, though he deplored his style and subject matter, and he confidently predicted a bright future for him. Garland, Gilder, and a few others accepted Crane as a potential writer of the first rank, but they insisted that he would attain that rank only with a more polished work than *Maggie*.

They did not have to wait long, for in 1895 Crane published the book that brought him instant international fame and lasting literary reputation, *The Red Badge of Courage*. The Civil War had long intrigued Crane; not only was it the national epic, but it was also the crucible of heroism, and that theme now occupied him more and more as he searched for the wellspring of human conduct. If he could explain heroism or grasp its fullest meaning, he might solve the question of conduct, might discover to what degree man understood and mastered the world around him.

Crane had had his fill of the posturing, sentimental novels of the war that flooded his generation. He thought it impossible that war consisted of swashbuckling knights and swooning ladies. Furthermore, he was not merely concerned with realism and war, but with the deeper meanings of the actions of the men who fought. Why did they fight, what did they feel, why did they commit valorous deeds, to what purpose did they give their lives, what constituted heroism, and was it extraordinary or commonplace? These were the questions he hoped to answer. He chose an ironic hero once again in the form of the youthful Henry Fleming, who went to war to find himself, who left his farm a boy and returned a hero, who tasted cowardice and felt victory and heroism.

As in *Maggie*, Crane pitched his story at a high level. He studied hard, amassing facts and dates, poring over maps and details of battles in the history of the war, all of which he filtered through his imagination. "I have spent ten nights writing a story of the war on my own responsibility but I am not sure that my facts are real and the books won't tell me what I want to know so I must do it all over again, I guess," [13] he wrote a friend while in the throes of composition.

The most prominent attitude in this chronicle of the boy-hero and his search for the fulfillment of battle is detachment. It is as if Crane surveyed the battle from a great height. He is not his hero, he is not part of his story; indeed, the author seems hardly evident anywhere. Henry realizes with a shock that his romantic dreams of war and the army are false. War was a life of hardship, dullness, and mud. He was not important. "He had grown to regard himself as a part of a vast blue demonstration." [14] If this was shocking to the ego, battle was even more shocking, for it had no glamour at all; it was an essay in detached confusion. "The battle was like the grinding of an immense and terrible machine to him. Its complexities and powers, its grim processes, fascinated him. He must go close and see it produce corpses." [15] That was the overpowering thing about war and battle, its impersonality, the machinelike manner in which it dwarfed the men who fought it.

Confused, beset by doubts, overawed by the relentless horror about him, Henry is tortured by the fear that he will be a coward, that he will fail the men around him, that he will fail himself by running away in battle. That is precisely what happens as he stumbles dazed from the field in search of peace and rest, fearful for his life, overcome by his guilt and cowardice. Valor, that splendid spark of war, has passed him by; he is not the stuff of heroes. He reflects bitterly on the uselessness of the idealism that brought him to this place of horror:

Reflecting, he saw a sort of humor in the point of view of himself and his fellows during the late encounter. They had taken themselves and the enemy very seriously and had imagined that they were deciding the war. Individuals must have supposed that they were cutting the letters of their names deep into everlasting tablets of brass, or enshrining their reputations forever on the hearts of their countrymen, while, as to fact, the affair would appear in printed reports under a meek and immaterial title.[16]

If that were so, what good was courage? Were men heroic only because they feared their reputation with other men, because others expected it, or because they were forced to be brave?

Henry could not believe it so, any more than Crane could believe it so despite his strong tendencies toward mechanism and the stoic view of life. There was something in courage: individualism, the expression of the one who thus spoke for the many. Henry must redeem himself by bravery. In some of his finest passages, Crane detailed the youth's quest for redemption. Henry had noticed earlier that his comrades seemed singularly unheroic. "The youth looked at the men nearest him, and saw, for the most part, expressions of deep interest, as if they were investigating something that had fascinated them." [17] With this tone he returns to battle and redeems himself by conspicuous gallantry in a charge. His heroism was not so important in showing that he was capable of nerve as in showing merely that it could be done. Heroism, courage, was common to all men who faced circumstances and rose above them. "It was not well to drive men into final corners; at those moments they could all develop teeth and claws," [18] Henry concluded. The story was essentially one of redemption: "He had slept and, awakening, found himself a knight." [19]

All in all, it was an astonishing performance. The English press and reading public seized on the book as evidence that American writing was emerging from the long Indian summer of sentimentalism and hailed Crane as a new light in the school of realism. In his own country, Crane's recognition was not so swift or sure, but gradually the book became a best-seller, was discussed in drawing rooms, colleges, and around country firesides. War veterans indignantly returned copies with remarks about patriotism and "The Cause" of the Civil War. Many were surprised to find that the author was not a veteran, but was barely twenty-four and had never experienced anything approaching a battle. Crane was also gratified by letters from veterans who reported that they had felt exactly like the men he described. The compositors who set up the novel, many of them veterans, were among the first to congratulate Crane.

In essence, the book had little to do with war: it was not a war novel, but a novel using a war setting. The war was but the testing ground of a higher ideal and a greater question in Crane's mind: what was the nature of courage? Was it common to all men, or to a few? Was it noble, and why? As in *Maggie*, his detachment and ease of writing combined with a truly extraordinary gift for words and facility with color impression to produce a powerful novel without preaching or moralizing. The characters seemed small to the reader, but they were not deliberately drawn that way; it was as if they existed independently of Crane and followed their own destinies. The sense of stoic mechanism which flavored the book did not dominate the reader; rather, it permeated the writing.

The success of *The Red Badge of Courage* seemed to establish Crane's future, and enabled him to repay some debts and to do many things that he had wanted to do for some time. Yet questions plagued him; his answer was not complete. A concise brevity was the mark of his successful style—he came in time to think that the brief *Red Badge of Courage* was too long—and he succeeded to his own best satisfaction in the short-story form. In many ways, he gave more fresh impetus to the form than any other American writer of his time. After 1893, he produced many short stories, some good, many bad, many more indifferent. Lacking the discipline necessary to formal, polished writing, his techniques failed steadily in his last years as pressures for money and of ill health mounted against him.

Yet he wrote perhaps a dozen classic short stories, the most celebrated of which is "The Open Boat." This story, in a few pages, displays all his talents for condensation, graphic description, and detached observation. The story is simple, drawn from his own experience after the sinking of a ship engaged in filibustering in Cuban waters prior to the Spanish-American War. Four men are set adrift in a tiny dinghy after shipwreck, prey to all the forces of an indifferent world. In one sense the story is a report of an actual event; in the largest sense, it is an expression of Crane's view of life, a microcosm in which Crane studied man and the universe as though they were in the palm of his hand. The story concerns the men's search for the shore, and for life.

"None of them knew the colour of the sky," the story begins, and Crane proceeded with deft incisiveness to describe their predicament. "Many a man ought to have a bathtub larger than the boat which here rode upon the sea." The sense of brooding isolation and loneliness is deftly sketched. "These two lights were the furniture of the world. Otherwise there was nothing but waves," he wrote of the two lights which the men could see. In two brief sentences he thus described their isolation more effectively than with volumes of mannered prose. But the protagonist of the story is really the sea, against whose indifference the men are pitted. Their heroism consists of salvation from her grasp. "She did not seem cruel to him then, nor beneficent, nor treacherous, nor wise. But she was indifferent, flatly indifferent." [20] That was more devastating to man than opposition, for he could not combat an indifferent adversary. All but one of the men are saved; their quest has its answer, but none of them feels important in the scheme of things they faced.

"The Open Boat," and other stories composed in 1897 and 1898, brought into sharp relief the outlines of Crane's philosophy. His emerging literary realism rested on several technical and philosophical bases. He was acknowledged as a word artist of the first importance, and his technical ability as well as his startling message insured him a wide audience. Not the least of his accomplishments was his abandonment of fashionable sentimentality. He hated sham because it was untrue and because it condescended toward both readers and the characters of fiction. The happy ending had little to do with life, and life was his major preoccupation.

This did not mean, of course, that Crane lacked sympathy. In their way, the clipped and dispassionate phrases that described Maggie's lot were far more eloquent than any amount of sentimental dress he could have offered. He was sympathetic but wise enough in his treatment to realize that one woe does not alter the world, and that injustice continues abroad long after it is condemned. He believed that injustice could be better combated with clear words than with sham and sentiment. Believing as he did that man goes much of his way alone, he could not bring himself to think that one man's sorrow should be elevated into a general principle.

Dark as much of his philosophy was, it was tempered by a belief in human goodness and kindness. "The final wall of the wise man's thoughts, however, is Human Kindness, of course," he wrote

Nellie Crouse. "If the road of disappointment, grief, pessimism, is followed far enough, it will arrive there. Pessimism itself is only a little, little way, and moreover it is ridiculously cheap. The cynical mind is an uneducated thing. Therefore I strive to be as kind and as just as may be to those about me and in my meager success at it, I find the solitary pleasure of life." [21]

Personally, he viewed the role of reformer with as much disdain as that of the sentimentalist; each was in essence a pose. He joined no movements, lent his name to no causes, asked nothing from public recognition. He reported that he "was a Socialist for two weeks but when a couple of Socialists assured me I had no right to think differently from any other Socialist and then quarreled with each other about what Socialism meant, I ran away." [22] It was the perfect expression of his view; he belonged in no camp. If life must be answered individually, it must be lived individually.

Crane was an artist, interested in his craft, yet many of the innovations he introduced into American writing were unconscious or afterthoughts. He wrote the way he felt; if that was new, the critics could make the most of it. He only knew that it was at best a hard lot. "It seems a pity that art should be a child of pain, and yet I think it is," [23] he wrote toward the end of his career. While Crane was not devoid of ego, he had a candid view of his own accomplishments. When he thought mankind inconsequential, he included himself, and he knew that much of his work was transitory. Unlike many successful writers, he hated the role of social lion and railed against the drawing rooms and tea parties which demanded his presence. It seemed to him that all the shallowness and pomposity of the age was focused in an author at a tea. He did not savor the heady wine of critical approval, but like it or not, he was an important contemporary influence, the spokesman for the rising cult of realism and naturalism in American literature that promised to obscure Howells' realism.

Crane intended to be realistic in his writing. "I try to give to readers a slice out of life; and if there is any moral or lesson in it, I do not try to point it out. I let the reader find it for himself." [24] That was essentially his credo, that of the superior reporter and observer. It cost him much to renounce "the clever school of literature," [25] in which he could have made a fortune and reputation, but he felt it a lack of ideals and integrity to surrender to the fashion of Rudyard Kipling.

His realism ran deeper than a mere "slice of life." He greatly disliked the French realists whom he was accused of copying, because he felt that their view of life was artificial and because they were cataloguers rather than artists. His own view was far more realistic, for he stripped it even of the clinical aspects of sociology which dominated so much of foreign realism. ". . . I understand that a man is born into the world with his own pair of eyes, and he is not at all responsible for his vision—he is merely responsible for his quality of personal honesty," he said in an often quoted remark. "To keep close to this personal honesty is my supreme ambition. There is a sublime egotism in talking of honesty. I, however, do not say that I am honest. I merely say that I am as nearly honest as a weak mental machinery will allow. This aim in life struck me as being the only thing worth while. A man is sure to fail at it, but there is something in the failure." [26]

Technically, he saw little else to it. "And my chiefest desire was to write plainly and unmistakably, so that all men (and some women) might read and understand. That to my mind is good writing." [27] To do this he developed the art of reporting in the best sense: terse words, exact description, the apt simile, the sense of being present. "He knew when to shut up," [28] Frank Norris said, putting it in a nutshell.

The strongest personal flavor in his work was irony, a difficult art which he mastered better than any other American writer. Perhaps in all of modern American literature there is not so fine an example of irony as the ending of *Maggie*, when the girl's death is announced to the besotted and depraved mother. The woman whose ways and standards had set her daughter upon the streets ironically clings to her false standard, insisting that Maggie was wicked and at fault. Persuaded by her forgiving neighbors, who had also hastened the girl's destruction, she relents and cries out: "Oh, yes, I'll fergive her! I'll fergive her!" [29] Quite as superbly in his shorter stories, such as "The Blue Hotel" and "Twelve O'clock," he sharpens the points of irony on which his characters impale themselves.

Yet for all his success, something tasted sour. "I get a little tired," he said in 1899, "of saying, Is this true?" He knew that literary naturalism had many of the limitations and tendencies toward artificiality of the saccharine literature he attacked. He knew also that one of his weaknesses was a tendency to preach surreptitiously. For this reason he cultivated the art of detachment in his writing, for he hated morality on every level when reduced to a fixed system or pedantic code. He liked Tolstoy, "But I confess that the conclusions of some of his novels, and the lectures he sticks in, leave me feeling that he regards his genius as the means to an end. I happen to be a preacher's son, but that heredity does not preclude—in me—a liking for sermons unmixed with other material . . . I mean that I like my art straight." [30]

To those who cared to probe deeper and assess the artist as well as the man, profounder currents were at work in his writing. The central theme of all his work, in one form or another, was courage. To Crane courage consisted of a disavowal of personality, a momentary abandonment of selfishness. Such moments came rarely to men, this "temporary but sublime absence of selfishness," [31] but they were a major quest in life. By forgetting self, the individual might rise above himself and thus survey the true extent and importance of his actions. Only thus could anyone assess his own potential and his contribution to life. Those rare moments of heroism that came to some men, whether in battle or by the fireside, were of grave importance, like the moment on the mountaintop when one saw in all directions the extent and meaning of life. The function of courage was to free man from himself and to define his context. Heroism was ironic to Crane; paradoxically, heroism was not egotistical, but humbling. The real hero was not the man who strutted his success before others, but the man who silently accepted the sublimity of his small personal accomplishment. The real badge of courage was not the outer red wound, but the inner understanding of what price bought the wound. The boy who traveled under fire on the seemingly foolish mission to fill his canteen before his fellows was technically a hero when he returned safely, yet he realized that his action was extraordinary only to the degree that it revealed his inner self. "This, then, was a hero. After all, heroes were not much." [32]

Crane was puzzled and challenged by the indifference with which supposedly heroic men regarded their deeds. "They do a thing and afterwards they find that they have done it because they have done it." [33] Once while reporting the Spanish-American War he saw men under cutting fire, seemingly indifferent to their fate and uninspired by any cause whatever; his mental flags of heroism fell in tatters as he realized that every heroic myth failed to describe real heroism. "There wasn't a high heroic face among them," he wrote in puzzled admiration.

They were all men intent on business. That was all. It may seem to you that I am trying to make everything a squalor. That would be wrong. I feel that things were often sublime. But they were *differently* sublime. They were not of our shallow and preposterous fictions. They stood out in a simple, majestic commonplace. It was the behaviour of men on the street. It was the behaviour of men. One cannot speak of it—the spectacle of the common man serenely doing his work, his appointed work. It is the one thing in the universe which makes one fling expression to the winds and be satisfied simply to feel.[34]

The behavior of men—that was the whole question. What made them act, heroically and otherwise? War fascinated him, and many charged that he sought personal fulfillment by participating in events after writing about them. But it was only a half-truth, for he need not travel far for any event; he lived chiefly in his own mind. Battle fascinated him not because of its excitement or because of its importance, but because of its paradoxes. Here men were grouped, yet alone; here the weak became strong and the strong weak; here men made decisions but were made by decisions. Battles, in short, were life. If he could discover the secrets of one he would understand the other. "It is because war is neither magnificent nor squalid; it is simply life, and an expression of life can always invade us," he wrote of his reasons for observing battles. "We can never tell life, one to another, although sometimes we think we can." [35] Once in battle, reality took the place of romance; the covering of culture fled from the truths of life. "War is death, and a plague of the lack of small things, and toil," [36] he noted tersely.

Still there were heroes, often unexpected, usually inexplicable, and they fascinated him. It was not heroism as such—the single moment of truth—that fascinated him so much as courage. An act of heroism presumably was but one reflection of a deeper courage, of a more enduring and more important thing—a code of personal conduct, a belief that given men will triumph over given circumstances in daily life as well as in battle. Courage, then, was an expression of individualism in a world that worked against individualism; it was an individual fulfillment in perspective, without selfishness and ego. It was the testing of all Crane's mechanistic theories and attitudes.

As his writing progressed, his mechanism and fatalism became more and more pronounced. Technically, his work resembled that of the continental realists abroad and Hamlin Garland and Howells at home; philosophically, he seemed ready to accept a far more pessimistic view of life and the world than the latter. As he progressed and traveled, observing men and their actions, he became more intrigued with "the inconsequence of individual tragedy—a message that is in the boom of the sea, the sliver of the wind through the grass-blades, the silken clash of hemlock boughs." [37] For himself, he had no illusions about men and their importance. "Each wise man in this world is concealed amid some twenty thousand fools," [38] he wrote in his unsuccessful novel, *The Third Violet* (1897).

He said much the same in "The Open Boat," in which the solemnity of the indifferent sea seemed to dwarf the tiny men upon it. Such an attitude permeated the short stories he wrote after a Western tour in 1895. The failure of the haunted Swede in "The Blue Hotel," his inability to redeem himself in any way except a foolish death, was offset by the weakness and failure of the men around him to prevent his death. The Swede at least had the courage to die for some sort of principle, which the others did not recognize. So much chance was involved, Crane seemed to be saying, so many small things that no man can recognize until it is too late.

Thus he viewed nature as a massive force, not to be arrested in its influence on man by that puny creature's efforts to control it. One fact impressed itself most on the mind of Henry Fleming, even at the height of the gigantic and cruel battle that engrossed him: "As he gazed around him the youth felt a flash of astonishment at the blue, pure sky and the sun gleaming on the trees and fields. It was surprising that Nature had gone tranquilly on with her golden process in the midst of so much devilment." [39] In "The Open Boat," he stated his attitude most succinctly:

When it occurs to a man that nature does not regard him as important and that she feels she would not maim the universe by disposing of him, he at first wishes to throw bricks at the temples, and he hates deeply the fact that there are no bricks and no temples. Any visible expression of nature would surely be pelleted with his jeers. . . . A high cold star on a winter's night is the word he feels that she says to him. Thereafter he knows the pathos of his situation.[40]

He set men in an indifferent universe which was in a sense more cruel than hostile, for man was helpless against it. George of "George's Mother" is the foil for Crane's irony in thinking that he will get drunk and avenge himself on the universe. "He was about to taste the delicious revenge of a partial self-destruction. The universe would regret its position when it saw him drunk." [41]

Crane was not bitter, nor was he angry; he realistically accepted what he thought was his condition. His quest for the substance of heroism was in large measure a testing of the limits of this determinism. Could man defy fate successfully? Could he escape, in a moment of heroism and through an expression of courage, the bonds of an indifferent world and the blind play of chance? Crane came to believe that man could escape, that courage, the willingness to admit the powers of the universe, tempered that power with endurance if not mercy. The world might not be changed by the hero's act, but the hero would have the secret knowledge that for a moment he rose above fate. That was his badge of courage.

The origins of this determinism, all the more startling because of its contemporary setting, remain Crane's private mystery. It may be that he was torn by fear of personal failure, that he fled perpetually from the shadows of doubt that pursued him. More than once in Cuba and elsewhere he seemed oblivious to personal danger, anxious to die the hero's death, eager to test the fiber of his own inner self. It may be that, personally insecure, he raised this insecurity to a principle. Yet such an answer is unlike Crane, for his lack of sentimentality denied such a conclusion. It is far more likely that the honesty of his conscience and the candor of his observing eye, coupled with intense inward experience, confirmed his belief that man was subject to chance and an indifferent universe.

Yet in this view as in others in his work it was not quite so simple as that. His lack of egotism told Crane that men were not as important as they liked to believe, yet neither were they mere pawns. It was a form of escape and self-indulgence to label the universe indifferent and the world malignant; it was the same kind of cowardice he had seen on the Bowery. It was in fact the negation of courage. This idea was suddenly borne in upon him when he read the reviews of his bitter poetry, *The Black Riders* (1895):

For the first time I saw the majestic forces which are arrayed against man's true success—not the world—the world is silly, changeable, any of its decisions can be reversed—but man's own colossal impulses more strong than chains, and I perceived that the fight was not going to be with the world but with myself. I had fought the world and had not bended nor moved an inch, but this other battle—it is to last on up through the years to my grave and only on that day am I to know if the word Victory will look well upon lips of mine.[42]

This, then, was the real profundity in his work and view of life. Nothing was ever simple to him, and naturalism and mechanism carried to their logical ends were too simple an explanation of man's condition. Heroism came from within, not from without; it was the product of the man, not the world. Environment acting on the weak made them weaker, but the flaw was hidden in their beings at first. Some, ironically like Maggie, rose against their environment, often in curious ways. They were the heroes.

Fame brought with it responsibilities; Crane must now maintain his reputation and insure his financial future. He turned once more to reporting, to writing for money out of desperation, for he realized that his health was ruined and that he had little time in which to provide for the wife he would leave. In 1897 he went to Greece to report the war with Turkey, but he was out of place, for he was still not a reporter. His eyes saw other things—the colors of the mountains, the customs of the people, the qualities of endurance and courage that the struggle left in its wake. The contest ended too quickly for his participation but he stayed to study the people. Out of the experience he wrote a poor novel, *Active Service* (1899), in a vain effort to right himself financially.

A dislike of the prying and tattling of American newspapers and the shallowness of American society and popular values drove him to England in 1898 where he lived his last years in a gloomy medieval castle, visited by Henry James and other literary lights, the victim of literally hundreds of unwanted guests and fortune followers. His health declined steadily as he desperately strove to solidify his place in letters and to earn enough money for a trip to Western America to recover his health.

The long-heralded war with Spain in 1898 interrupted his plans and he hastily won a reporting post and traveled to Cuba where he amazed and amused friends by his coolness under fire and his nonchalant attitude toward death and war. His keen eye missed few details, and some of his most graphic work in the form of short sketches and stories came from his Cuban experiences.

He was an important figure, a famous name, talked about in many circles, widely read, yet his notoriety brought him sour satisfaction. Rumors spread that he was an alcoholic, that he took drugs, that he gambled, that he was in constant trouble with the police, that he befriended the outcast and the loathsome. "When people see a banker taking a glass of beer in a cafe, they say, There is Smith," he said bitterly. "When they behold a writer taking a glass of beer, they say, Send for the police!" [43] From Cuba he wrote that "my friends will pile a mountain of lies on me but they will smoke my cigars as freely as I smoke theirs. That is cynicism." [44] The success for which he had worked through lean years had a hollow ring. "I was happier in the old days when I was always dreaming of the thing I have now attained. I am disappointed with success, and am tired of abuse." [45] He found in this what he had found in the rest of life: viewed without emotion, nothing is glamorous when touched—nothing save heroism.

Angered by charges that he copied or plagiarized, he often snapped back that he knew nothing of the French realists and worked from his own mind. His house guests in England persisted, clouding his last days. "They stand me against walls with a teacup in my hand and tell me how I have stolen all my things from De Maupassant, Zola, Loti and the bloke who wrote—I forget the book." [46] In the point of fact, Crane's genius was original and unique. He had studied little if at all before beginning his work. He carried with him less of literary tradition and continuity than any other major American writer. The dazzling quality of his genius is its unique character. [47]

For all the beauty of his words, the clipped precision—often ironic in itself—of his literary impressions, the personal kindness and generosity of the author and public figure, there is a dark side to Stephen Crane. His morbid reflections on death, his fascination with fate, his ever-present suspicion that the senses only confirm the deeper truth that man is indeed alone with himself and that even courage cannot overcome that loneliness, the dark magnet of the Bowery and other tawdry surroundings that drew him like steel filings—these and other things delineate a darkness in his personality. He was never sure, and sure he must be.

What to say of his accomplishment? He himself was wont to excuse rather than explain it, to insist that he had done nothing beyond report the world as it appeared to him. Yet he was too modest—or perhaps he himself did not perceive the full outlines of his work. He was not given to thinking in critical terms. Undeniably his technical accomplishments did much to elevate American literature from the surface sentimentality of his time. His precision, his demands for color and exactness of description constituted a brilliant model for later writers and readers.

The mysteries of his work are likely to escape many readers and critics, for much of his hidden meaning was in his life and died with him. An enigma in life, he remains an enigma in death. Yet he helped set in motion the clock of realism and naturalism that dominated American writing in the next two generations. Concerned with man's state in a world he cannot comprehend, he set the tone for many writers who followed.

But the challenge of Crane's work is not its influence but its uniqueness. It seems to have transpired in a vacuum, devoid of major derivations, original in the best sense of the word. In sum it is the small expression of a genius of great potential. The last of his short stories, some published posthumously, printed in *Midnight Sketches,* show a sharpening social consciousness under his great verbal skill. The body of his work varies from good to bad, but he will be best remembered for *The Red Badge of Courage,* and perhaps more importantly for his contributions to the short story form in "The Open Boat," "The Bride Comes to Yellow Sky," "The Blue Hotel," and other stories.

He died at twenty-eight, after England's damp climate hastened his inevitable end. "For my own part, I am minded to die in my thirty-fifth year," he had written years before. "I think that is all I care to stand. I don't like to make wise remarks on the aspect of life but I will say that it doesn't strike me as particularly worth the trouble." [48] On June 5, 1900, his wish was fulfilled, seven years too soon.

And so he passed, an old man for what he had seen in twenty-eight years. Still, the shadows of his personality cross the reader's path at every turn. Something fascinating remains unexplained. "The lives of some people are one long apology," he wrote to an early love. "Mine was once, but not now. I go through the world unexplained, I suppose." [49] Perhaps that was the epitaph he best deserved, and the only one he wished.

Edith Wharton: The Novelist of Manners and Morals

> Only children think that one can make a garden with flowers broken from the plant; only inexperience imagines that novelty is always synonymous with improvement.
>
> *French Ways and Their Meaning* (1919)

THE LITTLE GIRL who was Edith Newbold Jones had a prodigious liking for literature, and passed long hours in the sunlight "reading" various volumes, which often as not were held upside down in her childish hands. Her affection for reading was surprising not only because of her age, but because the people around her thought so little of it as a pastime. Born into the upper reaches of New York society in 1862, the last of the Jones children and the only daughter, she was not expected to become anything but an ornament to that society; that she might become a writer or have any serious connection with the arts was a foreign idea to her family and social class.[1]

Her family was not rich but "well off," in itself a more genteel term. Though her father took his family abroad yearly for his health, he also went because living there was cheaper. Her lineage dated to the beginnings of the nation and her family numbered among its members the very cream of Eastern society. Hers was a world controlled by fixed social forms, routines handed down like recipes from dim and distant fathers, and which were no more open to question than the fathers themselves. Some people were not admitted, some topics were not discussed, some things were not done, and everyone in the little caste understood why without asking. Good food, fine wines, the best clothing, expensive but unread books, the Episcopal church—these were some of the staples of her social group.

Edith's interest in reading matured as she grew. A momentary precocity with the pen produced her first story, at age nine,

which was set in an untidy drawing room. She showed it to her
mother, who returned it with the icy injunction: "Drawing rooms
are always tidy." [2] That comment delineated both the social and
intellectual horizon of her family and friends. Even though she
lacked an appreciative audience and adequate stimulation, the
girl continued her excursions into literature while enduring all
the training thought necessary to make her a lady. In her narrow
world, writing or any connection with the arts was met with
disfavor. Her peers viewed with alarm any of their number who
"filled the house with long-haired men and short-haired women." [3]
This attitude on the part of the class best situated to promote the
arts was to Mrs. Wharton one of the great failures of American
culture, and she lamented that no genuine patron class arose in her
native land as it had in Europe.

It was her business to become a lady, a task requiring study.
She was entrusted to private tutors. From them and from her
family and friends she imbibed attitudes and tastes which molded
her personality and marked her fiction. She later moved beyond
the intellectual standards of her group and attempted in her fiction
to widen her mental horizon, but she never abandoned the tastes
of her upbringing. To the end she was acutely conscious of her
social station.

She loved the ease, the sense of order and calm development,
the urbanity of her life. She was sensitive to beauty, a prime
requisite among her group: ". . . I was always vaguely frightened by ugliness." [4] She naturally avoided the public issues of the
day; she had no knowledge of the workaday world on which her
own gilded society rested. Her mother's advice rang in her ears:
"Never talk about money, and think about it as little as possible." [5]
She never forgot the taint which her society attached to business
and money-making and she never understood or accepted "the
innumerable army of American businessmen—the sallow, under-
sized, lacklustre drudges who have never lifted their heads from
the ledgers." [6]

Repelled by the values of the outside world, she felt that those
of her own group were little better. In due course she married an
older man, Edward Wharton, who apparently never understood
his wife's artistic leanings and who would have been content to

lead the life of the wandering gentleman which had characterized and consumed his ancestors.

But the young Mrs. Wharton was not content with the role of a society matron; she must have more mental stimulation than she found at her dinner table. She was bored with "the ideals of a world where conspicuousness passed for distinction, and the society column had become the role of fame." [7] Like Lily Bart in *The House of Mirth* (1905), she could scan her dinner guests and think: "How dreary and trivial these people were!" It was not that she disliked her set; they were kind and generous, if ignorant of the world, the victims of their circumstances just as much as the factory workers were of theirs. She appreciated them for what they were, but they were not enough. "Under the glitter of their opportunities she saw the poverty of their achievement." That was their failing—they knew nothing but each other, and all their splendid opportunities for intellectual growth and cultural activity were swallowed in the swamp of social convention. The point was not that they were trivial, but that they were nothing else.[8] She put her feeling in a nutshell in her first major novel, *The Valley of Decision* (1902), when she wrote: "None was more open than he [Prince Odo] to the seducements of luxurious living, the polish of manners, the tacit exclusion of all that is ugly or distressing; but it seemed to him that fine living should be but the flower of fine feeling, and that such external graces, when they adorned a dull and vapid society, were as incongruous as the royal purple on a clown." [9]

It was against this naïveté and provinciality, "the innocence that seals the mind against imagination and the heart against experience," [10] that she turned. For it was precisely the provinciality of her society that irritated her, the fact that it was as isolated from real intellectual currents as the lower classes. Her peers feared change, contented themselves with the past, lived in the shadows conversing with ghosts. "The weakness of the social structure of my parents' day was a blind dread of innovation, an instinctive shrinking from responsibility," [11] she remembered. Responsibility —that was her aim, responsibility for the development of the mind as well as the refinements of a well-set dinner table.

For all its faults, her inheritance was by no means empty; its greatest gift was the basis of her thought and life, "that background of beauty and old-established order" [12] which she cherished. It was to save this order, to insure the survival of the best qualities of her society that she turned her pen to it, covering it with the sudden light of irony and satire, hoping to salvage the best and destroy the worst.

Her entrance into the world of letters was not auspicious. Her first published works were poems, forwarded to editors in a rush of innocence with one of her calling cards. Her gratification at being published moved her to write more, an impulse fostered by the family physician who felt that her nervousness might be controlled if she channeled her energy into some creative pursuit. Her genre seemed at first to be the short story, a collection of which she published in 1899 under the title *The Greater Inclination*. This was preceded by a slender volume of verse and a book on interior decoration, the latter illustrating her abiding interest in the decor of her surroundings.

Her real interest, however, was the society in which she lived. As her concern over the disintegration of the old cultural order mounted, so did her determination to do her part to rescue it by revealing its follies. To reveal these, she mounted a double-pronged attack, branching in different directions but ultimately converging on a single point—the maintenance of the old values and standards by renovating them. First she must reveal her society's failures to its members; then she must assault the *nouveaux riches* who were rushing to buy their admission tickets into the old society.

As the new brownstone houses rose under the watchful eyes of the newly rich, the old standards fell. It was Mrs. Wharton's acutest observation that these old standards fell partly because the group which had established them was ossified from lack of change and fresh inspiration. She best stated her dislike of the new standards and the people who made them in *The Custom of the Country* (1913), whose heroine, surely one of the most devastating portraits in American letters, was the archetype of the crass, tasteless, overwealthy newcomers who were swamping the genteel boat of the old society. Undine Spragg, named after a hair curler invented by her father, summed up everything in the new order which Mrs. Wharton hated. She was the overdressed, unintelligent, grasping stereotype of a social climber. "Her entrances were always triumphs; but they had no sequel." [13] She had no standards and the horror of her example was that she never knew it. "Undine was fiercely independent and yet passionately imitative. She wanted to surprise everyone by her dash and originality, but she could not help modelling herself on the last person she met." [14]

Mrs. Wharton's favorite device was a character enriched by speculations or investments in the West who came East to find grace and status. She could ridicule the builders of the New West all the more effectively for not knowing them. Willa Cather found different strains in the pioneer expansion on the Western frontier, for unlike Mrs. Wharton, her concern was not with society but with individual courage and growth. It is an index to Mrs. Wharton's view that her concern was less with the heroism of an individual than with his place in his world and the action and reaction of his moral standards on those already established.

Mrs. Wharton wielded a double-edged sword. She would have been chagrined indeed had her set abandoned the ramparts before the invaders from the West, who smoothed their path by a combination of gold and brass. Her purpose was to stiffen resistance by pointing out both the weaknesses in the old moral order and the dangers posed by the new standardless culture. No one knew better than she the hollow aridity of a society which lives only on its past, the principal in its bank account, as it were, and her first aim was to expose this. Yet she would have been the last to pull the past down in favor of the new way. "What do you call the new way?" a character asked in *The Fruit of the Tree* (1907). "Launching one's boat over a human body—or several, as the case may be," [15] was the answer.

Because the danger was real to her, her assault was far from genteel. In truth, she knew little of the Westerners she lampooned except as she had seen them in her limited experience, but her fertile imagination did its best. The characters who peopled her pages dealing with the Western invasion revealed her acid attitude: Undine Spragg, Indiana Frusk, Claude Walsingham Popple, Ora

Prance Chattle, Mabel Blitch—these and a host of others showed her detestation of the social climbing, vulgar display, and lack of taste in the groups displacing her own old society.

Yet Mrs. Wharton did not dislike her characters because they rebelled; indeed, she considered herself a rebel and to the end of her work she greatly admired the man or woman with sufficient courage and integrity to accept his intellectual responsibilities and revolt. She did not so much oppose the *nouveaux riches* because of their wealth as because of their use of it. A steady stream of gold financed their assaults on the old moral order while they built nothing to replace it. Like its source, their money was vulgar. It corroded everything it touched.

Mrs. Wharton's writing reflected a basic philosophical cleavage that she never resolved and which explains much of the lack of focus in her work. Her persistent effort to clarify often merely added to the confusion, but was a tribute to the importance she accorded her ideas. Aware of the cultural crisis of her day, she was anxious to insure order in a time of transition by restoring a sense of value; retaining the old ethical standard of conduct in human dealings would insure integrity and individualism. To her credit, she clearly perceived that the redistribution of wealth and social status in her society had deep and permanent ramifications; it meant that new cultural and intellectual standards would be set by the new holders of wealth. In time, the masses themselves would hold wealth, and with it that same power and responsibility.

Mrs. Wharton considered herself a rebel; had she not endured censure for her work, and had her early fiction not been included as part of American literary naturalism and realism? The very fact that she wrote at all set her apart and made her sympathetic toward those who rebelled against the traditional order. But here exactly was the cleavage she could not heal. She committed herself to a system of *absolute* truth, which required an absolute code of conduct. But recognizing that men are weak, she sympathized with those who tried to attain that goal but fell short. Thus she accepted a code of relative truth in her efforts to achieve a working moral order. The test to her, as to a greater degree with Ellen Glasgow, was not so much attainment of the absolute as striving for it. Thus she could both berate her characters for failing and sympathize with their failures.

As she warmed to her subject she developed her art. It is curious that fiction to her seemed more a means than an end, and artistic theory as such did not intrigue her so much as the hidden meanings in the materials she handled. To the end she seemed a gifted amateur, and her work did not prevent her from leading the life of a great lady. ". . . I had never seen a writer in our old world who kept such state as she did," [16] Percy Lubbock remembered. Her tastes and interests ran beyond writing, and she took quite as much pleasure from good conversation, travel, and the social life as from writing. Her mind, essentially intellectual and nonromantic, more masculine than feminine in its tastes and attitudes, seemed to be compartmented, with doors and interests that she opened and closed at will.

Interest in the life around her, coupled with her wide reading and travel, equipped her for writing. A photographic memory and an eye for detail aided her work. She had only to see a thing to reproduce it at will from memory. The outline was always at hand, ready to be clothed with words. In her historical novels, the crowded page unfolds with the detail and color of a historical canvas. She had a sensitive eye for nature, but it was its decorative qualities, not its force, which impressed her. In none of her works, not even *Ethan Frome* (1911), does nature act as a major protagonist; it is always the stage, the background for human passions and actions. She was especially careful to delineate costumes, settings, houses, the countryside in which her characters lived and moved. The sense of decoration inherent in her training gave her work its wealth of detailed balance. To write *The Valley of Decision* required extensive original research in long-forgotten sources of Italian history, as well as travel through the Italian countryside.

Yet she was intrigued with the technique of fiction and the creative act, as is reflected in the general development of her work. "Modern fiction really began when the 'action' of the novel was transferred from the street to the soul," [17] she wrote. Her main purpose was not to display all of life, but to examine certain human experiences and thereby to illuminate certain truths. She once said that the good short story was "a shaft driven straight into the heart of human experience." [18] She disliked the sprawling, formless naturalistic novels of her later contemporaries. Just as she believed that form, control, experience were necessary in society, so she believed they were necessary in art. "True originality consists not in a new manner but in a new vision." [19] The conflicts of personality, the struggles of human beliefs, the weaknesses and strengths of men were the facets of life that intrigued her. "Drama, situation, is made out of the conflicts thus produced between the social order and individual appetites, and the art of rendering life in fiction can never, in the last analysis, be anything, or need be anything, but the disengaging of crucial moments from the welter of existence." [20] This conflict between the individual and his social, ethical, and moral order was the principal theme, in one guise or other, of her work. Her depiction of manners, social form, the function of society was but the means of defining the individual's status and position in his world. Her concern with depth rather than with sweep made her novels often seem overly long and tedious, two tendencies lamentably heightened in her late works. Yet at her best, in *Ethan Frome, The Custom of the Country, Summer* (1917), and *The Age of Innocence* (1920), her ability to dissect character and depict human conduct was unquestioned.

The central theme which emerged from Mrs. Wharton's work was not manners, but morality—the question of ethical conduct in society amid the problems of human relations. Two central points defined her moral attitude in her work: the aligning of a strong character with a weak one, with the ultimate threat to the strong one, and the question of individual ethical conduct. In all of her works there is an alliance or proposed alliance between incompatible natures, one strong and perceptive, the other weak and insensitive. The waste of human potential in these alliances is found in her best work. In *Ethan Frome* these incompatible natures are best and most sharply portrayed by her portrait of the tragic marriage between Ethan and Zeena Frome. Frome's tragedy is seen through three lenses, each of which focuses on and magnifies his trapped nature: his capture in a totally unhappy marriage, his enslavement to farming, an occupation for which he has neither taste nor aptitude, and the thwarting of his intellectual potential by his marriage. The tale, therefore, is one of trapped sensibilities, not merely a discussion of repressed New England life.

Frome's marriage was the product of both chance and generous impulse, the forces involved, in Mrs. Wharton's mind, in the making of tragedy. She feared impulsive action because it was impulsive; the human animal acting without the restraint afforded by reflection and thought was prone to error. In the broadest sense, her work implies that the strictly moral man acts with severe limitations in a world often without standards, and that he can survive and retain his moral standards and individual ethics only by taking shelter in the social conventions based on experience and wisdom. This whole attitude reflects her deep concern for absolute and relative truth, and absolute and relative conduct. For these reasons she had high regard for the social and ethical rules built up over long periods of time. Once trapped, the ethical man must suffer the penalty of his original action. He cannot remain moral by renouncing his ethics; his recourse is forbearance and discipline in his situation. Thus Frome, trapped into marriage with Zeena because of his gratitude to her for nursing his dying mother, must nonetheless accept his situation in the proper ethical context.

Frome's starved emotional life is set forth with bleak terseness. The girl Mattie is everything his wife is not. "She had an eye to see and an ear to hear: he could show her things and tell her things, and taste the bliss of feeling that all he imparted left long reverberations and echoes he could wake at will." [21] His true tragedy is his lack of communion, his failure to integrate his life with his surroundings. Yet he is faced with no real alternative to his dilemma; having chosen his path and having made his initial mistake, honor and morality require that he continue his relationship with his wife. His sacrifices have meant nothing to her, and there is no hope of redeeming her parched consciousness. Yet he shrinks from borrowing money under false pretenses to escape with Mattie; he cannot deceive his neighbors and violate his moral standards, even to escape. If he cannot leave as a man, he cannot leave at all. His final impulsive act, the disastrous sleigh ride with Mattie, which terribly injures them both and condemns them to a twisted life with Zeena, only plunges Frome deeper into his situation.

It is the same in Mrs. Wharton's other works. Character after character is faced with the dilemma of escaping his unhappy situation by unethical means or of remaining in his situation to avoid deceit and causing unhappiness for others. However cruel the alternatives, Mrs. Wharton's standards forbade any action which injured others. "I couldn't have my happiness made out of a wrong—a wrong to someone else," [22] a character protests in *The Age of Innocence*. "How young she is!" Archer muses in the same novel, watching his beautiful but uncomprehending wife, wondering how he can tell her that he loves another woman. "For what endless years this life will have to go on!" [23] Yet it must go on, for the alternatives encompass more than breakage of the marriage vows. The fault lay in the original impulsive act; another impulsive act will not remedy it. The individual trapped in unhappiness, without opportunities for understanding and communion, must realize that "certain renunciations might enrich where possession would have left a desert." [24]

Thus the ultimate moral test of any act is its effect on other people. Mrs. Wharton noted with a touch of sadness that "the bounds of a personality are not reproducible by a sharp black line, but . . . each of us flows imperceptibly into adjacent people and things." [25] Actions, like ripples on a pond, move ever outward in widening rings, exerting influence on people far removed from their causes. To violate these people, who are innocent of the original wrong, is unethical. Mrs. Wharton's view of life was such that she could hardly conclude otherwise. Like the hero of *The Valley of Decision*, she might have said: "He saw life as it was, an incomplete and shabby business, a patchwork of torn and ravelled effort." [26] In her own experience she had found that "life isn't a matter of abstract principles, but a succession of pitiful compromises with fate, of concessions to old tradition, old beliefs, old charities and frailties." [27]

To illuminate and define this quality of life was the major purpose of her fiction, for "the greatest novels have undoubtedly dealt with character and manners rather than with mere situation." [28] How much of this attitude is traceable to her own unhappy marriage, which ended in divorce in 1913, cannot be said, but it is likely that it ran far deeper than her personal life. At any rate, it became the central theme in her writing. "A good subject, then, must contain in itself something that sheds a light on our moral experience," she wrote, and her only criticism of Marcel Proust was that he lacked "the moral sensibility, that tuning fork of the novelist's art." [29]

Her morality and conception of ethical conduct reflected a profoundly conservative view of humanity. Not given to abstract thinking or formal academic logic, she developed no systematic philosophy except as it arose from her work, yet her bent by nature and training was toward a dark view of human nature. Because she believed that man needed restraint in his conduct and that such restraint produced civilized life, she valued the forms of control devised by society over centuries of growth. "Things are not always and everywhere well with the world, and each man has to find it out as he grows up," she wrote as the First World War was shattering her own ideals. "It is the finding out that makes him grow, and until he has faced the fact and digested the lesson he is not grown up—he is still in the nursery." [30] Manners, customs, represented the sum of a culture's development, and were as much symbols of growth as cathedrals and art works. They contained within themselves as much residue of human action as works of art. They not only provided stability in the social order, they were the mirror of the order's growth. They were also important as reflections of a deeper attitude in her, a profound respect for humanism, individualism, and social responsibility. Mrs. Wharton may have felt pessimistic about the human nature she saw around her, but her stoical humanism led her to prize the arts and culture that man had created in his long struggle away from animality. It is foolish and inaccurate to think of her as a snob, or to see in her personal pessimism any repudiation of human values and human works.

It was all very well to be an individual—none fought harder for it than she—but the individual was responsible to other individuals, and they in turn made up society. The question of responsibility to one's fellow men was always uppermost in her mind. "How mixed our passions are, and how elastic must be the word that would cover any one of them!" [31] She saw society as a thing of evolution, produced by centuries of slow development, change, counterchange; its values were not to be hazarded in a momentary desire to be rid of its faults. To be effective, change must come slowly, for "one stone rashly loosened from the laboriously erected bulwark of human society may produce remote fissures in that clumsy fabric." [32]

She met assertions of the goodness of human nature with an indulgent smile. She believed in the new, but it must exist with the old, blending into the larger fabric of society. The new was not progress if it violated the old. "Only children think that one can make a garden with flowers broken from the plant; only inexperience imagines that novelty is always synonymous with improvement." [33] She had watched her fellows too closely to succumb easily to doctrines of progress. She saw, like one of her characters, that "human relations [were] a tangled and deep-rooted growth, a dark forest through which the idealist cannot cut his straight path without hearing at each strike the cry of the severed branch: *'Why woundest thou me?'*" [34]

In two of her novels she dealt with reform of the social structure, *The Valley of Decision*, set in eighteenth-century Italy, and *The Fruit of the Tree*, set during the progressive movement at the beginning of the twentieth century in the United States. In neither was her conclusion sanguine. Reform was at best a mixed blessing, and controlling human passions was always a hard struggle. The dark side of human nature was submerged in the shadows of social convention and social restraint; man removed or altered them at his own risk. Men, if not evil, were at least weak; society protected them by exercising restraint. In her catalogue of Odo's struggles to enlighten his people in *The Valley of Decision*, Mrs. Wharton's sympathy was obviously with both the enlightened Prince and the downtrodden people he tried to raise, but her chief concern was the obstacles to his success. In the end, Odo's triumph was a thing of ashes, and he was left in ill health and with shattered ideals to muse on the enormity of the task he had set himself. Was the freedom worth the price, he asked:

For generations, for centuries, man had fought on; crying for liberty, dreaming it was won, waking to find himself the slave of the new forces he had generated, burning and being burned for the same beliefs under different guises, calling his instincts ideas and his ideas revelations; destroying, rebuilding, falling, rising, mending broken weapons, championing extinct illusions, mistaking his failures for achievements and planting his flag on the ramparts as they fell.[35]

This long view of the complexities of human society and the slight chance of transforming or improving it with hasty political or intellectual changes produced in her a jaundiced view of reformers. She was concerned with the world as it is, not as it might be. She trusted what she wished to believe. Hers was a classic conservatism.

Yet her view was more complex than simple conservatism. She is not easily classed with mechanistic thinkers and organic philosophers. In a sense, her view was a compound of both these, yet older than either. Just as her views on art sprang from an all-encompassing classicism, so did her view of man and society. There is a flavor of profound tragedy in all her work, a belief that man is the victim of circumstances in life not entirely of his own making and beyond his control; that life consists of giving hostages to the circumstances, while stoically accepting the burdens thrust upon mankind. But all of this is also tempered by a respect for man's individuality, a half-hidden hope that he will triumph in the end, and a deep respect for the growing tradition of beauty and intelligence which marks man's progress. "Life is the saddest thing there is, next to death," [36] she wrote at the end of her life. The pessimism that was intensified by her old age was present in all her work. Of all modern major American writers, her view of mankind is perhaps the darkest.

For all these reasons she rested her belief in the possibility of goodness and beauty not in social panaceas but in orderly development along historic lines. "The instinct to preserve that which has been slow and difficult in the making, that into which the long associations of the past are woven is a more constant element of progress than the Huguenot's idol-breaking hammer," [37] she wrote of the French, whom she greatly admired. With all its faults, an orderly society based on slow change and founded on time-tested principles afforded individuals something more priceless than quick reform and change. It gave them the "sense of being, not straws on a blind wind of chance, but units in an ordered force." [38] The fatal flaw in Undine Spragg of *The Custom of the Country*, the vile heroine who was the epitome of everything Mrs. Wharton hated, was her complete lack of roots, her failure to identify herself with anything beyond personal desire. Married at last to a French nobleman, she fails to understand his attachment to his family, his home, the art works that beautify his surroundings. They mean nothing to her except in terms of cash value, and she never understands that to a settled culture such as that of prewar France, Family and Tradition were sacred things because they provided unity and security.[39]

It came in the end to a question of responsibility; everyone's standards were at stake so no one person merited special consideration. Human frailty was such that society as constituted by time and change covered a multitude of sins and had evolved, like some intricate animal, to fulfill many conflicting purposes without destroying itself. As she saw life, so she saw her art. "Fashions in the arts come and go, and it is of little interest to try to analyze the work of any artist who does not give one the sense of being in some sort above them." [40] She herself had no desire to be "new" in an age that wanted newness more than anything else. Her dictum on Proust, that he was great because he was a renovator not an innovator, was her own standard.

Her search for this living tradition and the sense of continuity with the historical past led her in time to Europe, like that other celebrated pilgrim, her close friend Henry James. In 1907 she moved to Paris and remained in France until her death thirty years later, returning to the United States but once, in 1923, to receive an honorary degree from Yale. Was she then not American in her orientation? If familiarity with America is the criterion the answer must be no. Far less than James did she understand the culture of her native land. In fact, she knew little of the art or thought of the United States, and while she traveled the breadth and width of Europe, she never toured her own country. Buffalo, New York, was the beginning of the West to her, as to many other Easterners in her day, and the West was still populated by

Indians and heathens. Some innate fear of what lay beyond the Hudson kept her in New York and ultimately sent her in the opposite direction to Europe. Yet she was basically American in reflecting the changes that assaulted her society and in dealing with the American scene. Exile, to her as to James, did not mean ostracism; it was still voluntary.

The reasons for her sojourn abroad lie deeper than any temperamental dislike for her American surroundings. Her exodus rested on the conviction that her country was not unique, that it had not produced an art or culture that differed from the larger Western tradition on which it drew. To trace the roots of the older Western European civilization was more interesting to her. She enjoyed the cosmopolitan atmosphere of Paris and London society. Having traveled extensively, she was not satisfied with the narrow world of New York, or even of what she supposed to be the United States. In time she found in France what she missed in America: a civilization based on continuity rather than change, and a way of life attuned to slow assimilation rather than rapid accumulation. The settled Gallic pace and view of life appealed more to her than the hurry and change of the New World.

Yet she was not unaware of her country's development, and its lost potential always disturbed her. "It seems stupid to have discovered America only to make it into a copy of another country . . . Do you suppose Christopher Columbus would have taken all that trouble just to go to the Opera with the Selfridge Merrys?" [41] asked the Countess Olenska in *The Age of Innocence*. In France, Mrs. Wharton found the genteel conversation—epitomized by the *salon*—the respect for the arts, and the arts themselves which she never found in her own country. Yet the shadow of what America might have been lurked in the back of her mind: "The fact is that she could neither do with contemporary America nor do without it; she could neither forget nor forgive it; and as I don't think she had ever analysed or even stated the problem, her conscience was uneasy and her tongue sometimes bitter," [42] a contemporary remembered.

While in France, the World War burst upon her with overwhelming force, threatening to engulf everything she held dear. She rallied to the defense of her ideals and France with unusual zeal. She had never been interested in charity or philanthropy, two recognized outlets for ambitious or nervous ladies in her social milieu, but with so much in the balance she did not hesitate to plunge into volunteer hospital work, the Red Cross service, and other charitable labor. She raised funds, wrote books, made speeches, and even toured the front under the watchful eyes of powerful friends. To her the war was a conflict of ideals, the clash of alien and friendly civilizations. From her proximity to the struggle she perceived depths of meaning that escaped others. The threat to the whole culture which she prized had never been greater. France was France, but she was also an ideal, the symbol of everything Edith Wharton meant to save.

Her extensive work brought decorations from the French and Belgian governments. Her part in the struggle allied her even more closely to the ideals for which she fought, and she emerged from the ordeal more convinced than ever that man bore watching and could not be trusted when uncontrolled. If the war itself was tragic for her, that which followed was equally so. The standards loosened by the conflict now toppled one by one under the waves of the "new" postwar ideals. The passing of the old social conventions bewildered her, but the influx of the new and formless in the arts left her even more bitter. She never tired of attacking the "laborious monuments of schoolboy pornography" [43] which she felt constituted the sum of the new art. Both public and artists violated the canons of taste which she felt were fundamental to valid creativity. "The new novelists will learn that it is even more necessary to see life steadily than to recount it whole; and by that time a more thoughtful public may be ripe for the enjoyment of a riper art." [44]

Her world, like that of Willa Cather, broke in two after the war. "The world since 1914 has been like a house on fire. All the lodgers are on the stairs, in dishabille." [45] Given this attitude and her demand for a return to the classic molds of art, it is curious that she violated her own principles by descending into bad writing. Most of her postwar books do not show the marks of the careful revision and painstaking labor which she lavished on her early work. At their worst they seemed to emanate from some elegant factory. She seemed to lose her balance in her assaults on the new art and the new social order. The measure of the blows which the passing of the prewar culture dealt her is found in this failure of composure, in her almost frantic disavowal of everything new. It was as though she decided to show how bad the new standards were by showing what they had done to her writing.

Moreover, her attitude blinded her to the splendid opportunities for her pen during these years, for the play of social forces had never been starker. The same forces were at work in the 1920's as in the 1890's, tearing down and building up the social fabric; the danger was fully as great, the challenge quite as near, and it is curious that she ignored it. Perhaps she was tired, perhaps she did not care, or perhaps more truthfully the world of her old age was simply too alien for her to study. Yet, her posthumously published unfinished novel, *The Buccaneers* (1939), shows that her powers had not so much failed as they had been misapplied, for it rose at times to her old standards, illustrating that despite old age and bitterness she was still able to penetrate beyond the immediate in her quest for the eternal. The promise of further work was never fulfilled, for death ended her long career in 1937.

It is not easy to assess Edith Wharton's accomplishment, for her career, while long and varied, was peculiarly private. Much of her personal life and its relation to her work will doubtless remain hidden. She was not given to reminiscence, even among friends. Her life was too ceremonial, too enclosed in the armor of personal convention, too regulated by her awareness of her position to permit easy access to the heart of the fortress. It is surprising that she accomplished as much as she did, given the demands made upon her. "For me the wonder was that within this armature of her exacting taste she could pursue a literary task so remote from her daily life amongst us," [46] a friend recalled.

Undoubtedly her prewar novels were among the best of their kind produced by an American, and few writers matched the ability with which she delineated the stresses and strains under which her world labored with the impact of new ideas and alien forces. Her world was breaking down under the strain of new customs and manners, new ideas in the sciences and arts, new kinds of manners and intellect, and she mirrored the breakdown faithfully in her work. Her demands for order were efforts to save the viable parts of the Genteel Tradition which she prized. In this she was as American as Howells and other literary critics who sought to do the same. Her orientation was classical and she aimed her assaults at the romantic attitude; her view of art, man, and life removed her from the ranks of the optimistic. In an age which held itself strictly accountable for human perfectibility, and in a culture which fed upon the idea, she propounded the opposite doctrine. On the surface her adherence to proven form and tradition marks her as old-fashioned, but her work carried in it the seeds of naturalism that flowered in other hands. The solidity of her work alone sets it apart from the taste of the turn of the century, which was too often satisfied with sentimental fiction and transient muckraking.

For all its proportions, however, the sum of her work illustrates the conflicts of vision which hampered her writing. She chose to write about America, but knew little about it. Seeking a fixed point from which to measure actions she chose manners, a choice made inevitable by her background and bent of mind. The tragedy was that it narrowed her vision, for in time she came to see nothing beyond manners. As her world slipped away from her, she clung persistently to past convention and dead ideas.

There was a point of tension in her work which she never resolved, resting in the last analysis on her own feelings of insecurity. She could not break with the old or build with the new; her heart may have remained to the end with the rebel and his new standards, but her head was with the past and the security of tradition. Thus she stood between two fires, unable to warm herself at either, cold to the last, taking final comfort in forbearance and discipline, a kind of personal stoicism.

To the modern reader the bulk of Edith Wharton's writing is decidedly out-of-date. It savors everywhere of dust. Not merely new literary styles but the passing of her ideals has relegated most of her work to obscurity. Her fascination with degrees of truth fails to interest a later generation. The social standards she upheld have long since passed. The questions she asked remain to challenge, but her answers appeal to few. If her work undergoes any appreciable revival it will be because men realize that she dealt with eternal problems, and that the crisis of her time in moral conduct and ethical values still goes on.

With all its disappointments and shortcomings, her life had been rewarding. Her work and friends sustained her. "I am born happy every morning," [47] she used to say, and the blue and gold of every day could awaken in her both memory and expectation. Clouded as her final days were, skeptical as she was of the future, she found the course worth running. "The world is a welter and has always been one; but though all the cranks and theorists cannot master the old floundering monster, or force it for long into any of their neat plans of adjustment, here and there a saint or a genius suddenly sends a little ray through the fog, and helps humanity stumble on, and perhaps up," [48] she said in her memoirs. In this, as in everything, she tempered her skepticism with discipline and belief and even, perhaps, a kind of hope.

Ellen Glasgow: The Qualities of Endurance

I have done the work I wished to do for the sake of that work alone. And I have come, at last, from the fleeting rebellion of youth into the steadfast—or is it merely the seasonable—accord without surrender of the unreconciled heart.

The Woman Within (1954)

FEW SOUTHERNERS would dispute the fact that their geographic section awards more palms to the sword than to the pen. The South's proud traditions include a literary heritage, yet public recognition has gone to men of action rather than men of artistic creativity. But all in all, the South has given many fine writers to the American tradition; some have spoken for cultural regionalism, others have transcended their section to speak of and for dominant and universal strains in humanity's existence. Of the Southern writers of the first generation of this century, few attained such prestige and recognition as "Miss Ellen," Ellen Glasgow of Richmond, Virginia. Through most of her adult life she was the reigning queen of Southern letters. Much of her fame rested on her success at both portraying the problems of the South and setting them against the larger context of human values.

"Born without a skin," Ellen Glasgow's colored mammy once said of her tiny charge. She was not far wrong, for the child did indeed seem to lack an elemental protective covering for her heightened sensitivity to the world around her. Sickly, too ill to attend public schools, torn by family misfortunes that were sharpened by her intense inwardness, prey to doubts and fears, she yet managed to survive and probe with her art the limits of experience as she knew it.

Born in the Virginia of 1874, she knew secondhand the glories of Southern culture at its height. Her mother had been a belle, once moderately wealthy, whose fortune vanished in the grim days of Reconstruction. The daughter inherited from her the gentleness, beauty, and interest in people which characterized the best of the old tradition. From her father she took little except in a negative way, for she hated the strict, unemotional religion which dominated him. While her father read Calvin, his daughter read Darwin and the new thinkers of the day, and concluded that their view of man was also hers. "I cannot accept a creed that divides man from the rest of creation," she wrote many years later. "Evolution was in my blood and bone long before I had ever read Darwin." [1] Acutely conscious of the chaos of life that pressed in upon all mankind, Miss Glasgow thus accepted a view of mankind that placed him within his natural context and thereby gave some unity to the life he wrought.

Such precocity as the young Miss Glasgow displayed was not popular in the Virginia of her day. Her earliest rebellion against established convention took the form of allegiance to women's suffrage and a vague species of socialism. She mingled with such writers, thinkers, and reformers as Richmond afforded, absorbing their ideas, trying her best to bring order out of confusion, seeking always some medium through which she might ease the burden of her sensitivity. The burden was increasingly with her as she matured, and the inner woman registered the painful struggles faced by the outer woman. "Always I have had to learn for myself, from within. . . . To teach one's self is to be forced to learn twice." [2] She was different from other people, and the realization of her estrangement from the world only forced her further in upon herself and made brighter the lights of inner consciousness. She acquired a "sense of loss, of exile in solitude, which I was to bear with me to the end," [3] and which marked all her work. Yet her inwardness was not an entirely unhappy burden, for it compensated in some measure for her lack of worldly experience. It gave her the means to create, for she viewed every incident, felt every emotion, tasted every sensation in her limited life with an intensity denied to others. She was deeply aware of the hidden meanings in the life around her.

As a child she had written stories and shown an interest in reading and writing, which her education happily furthered rather than retarded. She undertook an apprenticeship of wide reading and critical writing which she later recommended for all writers.

Hers was a curiously iron determination in one so young, the product of a culture and a section which had not always properly rewarded the fruits of the pen, and seldom when that pen was wielded by a lady. But the knowledge that her audience might not only be limited but hostile only spurred her on. "I shall not divide my power or risk my future reputation," she insisted. "I will become a great novelist or none at all." [4] She hungered for fame, recognition, a lasting monument, and honestly admitted that "I do want my work to be widely recognized." [5]

Though her philosophy of art and life developed during her long career, she formed its central purposes early and they never wavered. "Only as a form of art has fiction ever concerned me," [6] she remembered, and it was with this in mind that she attacked the problem. It was not difficult to find subject matter; it lay everywhere at hand in the South of her day, in the conflict of orders, the rise of a new culture, and the friction among personalities. She needed first an understanding of her purpose, for only thus could she mold her art. "What I wanted was an interpretation of life," [7] she wrote later. For this she must touch experience, and "for my own purpose, I defined the art of fiction as experience illuminated." [8] Thus her central purpose was to illuminate man, to attempt to understand his actions and the motives from which they sprang; from this she might find something enduring. "The chief end of the novel, as indeed of all literature, I felt was to increase our understanding of life and heighten our consciousness." [9] To this task she brought that sensitivity which in others less disciplined would have been the making of tragedy, but which in her case was the source of her art. In thus managing to overcome the potentially fatal weakness of ultrasensitivity through personal discipline, Miss Glasgow mustered the stamina and dedication which she must unwittingly have gained from her father's puritanism. If she failed in her art, she failed herself. "For truth to art became in the end simple fidelity to one's own inner vision." [10]

The young Miss Glasgow had already expressed doubts about the social order and intellectual climate in which she moved. The 1890's was hardly an auspicious time for a young rebel to tear up roots which had been planted and nourished by older and stronger hands. But the demands for self-assertion lay deep within her. If she was disturbed by the social order, the literature which her contemporaries read and wrote upset her even more. Little as she knew about life at first hand, her common sense and education told her that the literature of the *fin de siecle* revealed very little, and hid far more than it revealed. It was against these "sugared falsehoods about life" [11] that she mounted her first literary crusade in an effort to bring realism and validity to Southern letters. Asked what she felt the South needed most, she once answered in a flash that became famous: "Blood and irony!"—blood for a new fiction of realism and artistic dimensions, irony for a rejuvenation of the culture she prized. To these two needs she kept her faith. "But, I have always looked through a veil of irony even in the days when all fiction wore fancy dress. Those were the days when one fattened and waxed rich on illusions, yet I kept even then to the bare and sober reality." [12]

Her insistence upon literary realism in an age which fled from reality into sentiment was not without drawbacks. Her first novel, *The Descendant* (1897), was published anonymously and was taken for the work of Harold Frederic. It seemed harmless enough, but the realistic treatment of new social themes, no matter with what gentility of pen, made the author suspect. With the turn of the century, her style developed and she gained some recognition in literary circles. She decided to belong to no derivative school. Her mature style consisted of a wealth of detail held in a smooth, flexible flow of words, and it did not come without concentration and labor. She often worked hours for the correct word or structure. Having broken into print and made her intentions clear, she placed her developing art at the service of the emerging literature of realism and revolt which dominated American letters through much of her lifetime.

To the Southerners of her day the Civil War period was the watershed from which flowed all the social, cultural, and intellectual order. It was, needless to say, the dominant subject in Southern literature of the time, and Miss Glasgow could not avoid it, even had she so wished. In *The Battleground* (1902), she attacked the subject from a new angle. Instead of sweetening her message, she let it stand for what it was. She described the antebellum period in detail, her pen often dipped in subtle irony, revealing the stresses and strains, the hidden flaws and inconsistencies which had brought the old order crashing down. The book was a major work in her early career, not only because it realistically described the war, but because she touched upon the themes which were to occupy her the rest of her life.

In the book she debunked myths about the glory of battle. Every white charger vanished before her pen, and every romantic, becurled Southern hero was reduced to the rags and filth in which he had actually fought the war. Not that she denied that courage and personal valor had carried more than one day for the South in its lost crusade; indeed, her treatment heightened the meaning of valor by setting it in its true perspective. No one admired more than she the strength and courage which Southerners had shown, but she treated them as elemental rather than sentimental forces. For her the great tragedy of the war was not that the South had fought for a principle, but that "abstract principle became, not a religion, but a romantic passion." [13] Romance—that was always the South's weakness.

To dispel this aura of romance, she determined to treat realistically the problems of her day. Her treatment of the Negro was at best ambiguous, and she never shook the Southern belief that the Negro was unequal to the white. But she was not blind to the injustice of his position. For her the evil in slavery was its denial of the basic human qualities of self-assertion and endurance in the face of life. She enjoyed the rich, primitive, earthy qualities and gifts of personality which made the Negro unique.[14] Her serious treatment of the Negro, whatever its limitations, raised her work above that of her contemporaries.

Just as she realized the flaws in slavery and the injustice in the Negro's position, she perceived the evils in the economic and social system that succeeded the war. Tenantry and sharecropping appeared to her merely as other forms of servitude. In each case the elemental human qualities of man were denied free access to the surface of life where they could grapple with the qualities of existence. In *The Battleground*, she described the character bred by the mountaintop as well as the plantation house, and in *Pinetop*, the illiterate farmer who saved the lives and fought for the causes of the landed gentry, she sketched her belief in the qualities of courage, endurance, and self-sacrifice, whatever their social origin.[15]

Having stated her purpose, she prepared to write a larger social history of Virginia. The South of the late nineteenth century afforded examples for her pen, for the old order did indeed pass. The plantation house gave way to the factory as the symbol and source of economic and social ascendancy, and with it came new men, new means, new aims. "The smoke of factories was already succeeding the smoke of the battlefields, and out of a vanquished idealism the spirit of commercial materialism was born," [16] she wrote. Here in the battle between the old order and the new currents of materialism and expansion was a perfect field for her writing. In the long series of novels which occupied her until her death she defined the themes that formed the loom on which she wove the fabric of her art.

Having so vigorously attacked the accepted tradition of her day, it was curious that she rallied to the defense of tradition with the force she displayed in her mature work. She had scant sympathy for the spurious tradition resting on genealogy which justified itself by "the endless lip-worship of a single moment in history," and the veneration of "dead grandfathers" left her cold.[17] But she did not deny the values of historical tradition. "It was not that I disliked legend," she insisted. "On the contrary, I still believe that a heroic legend is the noblest creation of man. But I believe also that legend to be a blessing must be re-created not in funeral wreaths, but in a dynamic tradition, and in the living character of a race." [18] In effect, she told her readers that the South had called tradition something which was in fact a romantic legend. The source of that legend—the real courage and vital sense of creativity and personal responsibility that produced the original heroism—was the real tradition which she wished to uncover.

It was not to destroy heritage and tradition, but to revivify them that she studied Southern culture. She was no enemy of tradition. Indeed, her basic aim was to strip away the artificial veneer of mere manners and social form in order to restore the older, deeper, more meaningful traditions of the South. If tradition did not build, it was false. All her fictional characters succeed through personal sacrifice in building something durable and ordered from their lives; this is the kind of tradition she had in mind, something resting upon basic human values. Only thus could order, cultural continuity, and logical development be gained. Her quarrel was not so much with the past as with the uses to which it had been put. It offered nothing to the present but itself. What she wanted was life "rooted, not in a decaying tradition, but in nature and in simple goodness of life [as] the part of tradition that lives on, by adjustment, that does not repudiate the unknown and the untried." [19] From the loneliness and intensity of her own life, she defined the need for the "certainty of a continuing tradition," and the necessity of a "vein of iron [to] hold all the generations together." [20]

Tradition put to the wrong purpose was vicious and retarding, for it merely bolstered a useless past. In *The Romance of a Plain Man* (1909), she traced the rise and fall of a New Southerner, the lower-class man who rose by sheer will and ability in the New South of the Gilded Age. His successes in business and finance and his ability to marry the daughter of an old established family illustrated the changes overtaking the Southern social structure. In her heroine's mouth, Miss Glasgow placed the words of protest against false tradition that motivated her attack on it: "What do I care for a dead arm that fought for a dead king? Both are dust today, and I am alive. No, no, give me, not honor and loyalty that have been dead five hundred years, but truth and courage that I can turn to today,—not chivalric phrases that are mere empty sound, but honesty and a strong arm that I can lean on." [21] The tradition which she disliked was the one that denied to the individual the chance to show his mettle, to meet life to its face, to display the values and virtues which were as unique as he himself. "I stand or fall by my own worth and by that alone," [22] spoke one of her heroes in a phrase worthy of Miss Glasgow's highest intent.

How to fashion this heritage, this cultural continuity, these bonds between generations? Surely not through mere forms, or obeisance to dead grandfathers who were hallowed merely because they were grandfathers. The roots of tradition, to be alive, must probe deeper than that. The basic need, in her mind, was a continuity between generations resting on lasting emotions and needs which would tide men through times of crisis. This understanding and continuity might be attained by discovering the basic qualities of character that motivate each generation.

Miss Glasgow contended that these basic qualities were the same in all generations. Character flowed from within as well as from without, and by probing the inner consciousness, as she herself had done, one generation could find the ties that held it to the past and future. "But it is the interior world that contains the deeper verities and the sounder realities," [23] she wrote. The burden of making order from chaos was predominantly personal; character was individual, thus culture was individual. The compound of individuals produced a larger social order. This whole concept explains much of her painful personal stoicism.

Institutions could provide continuity and unity if they were tempered with modernity and fresh thought. "From the past, then, I should like, were it possible, to retrieve a few individual graces of culture, while I would, at any sacrifice, seek to preserve and develop the broader comprehensions of what we may call the modern point of view," [24] she wrote. It would be too simple to say that she wanted new wine in old bottles. Her basic aims were freedom of individual action and an openness of mind functioning within the framework of a living cultural tradition that gave perspective to action. An understanding of the constructive achievements of the past was necessary to every man if he was to understand his world and be whole.

For all her sincere effort Ellen Glasgow never quite discovered the mold for that tradition. She could never quite lose her respect for the old social order based on the First Families of Virginia, nor could she ever really adopt the code of the rising lower classes which was replacing the old cultural order in her day. Her rustic heroes and heroines are redeemed and rewarded not for their rural origins or even for their innate virtues but for their forbearance in the face of a cruel life. As her work progressed, Miss Glasgow translated her concept of individual resistance to evil into a general principle of renunciation of experience as such. In part, this was inevitable, given her origins and isolation from the main currents of life. But the failure also reflected a personal bias which she never abandoned. Her answer to the social crisis of her time became almost too personal, a kind of forceful stoicism, a denial of life and its rewards that, carried to its logical conclusion, would have denied the living tradition she sought.

Her search was further complicated by her reluctance to sacrifice her own public position. For all her protestations, she carried in her a streak of romance and often of sentimentality, most obvious in her memoirs, that sometimes kept her work from genuine realism. Her treatment of women characters, marriage, social customs, and personal actions often savored of the romance she condemned in others. Apparently there was a repressed side of her that not even her armor of convention could totally conceal.

Much of her feeling for heritage and continuity sprang from her respect for the earth, a respect firmly rooted in most Southern literature. It was not merely a belief in rustic virtues and the hardihood and freedom of country life. Rather, she believed that the earth, the land as tilled and loved, represented the elemental natural forces in life; that the land shaped the qualities of mind and character in man; that it was the ultimate source of many of the virtues she so highly prized. Her demand that man not be separated from nature defined her attitude toward the land. "At rare intervals in the lives of all vigorous souls there comes this sense of kinship with external things, this passionate recognition of the appeal of the dumb world." [25] This was true unity, continuity, the stage upon which the dramas of life might be accurately played. "When I realize how invigorating contact with the earth may sometimes be, I find myself wondering how humanity ever consented to come so far away from the jungle," [26] she wrote in 1919.

This love of the land was joined with her demand for individual perseverance and stoicism. The land endured; the man who trusted and used it placed his faith in its mystical possibilities of unity. Since it was real, it could help man endure. "The spirit of the land was flowing into her, and her own spirit, strengthened and refreshed, was flowing out again toward life," she wrote in *Barren Ground* (1925), of the heroine who renounced human love for the love of the land. "This was the permanent self, she knew. This was what remained to her after the years had taken their bloom. She would find happiness again. Not the happiness for which she had once longed, but the serenity of mind which is above the conflict of frustrated desires." [27] Defeated in the temporary personal demands of love, this heroine abandons them for Miss Glasgow's concept of deeper fulfillment, inner satisfaction with stoicism. "While the soil endured, while the seasons bloomed and dropped, while the ancient, beneficent ritual of sowing and reaping moved in the fields," she knew that she could never despair of the necessity of an orientation toward the basic human qualities symbolized by the land; that each person comes to realize that "the only destiny worth cherishing at heart was the one that drew its roots from the homely soil." [28]

This land consciousness runs through all her work and is at the core of her quest for personal character and the force that shapes that character. In writing about her early works, she admitted her own need for the things of the soil: ". . . I had known that I must return to the familiar earth in which I was rooted and to the earliest fibers of my identity, which reached far down into a past that was deeper and richer than conscious recollection." [29] Sherwood Anderson also loved the land and the richness and primitivism it symbolized, but there is little similarity between his and Miss Glasgow's attitude; he viewed the land as a *source* of virtue, she as a *repository* of virtue. Anderson's quest was for an earthy and vital primitivism fed by land consciousness and individual creativity; Miss Glasgow's search was for the endurance and permanency of things of the land to fortify individual fortitude in the face of life.

The land and the qualities which it engendered in successive generations molded that peculiar quality of "race" which Miss Glasgow admired. The term had little ethnic connotation for her, but rather defined the qualities of given strains of temper which passed through successive generations, creating unity and continuity. The land was elemental in this process: "Had not the land entered into their souls and shaped their moods into permanent or impermanent forms?" [30] she asked. Like a magnet, the earth attracted or repelled the qualities of men, for to her its force was mystic in its full ramifications. A man could be made or broken by the challenge of the land; it was the test of his inner self.

Though she wrote several novels set in the city none possesses the intensity of feeling radiated by her novels set in the country. She was never drawn to "the rootless poverty of the streets," and if she moved to the city in her work it was temporary. "The time was when I didn't think it so; but I know now that there's as much life out there in that old field as in the tightest-packed city street I ever saw—purer life, praise God, and sweeter to the taste," [31] a character said in *The Deliverance* (1904). Always she returned to the primal forces symbolized by the land, and to the belief that "the land thought and felt, that it possessed a secret personal life of its own." [32]

Ellen Glasgow centered her work on the problems of the South, but there were deeper currents in her fiction than flowed from geographic environment. Her determination to be a great artist, to produce lasting work, could not rest upon so narrow a base as the Southern background. Great art must have a great theme, and her theme developed with each successive novel. By the late 1920's and early 1930's, that theme had defined itself into forbearance, personal courage, individual character, the willing-ness to meet life no matter what it offered and to perceive unity, reacting to the challenge of environment—that was her theme. She portrayed in her novels and devised in her life the personal courage "that had never valued an effortless heaven." [33]

In her mind the fatal flaw in life was not evil, but weakness, the refusal to meet life, the refusal to assert individual courage no matter what the material cost. Every victory was a victory of the spirit, a triumph of the soul; to fail to meet the challenge was to fail in life, for every vital experience was an inward one and every victory stiffened the fiber of soul. "For it was not sin that was punished in this world or the next; it was failure." [34] By exercising this courage, whose roots she had sought in natural unity and heritage, one might not only strengthen the individual will, but might also transcend oneself and perceive the true dimen-sions of life and experience. Forbearance itself was the triumph of life. "Yet he was not defeated," she wrote of the old philosopher,

John Fincastle, in *Vein of Iron* (1935). "Life had given him the thing he had wanted most. He had had his moment of victory, and he could look serenely ahead beyond the vanishing point in the perspective." [35]

This was the central purpose of her fiction, for as she said: "What I tried to do was to look through human nature and human behavior, and discover the motives, or qualities of endurance, that have enabled mankind to survive in any order under the sun." [36] Just as she had to fashion a code of courageous personal conduct, so she had to light her fiction with the fire of belief, and that belief in the end was a demand that every man utilize his full potential in the struggle to exist and grow. Her own life was saddened by illness, an increasing deafness that turned her even further in upon herself, and personal disappointments that convinced her she would never find happiness, and which ultimately turned her to personal fortitude.

From these wellsprings she drew the inspiration and the constancy to move forward in the search for a pattern in life. Like the heroine of *The Miller of Old Church* (1911), she believed "that just this attitude of soul—this steadfast courage in the face of circumstances—was the thing that life was meant to teach them both at the end." [37] She could have written her own epitaph with the words she used to describe her heroine in *Barren Ground:* "She saw, as she had seen in the night, that life is never what one dreamed, that it is seldom what one desired; yet for the vital spirit and the eager mind, the future will always hold the search for buried treasure and the possibilities of high adventure." [38]

She painted a far from cheerful picture. Her personal experience led her to believe that all things ultimately fade and vanish at the touch, and that only individual will endures. As her art developed, so did her conviction that nothing which the world cherishes is permanent, that even the love for which she yearned was transitory. At its starkest, her view was arid. "Life makes us and breaks us. We don't make life," she wrote in *Barren Ground*. "The best we can do is bear it." [39] In moments of gloom and reflection she was given to think, "Behind the little destinies of men and women, I felt always that unconquerable vastness in which nothing is everything." [40] She had no refuge—certainly not religion, for her father's hard Calvinism had turned her from dogma. She studied Greek and Roman stoicism for a time, and oriental mysticism, but the circle always turned and she knew that systems were inadequate for her. "But, in the end, nothing outside myself has ever really helped me very much." [41]

Determinism was undoubtedly a major force in her fiction and her view of life, yet it somehow remains curiously tangential, acting outside the personal character which fascinated her. In the last analysis, it was the response to life rather than the determinism in life that intrigued her. "Maybe we are grasshoppers, she thought, and something bigger will tread us into the ground, and our time will be over," mused the heroine of *Vein of Iron*. "But even then, a voice added within, I shall have something true to remember." [42] That something true to remember, the will to conquer or at least to meet life, was the vein of iron for all the generations.

Not all her work bespoke this stern stoicism. The irony of which she had spoken was applied with great wit and deftness of touch in the comedies of manners which engaged her between heavier novels. In *The Romantic Comedians* (1926), *They Stooped to Folly* (1929), *The Sheltered Life* (1932), and other books, she showed her concern with the light as well as the dark. The same pen that portrayed the dark character also portrayed the light, and many readers spent cheerful hours over the follies and foibles her lighter vein described. Her comedies are permeated by the same desires and aims of her more philosophical books; their chief virtue, aside from character delineation, is the wit and candor with which they attacked the shibboleths and false idols that she assaulted with heavier weapons in other works.

Though she continued to live a life of comparative seclusion, by 1930 her reputation as a leading American novelist was established. She realized that her demands for the art of fiction seemed old-fashioned as America moved from peace to war to peace and prosperity. But if she was not a "fashionable" American novelist in her middle years, she was at least widely recognized for her substantial contributions to the novel form. She quarreled with the aims and methods of the younger novelist who seemed unable and unwilling to accept the formidable literary discipline which she herself had acquired in her youth. The sociological novel, parading as realism, had little attraction for her because she considered it a mere surface description of life, lacking the true realism given by inner reflection and experience. The fact that her novels seemed old-fashioned left her untroubled, for her aim was to write lasting work.

She had begun her quest by revolting against the established order of the day; now that that revolt seemed to have matured, and the things for which she fought had come to pass, she turned her attention ever inward in quest of things that seemed as alien to the generation of the 1920's as women's suffrage had seemed to the generation of the 1890's. She craved fame, yet she refused to sacrifice her ideals for the world's rewards. "I know, at least, that I would not write down to a sensation-loving public for any amount of financial recompense, but I do want my work to be widely recognized," she had said honestly in 1900. "But for all that my methods don't belong to this generation—though I mean to stick to them." [43] She might easily have said the same thing a generation later.

As she matured and moved through the developmental phases common to any artist, her art concerned her more and more, and she was moved in her efforts by the hope and belief that she could fashion literature that would become part of the heritage she cherished. She had no illusions about the American scene and the rewards which her country was likely to bestow upon her. Travel in England and Europe convinced her that recognition for the artist was easier there. She often complained of living and working "in a world that 'encourages mediocrity' and in a country that consistently preferred the amateur to the artist." [44]

But this only made her fight more rewarding, and her struggle for recognition did not cause her to abandon or repudiate her basic Americanism. "Because I have painted an actual scene, my novels are fundamentally American in conception. Whatever their failings may be, they cannot, with truth, be called either derivative or imitative." [45] She was quick to defend her title to broader fame, pointing out that despite her seeming regionalism, her themes were applicable to the human condition without regard to time and circumstance. "It is true that I have portrayed the Southern landscape, with which I am familiar, that I have tried to be accurate in detail, to achieve external verisimilitude; but this outward fidelity, though important, is not essential to my interpretation of life," she insisted. "The significance of my work, the quickening spirit would not have varied, I believe, had I been born anywhere else." [46] Believing as she did that men were basically the same, she felt that geography could not limit her discussion of the human soul and its triumphs in life. For her "the ordinary is simply the universal observed from the surface," and "the direct approach to reality is not without, but within." [47] It was this inner vision, the demands of the artist within her, which she felt lifted her work above its locale. "Never from my earliest blind gropings after truth in art and truth in life had I felt an impulse to write of a single locality or of regional characteristics." [48]

But for all her efforts to the contrary, she was essentially Southern. The bulk of her writing, while not derivative in a technical sense, breathes the peculiar spirit that pervades Southern literature. The qualities of regionalism which mark her work flowed not so much from geography as from the attitudes inspired by Southern culture and Southern life. Even as she attacked the veils of Southern culture that she thought obstructed her path, she expressed in her work a consistent and profound nostalgia for the old South. Veneration of the past, admiration of a more or less rigid social order, dislike of change not accompanied by compensating order, respect for the land and the Southern locale and its people—these were the elements which made her Southern in her outlook. Only in the final stages of her writing, after a generation of agonized progress away from Southern tradition did she cast off the tangled skeins of myth. Her best works, *Barren Ground, Vein of Iron, In This Our Life* (1941), show that under the proper stimulus she could indeed sketch those human attributes that were timeless.

The philosophy which emerged from her inward and outward struggle with life was a singularly demanding one. It was at once narrow and broad—narrow in the experience on which it rested, broad in the view of human life which it took. For her, life was always an inner process, the reaction of the conscience and personal will to given circumstances in the outer world. In one sense she observed life but did not live it. Thus she consistently denied the validity of experience except as a test of will and conscience. Life as such and as it was to others meant little to her; her aim was not to amass experiences but to know fully those which she examined behind the armor of fortitude that she increasingly built around her as the years passed.

This was at once the weakness and the strength of her life and work. It gave her the will and the means to endure, and even in her way to triumph over life as she knew it, but it also robbed her of the broader experience and wider view that would have enabled her to understand more of life and which would have added growth and vitality to her view. In denying the validity of experience as such, in a sense she denied the meaning of life. She examined life as she knew it, but the narrow confines of her existence, however inwardly intense, bound the limits of her vision. Her sum of experience was really not sufficient to temper her courage with hope, or, ironically, with deeper understanding. Her tragedy was her isolation, and she could never join herself to any lasting ideal except self-exploration. That self-exploration, as far as it went, was valid, but it had too narrow a base on which to build a vital philosophy.

Perhaps it was because she had always lived an inner existence that the tragedies of her declining years did not move her to the impassioned bitterness of her talented contemporary, Willa Cather. By that time she had forged her inner resolution, her outer protection against the world which enabled her to endure her solitude. She was fond of saying that she felt younger at sixty than she had at twenty, and neither in art nor life would she abandon the modern temper for a return to the comparative security of her youth. "Although I may like better many aspects of other periods, both in art and in the actuality, still, taken together, and allowing for the defects of its qualities, I should prefer unquestionably to live in the age we have with us," [49] she said even in the midst of the Second World War. "I could laugh at the end, because I had had my life," [50] she said candidly in her memoirs, and if that life had not been fully permeated by all outward experience, she knew at least that she had lived an inner life which if not happy had been rewarding and meaningful. Age held few fears, for "the old not only *know*, they have *been*." [51]

Her death in 1945 closed one of the most prolific and widely recognized Southern literary careers. She left behind a body of work, some of which is undoubtedly destined to withstand the test of time. There remains a surprising modernity about her best writing. In spite of a certain quaintness it does not seem a generation old.

Like Mrs. Wharton, Miss Glasgow based her view of life and the substance of her work on what she called tradition. Yet it differed from Mrs. Wharton's view in that Miss Glasgow never fully understood the changes with which she dealt. She was a rebel and championed the new, while never really accepting it. What she really favored was the new *attitude* rather than the new *thing*. On the one hand she favored the New South of industrialism, changed social attitudes, and new ideas. But on the other hand she did not fathom the full meanings of the changes that these new forces introduced. She could not wholly accept the new generation because it dealt in a coinage as debased as that of the old. The fault of her view was its lack of focus. Hoping to preserve the old ideals with new means, she did not see that those very ideals were doomed to destruction. Anxious to affirm the innate dignity of free thought and the importance of ideas, she could not bring herself to accept fully the rebellion of which she was considered a part. Her dilemma vividly illustrates Southern literature in the first generation of the twentieth century.

Narrow and demanding as her philosophy of life ultimately was, there is something infinitely admirable about the struggle which Ellen Glasgow made to understand her world. That so acutely sensitive and withdrawn a figure should yet plumb the depths, the lights, the shadows of her experiences and emotions and emerge the wiser for the quest; that she should have benefited from and understood so much more of life than many of her contemporaries who "lived" more is the measure of her artistry and personality. The object of her quest had been to discover the inner truths, the character, the motives that impelled men to action. She had tried not merely to understand but to test the fibers that formed the life of man. If her characters moved at times in bleakness, it was because life as she knew it was often bleak. Yet each, author and character, had rewards.

It is safe to say that Ellen Glasgow stood as true to the inward test as did any of the characters she created. Often despairing of attaining her goal, fearful of failure, shunning the world's pain yet intensely aware of it, it seemed at times that she might break under the strain. Yet she had the satisfaction of knowing at the end that she had withstood the test. "As you know, I am not sanguine about our destiny," she wrote toward the end of her life. ". . . But I believe in a gallant endeavor, whether or not we are ever to come into a finer inheritance." [52] In that gallant endeavor she succeeded, for it was her philosophy, the secret of her quest, her vein of iron.

Willa Cather: The Artist's Quest

> Life was so short that it meant nothing at all unless it were
> continually reinforced by something that endured; unless
> the shadows of individual existence came and went against
> a background that held together.
>
> *One of Ours* (1922)

WHEN WILLA CATHER was a little girl she often set herself too
big a task and when help was offered she cried out: "Self-alone,
self-alone!" [1] The remark illuminates her whole career, for she
early displayed a stubbornness and personal independence that
was reflected throughout her life and work, and which left enduring marks on everything she did. Her family were of hardy
stock, whose ancestry stretched back into American history. She
spent her early childhood in Virginia, where she was born in
1873, a product of a stable society with old traditions to which
she returned, characteristically, in her last novel.

Virginia, however, was not the environment that she remembered and which provided the substance and the setting for most
of her work. It was in Nebraska, to which her family moved in
1883, that Willa Cather acquired the fundamental attitudes and
ideas which she elaborated in her fiction. Many years later when
she was famous, she said that the "years from eight to fifteen
are the formative period in a writer's life, when he unconsciously
gathers basic material. He may acquire a great many interesting
and vivid impressions in his mature years but his thematic material
he acquires under fifteen years of age." [2]

The chief influences in her youth were frontier Nebraska and
its culture. As a child she displayed extraordinary interest in the
life and people around her, and seemed to realize the influence
which the country exercised upon her. Many of the vivid impressions, ideas, and much of her education came from the towns-
people and neighbors whom she observed. She stored up impressions and facts about them and years later they emerged as living

characters in the pages of her books after they had passed through the filter of her memory. She talked, watched, listened to, and observed them all. When a neighbor with a love of classical literature felt that his children were missing too much in the primitive frontier school, he introduced them and Willa to the Latin and Greek poets. His learning and desire to transmit it struck her as peculiar, almost heroic, and his image must have provoked her to say: "There are always dreamers on the frontier," [3] when she wrote her first major novel, *O Pioneers!* (1913). She possessed a remarkable ability to enlarge her experience with imagination, and thus perceived hidden meanings in the things around her. "From earliest childhood, everything in her life—books, people, places, her own thoughts—had taken the form of imaginative experience," [4] wrote her friend Edith Lewis. This quality of imaginative insight, coupled with a great ability to imbue everything with the touch of memory, characterized her work.

Red Cloud, Nebraska, was her home, sitting on the great frontier, a Western settlement in her day, pervaded with both the freedom and the narrowness that she used so deftly in her work, and which she observed so closely in her life. Her father was involved in both farming and business and managed to maintain good intellectual standards in his family. Known as a girl with unusual perception and interests, Willa Cather was determined to study, to learn more of the world's great art, and perhaps to contribute to that art herself. She stored up her hopes like her memories, looking always to the day when she could fulfill them. "To fulfill the dreams of one's youth; that is the best that can happen to a man," she wrote years later. "No worldly success can take the place of that." [5]

To fulfill those dreams she must study something more than the life around her; she must combine her curiosity with great literature, art, music—all of which she loved and which not only stimulated her art, but served as something enduring in a shifting world. To fulfill her promise she went to the state university at Lincoln, where she was both elated and depressed by the academic world. She found much in the university to reward and delight her, but she also encountered aridity and pedantry. Though she was interested in literature and the arts, it was from the artist's, not the scholar's viewpoint; she wished to perceive the meaning of a work of art through feeling rather than through analyzing it. Nothing depressed her more than the routine and lack of insight that characterized so much scholarly work, and she quickly realized that while it might be a means with her it could never be an end. Like Jim Burden in *My Antonia* (1918), "I was not deceived about myself; I knew that I should never be a scholar. I could never lose myself for long among impersonal things. Mental excitement was apt to send me with a rush back to my own naked land and the figures scattered upon it." [6] This feeling for people and the land was a good index to the vigor, personal strength, and vitality which she exuded even as a young woman.

Willa Cather worked hard at the university. In addition to a grueling routine of daily study she wrote reviews of plays and helped produce the university newspaper and annual yearbook. The hard times of the 1890's hit Nebraska and her family with full force while she was in college and she supplemented the family income with her meager earnings. "Life is one damned grind, Cather," [7] an English instructor once told her in a moment of candor that she must have remembered as she moved through the long apprenticeship that preceded her literary career.

All the while she continued to gather and store up impressions of the life around her, influenced at every turn by the mixture of good and bad, heroism and pettiness which abounded in her surroundings. She worked in Pittsburgh on a magazine, editing, producing copy, moving in a circle of friends, living a crowded life which she knew was not permanent. She went to Europe and recorded her impressions, noting how much certain aspects of the Old World reminded her of the New, furnishing evidence that much of life was everywhere the same, leading her nearer the sources of stability and enduring values. Always she returned to the frontier environment which she could never entirely leave, and slowly her impressions, beliefs, and ideals gathered around the pole of her emerging art. She taught school in a classical curriculum and published her first books, a selection of verse, *April Twilights* (1903), and a collection of short stories, *The Troll Garden* (1905).

The publication of her poetry and short stories did not attract a great deal of attention but did lead to an editorial job on the magazine staff of the brilliant but erratic S. S. McClure. She was an excellent editor, for she impressed her own exacting standards on the people around her. Although she did not feel that editing, however constructive, could be her life's work, she profited from her years in magazine work. Between 1905 and 1912 she met a variety of people, traveled widely, and turned her hand at many kinds of writing. S. S. McClure could be generous and understanding as well as irritating and he recognized in Willa Cather a person of high qualities and great potential. When she left her position in 1912, verging on forty and having come at last to the end of her long apprenticeship, she went with his blessing and they remained friends until parted by death.

Once independent, determined to nurse her art into its full potential, Willa Cather traveled, but always had a home, the Nebraska frontier of her memory and artistic imagination. By the time she set to work in earnest, her memory was crowded with characters, events, ideas, and impressions enough for any major writer. Hers was the gift and the genius to exploit this memory to the fullest. Though she had written *Alexander's Bridge*, a minor novel, in 1912, she published no important work until her final decision to be a writer gave her the time and means to concentrate on her art.

She came to the task equipped by fact and inspiration gained from wide reading as well as close observation and formal education. Her earliest models in the novel were the works of Henry James and Edith Wharton, from both of whom she quickly turned. She came to prefer instead *The Scarlet Letter* and *Huckleberry Finn*, two books which she thought truly great.[8] Later she developed her own theory of the novel, the *nouvelle démeublé*. In reality she was less influenced by other novelists than by her surroundings and the qualities of her personal genius. Though she produced fine short stories, the novel was her medium, and she felt that through it, more than any other literary form, could the artist express his feelings. It was said of Stephen Crane that he wrote of a thing and then lived it. It can be said with better truth of Willa Cather that she lived a thing and then wrote of it. Nearly everyone and everything of importance that she remembered found a place in her work.

Art was the supreme demand of her life and she turned her whole being to it. Early in her career, long before she had begun her great works, she wrote: "The further the world advances the more it becomes evident that an author's only safe course is to cling to the skirts of his art, forsaking all others, and keep unto her as long as they two shall live." [9] She chose the novel as her form because of its freedom and artistic possibilities, and she always deprecated those who used it as a platform for reporting or propagandizing. "If the novel is a form of imaginative art, it cannot be at the same time a vivid and brilliant form of journalism. Out of the teeming, gleaming stream of the present it must select the eternal material of art." [10] This sense of craftsmanship, resting on the whole tradition of humanistic art, made her work technically outstanding and rapidly gained her an audience that has persisted long after her death. Her quest for the permanent and enduring meanings in life, described with this technical ability and humanistic outlook, make much of her work great.

She sought eternal material all her life, for caught in the midst of a changing world she was determined above all else to find stability. Failing to find it in the world around her, she hoped to build it in her art. It was a challenge which she had to meet to retain her integrity, and though in later years she seemed to turn from the world rather than face it, her work is an enduring monument to that quest. Art as such was sacred to her, for the inspiration that produced it never changed and was found in all times and circumstances where man had risen above the animal. Art was the testament of humanity. "The major arts (poetry, painting, architecture, sculpture, music) have a pedigree all their own," she wrote. "They did not come into being as a means of increasing the game supply or promoting tribal security. They sprang from an unaccountable predilection of the one unaccountable thing in man." [11] And whatever its form, the substance of art was always the same: "One is bumped up smartly against the truth, old enough but always new, that in novels, as in poetry, the facts are nothing, the feeling is everything." [12] Art was crucial to her because it stood unchallenged and enduring. In all the world of change and chance the monuments of art alone stood as evidence of man's answers to the challenges that confronted him.

In later years, she combined art and religion and came to believe that they were the same—both were essentially spiritual, both were products of the individual mind, both were testaments of identification with life and of the individual's quest for truth and a form of salvation from animality through creativity. Indeed, she once defined art as "a refining of the sense of truthfulness." [13] The endurance of art is a basic theme in all her work; it formed for her the reason for life and gave stability where there was none. "Life was so short that it meant nothing at all unless it were continually reinforced by something that endured; unless the shadows of individual existence came and went against a background that held together," [14] she wrote in *One of Ours* (1922), at a time when that background seemed less stable than ever. She perceived that regardless of how much man's civilization changed, his basic needs and desires as reflected in his arts changed little. "Isn't it queer," Carl asks in *O Pioneers!*, "there are only two or three human stories, and they go on repeating themselves as fiercely as if they had never happened before; like the larks in this country, that have been singing the same five notes for thousands of years." [15] The Indians whom she first portrayed in *The Song of the Lark* (1915) had long since vanished, but significantly the relics of their passage, the evidences of their existence, were clay pottery and other art works. Here was the past in the present, all that could survive—the individual products of the imagination.

What sources could give life to the imagination, provide a fund of permanence and material upon which it could draw? For Willa Cather, the land symbolized that permanence, especially the land she knew best, the great West. She looked to that area because of the freedom it afforded the spirit, the scope which it gave to the imagination, and the timelessness and sense of endurance with which it imbued the sensitive onlooker. Yet her attitude toward the West was ambivalent in her early work. Not until she fused her feeling for the plains with her feeling for the Southwest and the vanished life it had nourished did she settle the dichotomy in her early work. She knew that the frontier could foster meanness as well as kindness, narrowness as well as freedom. She had not always loved her Nebraska environment. It was a life of ironies and contrasts and one has only to read her early short stories to realize how fully and how well she understood the limitations as well as the possibilities of frontier life. But the land itself became a personal thing to her; it had more than being—it had a life of its own. Regardless of its restrictions the West afforded more opportunity for personal development and artistic inspiration than any other place she knew. Whatever narrowness she found there came not so much from the land as from the people, who took much from it and returned little, who ruined its freedom with mental as well as actual fences.

Willa Cather looked upon the earth and nature as the personal, basic, primeval forces that sustained and enriched life and the creative force. "We come and go, but the land is always here," Alexandra muses in *O Pioneers!* "And the people who love it and understand it are the people who own it—for a little while." [16] The earth symbolized for her the enduring qualities which she so needed in her own life, and not to perceive these qualities robbed man of his basic inheritance. "To be a landless man was to be a wage-earner, a slave, all your life; to have nothing, to be nothing,"[17] she wrote in one of her best short stories, "Neighbour Rosicky." However great a man himself might be, his art, his being were unfulfilled if he lacked the continuity with life which came through contact with the earth. "He had missed the deepest of all companionships, a relationship with the earth itself, with a countryside and a people," she wrote of the famous singer in *Lucy Gayheart* (1935). "That relationship, he knew, cannot be gone after and found; it must be long and deliberate, unconscious. It must, indeed, be a way of living." [18] The identification of the individual with the land and all it symbolized was a primary form of the cultural and spiritual order and unity which she desired.

The pioneer, the builder, the doer and mover and shaker, the man of courage and will and integrity, is the central figure in Willa Cather's work. In him she found the perfect vehicle to express her admiration for the constructive qualities of creative individualism; in him she outlined the means whereby every man might make order in his life for himself, through building something creative. She returned time and time again to the earth, and Antaeus-like, she was made stronger by each journey.

The pioneer was doubly significant for her. Faced with a hostile environment, he conquered and imposed order upon it. Especially in her early works, the pioneer also tamed and enriched the land by bringing culture to it. She did not choose foreigners so often as heroes accidentally. The hardy Swedes, Bohemians, and Norwegians she dealt with in *O Pioneers!* and *My Antonia* came from an Old World rich with customs and cultural order to a New World lawless and uncultured, a thing of untamed beauty and strife. These pioneers not only conquered the land physically, they passed on their old ways of life, settled customs and culture, a sense of unity and order that enriched both the land and the new life it bred. The frontier also offered the immigrant one thing he had not had before—freedom of will, individualism, the chance to exercise his pioneer spirit.

Art, then, was Willa Cather's way of discovering the eternal. She has often been accused of loving the past for its own sake, but that is too simple a judgment. She loved nothing because it was old. That a thing had survived did not endear it to her, but if it showed evidence of travail and spiritual quest, she revered it. Thus she turned to the land, oldest and most enduring of forces, as a symbol of survival and birth, just as she turned to the Swedes, Bohemians, and Norwegians of the Nebraska plains, not only because she knew them, but because they transmitted in their persons customs, feelings, ways of life that stretched beyond any man's memory. "There was nothing of the antiquarian in her," Edith Lewis noted; "she did not care for old things because they were old or curious or rare—she cared for them only as they expressed the human spirit and the human lot on earth." [19] Late in life, Willa Cather was certainly guilty of nostalgia, of wishing fervently to return to a past that doubtless was far less beautiful than she remembered or imagined. "She never altogether lost the past in the present—and sometimes the beauty and stimulus of the new only heightened nostalgia and regret for the old," [20] this same friend remembered. And Willa Cather herself wrote: "Some memories are realities, and are better than anything that can ever happen to one again." [21]

In the great works of her mature years, before her vision was narrowed by her distaste for all that was modern, the best sense of the past—"the precious, the incommunicable past"—was in all her work. Yet it was no mere flight from reality or evasion of responsibility. She was willing to face the new world's problems, but she preferred to do so with the tools, ideas, and inspirations that had proved themselves by withstanding time. What she sought was not so much the past itself, but the order, stability, and continuity which were linked in her mind to a respect for the poet's great works and thoughts.

The idea of timelessness often led her to minimize the present and to view it as one facet of an incalculably long span of history; thus, its works, however great they might seem in the present, were in reality of little or no relevance unless they were linked to the heritage that produced them. Experimentation was dangerous if it denied orderly development and continuity. Actions were unimportant for her unless they reflected something enduring. "The world is little, people are little, human life is little," old Wunsch tells Thea in *The Song of the Lark*. "There is only one big thing—desire. And before it, when it is big, all else is little." [22]

The spacious settings of her work and the vision of her world in general lend themselves to the ideas of chance and fate as controlling forces in human life. A thread of determinism runs through her work, a belief that "fortunate accidents will always happen," [23] and that the wise man seizes upon those accidents as means of his development. Feelings such as these often made her think of fate and may have plunged her into those moods of melancholy that increased over the years. Her best friend noted that "there was in her also a deep strain of melancholy. It did not often emerge. Perhaps it even gave intensity to her delight in things—this sense that human destiny was ultimately, and necessarily, tragic." [24]

Yet feelings of fate and chance worked as subtle undercurrents, not dominant themes, in her great work, and she never felt that man was helpless before fate or evil in his intent. Her belief in individual creativity and potential counteracted any inclinations toward mechanism. Her interest lay not in fate or chance, but in the act that overcame them as an expression of individualism. That was why she wrote of pioneers; theirs was the personal character, integrity, and humanity that met and mastered challenges. Individual creativity and artistic perception could work that strange alchemy that transformed potential wrong into right, the transitory into the permanent. Like a character in *O Pioneers!*, she felt in the end that "good was, after all, stronger than evil, and that good was possible to men." [25]

As an artist concerned with the durable materials of art, Willa Cather cared little for the great social and political issues of her day. Her service with S. S. McClure had given her a surfeit of reformers. She joined no crusades, lent her name to no movements, partook of no efforts to reform the world outside of her art. She refused to do so precisely because she believed that reformers lacked insight into the human process which alone could make their efforts successful. Their usual insistence that economic security would solve the problems of the day struck her as terribly shortsighted, and in the end seemed only to threaten the individualism which produced and appreciated great art.

The production of art, the exploration of the human mind and emotions, and the magnification of the human spirit through art were to her the means of bettering mankind. That art to Willa Cather consisted of more than artifacts; it was, in fact, a kind of love, a feeling of spirit that tied the artist and his audience together, that gave them common bonds for common things, that in short produced unity and order from the world's disorder. She cared little for man in the mass, though she was perpetually curious about the people around her. She was interested in particular men. This indifference to the mass was neither blind nor cruel; it sprang from her belief that men were worthy of individual consideration. She had great respect for civilization, provided it had produced something enduring. "Wherever humanity has made that hardest of all starts and lifted itself out of mere brutality, is a sacred spot," [26] the priest said of the Mesa civilization in *The Professor's House* (1925).

All of her life Willa Cather fought against the inroads which her era made into individualism. Nothing was possible if the individual mind were not free. It must be its own frontier. She often carried this idea too far, and her own strong will hampered her vision late in life; her refusal to compromise too often resulted in mere escape. But the principle behind her belief operated everywhere in her fiction, culminating in her last novel, *Sapphira and the Slave Girl* (1940), one of whose themes is the necessity of freedom. Believing as she did that security against the world provoked no challenge of individual response, it is not to be wondered that she hated the New Deal and the growing statism of her old age. "To be assured, at his age, of three meals a day and plenty of sleep, was like being assured of a decent burial," she wrote in *One of Ours*. "Safety, security; if you followed that reasoning out, then the unborn, those who would never be born, were the safest of all; nothing could ever happen to them." [27]

By the advent of the First World War, Willa Cather had produced some of her best work and had attained recognition for *O Pioneers!*, *The Song of the Lark*, and *My Antonia* along with her earlier works. Perhaps it is impossible for current generations attuned to tension, to understand the crushing impact which the World War had on the values and personal lives of the generation of the Edwardian Era. The settled society, personal security, freedom, and lack of entangling obligations which that era took for granted were swept away in one sudden and devastating blow. A whole way of life vanished with incredible swiftness and horror to the generation which had built a world of peace and which had assumed that its safety would never again be threatened.

For Willa Cather, the conflict had deeper meanings: it brought into question her belief in the superior man, the pioneering hero who was able to conquer his surroundings and impose his will and artistic culture on life. The idea that the superior man could control life rather than have it control him was badly shaken. Suddenly the war put in focus all the disquieting tendencies in life which she had observed for years. The world, the very mental order to which she had attached such importance, was lost in the crisis. Never given to compromise, she steadily retreated rather than face the new order which replaced the old. Henceforth, her work became increasingly introspective, torn between the desire to meet the new and a hardening belief that greatness lay in the past, not the future. The old conflicts which she had thought settled—the nature of man, the possibilities of individualism, city versus country, the artist versus the world— now rose again in more threatening forms.

The postwar generation brought new concepts to literature and art, and brought to fruition the ideas of naturalism and realism that had been developing during the prewar period. The new artists seemed to care little for the classic works of the past which Willa Cather thought enduring and instructive. Their interest was in the new, and from the first she bitterly disliked their work. Her assault on the new lacked Mrs. Wharton's understanding that a whole cultural and social order was passing, but rested on the same belief that standards were being destroyed without being replaced. Never an experimentalist, she disliked both the new subject matter and form. "Just how did this change come about, one wonders," she asked with bewilderment. "When and where were the Arnolds overthrown and the Brownings devaluated? Was it at the Marne? At Versailles, when a new geography was being made on paper? Certainly the literary world which emerged from the war used a new coinage." [28]

Aside from what she considered their poor craftsmanship, her chief argument against the novelists of the 1920's was that their emphasis lay too much on problems of the present and not enough on the eternal problems that constituted great artistic themes. They looked for something new with which to solve new problems; she looked for something tested, durable, proved, with which to meet old problems. The promise of the new generation never matured for her. "They were to bring about a renaissance within a decade or so," she noted. "Failing in this, they made a career of destroying the past. The only new thing they offered us was contempt for the old." [29] The craft of the new novelists repelled her; they were mere cataloguers "accounting for everything, as trustees of an estate are supposed to do—thoroughly good business methods applied to art; 'doing' landscapes and interiors like houses—decorators, putting up the curtains and tacking down the carpets." [30]

But it seemed to her the assault on the old in art was not the only or perhaps even the major result of the war. It seemed as though her whole way of life, which had given some stability and purpose to her art, was doomed to vanish before the guns of the Marne and the Peace of Versailles. "The world broke in two in 1922 or thereabouts," she noted with considerable bitterness in the preface to a book of critical essays in 1936. "It is for the backward, and by one of their number, that these sketches were written." [31]

This postwar revolution in values had considerable impact on her art, but in large measure it merely completed the cycle of change that was perceptible in her earlier writing. In her bewilderment in the 1920's she turned the circle, returning to the basic ideas and themes that had occupied her from the first. The war prompted her to write *One of Ours*, which won a Pulitzer Prize in 1922. But that book was basically not a war story so much as a story about the war, whose themes ran far deeper than the surface to touch upon man's quest for order and security, the need for idealism, individualism, and art.

Several of the themes which she had developed in her early work attained new emphasis because of her uncertainty in the decade that followed the war. Her distrust of and distaste for the new social and intellectual order took the form of increased suspicion of three forces which the revolution in values augmented: science, the machine, and the city.

To Miss Cather, science was never speculative but utilitarian. In this she betrayed her nineteenth-century attitudes which thought of science as inventive and technological rather than philosophical. For her, science had less to do with theory than with practice. Science, therefore, meant mass production. The real horror of the scientific and mechanical revolution was its impersonality: once established, the machine was really beyond man's control. Science knew no limits in its assault on humanism.

Her skeptical attitude toward science rested on a fear that the scientific process did not test that which was durable, but destroyed it for the new. In her deeply introspective novel, *The Professor's House*, written when the rising emphasis on science concerned her, the Professor spoke for the author when he said: "I don't myself think much of science as a phase of human development. It has given us a lot of ingenious toys; they take our attention away from the real problems, of course, and since the problems are insoluble, I suppose we ought to be grateful for the distraction." Or should man be grateful for distraction?

But the fact is, the human mind, the individual mind, has always been made more interesting by dwelling on the old riddles, even if it makes nothing new of them. Science hasn't given us any new amazements, except of the superficial kind we get from witnessing dexterity and sleight-of-hand. It hasn't given us any richer pleasures, as the Renaissance did, nor any new sins—not one! Indeed, it takes our good old ones away. It's the laboratory, not the Lamb of God, that taketh away the sins of the world. . . . I don't think you help people by making their conduct of no importance—you impoverish them. . . . Art and religion (they are the same thing, in the end of course) have given man the only happiness he has ever had.[32]

To the Professor and to Willa Cather, science had done nothing positive beyond "making us very comfortable."

The Professor's two houses, the old and the new, which form the basis of the novel's plot, symbolize the two orders, old and new, between which Willa Cather and her generation were torn. If art and religion were indeed the same thing—the exploration and development of the individual mind, the creation of great art, the linking of one man to many and to the past and present through individual insight—then they were indeed threatened by the scientific revolution. To the end she refused to accept the "advances" of science on the grounds that they were products of the mind alone, not of the heart and spirit as well. In this, as in so many things, there was no compromise for Willa Cather.

The product of science which she disliked most was the machine, and her suspicion of its force and potential in her early works hardened later into a refusal to accept it as anything but disastrous. She feared the machine because it threatened her heroic pioneer; if man could not control machinery, and there was evidence to her that he could not, the machine would then control him, depersonalizing his world and closing man's frontiers of knowledge and the spirit. The machine also made life easier, thereby removing challenges that would bring greater responses from man. It produced things also, thus curbing man's opportunities for creativity and individual expression.

The generation that emerged from World War I was machine-ruled. In *One of Ours*, she deftly set Claude Wheeler and his values against those of his brother. While Claude embodied the virtues of the frontier—individualism, freedom, endurance, continuity—his brother was machinebound, narrow-minded, money-oriented, and unaware of the natural beauty and human potential around him. Watching him and others like him made Claude aware of the peculiarly unhuman qualities of machinery. "Machines, Claude decided, could not make pleasure, whatever else they could do." [33] The "mechanical gear" of the postwar world directed "every moment of modern life toward accuracy," [34] and left nothing to individual challenge and chance discovery. "The generation now in the driver's seat hates to make anything, wants to live and die in an automobile, scudding past those acres where the old men used to follow the long corn rows up and down," she wrote in 1923. "They want to buy everything ready-made: clothes, food, education, music, pleasure." [35] Hart Crane and Sherwood Anderson might devise a hopeful role for the machine in modern life, but not Willa Cather.

Her demands for order, art, and continuity seemed to fall on deaf ears in her later years, and she blamed that indifference in no small degree on the mechanical revolution of her time. "It is possible that machinery has finished us as far as this is concerned. Nobody stays at home any more; nobody makes anything beautiful anymore," [36] she said in a moment of the sad and often angry candor that more and more came to dominate her thinking.

The increasing emphasis on mechanization and science was met by an equal growth of city life. Willa Cather had always distrusted the city, and though her early attitudes toward town life were mixed, there was never any doubt of her belief in the rural virtues. While she admired many aspects of city life—the cultural advantages, the sense of life, the nearness of human potential—the return to the country from the city was always a triumph for her, proof that the city's glitter could not match the country's gold. Like Thea Kronborg, when returning from the city "she had the sense of going back to a friendly soil, whose friendship was somehow going to strengthen her; a naive, generous country that gave one its joyous force, its large-hearted, childlike power to love, just as it gave one its coarse, brilliant flowers." [37]

She knew the narrowness bred in small towns, the hatreds and fears that often stifled thought, but in her mind the impact of the town and its frontier environment upon the people was far less destructive than that of the large city. She could never quite forgive the great cities that rose from her beloved plains for the destructive forces which they unleashed upon the rural virtues that she prized so highly. Whatever the city might offer, it could not overcome her feeling that urbanization violated the life force itself; the city pushed the individual spirit into a mold of hurry, indifference to fellow men, and blindness to anything durable or artistic. Ironically to her, there in the midst of masses of individuals there was no individualism. "Here," Carl says in *O Pioneers!*, "you are an individual, you have a background of your own, you would be missed. But off there in the cities there are thousands of rolling stones like me. We are all alike; we have no ties, we know nobody, we owe nothing." [38] *You would be missed*—there was the heart of the matter. The city robbed man of his individuality, set him in the midst of mass, without roots, heritage, or continuity of feeling with the earth and his fellow men.

In one of her best short stories, "Neighbour Rosicky," she treated the climb of an immigrant from poverty and personal desolation in the great cities to peace and fulfillment on the frontier. "It struck young Rosicky that this was the trouble with big cities," she wrote of his trials; "they built you in from the earth itself, cemented you away from any contact with the ground." [39] Willa Cather lived to see the city encroach upon and threaten to devour the plains and the way of life they nurtured and she could never accept it. Firmly planted in the American tradition of respect for the earth, those forces which defiled it were alien to her. In this sense she spoke for her age and the old rural American way which was a victim of the twentieth century. Her belief in the ideals held by that age was heightened by the medium through which she viewed them, the rural virtues which have formed a part of American thinking at least since Jefferson.

By the mid-1920's a great sadness, together with an increasing refusal to compromise with modern life, overtook Willa Cather. The stimulus of these new forces turned her increasingly to the past in search of weapons to combat the crisis. She had discovered the Southwest before World War I, and recorded its beauties first in *The Song of the Lark*. Now in the years after the war, she returned to it, and this renewed contact reinforced the mental images which she had gathered in former times, to be recorded in *Death Comes for the Archbishop* (1927).

Her feeling for the Southwest was in essence an extension of her first feelings toward the Nebraska frontier. In the Southwest she found one thing which she had not encountered before: evidence of a superior civilization whose works had endured despite the passing of the hands that made them. Visits to her brother, who worked on the railroad in Winslow, Arizona, and her illuminating trips to the great cliff dwellings of Walnut Canyon, Arizona, impressed upon her the richness and timelessness of the Indian civilizations. Here indeed was the basic object of her lifelong quest: endurance and continuity of civilization in a natural setting which guaranteed freedom and individuality. Though centuries and a vastly different point of view separated the ancient Indian civilizations from their modern successors, art in its human and cultural context remained as an expression of man's basic needs and desires.

In the Southwest she encountered space, freedom, and inspiration that flowed from the land itself as well as from human consciousness. It was as though she looked upon the world before the coming of civilization. "This mesa plain had an appearance of great antiquity and of incompleteness; as if, with all the materials for world-making assembled, the Creator had desisted, gone away, and left everything on the point of being brought together, on the eve of being arranged into mountain, plain, plateau. The country was still waiting to be made into a landscape." [40] Everything she saw here was "fresh, individual, first-hand." [41] Here at least the machine and its manufactured culture had not yet dominated and there was time for personal expression. Objects still had "that irregular and intimate quality of things made entirely by the human hand." [42]

She respected the Indians and their civilization. "There was purpose and conviction behind their inscrutable reserve; something active and quick, something with an edge." [43] The Indians' desire to blend themselves with their surroundings, to draw from the land rather than take from it, appealed to her. "They seemed to have none of the European's desire to 'master' nature, to rearrange and recreate. They spent their ingenuity in the other direction; in accommodating themselves to the scene in which they found themselves. This was not so much from indolence, the Bishop thought, as from an inherited caution and respect." [44] Here at last was a civilization that utilized rather than exploited, that looked to primary forces for life rather than to superficial technical improvements.

The challenge of white civilizations, represented by the early missionaries, to the ancient Indian civilization fascinated Willa Cather. To her the biographies of the padres were living testaments of the conviction, courage, and personal needs that impelled men to face and accommodate themselves to an older way of life in their search for God and for themselves. They were classic pioneers to her, worthy of study and respect for the manner in which they had met life's challenges. "Those early missionaries threw themselves naked upon the hard heart of a country that was calculated to try the endurance of giants." [45] She respected their quest and was fascinated by their accomplishments.

This fascination produced one of her greatest characters, the Archbishop. Most of her earlier characters had been torn between extremes—city versus country, individual versus mass, art versus worldly success. But one supreme goal motivated the Archbishop, toward which all of his actions led: the glorification of God through the development of his individual capacities and an understanding of the men around him; indeed, he worked in a physical and mental environment that impelled rather than impeded his quest. He had no basic doubts about the purpose of his life.

The religious qualities of this novel were pronounced and marked Willa Cather's further movement toward the spiritual aspects of life, which she brought to a conclusion in her last major work, *Shadows on the Rock* (1931). The latter novel suffers from nostalgia and a historical setting which she admired but did not wholly understand. In her later years she turned to

religion for solace and understanding. But it was not so much a
formal and dogmatic religion as it was the religion of mind and
creative insight which she had always connected with art. To
Willa Cather, art and religion were mutually sustaining forces,
since both flowed from the same source, the desire of the individual for identification with life and cultural continuity. "After all,
the supreme virtue in art is soul," she wrote in her early years;
"perhaps it is the only thing which gives art the right to be." [46]

By 1930 she had attained a prominent position in American
letters, and though she felt even then that her themes were out-
moded among much of the public, her craft remained a model to
many writers and her works enjoyed considerable popularity.
She wrote a final novel, *Sapphira and the Slave Girl,* and she
collected her essays and short stories. Her later years were clouded
by the inevitable passing of her friends and relatives, precious links
to the past, and by world events which seemed to intrude upon
her life no matter how hard she combated them. Uncompromising
to the end about her art, she consistently refused all commercial
advantages, most of the demands made upon her as a public
figure, and withdrew into retirement.

The unrest of the 1930's, culminating in a second world war,
seemed to destroy all that she had salvaged from the first. "There
seems to be no future at all for people of my generation," [47] she
said as France fell to Hitler's armies. She deprecated the New
Deal as an invasion against individualism which would ultimately
stifle creativity, and time only solidified her belief that the new
world was not hers and that new attitudes had already destroyed
most of what she held dear. Well might she have said with the
old Navajo in *Death Comes for the Archbishop:* "Men travel
faster now, but I do not know if they go to better things." And
she could have answered with the Archbishop: "We must not try
to know the future, Eusabio. It is better not." [48]

Unquestionably, Willa Cather's view narrowed as the curtains
of age and time drew together before her and as the new cultural
order threatened everything she had worked to sustain. Despite
her careful craftsmanship and call for fresh vision, a strong note
of nostalgia and complaint is evident in her late work. She began
increasingly to feel that she wrote for an audience that was not

there, much like the actor who performs for a half-empty house. She had said of Sarah Orne Jewett, whose work she greatly admired, that she wrote for a select audience that would always be present, and perhaps she felt the same way about her own work now. "The courage to go on without compromise does not come to a writer all at once—nor, for that matter, does the ability," she wrote in a late essay. "Both are phases of natural development."[49] That courage to go on and that ability to do so sustained her until her death on April 24, 1947.

There is a point beyond which refusal to compromise becomes mere intransigence and refusal to meet challenge, and in her personal attitudes Willa Cather came dangerously close to that point. The high level of perception which she demanded made some of her work difficult for the average reader, and left her open to critics who held that the major function of art is to promote man's welfare in concrete terms. She could not descend to that level; nothing would have been less characteristic of her. She would have answered these critics that the artist's function is not merely to reform but to enlighten man, and that the questions she asked and tried to answer would in the end be far more important than any social or political themes she might have developed.

Like Mrs. Wharton, Miss Cather came in the end to savor the past for its coherence and order, and to denounce the present for its insecurity and barbarous tastes. Yet the similarities between the two are not so simply stated. Mrs. Wharton's reliance on custom and tradition at least had the merit of consistency, for it formed the basis of her personal philosophy as well as her work. Miss Cather's turn toward the past, on the other hand, seems to reveal a more obvious change. She had always favored the rebel in society, the strongest will, the deepest pioneer spirit; after 1920 she could not accept rebellion and change. The vitality with which she had so successfully filled her novels seemed progressively to wither and die in what to her were the arid years after 1920. Certainly her concept of social stability and culture differed more sharply with the new forces than Mrs. Wharton's precisely because she had been less consciously concerned with them. Her basic search had always been esthetic, resting on art rather than social views. She had looked for the enduring man and enduring art, while

Mrs. Wharton persistently broadened this outlook into a general view of culture. In a sense, Miss Cather betrayed her origins in suffering so sharp a shock. Mrs. Wharton's view had always been more cosmopolitan, more aware of the complex society around her.

Yet, in another and deeper sense, Miss Cather's turn from her world was only the logical culmination of her career. It did not really mark a major departure in her work and view of life, for it involved an affirmation as well as a denial. If she could no longer believe in the America she saw around her, and if she did indeed believe that the new generation's ideals were false, less compelling and vital than those of her youth, she could move beyond these limits. She could and did then affirm the larger living tradition of Western art and humanism by studying the past. Her interest in the past was far more profound than critics have realized, for she was not simply an escapist. She still wrote of pioneers, builders, and makers; only the scene had changed. The Archbishop and the people of *Shadows on the Rock* were of a piece with her earlier enduring characters of *O Pioneers!* and *My Antonia*.

Her rejection of the modern did not imply a rejection of American culture or ideals, but of contemporary taste. She did not turn from life, but from her world. In her early career, when it was fashionable to go abroad for themes and characters, she wrote of the American scene she knew. Despite her increasing dislike of modern life, she aimed her criticisms at the age, not the country, and she remained a basically American figure. Her sojourns in Europe impressed upon her the beauties and qualities of that older civilization, but she never forsook her native land. There was "a quality of voice" about America, especially the West, which she found nowhere else and which drew her unceasingly to the sources of her art—the land and the people.

Even to a reading public inured to indifferent writing and static novels, Miss Cather's work is filled with compelling beauty and meaning. The quality of her craftsmanship, the depth of her feeling for nature and art, her profound humanism, and her ability to portray character offset the limitations of her social views. Many readers of an earlier generation eagerly awaited her newest book, and much of her work is still in print today as a testament to the endurance which her work has attained.

She occupies an important position in the main stream of American writing. Writing in times of cultural and social transition, she affords a prime example of withdrawal from the force of that transition. Yet the things in which she sought refuge are indexes to what was passing in her day—rural America, pioneer individualism, fixed standards of artistic judgment, unity among men. She is one of the most important of that group of American writers who felt it their duty to preserve and augment the best artistic works from the past in an effort to insure order and continuity in society. In her search for something lasting and durable, something permanent in a world of change, she spoke for an older generation adjusting to a new way of life. She answered the personal crisis of the first generation of the twentieth century by her quest for tested values, her return to the America of her youth, forever lost before the guns of the First World War. Her work, as befits her artistry, stands not only as an artistic success but as a revealing and human social document, reflecting many of the basic historic currents of her time.

To this generation, still concerned with individualism, humanism, and the pioneer attitude, her work has much to say. Time undoubtedly will challenge much of her writing, but she produced at least two of the best modern American novels, *My Antonia* and *Death Comes for the Archbishop*. Not everyone will understand the full beauty and hidden meanings of her work, and will prefer instead the great social novels which overtook her. But "to note an artist's limitations is but to define his talent," she said in her celebrated essay on Sarah Orne Jewett. Her work will endure and will be read in that light. She would ask no more.

Sherwood Anderson: The Search for Unity

> When I walk here in the country and see a man ploughing,
> say, on a hillside field, I hunger to have the man know the
> beauty of the gesture, in himself and his horses, involved in
> the act of ploughing. I want him to know this in relation
> to earth, sky, trees, river, etc. It may be that is all we are
> after—that he shall know.
>
> Sherwood Anderson, 1936

THE AMERICAN MIDWEST of the late nineteenth century was in
many ways a fortunate and a pleasant place in which to live. A
land predominantly of small towns and settled ways, it offered a
life of abundance and ease. In the days before industry and commerce dominated the region the towns of the Midwest were
sleepy places, devoted to small crafts, farming, and business. Men
worked the land, carried on their dealings with a certain faith in
each other, and honored the tenets of their society. The literary
spokesmen of the region had not yet delved deeply into naturalism
and realism, and William Dean Howells was considered con-
troversial enough by those who read "high-class" literature.

Few men enjoyed these surroundings more than Sherwood
Anderson, born in Camden, Ohio, on September 13, 1876, the
third child of a harnessmaker.[1] Anderson fondly remembered his
childhood in his *Memoirs* (1941) and in the nostalgic *Tar: A Midwestern Childhood* (1927). His father, who figured prominently
in many of his works, was a colorful and improvident craftsman
with a large family, who changed occupations and locale often in
a disorderly search for economic security. Like Thomas Wolfe,
though without the latter's almost total recall, Sherwood Anderson was to recollect and reconstruct much of the society and way
of life of his childhood, never forgetting its agonies while celebrating its triumphs. When the Midwest changed, when agricul-
ture and its civilization fell before industry, Anderson recorded
that change in his work. Just as Ellen Glasgow spoke for a South-

ern tradition that was passing in her day, so Anderson spoke for a Midwestern tradition that was crumbling in his time.

In 1884, the family moved to Clyde, Ohio. Acquiring the customary education in local schools, Anderson as a boy also gained a reputation for "go-getting" and "hustling" by his efforts to offset his family's poverty through hard work and diligent application. Never a student or a serious reader, his early education consisted primarily of impressions gathered from the life around him. Though he did read, he frankly admitted later that his early ideas were derivative and of little importance. The necessity of making a living early in life and his natural distaste for formal learning combined to plant the love of observation in him that later provided such rich material for his fiction.

In 1896, Anderson left his Ohio home and went to Chicago, the mecca of ambitious young men from the Midwest. For a time he worked in warehouses and factories as an unskilled laborer, feeling acutely the hard times of the middle 1890's. Somewhat weak as a youngster, he was inclined to physical slightness, and hard work did not brighten his outlook on life. Endowed with a certain vanity, which he never denied, he offset this with an almost feminine sense of sympathy and understanding toward the people around him. This rich strain of understanding was his greatest asset as a writer.

The industrialization which he saw in Chicago impressed him; even before he left his Ohio home he had been aware of the increasing invasion of the old Midwest by Eastern industry. "Out through the coal and iron regions of Pennsylvania, into Ohio and Indiana, and on westward into the States bordering on the Mississippi River, industry crept," he wrote later in *Poor White* (1920). "Gas and oil were discovered in Ohio and Indiana. Overnight, towns grew into cities. A madness took hold of the people." [2] Just as Edith Wharton chronicled the Western invasion of the East, so Sherwood Anderson related the story of the Eastern industrial invasion of the old agricultural Midwest. Tiring of his work, and ambitious to succeed at writing, Anderson left his job in 1898 to fight in the war with Spain, feeling that this experience would further equip him for writing. Service in Cuba was far from glamorous but gave him a somewhat broadened outlook on life.

The rising advertising industry of the turn of the century attracted him after his military service, not because he liked it, but because he at first considered it a steppingstone to creative writing. In 1900 he began to work for a prominent advertising firm, writing copy used in national publications. Like Hart Crane, Anderson found the work tiring and superficial, a hindrance rather than a help to his real ambitions. Nonetheless, he had no real alternative. His marriage in 1904 made him reluctant to embark on the literary career he longed for, and by 1906 he had acquired sufficient capital to enter the paint business in Elyria, Ohio. For several years he grimly pursued the task of settling his family and accepting his social responsibilities.

The conflicts of loyalty and the strains of business, which he never liked, proved too much, and on November 27, 1912, he suffered a nervous breakdown in his factory, walked from his office in a daze, and disappeared for some time. He did not return to his business, but decided to become a writer. It was an unusual step for a man of thirty-six with a family and a business career. He could not, however, fulfill his hope of becoming a free writer and in 1913 he became a copywriter in a Chicago office.

Anderson now mixed with the members of the "Chicago Renaissance" that flourished in the Windy City in the decade before the First World War. He circulated among the poets, painters, novelists, and experimental artists of all kinds who were bringing new forms and fresh life into the stream of American art. Anderson was never especially fond of many intellectuals, and came in time to disavow much of this phase of his career. But he published short stories and poetry in experimental quarterlies and made many friendships that stood him in good stead in his period of mature writing.

After scattered publications in little magazines and reviews, Anderson began his literary career with a novel, *Windy Mc-Pherson's Son* (1916). Frankly autobiographical, the novel described the rise of a small-town boy to limited success in the business world; ultimately the hero renounces the business ethic and quest for wealth in favor of more durable virtues of love and settled society. The book drew praise from the new reviewers, but fell far short of a major work, for its last half was a fumbling effort to resolve several conflicting theories on the nature of human relationships.

Though it lacked finish and the rich detail of Theodore Dreiser's novels of the business world or the flashes of insight in the best of Frank Norris, *Windy McPherson's Son* dealt with many of the same themes. Anderson too was fascinated by the power of material wealth, the complexity of the business world, and its impact on the people involved. He realized that business was the wave of the future and that economic changes also meant cultural changes. Anderson tried to say in his first novel many of the things he later said better: money is power, men are often ruthless in their dealings, society is complex and often blind to individuals. For all its technical faults, the novel carried the message that was central in Anderson's later work: man's greatest need is for unity in the midst of chaos, and that unity can be attained only through human love.

The businessman and the world he created fascinated Anderson. Desiring unity and identification with as much of life as possible, Anderson believed that the modern businessman who wrested order from chaos and at the same time created a world of his own was as creative as the artist. He could, in fact, be a kind of artist. The power and the unified force of great business and the creative drive of industry satisfied some deep urge in Anderson. The businessman was in reality the key figure in the great transition from agrarianism to industrialism in the Midwest of Anderson's day. He lamented that so few businessmen were aware of their potential power, or raised their ideals above materialism. Those who did realize their creative role were leaders. "To these men America is looking," he wrote in *Windy*. "It is asking them to keep the faith, to stand themselves up against the force of the brute trader, the dollar man, the man who with his one cunning wolf quality of acquisitiveness has too long ruled the business of the nation." [3]

In most of his work, Anderson presents a study of divided personality, well illustrated by this attitude. On the one hand, he detested the materialism of business; on the other, he clearly saw its potential for good if men would use it in a truly creative way.

Similarly, he was ambivalent in his attitude toward the machine; he believed that ultimately it might prove a great force for unity, yet he hated it for displacing the older and more personal crafts.

While he greatly prized individuality, he also admired the strength of purpose and power inherent in a group motivated by a single purpose. His second novel, *Marching Men* (1917), again technically imperfect, centered on a coal miner's son, Beaut McGregor, who rose from the West Virginia mines to a famous law practice in Chicago. Deeply impressed by the brutality and thwarted goodness of his youthful surroundings, McGregor burns with the desire to organize the poor and the workers into battalions which would use the strength of their numbers to remake society and at the same time would give every individual a sense of identification with his fellow men. The novel was partly autobiographical, filled with suppressed youthful longings for power and fame, and revealed an often mordant determinism that recurred in Anderson's work. "He began to feel that he was in the midst of something too vast to be moved by the efforts of any one man. The pitiful insignificance of the individual was apparent." [4] Thus Anderson early developed what became a major theme: individualism is sterile unless it is co-ordinated with love for other individuals. Love, a form of heroic sacrifice, would achieve human understanding.

The book had implications which are frightening to a later generation. The battalions are organized, and for a time are successful, but the terrible force inherent in them causes their ruin and the failure of McGregor's movement. For all its crudeness, *Marching Men* contained a subtler theme. McGregor, like Anderson, sought the unity of individuals with other individuals and thus a deeper identification with life and the world around them. By using a negative example, Anderson tried to show the strength that could come from such unity when tempered by sympathy and love. "He will make them conquer, not one another, but the terrifying disorder of life . . ." he wrote. "Love invaded his spirit and made his body tingle." [5] Anderson seemed to say in *Marching Men* that McGregor's movement failed not because its aims were wrong but because it did not rest on love and regard for humanity.

Anderson's beginning as a novelist was not spectacular. The

Chicago group proclaimed him a major newcomer and praised the vitality and richness of his first two novels, though they deplored, as did more academic critics, the lack of technical ability which Anderson displayed in the books. For himself, Anderson had little patience with critics and less with those who condemned his lack of "form." He felt with Thomas Wolfe that form in fiction or any creative art was a thing to be felt instead of manufactured. "You see, Pearson, I have the belief that in this matter of form it is largely a matter of depth of feeling," he wrote to Norman Holmes Pearson late in life when summing up what he felt about the subject. "How deeply do you feel it? Feel it deeply enough, and you will be torn inside and driven on until form comes." [6]

Anderson never considered himself a novelist, but a storyteller, and his reputation as a writer rested and rests largely on his short stories. He deemed it his primary task to report his observations. Lacking literary discipline, he made little effort to perfect the manner in which he worked; the story, not its form, was his concern. "I'll never preach at anyone, anyhow!" he wrote in *Many Marriages* (1923). "If by chance I ever do become a writer I'll only try to tell people what I have seen and heard in life and besides that I'll spend my time walking up and down looking and listening." [7] Anderson was hungry for life, and the saving grace of his work was the successful way in which he instilled that vital hunger into his writing. He was desperately eager to transcend self, "to escape out of old minds, old thoughts, put into my head by others, into my own thoughts, my own feelings." [8] If this required a sacrifice of accepted form, he was willing to make it. "Form is, of course, content. It is nothing else, can be nothing else." [9] He had circulated enough in literary circles to detest the smartness that often passed for form. "The object drawn doesn't matter so much," he later wrote to his son John. "It's what you feel about it, what it means to you. . . . Try to remain humble. Smartness kills everything." [10] Early in his career he formulated his final answer for critics. "I often wonder, if I wrapped my packages up more neatly, if the same large, loose sense of life could be attained." [11]

Despite the controversy over the form of his work, Anderson's success was considerable in the light of his chaotic apprenticeship and background. His work did not provide him with an income and he continued to work in advertising, but he slowly gathered a group of followers and attained some recognition in the new literature that was rising as America verged on the 1920's. Anderson enjoyed writing; it gave him a sense of purpose and accomplishment that no other work afforded. Personally as well as artistically his one basic aim was for unity with life. "I presume that we all who begin the practice of an art begin out of a great hunger for order. We want brought into consciousness something that is always there but that gets so terribly lost." [12] In *Marching Men* he spelled it out specifically: "In the heart of all men lies sleeping the love of order. How to achieve order out of our strange jumble of forms, out of democracies and monarchies, dreams and endeavors is the riddle of the Universe, and the thing that in the artist is called the passion for form and for which he will also laugh in the face of death is in all men." [13]

If Anderson's novels lack the focus and technical cohesion necessary for that order, the same cannot be said of his short stories. His sense of vitality, his keen eye for detail, and his straightforward and compelling style made him a talented and successful short-story writer. The proof of this ability is *Winesburg, Ohio* (1919), a collection of short stories centered on fictional characters living in a supposedly fictional Ohio town. [14]

The America which had just experienced the First World War was startled by the themes explored in *Winesburg*. Anderson later insisted that he had not meant to be sensational and had never wished to exploit forbidden themes in *Winesburg* or any of his work. When told that the stories were indecent, he merely replied that he had never felt cleaner than when writing them. The tales dealt with homosexuality, the suppressed sexual yearnings of young men and women, the tragedies inherent in unhappy marriages, and other personal and sexual problems that the society of the early 1920's considered shocking.

Such subjects and people attracted Anderson because he had observed them in his own youth, and in his imagination as well as in fact had peeked behind the walls that hid them. "There are walls everywhere, about individuals, about groups. The houses are mussy. People die inside walls without ever having seen the light. I want the houses cleaned, the doorsteps washed, the walls broken away," [15] he wrote in 1921.

His personal sympathy as well as the recollection of his own troubled youth drew him to the so-called misfits of society on the assumption that they too could enrich the stream of human consciousness. In them, as in every man, there was something common to all men, something from which the world and certainly the artist could profit. "Only the few know the sweetness of the twisted apples," [16] he wrote in *Winesburg*. "Tales are everywhere," he wrote a few years later. "Every man, woman and child you meet on the street has a tale for you." [17] True to the tradition of personal revolt which had brought him to writing, and reflecting the demands of the new generation that no themes be denied the sympathetic and creative artist, Anderson refused to turn from those whom society denied.

Anderson wrote his short stories with a matter-of-factness, a rugged vernacular style, and a deep sympathy that made them compelling, and made *Winesburg, Ohio* one of the most talked-about books of the decade. It marked his arrival as an artist of national reputation, though for financial reasons he still was not able to abandon his advertising work.

Winesburg rested on four basic assumptions, which Anderson had already elaborated, and which occupied all his work: there is a hidden side of every man that should be exposed and understood; loneliness is a common factor in all of life and is destructive if unchecked; love and human sympathy, based on understanding and self-sacrifice, may eliminate loneliness and bring life to full fruition; every man is in his way striving to identify himself with the world around him to the extent of his ability, and his actions, however perverse they may appear, must be understood and valued in that light. The power of loneliness and the need for love were reiterated in all the stories and made the book a continuous narrative.

Another of Anderson's themes was projected more sharply in *Winesburg*: a dry fatalism, an attitude that men are prone to error and are often the victims of circumstances beyond their control, that life's relationships are essentially tragic. All of his characters show an insistent groping toward full consciousness that is never fulfilled, and which leaves the reader with the impression that such groping is the lot of much of mankind. Understanding, if it comes, is so rare as to be precious, hence Anderson's fascination with the power of love in human relationships.

Yet Anderson never quite expressed the degree of fatalism found in Stephen Crane or Theodore Dreiser. Characteristically, Anderson evolved no theory of determinism, although he believed in chance and fate in human affairs. "Life was an experience full of queer accidents," [18] he wrote in a late novel. And recalling the poignant bitterness of adolescence and youth verging on manhood, he could write: "He knows that in spite of all the stout talk of his fellows he must live and die in uncertainty, a thing blown by the winds, a thing destined like corn to wilt in the sun." [19] But he tempered this fatalism with sympathy for humanity, even when humanity was foolish, and with a profoundly felt belief that love and communion among men could sweep away all problems.

This belief in mankind, and the vitality that filled his better works, arose from Anderson's feeling for the soil of the Midwest and for the poor and oppressed. Never materialistic, he cared little for wealth and lived on the edge of poverty most of his life. The poor and the backward fascinated him because to him they were more elemental than their more fortunate fellows. They were in fact a link from former times to the present; the bridge over which the old in society and human consciousness passed to mingle with the new. At home with the poor, he often felt insecure in the presence of the learned. He was not pretentious, though sensitive about criticisms of his themes. "I am immature, will live and die immature," [20] he wrote Van Wyck Brooks, who was his personal opposite, in 1919.

In his memoirs, Anderson justified his earthy primitivism and his interest in the unsophisticated on the grounds that they were the poet's responsibility; from these wellsprings flowed the sources of any living and meaningful art. Just as the supposedly perverted characters of *Winesburg, Ohio* had something to offer their fellow men, so did the Negroes and poor whites of the South, whom he had come to love. "It is in the nature of the poet to have something primitive in him. The poet is in some odd way akin to the savage. It cannot be denied. When he is a true poet he is tender, cruel, isolated from others, intensely a part of others in a way the generality of men will never understand." [21]

If the artist's chief function was to discover the sources of conduct and to define the actions and relationships of men, Anderson felt that study of the primitive and backward was crucial; their lives still contained attitudes and customs, obscured in other groups by cultural change, which might lead the artist back to the sources of life itself. The frontier period of Midwestern history fascinated Anderson as Abraham Lincoln fascinated him. He believed that the pioneer's close contact with the earth, combined with his personal primitivism, gave him a unity with his fellow men and his natural world that his modern successors never attained:

A curious notion often comes to me. Is it not likely that when the country was new and men were often alone in the fields and forests, they got a sense of bigness outside themselves that has now in some way been lost? I don't mean the conventional religious thing that is still prevalent and that is nowadays being retailed to the people by the most up-to-date commercial methods, but something else. The people, I fancy, had a savagery superior to our own. Mystery whispered in the grass, played in the branches of trees overhead, was caught up and blown across the horizon line in clouds of dust at evening on the prairies.[22]

For this same reason, he loved animals because their qualities were more earthy and primitive, and therefore closer to the main streams of life. It is not accidental that horses play so large a part in his short stories. *Poor White* (1920), *Horses and Men* (1923), *Dark Laughter* (1925), his one best-seller, and *Death in the Woods* (1933) contain his best statements of this primitivism. He admired the poor because they were simple. "When I want peace I go among the poor. They are poor because they are not clever, cannot get the best of me or anyone." [23]

In 1922, Anderson left advertising and vowed to endure poverty in order to write full time. His early life had been unhappy. He was married four times, yet he had managed to travel freely and make careful observations. Next to the old Midwest, the South, to which he moved in 1922, fascinated him most. Its rural isolation, simplicity, natural beauty, and varied population provided him with personal pleasure as well as literary material. When industry invaded that South in the 1920's and 1930's, he turned his attention to its problems just as he had done when his Midwest fell before the onslaught of industrialized materialism.

With the proceeds from his one financial success, *Dark Laughter*, Anderson purchased a farm on Ripshin Creek in Virginia, and with the help of neighbors built a large stone house where he lived and worked most of the rest of his life. Later, with the assistance of a friend, he bought two small newspapers in Marion, Virginia, which his sons later directed, and which he hoped would keep him financially solvent while he wrote. It was no accident that he settled in the South, nor was it accidental that he sang the praises of the hillbillies, poor whites, and Negroes in this section. He admired them because they had made a marriage with the land and their natural world; they owned little but were part of everything. In their way they had found the unity that he himself sought.

Anderson's self-avowed primitivism was in part a manifestation of his desire to rediscover the power of the natural world in human affairs. To Ellen Glasgow the land symbolized eternity and a kind of determinism; to Willa Cather it was a force for man to join. But neither of these authors was a primitivist in the sense that Anderson was, for their attitude was intellectual rather than emotional. He himself did not lack intellect but the intellectual attitude. He did not read, he wrote. He was not a craftsman, but a storyteller. He did feel that man must study nature to understand life. "It may sound childish, but men will have to go back to nature more," he wrote in *Perhaps Women* (1931). "They will have to go to the fields and the rivers. There will have to be a new religion, more pagan, something more closely connected with fields and rivers." Nature's secrets might solve many of man's problems. "There will have to be built up a new and stronger sympathy as between man and man. We may find the new mystery there." [24]

Feeling that men were closer to the earth and nature in the South than in the industrialized East, Anderson hoped they might there preserve and enhance the continuity and unity of life. "There still is, however, in the hill country, a way of life that is outside the tone of most America just now," he remembered in his *Memoirs*. "The machine has not penetrated deeply into the hills. Hand weaving is still being done. Grain is still cut with a cradle." [25]

The passing of this way of life before the machine and industrialization furnished the central theme of Anderson's later work. The 1920's and early 1930's rapidly brought industry to the South, an area with a supply of cheap labor and undeveloped natural resources. Anderson believed that this changing economy was the crucial event of his time, for it meant a change in social and spiritual values. Although he disliked much of his world, Anderson was never an escapist. And although early in his career he had dabbled freely with bohemianism in Chicago, he was never a dilettante. He understood the social as well as artistic responsibilities of the writer, and he freely accepted the challenge of divergent social forces that worked such far-reaching changes in his time. He had no use for the expatriates. "Unlike many American writers, when the change in life became apparent, when it became obvious, when mechanical invention followed mechanical invention, the automobile coming, the flying machine, the radio, when the world about became filled with new noises, when speed took the place of purpose, when it became more and more difficult for men like myself to live, I at least had not tried to get out of it all by fleeing to Europe. I had at least not gone to Paris, to sit eternally in cafes, talking of art." [26]

It required no great stretch of memory for Anderson to recall what had happened in the Ohio towns of his boyhood, and to see it happening again in the South. The old personalized handicrafts fell before mass production and cheap goods; the workman's identification with his materials faded before mechanized progress. The railroads came, bringing an influx of people; the land itself was exploited, often ravaged, by industry.

It was easy to justify the machine. It meant less labor for the common man, cheaper goods within his reach, and more leisure. These themes were treated in *Poor White*, a book in which Anderson traced the rise of a poor Southern white to fame as an inventor of industrial machinery that was supposed to lighten the labor load of the Midwestern farmer. Anderson developed his old idea that without love there is no progress; without understanding among people, machines become masters.

Anderson did not look upon the destruction of the countryside, the low wages and long hours, the poor working conditions in the mills and factories as industrialization's greatest evils. These were, in a way, tangential to the major problem, which lay far deeper. To Anderson, as an artist and social observer, the machine's destructive power was far more subtle; its major assault was not on the physical well-being of the men who tended it but on their souls. The separation of the worker from his materials and tools broke the unity of forms that Anderson prized. "Where we are all most robbed is in the dreadful decay of taste, the separation of men from the sense of tools and materials." [27]

Anderson's father was a harnessmaker. Although he failed for lack of application and endeavor, he loved his trade. His son never forgot the pride of craftsmanship, and the fall of the individual craftsman before the machine recurs repeatedly in his fiction. The maker of goods was himself an artist to Anderson, just as the writer, painter, or musician was an artist. Not every man could create on these high levels, but every man was endowed with some creative talent, generally the gift of work. The tools and materials which he used and to which he gave form and purpose thus became expressions of his individual art. Just as much as a painting, a finely made harness made its maker a part of his world. When the materials were fashioned by a machine controlled by a man, the worker was denied self-expression. "Might it not be that with the coming into general use of machinery men did lose the grip of what is perhaps the most truly important of man's functions in life—the right every man has always before held dearest of all his human possessions, the right in short to stand alone in the presence of his tools and his materials and with those tools and materials to attempt to twist, to bend, to form something that will be the expression of his inner hunger for the truth that is his own and that is beauty?" [28] he asked.

Anderson always complained that his own social sense was deficient, but he could not help noting the deep and lasting effects which industry and science had upon thought. "Science has succeeded in killing most of the old mystery. Who dares question the assertion? . . . the scientists have taken from us old mysteries and, as yet, no poets have arisen who can give us new ones." [29]

Among artists contemporary with Anderson, Hart Crane tried hardest to come to grips with the problem of the machine in modern life, and that brilliant poet also concluded that in time the artist might help society adjust to the new changes. Both men accepted the challenge; neither retreated from the task, and both were aware that however much they might wish it, they could never return to the nostalgic Midwest from which they sprang. "We will have to keep the machine and control it," [30] Anderson noted tersely in 1931. "I tried to say that the new world of which men sometimes talk was not to be born, but had been born," he wrote a friend in 1930. "The machine had made the new world. It was a question of going into the new world, opening doors, going in. Like a new house standing ready." [31]

In accepting the social challenge as an artistic challenge, Hart Crane drew on the tradition of Walt Whitman, who held that the poet must be a social innovator and that the artist must learn to bridge the cultural transitions from old to new, thus helping man in his progress. Using this reasoning, Anderson condemned the faddists and escapists in the arts of the 1920's. "To me it seems that as writers we shall have to throw ourselves with greater daring into life," he wrote in 1926. "We shall have to begin to write out of the people and not for the people. We shall have to find within ourselves a little of that courage. To continue along the road we are travelling is unthinkable. To draw ourselves apart, to live in little groups and console ourselves with the thought that we are achieving intellectuality is to get nowhere. By such a road we can hope only to go on producing a literature that has nothing to do with life as it is lived in these United States." [32]

Anderson did not mean that the artist should become the social spokesman as such; he always believed that the artist's proper function was to create lasting art, and he decried the loss of many brilliant friends who were caught up and spent in reform movements.[33] He wanted a social consciousness deeper than a mere awareness of current problems. Like Hart Crane, he wanted the creative artist to put his heightened sensibilities at the service of mankind in the midst of social change. The artist could see beyond the current problems, could test the solutions offered in the light of heightened consciousness. The problem was not one of low wages and long hours; it was essentially a crisis of the spirit. "Basically, I do believe that the robbing of man of his craft, his touch with tools and materials by modern industry does tend to make him spiritually impotent. I believe that spiritual impotence eventually leads to physical impotence. This belief is basic in me. The darkness is a darkness of the soul." [34] The creative artist who bridged the transition from old to new might alleviate that darkness.

It was, to say the least, a mystical attitude, but not without its practical applications. Anderson himself had to lecture for money, a task he hated, and in the 1920's and 1930's he participated in many writers' conferences. When the Great Depression brought hunger and poverty to the mill towns and factory sites of the South, Anderson lent his name and prestige to movements to help the underprivileged. Accused of communist sympathies, he never in fact adopted communism. The blight and poverty around him deeply touched his sense of humanity, but in a larger sense he was merely trying to fulfill his ideas of the artist as a social leader.

Though he accepted the machine as an evil that had come to stay, its potentialities also fascinated Anderson. Tours in factories and close observation of workers convinced him that the machine might even in time become a great force for unity among men. He felt that the machine had dehumanized the worker, yet it had also brought a kind of unity. "I think it must have been the vast order in the mass of steel parts, all in movement, that had caught and held me so," [35] he wrote after a tour through a factory.

Perhaps because he wanted to convince himself that there was hope through the machine, or perhaps simply because of his emotional attitude, Anderson came to feel that the machine could work for unity. "There was something exultant in Red, working in that place," he wrote of the factory in *Beyond Desire* (1933). "On some days all the nerves in his body seemed to dance and run with the machines." [36] Though the worker might often feel dehumanized, he could also learn to love his machine, much as he would a horse or cow with which he might work. "There was even, Red thought, a certain affinity between the girls in the spinning-room and the machines they tended," he wrote in the same novel. "They seemed at times to become all one thing." [37] Anderson's viewpoint was certainly that of the mystical artist; he never worked with a factory machine. Yet he had seen firsthand both sides of the new industrialism, its hard poverty and harsh dehumanization, and this sense of mystical identification between workers and machines. This attitude never really crystallized in favor of the machine, for Anderson could not forget the impersonal brutality with which industry treated its workers. He also hated the cheapening of taste that characterized manufactured goods.

In another sense the machine had profoundly changed human relationships for Anderson. He believed insistently that a basic fault in modern society was the domination of women. In a somewhat halting and confused manner he developed the theory that the relationship of love between men was basic to social progress, and that the American failure to exploit that ideal had resulted in a woman-dominated society. Replacing hand tools with machines furthered this process of masculine isolation; it robbed the male of his only chance for real creativity. Women bore children; their creative role and desire for immortality was thus biologically secured. But men created things; when that power was denied them they became rootless and, Anderson believed, in time would become powerless. "Your male should be the adventurer," he wrote. "He should be careless of possessions, should throw them aside." [38] The woman's desire for material security tied the man to the machine but did not rob her of her basic power to create by bearing other life.

Anderson noted, to his satisfaction at least, that women workers in factories seemed less disturbed by their labor than men. It was not an empty gesture to him. "In the factories the men employees seem to feel smaller than the women. The women are affected less. It must be because every woman has a life within herself that nothing outside her can really touch except maybe a mate." [39] However right or wrong this theory may have been, it occurs in almost all of Anderson's work during the Great Depression.

The whole question of the changed relationship between men and women was only part of the much larger problem of unity among men and the overarching concept of love that unified Anderson's work. Anderson's personality accounted for much of his interest in the concept of human love, for he himself had felt loneliness and isolation. His unhappy personal life also sharpened his consciousness of the need of love. He not only observed life but participated in it. "I float in many lives, am distressed, made gay, made happy—a thousand times each day." [40] The sense of comradeship with men and things, a state of exalted participation in life, a feeling of unity with creation was at the heart of his concept of love.

As a writer concerned with sex in a generation that was first exposed to an emancipated literature, he had done his share to make this literature acceptable. He had suffered as well as profited from that aspect of his work. He wisely divorced his concept of love from sex; the former was an emotion, while the latter was a sensation. Love was rare; sex was not. Love, this sense of communion and participation with a person, thing, or event rose above self and personality to combine disparate emotions and persons into an exalted sense of unity. For Stephen Crane an act of personal heroism was at once an expression of individualism and a triumph over the world's limitations, as well as a close identification with life itself. For Sherwood Anderson a deeply felt emotion of love fulfilled the same purpose. It permitted one to abandon and yet to comprehend more fully the self and other selves. It was, after all, the supreme courage.

Anderson came in the end to a remarkably frank and critical estimate of his work. He knew from personal experience the power of selfishness and the lack of true self-sacrifice in most men. "Self is the grand disease," he once advised his son. "It is what we are all trying to lose." [41]

Anderson, like Hart Crane, believed that the application of this mystical concept of love in daily affairs might work the miracle of unity in chaos. Deeply aware of his own insignificance in the sum of the universe, he believed that love would save him. "I am a little thing, a tiny thing on the vast prairies. I know nothing. My mouth is dirty. I cannot tell what I want. My feet are sunk in the black swampy land, but I am a lover. I love life. In the end love shall save me." [42]

Willingness to help others by sacrificing selfish desires was a responsibility especially incumbent upon the creative artist. To fulfill his role of social builder and utilize his sensitivity, the artist must base his work upon the positive principle that love can break down the walls between men and make life meaningful. "Few enough people realize that all art that has vitality must have its basis in love," [43] he wrote in 1926.

Anderson's abiding interest in humanity and his deep respect for individualism and man's works depended upon the assumption that every man carried in himself something common to all other men. The discovery of this fragment of love in every man would tie all men together and bring the unity for which he worked. "I believe . . . that it is this universal thing, scattered about in many people, a fragment of it here, a fragment there, this thing we call love that we have to keep on trying to tap." [44] For himself as a writer his basic search was for unity through love. "Well, after all, that terribly abused word 'love' is at the bottom of all the decay," he wrote his brother Karl as early as 1922. "When men do not dare to love, they cannot live, and the men of our day did not dare love either God or their fellow men." [45]

This seemed to many an impractical ideal, and in truth it was an ideal that Anderson never fully explained, for he felt it more than he understood it. It was based on emotion rather than reason. Nothing was more characteristic of the man than this ideal, for it reflected his unsophisticated, primitive, sympathetic nature. Anxious to discover means whereby every man might survive the transitions and stresses that were remaking society, Anderson's intuition led him to focus on the most common denominator, the emotion possible to most men, love; whatever the imperfections of the theory as a formal idea, many men have propounded worse doctrines. If Anderson's work survives the test of time, it will be in large measure because he spoke to his fellows with this voice of love and because he delineated in it a vision open to all men caught as he was between conflicting forces.

By 1930 Anderson had attained considerable reputation as an American writer and as a spokesman for free thought and the underprivileged. A whole generation, maturing in the Jazz Age, had taken *Winesburg, Ohio* as a kind of Bible. His reputation grew slowly but surely with the years. He was not famous as a novelist, but his short stories and books devoted to current events reached a large audience. The Great Depression had struck America with terrible force and stirred Anderson to greater work on behalf of the poverty-stricken workers of the South and elsewhere in the country. He lent his name freely and often naively to a multitude of causes and wrote several books dealing with social issues. *Hello Towns!* (1929) and *Puzzled America* (1935) were journalistic pieces—some gathered from his Virginia newspapers—designed to report the true status of the unfortunate and downtrodden. Anderson spoke at many strikes, reported social unrest, and flirted with radical groups who vied for the prestige of his name and pen.

Anderson's sympathies were deeply touched by the economic and social crisis of the 1930's, and he never regretted what little he did on behalf of the less fortunate. Yet he was not a social theorist. "The one thing I detest, because it makes me feel detestable, is preaching or being wise man or seer," he wrote as early as 1924. He adhered to that standard as much as possible in later and darker years. "The whole secret lies in the fact that it is also my problem to be 'just the man, walking alone, seeing, smelling.' " [46]

He had watched the long shift from agrarianism to industrialism and looked upon the depression as the logical culmination of the whole movement. He was acutely aware that his own life spanned two quite different eras. "Men are a good deal lost in our time," he wrote in 1936. "They have lost the sense of being a part of the big complex thing in which we seem to be caught. They want that, to feel a part of something big going on. Until the turn of the century there was such a feeling. Read the histories written up to that time. There was apparently the belief that we were all marching onward, upward. I do think that feeling is lost." [47]

Thus Sherwood Anderson, the supposedly naive artist of unstable theories, clearly perceived the destruction of unity ushered in by the power conflicts of the twentieth century. Industrialization, the First World War, America's social experiments in the 1930's, economic dislocation—all had served to drive men apart. Anderson gave the only answer he could to this historic change: man must accept the facts and triumph over them by using the means at hand. Anderson was accused of communistic leanings; he did belong to radical groups, but he never accepted anything approximating formal communism. In one of the moments of insight that marked his shrewdness as a judge of men and motives, Anderson perceived the flaw in communism. "I am puzzled about Communism, as I am sure you may be," he wrote his old friend Theodore Dreiser. "It may be the answer, and then it may only be a new sort of Puritanism, more deadly than the old moral Puritanism, a new kind of Puritanism at last got power in one place to push its rigid Puritanism home." [48]

Anderson believed that the old economic and social fabric of America must undergo radical change to insure the survival of basic American institutions, but he never lost his belief that America was the land of artistic opportunity. If his fellow countrymen would awake and use their potential, Anderson felt that "the center of culture for the whole western world may be shifted to America. In short America may become the center for a new channeling of life through the arts, for a new renaissance." [49]

Anderson's talents as a novelist progressively deteriorated, a deterioration to be epitomized in *Kit Brandon* (1936), a wandering, ill-defined, verbose story of a mill-town girl who became a rumrunner during Prohibition. As he scattered his talents, his audience dwindled and his reputation increasingly began to rest on works done prior to the depression. Whatever the faults of his novels, his short stories insured his standing as at least a secondary figure in American literature. *Winesburg, Ohio, The Triumph of the Egg* (1921), *Horses and Men*, and *Death in the Woods* contain by far his best and most vital short-story writing.

All in all, his career was indeed remarkable. A middle-aged paint manufacturer, a veteran of the advertising business, a family man with definite emotional problems, totally untrained in formal writing, essentially uneducated when he began to write, he became a distinguished and widely read author and an influence in the writing of his time. His interest in life, the vitality with which he re-created that interest in words insured his success. Anderson kept to his own code, costly as it was. "There is no golden key that unlocks all doors," he wrote toward the end of his life. "There is only the joy of living as richly as you can, always feeling more, absorbing more, and, if you are by nature a teller of tales, the realization that by faking, trying to give people what they think they want, you are in danger of dulling and in the end quite destroying what may be your own road into life." [50]

Anderson did his best to live the fullness of the life accorded him. His standing as a public figure caused him to accept a magazine assignment to travel in South America in 1941 as an unofficial ambassador of good will. In the Canal Zone, he was stricken with peritonitis and died suddenly on March 8, 1941.

The years have not dealt kindly with Anderson's writings, and though various of his shorter selections enjoy continued popularity, critics and readers have not favored the corpus of his work. Much of the form and content of his books seems old-fashioned. The most ironic aspect of Anderson's work is that while he was accused of radicalism and innovation, of introducing new and forbidden themes in his early work, he was in fact concerned with older ideas derived from his American experience. The ideas of unity and love, which underlay even his most radical books, were older than any technique he employed. Yet the rejection of a machine society, the glorification of the agrarian Midwest, his interest in nature and primitivism all stamped Sherwood Anderson as a writer of the old school. In one sense he seems to have come upon writing too late in life.

But in a larger sense he was not old-fashioned. In his way he was one of the pioneers he admired, for he perceived that the increasing disunity of modern life must sooner or later call order into being or man would perish. He saw also that evil as the machine was, it must be met and mastered, that however much the land and the civilization might change under the impact of new forces, these forces must be met. He saw the dangers to individualism and took the only course open to sensitive realists—not rejection but acceptance of the change and an attempt to identify himself with all of life. Desperate to salvage something from the wreckage of change, he chose, like Thomas Wolfe and Hart Crane, to fashion a new ethic that placed the artist in the midst of social change. Above all, he perceived that the crisis of his time would be of long duration, and that it was not essentially one of economics or politics but of the human spirit.

As a figure of cultural transition, Sherwood Anderson suffered more than Ellen Glasgow or Willa Cather. Essentially unlettered and uncultured, he lacked the perspective on the past and the training in art that sustained these two contemporaries. He often said that he had little concept of the past or future but lived for the present. The lack of orderly development and growth marks his severest limitation as a writer.

The theories which he devised to save his situation were often flavored by naïve and loose thinking and are easily condemned for their lack of concreteness. Yet who is to say that the emotions he felt and the attitudes he developed will not indicate the road to a deeper kind of human understanding as well as, if not better than, the more learned disquisitions of his contemporaries? Whatever his faults, Anderson understood the people and their life with a profundity that has escaped many readers and critics. His solutions will have greater validity than even he dreamed, if mankind reaches the state of consciousness he felt was imminent.

Disliking materialism and shy of display, Anderson had no taste for celebrities and studiously avoided such a role for himself. Candid about his own work, he knew that he was a minor figure in American letters, yet he hoped that at least a few in the future would read his words. "I have been all my life a wanderer but my wandering has been to some purpose," he wrote in his *Memoirs*. "America is a vast country. I have wanted to feel all of it in its thousand phases, see it, walk upon it—its plains, mountains, towns, cities, rivers, lakes, forests and plowed lands. I have been a true son of God in my meager love for and appreciation of nature. It is only through nature and art that men really live." [51] Perhaps that is the best there is to say for his life and work. Surely, for such a man, so vital and dynamic even in his faults, so close to the earth and to life itself, so fascinated by the human procession, there can be no better judgment than the epitaph he fashioned for himself: "Life, not Death, is the great adventure."

Hart Crane: Spokesman of Vision

> The Imaged Word, it is, that holds
> Hushed willows anchored in its glow.
> It is the unbetrayable reply,
> Whose accents no farewell can know.
>
> "Voyages: VI" (1926)

HART CRANE was born in Ohio in 1899, on the eve of the twentieth century. The Ohio of his youth was a rich and varied land, far removed from its frontier origins yet filled with fables and stories enough to amuse the sturdy Crane child. He listened with eager and often somber fascination to the tales of the early days told to him by the older residents of his home town. He was his parents' only child and it was his tragedy to be a pawn between them in later years when their marriage fell to pieces amid recriminations, unsettled affairs, and mental anguish.[1]

He was an alert child, endowed with unusual sensitivity to light and color, and often seemed more mature than his years allowed. His early childhood was not extraordinary. He played games, listened to his grandmother's stories, wandered the neighborhood in search of boyish adventure, and passed the years of youth in much the same way as others have done. He launched monoplanes "with paper wings and twisted rubber bands," or "stoned the family of young garter snakes under," or poked in ash heaps in search of "some sunning inch of unsuspecting fiver," always rejoicing when "it flashed back at your thrust, as clean as fire." He remembered his mother and father before the shadows of matrimonial strife darkened their home. He was not without less pleasant memories of "the whip stripped from the lilac tree one day in spring my father took to me . . ."[2] His early pictures reveal a sturdy child, large-eyed and somewhat heavy-cheeked, who stared back at the camera with determination and something akin to amusement.

It was not long before the pleasant, busy years of childhood passed, however, and heightened sensitivity to the things around him made him more and more aware of the unhappiness in his life. His father and mother quarreled, separated, and reconciled in constant cycles that racked the boy. As he grew into adolescence and manhood he could remember little but household battles. His father, by now a successful candy manufacturer in Ohio, did not understand his son's literary inclinations; nor did he accept the twist of fate that had given him a poet instead of a businessman for a son. The boy sided with his mother in the family quarrels, angering his father more, and wedges of separation were driven between the two men that kept them apart until nearly the end of their lives.

As a youth, Crane read widely and indiscriminately, eagerly devouring such diverse authors as Chaucer, D. H. Lawrence, Henry James, Plato, and Mark Twain.[3] In high school he seemed uninterested in the students around him, preferring to have a few friends and to devote the rest of his time to study, music, and poetry. "Popularity is not my aim," he wrote his grandmother, "though it were easy to win by laughing when they do at nothing and always making a general ass of oneself." [4]

He groped to find himself in his youth, realizing that these were years of preparation. Though his reading often lacked direction, he sometimes showed great insight into the works he read. He liked the brilliant hardness in the work of his friend Matthew Josephson, but he was more drawn to the basic, native qualities of Sherwood Anderson. "Somewhere between them is Hart Crane with a kind of wistful indetermination, still much puzzled," [5] he wrote as he verged on twenty.

Though Crane worked for his father at intervals, he could not bear the strain imposed by such contact and fled to New York to try his hand at advertising work, newspaper reporting, and odd jobs of any kind that would enable him to follow his muse. At eighteen he had published verse in several obscure magazines, had made a wide variety of contacts with fellow artists in New York, and had glimpsed moments of vision and ecstasy that seemed to herald a brilliant future. "I realize more entirely every day, that I am preparing for a fine life," he wrote his father in

1917, "that I have powers, which, if correctly balanced, will enable me to mount to extraordinary latitudes. There is constantly an inward struggle, but the time to worry is only when there is no inward debate, and consequently there is smooth sliding to the devil. There is only one harmony, that is the equilibrium maintained by two opposite forces, equally strong." [6] It was an acute analysis for one of his age. He spent the rest of his life in search of the elusive balance between his personal desires and the demands made upon him by his art. In the end he found balance in his art but not in himself. His greatest enemy was always Hart Crane.

In New York in the early 1920's, writing advertising copy about cheese, hot-water heaters, and other products during the day and trying to write poetry at night, Crane was faced with the necessity of disciplining the forces that worked within him. He became stubborn about it. Bitter at times at being forced to work at such things as advertising in order to live, he was nonetheless determined to be a poet. "Our age tries hard enough to kill us, but I begin to feel pleasure in sheer stubbornness, and will possibly turn in time into some sort of a beautiful crank." [7] Study helped him channel his thoughts and find direction. He had already discovered the leading French poets, especially Rimbaud and Verlaine; and he went back time and again to what he considered the foundations of English literature, the Elizabethans. "The people I am closest to in English are Yeats, Eliot, Pound, and the dear great Elizabethans like Marlowe, Webster, Donne and Drayton, whom I never weary of." [8] Their influences often appear in his later work, and he studied them with renewed fascination before writing his own great work, The Bridge (1930).

He knew well the precarious position occupied by the artist in the America of his day. Yet he had little sympathy, then or later, with the perpetual complaints about the artist's insecurity; nor did he recommend flight from reality. "The modern artist has got to harden himself, and the walls of an ivory tower are too delicate and brittle a coat of mail for substitute," [9] he wrote in 1920. In his middle twenties, as he approached his most productive period, he admitted that his road had been hard, but not without its rewards. The artist had never led an easy life, even in the best of circumstances. "The darkness is part of his business," [10] he told Waldo Frank.

In the midst of the struggle his reading continued. He had great respect for the work of T. S. Eliot, who was gaining prominence in the early 1920's. He read and reread Eliot's poetry with interest and appreciation, but its greatest service was to send him back to the Elizabethans whom Eliot echoed. From the first he was suspicious of Eliot's pessimism and warned that "Eliot's influence threatens to predominate the new English." [11] He thought *The Wasteland* was good, "but so damned dead." [12]

It was not that Crane disparaged Eliot's demands for purity of form and careful craftsmanship; on the contrary, this aspect of Eliot's work, together with his great verbal facility, appealed most to Crane. But Eliot seemed to be making a science of poetry and Crane feared the end result. He was afraid that form might triumph over vision and that the hollow sounding of doom implicit in the whole Eliot school would be taken as prophecy rather than as interpretation. "There is no one writing in English who can command so much respect, to my mind, as Eliot," Crane wrote in 1923 as Eliot's reputation and influence began their long upward climb. "However, I take Eliot as a point of departure toward an almost complete reversal of direction. His pessimism is amply justified, in his own case, but I would apply as much of his erudition and technique as I can absorb and assemble toward a more positive goal, or . . . ecstatic goal." Feeling that the Eliot school overlooked much positive material in favor of the darkness, he could not help believing that the Eliot movement would generate something more hopeful. "After this perfection of death —nothing is possible in motion but a resurrection of some kind." [13] He freely admitted, "The poetry of negation is beautiful," but insisted in the same breath, "I am trying to break away from it . . . Let us invent an idiom for the proper transposition of jazz into words! Something clean, sparkling, elusive!" [14]

In later years when some reputation had come to him and when he could count the influences that had affected him, he acknowledged his debt to Eliot, but still deplored "the fashionable pessimism of the hour." [15] Always in search of a positive attitude,

Crane doubted that the straw and ashes of the pessimists offered much to build on. ". . . I doubt if any remedy will be forthcoming from so nostalgic an attitude as the Thomists betray, and moreover a strictly European system of values, at that." [16] By way of influence, Crane owed far more to his own wide reading, the conversation of the loyal friends who endured him at his chatty best and violent worst, and to an inner demand for creativity that eventually drew him to an enduring source of inspiration, the work of Walt Whitman.

The great underlying spirit of Crane's whole work was a genuine belief in life of and for itself, as well as life for the purpose of artistic creation. Critics have often misread his criticisms of America as reflections of doubts and alienations that he never really felt. His personal troubles—compounded of an unhappy childhood, poverty, unproductive daily work, acute nervousness, alcohol, and homosexuality—often intruded on his work, producing long periods of arid contemplation. But these periods were broken by productive effort. However much these forces and events intruded on his work, his bitterness was transitory not permanent, and the sum of his poetry is wrought of light not darkness. He felt no basic alienation from his country or culture, although he criticized them at times, for he recognized their worst aspects as temporary and believed in the possibilities for good that would come from his world. Even in the depths of the despair that resulted finally in his suicide, Crane could write, when asked for articles on his impressions of Mexico: "I'm too attached to the consciousness of my own land to write 'tourist sketches' elsewhere." [17]

His progressive interest in America, her poetic past and future possibilities, pulled Crane toward Walt Whitman whose optimism and belief in life he admired. He struggled hard that his success might be the same as Whitman's: "thy wand has beat a song O Walt," he cried in *The Bridge,* hoping that that wand might also touch his song. It was for this that he proclaimed Whitman's greatness in such rhapsodic terms in the "Cape Hatteras" section of *The Bridge:*

The stars have grooved our eyes with old persuasions
Of love and hatred, birth,—surcease of nations . . .

But who has held the heights more sure than thou,
O Walt!—Ascensions of thee hover in me now.

It was not only because Whitman had revealed his soul, or because he had proclaimed his heartfelt beliefs to a heedless generation, or even because he had made new forms for poetry that Crane turned to him for instruction and inspiration. It was Whitman's belief in the goodness of man, his hopes for a better future that caused Crane to study his insights. He was caught, like Whitman, in "years of the modern," and he tried to answer the questions that besieged him by recording his belief that the future could be better if men worked toward better goals.

Crane responded to Whitman's idea that the poet's function was to show man his own potentialities and to tie him to the rest of life:

O upward from the dead
Thou bringest tally, and a pact, new bound,
Of living brotherhood!

Whitman's insistence that art must be a living rather than a dead thing, must act as an agent of understanding between men, tying them to past and future, ordering chaos, struck a chord in Crane:

O something
green,
Beyond all sesames of science was thy choice
Wherewith to bind us throbbing with one voice.

He knew that Whitman had been spurned by his own generation, and Crane must have seen his own face when he wrote the words:

Recorders ages hence, yes, they shall hear
In their own veins uncancelled thy sure tread
And read thee by the aureole 'round thy head
Of pasture—shine, *Panis Angelicus!*

Crane knew that he passed from criticism to rhapsody in evaluating Whitman. "It's true that my rhapsodic address to him in *The Bridge* exceeds any exact evaluation of the man." [18] Yet he felt that he had touched strains and fibers in Whitman's work that summed up the poet's essential greatness. He was determined not to be sidetracked into the fashionable wailing of the Lost Generation, whom he never joined, and desired to turn instead to hopeful and constructive work. Whitman gave him more food for thought than Eliot, and Crane could not but feel that he reflected greater currents and offered more possibilities than any other figure to whom he could look:

The most typical and valid expression of the American *psychosis* seems to me still to be found in Whitman. His faults as a technician and his clumsy and indiscriminate enthusiasm are somewhat beside the point. He, better than any other, was able to coordinate those forces in America which seem most intractable, fusing them into a universal vision which takes on additional significance as time goes on. He was a revolutionist beyond the strict meaning of Coleridge's definition of genius, but his bequest is still to be realized in all its implications.[19]

Even in the twilight of self-doubt that racked him after the completion of *The Bridge*, he could still vow his "allegiance to the Positive and universal tendencies implicit in nearly all his [Whitman's] best work." [20]

Crane not only studied Whitman, but also Poe, Melville, and other Americans, as well as the English authors, in the years of preparation that produced *The Bridge*. From this multiplicity of sources and his own creativity he gathered the variety of forms and imagery that made him famous in his own time, and later, as one of the most difficult modern American poets.

Crane had discovered that alcohol exerted a powerful influence on him. It served as a stimulant to his already supersensitive personality, and under its influence his subconscious mind would go "rioting out through gates that only alcohol has the power to open." [21] Once within its grip new worlds seemed to open for him. Wine, music, conversation—all could open his inner mind and produce "This competence—to travel in a tear, sparkling alone, with another's will." But it would be a mistake to assume that Crane's poetry resulted largely from the wine. He possessed a truly mystic ability to transcend time and circumstance without alcohol's help. Though he had to be deeply stirred to write, alcohol was only one of the keys that unlocked the doors of creative activity.

Despite his lack of formal education, which embarrassed him

at times, he understood poetic rules and he did not hesitate to use them as well as adapt them to his needs. He was quick to defend himself against charges of willful obscurity. " 'Make my dark poem light, and light,' however, is the text I chose from Donne some time ago as my direction. I have always been working hard for a more perfect lucidity, and it never pleases me to be taken as wilfully obscure or esoteric." [22]

Wide reading, study of the masters of the past, heightened sensibility, and a willingness to experiment afforded Crane the materials for an astonishing range of form and symbol. The English poets gave him his solid base of language, and the French gave him a sense of color and perception that lifted his poetry to ecstatic levels. To these he added his own creative talent, his gift for words, and his almost uncanny ability to capture in images the visions he saw. Who of his contemporaries could match his changes of style, tempo, his use of visual color, his variety of formal rhyme, now restrained, now dazzling? He moved with ease from solidity:

> Damp tonnage and alluvial march of days—
> Nights turbid, vascular with silted shale
> And roots surrendered down of moraine clays:
> The Mississippi drinks the farthest dale.

to elegiac tones:

> Under the Ozarks, domed by Iron Mountain,
> The old gods of the rain lie wrapped in pools
> Where eyeless fish curvet a sunken fountain
> And re-descend with corn from querulous crows.
> Such pilferings make up their timeless eatage,
> Propitiate them for their timber torn
> By iron, iron—always the iron dealt cleavage!
> They doze now below axe and powder horn.

to the tenderness of love lyrics:

> *your hands within my hands are deeds:*
> *my tongue upon your throat—singing*
> *arms close; eyes wide, undoubtful*
> *dark*
> *drink the dawn—*
> *a forest shudders in your hair!*

and taut symbolism:

> The phonographs of hades in the brain
> Are tunnels that rewind themselves, and love
> A burnt match skating in a urinal

It was Crane's greatest technical accomplishment to balance incongruities of image. The poetic forms he used seemed new, yet they were in fact traditional; he was able to join language and a transcendent vision in a way that triumphed over both old and new. "The imagination is the only thing worth a damn," [23] he told Gorham Munson before he began The Bridge, and he was determined to remain unfettered in his search for new dimensions of the imagination.

Composition was desperately hard for him, for he felt both the compelling urge to write and the exhaustion that came with it. He was hounded by poverty, disagreeable work, family troubles, lack of time, and besieged by outbursts of debauchery that drained both strength and inspiration. Yet he managed to write, working steadily toward The Bridge. "Oh! it is hard! One must be drenched in words, literally soaked with them to have the right ones form themselves into the proper patterns at the right moment." [24]

To those who criticized his new attitudes and fresh techniques and who accused him of being cryptic, he answered that he was only trying to explore old questions with new devices. It was not easy. "There is little to [be] gained in any art so far as I can see, except with much conscious effort." [25] He had little patience with criticisms of his "newness." "If the poet is to be held completely to the already evolved and exploited sequence of imagery and logic—what field of added consciousness and increased perceptions (the actual province of poetry, if not lullabys) can be expected when one has to relatively return to the alphabet every breath or so?" [26] he asked Harriet Munroe in 1926. "I am only interested in adding what seems to me something really new to what has been written. Unless one has some new, intensely personal viewpoint to record . . . why write about it?" [27] he told a friend early in his career.

Crane was not merely a brilliant technician; he was also deeply concerned with the society around him, with the problems that beset not only the artist but man in general. He quickly perceived that machine civilization posed a threat to both the artist and the man on the street. In an early review of Sherwood Anderson's work he praised his attack on the machine, and lauded his return to the basic, premachine influences in life. The problem loomed large to Crane when he undertook *The Bridge*. To him the machine was "the monster that is upon us all. No one who treats however slightly of the lives of the poor or middle classes can escape the issues of its present hold upon us. It has seduced the strongest from the land to the cities, and in most cases made empty and meaningless their lives. It has cheapened the worth of all human commodities and even the value of human lives. It has destroyed the pride and pleasure of the craftsman in his work." [28]

Like Sherwood Anderson, Crane mirrored the cultural conflicts introduced by triumphant industrialism. He, too, cherished the recollections of an agrarian childhood in the Midwest and condemned the machine for its destruction of spiritual values. And, he clearly saw that the crisis was one of the soul and the imagination, not merely of politics or economics. Crane, too, valued the primitivism and earthy naturalness of life that he felt the machine had crushed out.

Yet this bitter rejection of the machine and the civilization that it was making in America was not accompanied by any nostalgic demand for a return to the past. As time passed and his own perceptions increased, Crane looked upon the machine in a different light. Like Anderson, he came to believe that it had potentialities for unity as well as disorder, and though he continued to distrust it and the esthetic insensitivity it produced, he determined to cope with it. The evil flaw in machinery was not the machine itself, but the uses to which man put it. "The emotional stimulus of machinery is on an entirely different psychic plane from that of poetry," he observed in an essay on modern poetry. But he did not feel that the machine needed necessarily to dominate life, "Its only menace lies in its capacity for facile entertainment, so easily accessible as to arrest the development of any but the most negligible esthetic responses." [29] There was the machine's real threat—its power to dull men's sensitivity to the possibilities inherent in the life around them.

The machine was a great challenge to him as a poet and he deemed it the artist's greatest task to meet it. "For unless poetry can absorb the machine, i.e., *acclimatize* it as naturally and casually as trees, cattle, galleons, castles and all other human associations of the past, then poetry has failed of its full contemporary function." [30] He felt that once the creative artist attacked the problem, explored its ramifications, and pointed out the alternatives, the threat would recede. "Machinery will tend to lose its sensational glamour and appear in its true subsidiary order in human life as use and continual poetic allusion subdue its novelty" [31]

While he attacked the machine and the sterility of science in general, he recognized them as forces that would have to be met and mastered if men were to progress. Here the poet must place his heightened sensitivity at man's disposal to show how this could be done. Crane saw that machinery was but one aspect of the threat that faced him. "But the main faults are not of our city, alone," he wrote as early as 1922. "They are of the age. A period that is loose at all ends, without apparent direction of any sort. In some ways the most amazing age there ever was. Appalling and dull at the same time." [32] Thus it was to combat "a world of chaotic values and frightful spiritual depression" [33] that Crane undertook *The Bridge*, and nothing is so characteristic of the man or so illuminating of his purpose as this positive act in the face of negative challenge. While others fled into academicism or Dada, Crane investigated, challenged, and in his way tried to subdue the evils of the day.

Realizing the full dimensions of the machine-made threat, aware of public indifference to his art, Crane nevertheless fought for a positive conception of the artist's role in society. He read Spengler, and sometimes conceded that he might be right, but disliked the philosophers of gloom. He was disturbed by his generation's concern with the future and thought it was a great danger to the arts. "It seems as though the imagination had ceased all attempts at any creative activity—and had become simply a great bulging eye ogling the foetus of the next century," [34] he wrote toward the end of the 1920's.

It was precisely here, he thought, that the artist could do himself and his fellow men most good, for he possessed something that could transcend both today and tomorrow: heightened sensitivity to the possibilities of creative vision. The poet's vision was to him "a peculiar type of perception, capable of apprehending some absolute and timeless concept of the imagination with astounding clarity and conviction." [35] With this greater degree of perception and understanding, the poet and artist could perceive hidden possibilities and meanings in the world around him, visions denied to other men and which he must make explicit in his art. "The imagination spans beyond despair, Outpacing bargain, vocable and prayer," he wrote in an early poem "For the Marriage of Faust and Helen." The artist might through imagination transmit continuity and order in times of intellectual and cultural transition. He might, in short, make the world meaningful.

Crane advised a deeper study of mankind for those who doubted the future. He wrote Allen Tate that while he admired his poems, he would like to see "their upward slant into something broadly human. Launch into praise." [36] And he recommended that the poet return to the sources which had always given him fresh vigor and inspiration. He himself mixed with a wide variety of people in the places where he worked and lived, and he never tired of their vitality and wholesomeness. "We must somehow touch the clearest veins of eternity flowing through the crowds around us—or risk becoming the kind of glorious cripples that have missed some vital part of their inheritance." [37]

Love would break the power of the machine and order the world's chaos. Crane's early lyrical poetry, best exemplified by the incomparably beautiful "Voyages," speaks of an intensely personal love that was also a part of his desire to bind himself to all humanity. In the "Atlantis" section of *The Bridge*, this love became part of his paean to the bridge and to humanity itself; it was depicted as the basic force that could insure unity in all of life. Loving was in itself a creative act for Crane, because it lifted the loved and the lover to new levels of consciousness. This personal love could become universal, the fulfillment of the poet's vision of the possibilities inherent in reality. It was a means of uniting the self with all of life:

> I dreamed that all men dropped their names, and sang
> As only they can praise, who build their days

With fin and hoof, with wing and sweetened fang
Struck free and holy in one Name always.

Like Sherwood Anderson, he believed that should human love be given the opportunity to function, it would cure the loneliness of life and bridge the gap between individuals and eras.

Human love in his verse became a form of communion. That he was denied the opportunity to realize this love in his own life was the source of Crane's greatest despair, and became a factor contributing to his suicide. But the possible triumph of such love remained one of the basic motives that impelled him to write. His biographer noted that "despite the long years of disillusionment and frustrations his belief in love as the transcendent force of life remained the steadfast lodestar of his imagination and work." [38]

Was the situation worse in America than in Europe? Was Crane's native land immune to art, callous in its attitudes toward the artist, inherently unable to cope with so great a moral and spiritual crisis as the times presented? Did Crane in fact repudiate the American past and deny its future, as some critics have suggested? [39] Crane alternated between fits of despair and fits of hope for the future of America, depending largely on how successfully his work of the moment was going. He condemned freely the lack of esthetic sense and appreciation of the arts which he confronted on every hand. He would easily burst out at his countrymen's inability to appreciate the dancing of Isadora Duncan, the subtle mimicry of Charlie Chaplin, and the work of himself and other artists. "Our people have no *atom* of a conception of beauty—and don't want it," [40] he would angrily erupt.

Yet, as he developed as an artist and as he became more and more intrigued with American history and the possibility of defining the chaos of his age in terms of an epic poem about America, he doubted that his country was any worse or more shallow in its insights and tastes than Europe. "The world is fast becoming standardized,—and who knows but what our American scene will be the most intricate and absorbing one in fifty years or so? Something is happening. Some kind of aristocracy of taste is being established,—and there is more evidenced every year." [41] He was generally unmoved by outcries from his fellow artists that they were neglected. "And I am as completely out of sympathy with the familiar whimpering caricature of the artist and his 'divine rights' as you seem to be," [42] he wrote Yvor Winters in 1927. If the artist was oppressed, he must react to the challenge and attempt to rectify it.

This whole attitude was only another facet of Crane's demand for positive goals. Artistic failure could not be blamed on external causes. "If you ARE an artist then, you will create spontaneously." [43] He knew what many of his contemporaries never seemed to grasp: there is generally a long period of waiting in the wings before a new creation of merit is afforded the center of the stage. Though the public did not understand the new art, Crane believed that it could in time, and that it was America's historic mission to present new artistic conceptions to the rest of the world. "The American public is still strangely unprepared for its men of higher talents," he wrote his mother in 1924 with a trace of irritation that ended on hope, "while Europe looks more to America for the renascence of creative spirit." [44]

In the meantime, the artist would have to endure and pursue his work. "The true idea of God is the only thing that can give happiness,—and that is the identification of yourself with *all of life*," [45] he insisted emphatically. The artist must not only project himself into life, but must try to affect and to become a part of all of life in order to utilize all aspects of his art.[46] That was why he had so little sympathy with the Dadaists and other faddists who abounded in the 1920's; they produced nothing ultimately tied to life, and their quest was for escape from life, not for identification with it.[47]

The artist's mission in the midst of confusion was to try to unify the forces around him. Crane looked to Whitman with such reverence because he had also lived in an age of transition. And yet Whitman had not called for despair or withdrawal, but for a new belief in humanity. Whitman had posited the poet as an active agent in the salvation of humanity; an artistic renaissance could not fail to affect more of life than the arts. This idea of mission, of being an agent of unification in times of chaos appealed to Crane because it afforded him the chance and the means to be human in the broadest sense of the word.[48]

With all this in mind, Crane came to compose *The Bridge*.[49]

Hounded almost beyond endurance by poverty, personal insecurity, dulling labor, and unable to raise funds from friends, Crane at last appealed to the noted banker Otto Kahn, who had subsidized the work of several young artists. Kahn met Crane, listened to the outline of his proposed project, and then advanced a generous sum so that Crane could begin work on the epic poem.

Crane had once said that he felt he could become "the greatest singer of our generation," [50] and this was his chance to prove it. The critical acclaim accorded his first book, *White Buildings* (1926), his own satisfaction with much of his work, the long period of preparation, and the encouragement of friends convinced him that there were materials at hand for an epic of America that could also be an epic of mankind. He was eager to undertake the task; some such conception had dwelled in his mind for years.

It was an ambitious plan, even for a poet of Crane's competence, but he was driven by a desperate need to compose it. Hoping that he might at last see the ultimate vision, Crane worked at the poem in a frenzy of activity in 1926. "Sometimes the words come and go, presented like a rose that yields only its light, never its composite form," he wrote Waldo Frank in the midst of agonized composition. But "to handle the beautiful skeins of this myth of America—to realize suddenly, as I seem to, how much of the past is living under only slightly altered forms, even in machinery and such-like, is extremely exciting." [51]

He worked on the various sections of the poem, alternating from one to another, pausing in the midst of composition to write Otto Kahn of his progress:

What I am really handling you see, is the Myth of America. Thousands of strands have had to be searched for, sorted and interwoven. In a sense I have had to do a great deal of pioneering myself. It has taken a great deal of energy—which has not been so difficult to summon as the necessary patience to wait, simply wait much of the time—until my instincts assured me that I had assembled my materials in proper order for a final welding into their natural form. For each section of the entire poem has presented its own unique problem of form, not alone in relation to the materials embodied in its separate confines, but also in relation to the other parts, *in series,* of the major design of the entire poem. Each is a separate canvas, as it were, yet none yields its entire significance when seen apart from the others. One might take the Sistine Chapel as an analogy.[52]

Taken together, these separate canvases were Crane's effort to explain the past, its continuity with the present, its promise for the future, and its meaning for the artist as a source of inspiration. "*The Bridge*, in becoming a ship, a world, a woman, a tremendous harp (as it does finally) seems really to have a career," [53] he wrote Waldo Frank as the poem's outline first became clear in his mind.

The Bridge, as finally published, was divided into eight major sections, preceded by an introduction. Crane had planned other sections but they were never finished and his original outline of the poem was considerably altered. The introductory "Poem" set forth the object of the entire poem, the bridge, a symbol of America, "a symbol of our constructive future, our unique identity, in which is included also our scientific hopes and achievements of the future." [54]

In the "Ave Maria" section of the poem, Crane describes Columbus in search of a new world, but this is not the Columbus of history books. Crane depicts him as seeking a New Jerusalem, a new consciousness as well as a new world; he, like Crane, is a man of transcendent vision who could probe beyond the mundane for the essential spiritual vision:

> For I have seen now what no perjured breath
> Of clown nor sage can riddle or gainsay;—
> To you, too, Juan Perez, whose counsel fear
> And greed adjourned,—I bring you back Cathay!

Here is the object of the ultimate quest, symbolized by mythical Cathay—new vision, new hope.

The second section of the poem, "Powhatan's Daughter," is a symbolic reaffirmation of Crane's old demand to return to first principles for inspiration and true beliefs. The Indian princess symbolizes the American earth, unsullied flesh, "the mother of our dreams." [55] In the "Van Winkle" part of this section he moves among familiar surroundings in New York, through a cross-country passage in "The River," followed by the beautiful "Dance" section, which extols the primeval virtues, the powerful earthy attractions of the symbolic savage who danced for Mother America. "Lie to us,—dance us back the tribal morn!" he begs plaintively. In "Indiana," though describing the frustrations and bitterness in the heart of a pioneer mother, the poet reaffirms the possibilities of life.

In "Cutty Sark," the third major section of the poem, Crane is once more fascinated by the sea as an agent and source of both life and death, holding promises of good as well as tragedy. Here the protagonist of the poem falls in with a drunken sailor who mouths the names of distant lands and faraway places, heading at last for the sea once again.

The poem's fourth major section, "Cape Hatteras," sings praises to Walt Whitman. Here Crane descends from the universal to the particular, which sets this section (like "Indiana") apart from the universality of the others. The old love of Whitman surges forth once more for final and complete identification with America and the symbol which Crane has set for her, the bridge:

> Our Meistersinger, thou set breath in steel;
> And it was thou who on the boldest heel
> Stood up and flung the span on even wing
> Of that great Bridge, our Myth, whereof I sing!

In "Three Songs," the poet sings his praises to woman, but a greater woman than of the flesh, for here once more she symbolizes life and basic sources. This section of the poem, coming after the frenzied accolade to Whitman, is "a pause for humbler music." [56]

But once again the poet attempts to grasp new inspiration, trying in "Quaker Hill" to set all his own personal past in some cosmic order. Here rise before him the visions and memories that are peculiarly his own and yet which belong to a larger audience, for his life has been that of all mankind. Here his exuberance wanes as the poet contemplates the changes that have marred the face of America. Moments of optimism mingle with moments of pessimism:

> Who holds the lease on time and on disgrace?
> What eats the pattern with ubiquity?
> Where are my kinsmen and the patriarch race?

A sense of resignation and bitterness prevails, yet Crane demands that the poet sing and thereby elevate himself and his audience:

> Yes, while the heart is wrung,
> Arise—yes, take this sheaf of dust upon your tongue!
> In one last angelus lift throbbing throat—
> Listen, transmuting silence with that silly note
> Of pain that Emily, that Isadora knew!

In "The Tunnel" the poet is once again dropped back into daily life, homeward bound by subway, the great bridge that spans the underworld as the other bridge spans the river. The tunnel is a place of visions and nightmares. It "is a kind of hell. But it has dynamic direction, it is moving!" [57] The poet sees the face of Poe, as if in grim premonition of his own fate: "And why do I often meet your visage here, Your eyes like agate lanterns—" he asks of the apparition.

The final section, "Atlantis," completes the circle. Atlantis now unites with Cathay to complete the journey in time and metaphor and provokes the poet's most rhapsodic tribute to the bridge symbol:

> From gulfs unfolding, terrible of drums,
> Tall Vision-of-the-Voyage, tensely spare—
> Bridge, lifting night to cycloramic crest
> Of deepest day—O Choir, translating time
> Into what multitudinous Verb the suns
> And synergy of waters ever fuse, recast
> In myriad syllables,—Psalm of Cathay!
> O Love, thy white, pervasive Paradigm . . .

And here the myth comes to life and is real to Crane in one last burst of song and homage. It dances on the waters of his mind, singing out the powers of love, no longer myth to him but reality itself:

> Unspeakable Thou Bridge to Thee, O Love.
> Thy pardon for this history, whitest Flower,
> O Answerer of all,—Anemone,—
> Now while thy petals spend the suns about us, hold—
> (O Thou whose radiance doth inherit me)
> Atlantis,—hold thy floating singer late!

Thus Crane concluded his greatest work, his effort to make his individual vision a universal vision, his attempt to find "One Song, One Bridge of Fire!" He had poured into its composition all his ideas of the function of art, the poet's responsibility, his hope of unity in the midst of chaos. "What Crane was really trying to do, as a poet, was to give an inward, spiritual significance to the material, outward conditions of twentieth-century civilization," [58] one critic has noted. How well he had succeeded in doing this was a question that began to plague Crane long before he finished his poem.

As Crane's work on the intricate poem progressed, there were times when his inspiration flagged and when the high hopes with which he had begun dimmed. Besieged by personal doubts, fearful that the poem would be his tomb instead of his monument, Crane himself was dissatisfied with the final form of *The Bridge*. His private world had begun to crumble in the midst of composition, inevitably affecting his outlook and work. His old self-doubts reasserted themselves, and as he lost faith in his creative powers, he also lost faith in the validity of the task he had set himself. "So much is expected of me via that poem—that if I fail on it I shall become a laughing stock and my career closed," [59] he wrote his mother when he first began the poem. Crane's anxieties about the validity of his concept and his declining faith in his original inspiration were prompted more by personal problems than by any sustained loss of belief in the possibilities he had sensed and even seen while working on the poem.

Reviews of the work were mixed, though many rang with high praise. The fact that some of his friends and critics had reservations about the poem only made Crane feel more insecure and uncertain about his accomplishment. Many critics were irritated by his loose use of historical fact, complaining that history seemed to be a series of romantic tableaux to Crane. None could deny, least of all Crane himself, that the interpretation of historical fact was very free in the poem. But to judge *The Bridge* in terms of its adherence to facts is to view it through a narrow prism, missing the poem's point.[60] It lacks perfect unity, yet as Crane had pointed out, each section was designed as an entity, forming a larger more complete picture when combined with other sections. To conclude that the work as a whole is pessimistic is to fail to see the essential vision, that of infinite possibilities inherent in the materials of life, outlined in the poem.

Nothing better illustrates Crane's attitude than this absorbing interest in possibilities. He had set himself a larger task than that of the historian. "I am really writing an epic of the modern consciousness," [61] he explained to Otto Kahn. While his poem may have failed to achieve perfect technical unity to the satisfaction of literary critics, and while it may not have maintained the heights of inspiration he and his admirers had hoped for, it nonetheless remains an enduring monument to his quest and one of the greatest modern poems. It needs no apologies. The poem's depiction of the varieties of modern life, the machine, and the mystical vision possible through love make it compelling in its entirety. Language alone will insure the poem a long life, but it will survive and be studied not merely as a source of technical virtuosity, but also for the evidence it contains of the disparate forms, forces, fears, hopes, and triumphs which made up the world of Crane and his generation.

Out of the struggle with himself, the revolt and attraction which the world held for him, and his intense emotional problems, Crane had perceived a great truth: chaos, like order, can be used to define itself. That very definition then became the springboard to discover the means of challenging chaos and creating unity. This was necessary for Crane, for his acute sensitivity made chaos very real to him. Crane succeeded in showing the possibility of unity in *The Bridge* to this extent: he showed that his old belief in the power of love as a unifying force was as strong as ever, and out of his demand for a positive artistic role came moments of personal vision that showed him the reality of his vision. In the end, these concepts as much as American history gave order to the poem. Vision more than facts unified *The Bridge*.

Once the poem was finished, Crane seemed to lose the will to continue his work. "In falling short of the extreme goal he had set himself, in failing to achieve the complete and radiant vision of the mysticism he so vividly felt and so sadly misunderstood and abused, he seems to have done his spirit an irreparable injury from which it never recovered." [62] He won a Guggenheim Fellowship in 1931-1932 and went to Mexico with the outline of an epic of the Conquest hazy in his mind. But he spent his time and energy in self-recrimination and debauchery. On April 27, 1932, returning from his year in Mexico, he jumped from a northbound steamer, ending his career in suicide.

Was this final act of despair an admission that he and *The Bridge* had failed their purpose? The question can never be answered, for no one will ever know what dark images passed before the mirror of his mind in the days and hours before his death. Visions from the wreckage of his past and dark intimations of the future must have risen up to combine with the grayness of his present to test his failing strength. He feared that he had written himself out. "Have we the patience to endure? I say YES!" [63] he wrote shortly before his death. But flesh and mind had withstood much since the ecstatic days that produced his best work and he must have felt a constant uncertainty that he could ever scale the heights of inspiration again.

Moreover, his fears of age and time took on new dimensions as he counted the years that lay behind. He had spent much of his youth in a desperate search for stability and beauty and he must have wondered as he verged on middle age if added years could bring anything but decline. He feared the things that travel in time's wake—continued insecurity, failing powers, the dangers of complacency as the body slowed down. He had worked too long and endured too much to settle into a life of lesser intensity. If he forced himself to write, he might reveal that his powers had failed. He could not face such a prospect, for only his art and the towers of vision had sustained him.

In sum, the reason for Crane's suicide was not the loss of faith in his art or belief in its possibilities; nor was he driven to death by a callous society. Crane committed suicide because he could no longer endure his lack of personal balance. In any discussion of his death the poet must be separated from the man. "The poet was clearer and shrewder than the man," [64] his friend Waldo Frank clearly perceived.

And the summing up? What had he done to insure his future survival through his art? He had always been sure that much of his work would survive as testimony to the validity of his concepts. He once tried to explain to his father why he wrote poetry and told him "you may live to see the name 'Crane' stand for something where literature is talked about, not only in New York but in London and abroad." [65] Even his agonizing doubts gave way before the belief that his work would not perish with him. His concepts of the artist's role in society, his hopes for the future remained optimistic to the end. He had done more than his share for modern poetry, having produced new concepts of word functions, new meters, language, symbols, and purpose that would make his work endure.[66]

Crane's poetry will be studied in the future not merely for its brilliant language but because it is the record of struggle, creative endeavor, and experience that he endured and which others will endure in the future. With time and study and the striving of readers themselves toward those same high levels of consciousness that impelled Crane to live and work, the full outlines of his contributions to poetry and to human consciousness will be realized.

Crane's work is as yet relatively undiscovered, and its technical difficulty and symbolism obscure for many its innate beauty and vibrant vision. But along with Thomas Wolfe, he spoke for an America that had not yet come into its own, an America which he believed stood on the threshold of a great artistic awakening. His avowed purpose was to awaken a consciousness of that potential by writing *The Bridge*. Whatever his faults and shortcomings, Crane had the courage to follow the full course of his vision and art. In an age of materialism, he spurned the gods of both wealth and power and strove to realize in poetry what he had glimpsed in his imagination.

Like Thomas Wolfe, Crane suffered from his long and agonized search; the role of the artist was never an easy one for him. America will owe him a great deal if her arts reach that fruition for which he worked. When that day comes, he should be recognized as a dominant poet of his time, a creator of lasting beauty, and spokesman of a vision and ideals that may yet present practical answers to mankind's problems. He will then indeed be "the greatest singer of our generation."

Thomas Wolfe: The Web of Memory

> In one sense, my whole effort for years might be described as an effort to fathom my own design, to explore my own channels, to discover my own ways . . . I believe I have found my language, I think I know my way. And I shall wreak out my vision of this life, this way, this world and this America, to the top of my bent, to the height of my ability, but with an unswerving devotion, integrity and purity of purpose that shall not be menaced, altered or weakened by anyone.
>
> Thomas Wolfe (1936)

FEW MEN have been the subject of so many legends as Thomas Wolfe.[1] How many stories surround his rise to fame in American letters, telling of his huge appetite; his tall frame whose shadow fell across so many lives; his voracious desire to read every book at Harvard and to know everyone in New York; his frantic effort to find himself and his production of four sprawling novels in the process of that quest; his frenzied work, during which he consumed gallons of coffee and dozens of cigarettes a day, writing on the top of an icebox because tables were too short for him; his tragic death at the height of his powers.

He was born in Asheville, in the mountains of North Carolina, on October 3, 1900. The Asheville from which he came, the Altamont of his later work, was a mixture of cultures, and the crosscurrents and conflicts which gave it life profoundly influenced him. Asheville was, to all appearances, a pleasant, moderately prosperous town. A resort center, and later a focus of land speculation, it was a place of beauty and rural charm. During and after the First World War, Asheville, like many other sections of the South, fell victim to real-estate speculation and industrialization. Waves of commercial expansion that signaled the approach of a New South broke over the little city and the state in the 1920's, bringing a boom spirit to the whole area. The town that Wolfe loved as a child became a city. In all of this the young Tom Wolfe saw the conflict of cultures and ideals, mountain spirit meeting urban enterprise, the past yielding to the future, the present often a victim of exploitation and moral decay.

As he watched, the gangling, awkward boy recorded everything he saw. Every symbol cast a shadow, tantalizing in its hidden meanings. Here indeed was the stuff of many novels.

His family even more than the town molded Wolfe's personality and gave him the resources for his work. Few men have ever had a family so full of color and emotion. His father, who became old Gant in his son's first novel, was built on heroic proportions: tall of limb, broad of girth, filled with the insatiable desires and lusts of his country origins. He built roaring fires, ate huge meals, drank raw whiskey on periodic binges, a man for whom the world was Lilliput to his Gulliver.

Wolfe's mother differed sharply from her husband. He was rash and impatient, but she was as silent and timeless as the earth itself, patient in her knowledge that most things come to him who waits. Parsimonious to the point of stinginess, she saved string and sticks, begrudging her family even necessities, denying herself many small pleasures to satisfy her lust for ownership. Her mind, like her son's, tenaciously stored memories. Her brain was a warehouse, her home a collection of junk.

All of Wolfe's family found its way into his fiction: the gentle Grover, dead of typhus as a child; the pathetic, tragic Ben, cut off in youth; the quarrelsome, rugged sister Mabel, so much like her father. These and many of the population of Asheville people the pages of his writing. The young Tom Wolfe suffered all of the frustrations, desires, doubts, and despairs of his adult life. Always hungry, always restless, he grew up in a world that smirked at his pretensions and dreams. The gods seemed to heighten his pain by making him stand out, and he suffered much because of his size and awkwardness. School had few charms for him. Except for one teacher, Margaret Roberts, and a few books, it was the town's life that intrigued him even as an adolescent.

Money was the yardstick of success for his family, but never for him. "Eugene wanted the two things all men want," he wrote of his fictional counterpart in *Look Homeward, Angel* (1929);

"he wanted to be loved, and he wanted to be famous." [2] That fame, he knew, would not come to him through business or politics, but through art, the writing he would do.

It was a strange ambition for his section and his origins, for the South accorded few rewards to writers. Writers were people like Longfellow and Tennyson, he remembered, and were as distant as the moon to his contemporaries. The normal confusions of boyhood were complicated for him by his realization that his ambitions were different. There was a mystical quality in his confusion. From the darkness of his troubled life and in the midst of his aching growing pains, he realized that there was magic at his finger tips. "He wanted opulent solitude," he recalled. "His dark vision burned on kingdoms under the sea, on windy castle crags, and on the deep elf kingdoms at the earth's core. He groped for the doorless land of the faery, that illimitable haunted country that opened somewhere below a leaf or a stone. And no birds sing." [3]

His father, whom he deeply loved, was a master stonecutter, an artist in his way as well as a workman, but his son had no such talent. Instead, Wolfe convinced his family that college would equip him for life, and with divided blessings he enrolled in the University of North Carolina in 1915. Fully alive to his country origins and lack of polish, Wolfe was often unhappy in college. His engaging sense of humor, his capacity for work, and his gusto helped him through the years of study.

From his confusion of purpose, Wolfe distilled the desire to write plays. For years he labored to put what he wished to say on the stage. The task was a fruitless one, though he produced some creditable drama as an undergraduate and later at Harvard. Time and deeper reflection convinced him that only the breadth and sweep of the novel afforded him a proper vehicle.

The First World War interrupted his schooling. He left the university briefly after quarreling with his family and worked in war industry at Newport News, still absorbing like a sponge the life that he saw around him. Graduating in 1920, he convinced his parents that graduate study would bring his talents to fruition, an unprecedented step in his family and circle, who viewed further education as a waste of time. He chose Harvard because of its celebrated drama department and enrolled in the famous 47 Workshop of Professor George Pierce Baker. Harvard was a new world to him, a world of the city, of glamour and learning, and of sophistication. The years at Harvard taught him that he could not read every book in Widener Library, and also that he was destined to write. "I don't know how I became a writer, but I think it was because of a certain force in me that had to write and that finally burst through and found a channel," [4] he said later.

Graduate study and writing also brought into focus a belief that did more than merely justify what he wished to do. "The only Progress is spiritual," he wrote his mother in 1924, "the only lasting thing is Beauty—created by an artist." [5] Wolfe would weave this beauty from the thread of memory, using his past and its rich materials for his writings. Just as his mother had an insatiate lust to possess things, so her son had a similar lust to own his past, to relive it in his writing. He laid himself open to the charge of autobiographical writing, but founded his art in a deep consciousness of life and a rich variety of experience that few artists of his time could match.

For it was life that intrigued him, not study; he was an indifferent scholar and studied drama as a technique rather than a discipline. As he grew he realized as all men do that the life he had been taught was not the life that he saw in reality. He wished to present both, myth and reality, and thus find from the fusion of the two the secret of existence. "I want to know life and understand it and interpret it without fear or favor," [6] he wrote his mother in 1923. For Wolfe such an ambition was founded on more than the exuberance of youth. The very frustrations and tortures that compelled him to write contained a force, he felt, that would enable him to fulfill his task. "I will meet all the people I can. I will think all the thoughts, feel all the emotions I am able, and I will write, write, write." [7]

The passions of his family and the conflicting purposes of his youth had not given him personal security. Recognizing his sensitivity, while unable to control it, he saw clearly that his only salvation lay in creating. The purpose of his frenzied search was to find a central design in life, to give it meaning and order. "He

believed in beauty and in order, and that he would wreak out
their mighty forms upon the distressful chaos of his life," [8] he
wrote in his first novel. It was the artist's purpose to see beauty
and immortality, and thereby to make unity in life possible. "Our
effort is to wreak out of chaos and the impermanent hours some
lasting beauty," he wrote in later years; "the effort usually fails,
but it is a thing for the strong and faithful to try for." [9]

In many ways, the youthful Wolfe was bitter at his world,
which denied him recognition and trampled into the mud of
false values the ideas that he and his fellow creators held dear.
But he was not a rebel in the fullest sense; neither then nor later
did he join any Lost Generation, nor did he feel at war with his
fellows. Then as always his revolt was within himself; it was
inner and artistic, and that was its power, for that revolt combined with his loneliness and insecurity to produce a view of life
and a kind of writing that influenced much of his generation. He
felt, as he wrote his mother from Harvard, that only death could
deny him triumph. That sense of inevitable triumph was in itself
a form of enslavement; it gave him reassurance, but it also denied
him freedom, for he believed that he must suffer through his
creativity.

Graduation with a Master's degree from Harvard in 1922 did
not alter his sense of loneliness and isolation. He resigned himself to drudgery while trying to write. His family helped support
his efforts without understanding his ideas. He taught at the
Washington Square College of New York University, a post he
held first in 1924 and again several years later while writing his
first novel, *Look Homeward, Angel.* Though he considered himself a bad teacher, his students profited from his rather unorthodox
approach to learning.

Living simply on his slender means, he threw himself into his
writing with characteristic energy. All other things faded as he
attacked his memory, hacking from it day by day, word by word,
scene by scene, the immense stone that became "the Angel."
"While the fury of creation was upon him, it meant sixty
cigarettes a day, twenty cups of coffee, meals snatched anyhow
and anywhere, and at whatever time of day or night he happened to remember he was hungry. It meant sleeplessness, and

miles of walking to bring on the physical fatigue without which he could not sleep, then nightmares, nerves, and exhaustion in the morning," [10] he wrote of his fictional self years later.

While writing his first novel, Wolfe was imprisoned in a double image of time, the recollection of his childhood that shaped the novel, and his exultation in his present youthful strength which enabled him to work. "Oh, what a land, a life, a time was that, the world of youth and no return," [11] he recalled. His writing was interspersed with trips to Europe, teaching, and times of despair. By 1929 all his suffering had produced an immense manuscript, *Look Homeward, Angel.*

Loath to cut off a single branch from the tree of memory, or to deny the validity of any moment in time, Wolfe had poured out everything he remembered. He had no contacts with the publishing world; rejection of the manuscript plunged him into despair until it was accepted by Scribners. Then began his long and fruitful association with the publishing house and with its great editor, Maxwell Perkins.

His work on the novel had only begun. He and Perkins spent tiresome weeks in revising the manuscript, during which all Wolfe's faults as a writer were magnified tenfold. Told to cut 50,000 words, he often wrote 100,000 to fill the gap thus created; his notes were difficult to follow; he fought to retain everything that he could recall. But his gradual realization that creative art differed from recollection helped him produce a finished manuscript that was given to the world at the inopportune moment of the Great Crash of 1929.

By any standard, *Look Homeward, Angel* was an impressive first novel. It purported to be the long chronicle of a mythical boy in a mythical family situated in a mythical mountain town named Altamont. In fact, it was the story of Wolfe's own childhood, immense in scope and meticulous in detail. His father was the central character of the book, with his mother and family rotating around this center. The book was episodic and lacked technical finish, but the language was rich; the pace was slow, but the force of the images was often haunting. Like a river, it moved grandly to its conclusion. Its length was formidable, its detail myriad, but its impact on those who read and appreciated it was great. Everyone who read it sensed the return of a part of his own youth. If readers complained of its length, they admired its richness. If they scorned its sentimentality, they would not deny the accuracy of many of its attitudes. If they cried that it lacked form, they admitted that it had substance. Few recent novels have been so alive with the joys, terrors, frustrations, and triumphs of youth as *Look Homeward, Angel*.

Its reception was gratifying to Wolfe. The publisher had feared it to be too long, but it paid its way. Reviewers were unkind toward its form but praised its content and purpose. The inevitable coterie of admirers flocked around Wolfe, bringing him some measure of the recognition he had craved. In Asheville, hundreds of copies crossed the book counters and angry condemnation reached Wolfe from his home town. He had said too much too accurately to escape offending the sensitive pride of his Southern kin and friends.

For Wolfe, the book's reception was a different story. He knew its faults, knew that he lacked literary discipline, was tortured by bad reviews, and was surprised and hurt by the book's reception at home. But he had arrived as an author; he had redeemed his promise and had said enough in his first book to warrant continuing to write.

He was now a citizen of New York in fact and in spirit. He disliked teaching, by which he had supported himself most of the time since leaving Harvard, but his income had not been sufficient to permit full-time writing. *Look Homeward, Angel* furnished him this means at last, and the receipt of a Guggenheim Fellowship in 1930-1931 enabled him to travel abroad once more and to plan his second book.

Wolfe went to Europe to gain perspective on the work that lay ahead. He knew that the agony that had produced his first book had only begun and that for him the struggles of composition and creation would always be a travail of birth. Europe fascinated him for a while, for the play of human emotions in an older civilization was intriguing. But he returned to the only home he really knew, America, determined to exploit her themes in his writing. Already he believed that his native land would occupy his future work and become not merely the vehicle of his writing but the vehicle of his life itself.

He returned to the United States in 1931 at the end of his fellowship and moved to Brooklyn where he resolved to sweep away his self-doubts by writing a second book. He would prove to himself and to the world that he was not a one-book novelist. *Look Homeward, Angel* had ended with the protagonist on the eve of his departure for the fabled land of the north and study at Harvard. Between 1931 and 1934, barely subsisting on his income in these depression years, Wolfe worked on the continuation of this story, *Of Time and the River* (1935). This volume, and two collections of short stories, *The Hills Beyond* (1941) and *From Death to Morning* (1935), together with the last two great posthumous novels, *The Web and the Rock* (1939) and *You Can't Go Home Again* (1940), make up the bulk of his work.

Of Time and the River continued the saga of Eugene Gant and his family, carrying Eugene through his first years in Boston and New York. Richly humorous, containing fine descriptions of personalities and long stretches of lyrical narrative, the book also showed Wolfe's growing awareness of the design he wished now to complete. It also portrayed his life abroad and his awakening belief that America and her themes would be the source of his future work.

The Web and the Rock introduced a new character, a young writer named George Webber, who Wolfe insisted was different from Eugene Gant. In fact, he was as much Thomas Wolfe as Gant had been, and the long novel depicted his struggles as a rising young writer in the whirl of city life in New York. Though verbose and stilted at times, the book contained vignettes and passages fully as brilliant as those in *Look Homeward, Angel* and *Of Time and the River*. The central themes of the book were the city, the rock, and its impact on the artist, and the artist's struggle to make a viable thing of memory and his own materials, the web.

You Can't Go Home Again was both Wolfe's poorest and his best novel. It lacked polish and badly needed condensation, yet it was crucial in his development, for it chronicled the years of his greatest change and marked his final acceptance of the belief in America that haunted his last years. For lyrical beauty some of its prose passages have few equals in modern American literature, and like *Look Homeward, Angel*, it contained much of the agony and bittersweet glory of developing youth and growing artistic talent.

From Death to Morning and *The Hills Beyond* were collections of his short stories, most of which were passages that had been cut from his original novel manuscripts. In their message, their verbal artistry, and their immediacy they were worthy counterparts to his longer works.

The 1930's were years of crisis and personal agony for Thomas Wolfe, but from millions of words which he wrote awkwardly in big ledgers and stored in a packing crate, he produced a series of literary and social themes that set him apart from the writers of his time and which account for his appeal to much of his generation.

Wolfe never liked artistic theory. Craft did not interest him; he relied on the freshness, vividness, and interest of his materials to carry his story. Critics and many readers objected to the lack of form in his novels, to their sprawling, often incoherent stream-of-consciousness style. Wolfe himself admitted candidly that he was not concerned with technical form and knew that much of his outpouring looked like posturing to others. "I seem to have been born a freshman—and in many ways I'm afraid I'll continue to be one," [12] he wrote to a friend as *Look Homeward, Angel* appeared.

If Wolfe was uninterested in the forms of art, he was deeply interested in the artistic process and especially in the artist's role in society. He had seen too many brilliant men—men like Starwick in *Of Time and the River*—come to nothing because of their preoccupation with form and their lack of real subject matter not to know that what an artist says is more important than how he says it.

This was not a rationalization of his own shortcomings, but a deeply held conviction that the creator of literary beauty must deal in universal truths. Those universal truths were self-evident, for to know one man was to know all men; to understand the simple was to grasp the complex, for all things tended to be one.

Wolfe believed that unity in life was possible and that the artist could fashion it. The only validity in life was experience. "But I think you know that fiction is not spun out of air," he wrote Margaret Roberts in 1929; "it is made from the solid stuff of human experience—any other way is unthinkable." [13]

Wolfe's passion for detail revealed his deep and unswerving realism; he would sacrifice nothing from his story because it was weak, or sentimental, or tragic, or ribald. But it also revealed a deep flaw in his talent, a lack of sure judgment as to the significance of events. Only late in his career did he finally realize that he must have a central purpose in his writing to focus his art.

Nevertheless his hoarded memories could contain the key. The key that unlocked one thing could unlock all; the secret of life within every day might be his through art. "For, it is the union of the ordinary and the miraculous that makes wonder," [14] he wrote in *Look Homeward, Angel,* in justifying his approach. Thus the proper study of mankind was indeed man, and the struggles of one man. "In every man there are two hemispheres of light and dark, two worlds discrete, two countries of his soul's adventure," [15] he wrote in *The Web and the Rock.*

All his work pointed to this ideal; he lived to know mankind through himself and himself through mankind. "It is to snare the spirits of mankind in nets of magic, to make his life prevail through his creation, to wreak the vision of his life, the rude and painful substance of his own experience, into the congruence of blazing and enchanted images that are themselves the core of life, the essential pattern whence all other things proceed, the kernel of eternity." [16] If he could dissect a single moment, he might capture time; if he could know a single man, even himself, he might find the ultimate unity of all men.

The criticism that his books were merely autobiographical hurt him most. They were in fact, his critics said, the proliferations of a monstrous ego bent on self-enshrinement. Wolfe admitted freely that his work was autobiographical but denied that this subjectivity was a false standard. "As I have said, my conviction is that all serious creative work must be at bottom autobiographical, and that man must use the material and experience of his own life if he is to create anything that has substantial value," [17] he said in *The Story of a Novel* (1936). As he believed that every man was not one but many beings, not a single theme but the sum of all the themes of his life, he believed that autobiography was a valid fictional approach. The artist's first duty was "to derive from his own experience—as the fruit of all his seeing, feeling, living, joy and bitter anguish—the palpable and living substance of his art." [18]

There was a side to his autobiographical writing that eluded many critics. Paradoxically, Wolfe tried to transcend himself by studying himself. His work was not the reflection of a monstrous ego, but a catalogue of experience from which he hoped to derive a key to the door that forever eluded him. From his experience he might form a pattern that would satisfy his unending voracity to consume everything and everyone he knew. "It was a feeling that every man on earth held in the little tenement of his flesh and spirit the whole ocean of human life and time." [19]

Thus all his work rested on his memory, that voluminous storeroom which yielded nothing without a fierce struggle. He knew that he was at its mercy. "The vast fruitage of my years of hunger, my prodigies of reading, my infinite stores of memories, my hundreds of books and notes, return to drown me—sometimes I feel as if I shall compass and devour them, again be devoured by them," [20] he wrote to Maxwell Perkins while writing his second book.

He spent all his youth trying to find a way back home and found in the end the lesson that most men learn earlier: you can't go back to the world of childhood. His last book, *You Can't Go Home Again*, full of that realization, stands as a monument to his final understanding that the world of youth passes. His memory was that other world, however, and he drew on it freely, trying to understand what had made him so. "We are the sum of all the moments of our lives—all that is ours is in them; we cannot escape or conceal it," he wrote in the dedication of *Look Homeward, Angel*. "Each moment is the fruit of forty thousand years. The minute-winning days, like flies, buzz home to death, and every moment is a window on all time." [21] Time as symbolized by memory, lost time, fascinated him, though he knew that seeking it was in vain. "There is a great sadness in knowing you can never recall the scene except the memory," he wrote to his mother about a moment in his childhood; ". . . even if all were here you could not bring it back." [22]

Three kinds of time intrigued him: the time of the present, in which characters lived and moved; past time, acting upon men in the present through the accumulated experience of the past; and immutable time, oblivious to individual actions, "a kind of eternal and unchanging universe of time against which would be projected the transience of man's life, the bitter briefness of his days." [23] As an artist he moved through all three phases of this complex scheme of time, beginning with the simplicity of the present, to a final belief that life itself was a form of time.

Wolfe loved train rides because the train defeated time. It moved through time, carrying degrees of time with it, past the immutable earth, which also symbolized time. "The weird combination of fixity and change, the terrible moment of immobility stamped with eternity" [24] of the passing train held him like a magnet. As he matured, his fascination with time transposed itself into a sense of loss, a belief that time outstripped him wherever he turned and whatever he did:

Strange time, forever lost, forever flowing like the river! Lost time, lost people, and lost love—forever lost! There's nothing you can hold there in the river! There's nothing you can keep there in the river! It takes your love, it takes your life, it takes great ships going out to sea, and it takes time, dark, delicate time, the little ticking moments of strange time that count us unto death. Now in the dark I hear the passing of dark time, and all the sad and secret flowing of my life. All of my life is passing like the river, I dream and talk and feel just like the river, as it flows by me, by me, by me, to the sea.[25]

Only his writing and the understanding of experience afforded security in the deluge. He could conquer time by reliving the past and by understanding his relation to time. Then he could go home again.

The essence of the art which sustained this belief was truth, fidelity to fact. "And it all boiled down to this: honesty, sincerity, no compromise with truth—these were the essentials of any art—

and a writer, no matter what else he had, was just a hack without them." [26] He grew to maturity in the 1920's when it was fashionable either to belittle art based on direct experience or to make something artificial as a refuge from life. He disliked and feared both approaches; like Hart Crane, he would understand life by knowing it. "You ask if I look upon writing as an escape from reality; in no sense of the word does it seem to me to be an escape from reality; I should rather say that it is an attempt to approach and penetrate reality." [27]

For this reason the esthetes and dilettantes whom he met by the score at home and abroad, and who are so brilliantly pilloried in *Of Time and the River*, never converted him. They clung to style in art. "And the great danger of this glib and easy jargon of the arts was this: that instead of knowledge, the experience of hard work and patient living, they were given a formula for knowledge; a language that sounded very knowing, expert and assured, and yet that knew nothing, was experienced in nothing, was sure of nothing." [28]

Though he countered the attacks on him from his home and family after the publication of *Look Homeward, Angel* by pleading his honest intent and their misunderstanding, he must have known that his acid sketches and frank judgments on the people he had known would cause anger.

The great unifying idea, the idea that urged him on, was a sense of loneliness so overpowering that he concluded that life itself was a form of isolation, since one man could only rarely and with great pain extend himself into the lives of others. "Loneliness, far from being a rare and curious circumstance, is and always has been the central and inevitable experience of every man." [29] This was the sum of his belief early in life, the motto of his early fiction: we are born alone, we live alone, and we die alone. But memory was a form of immortality, insurance against the future and the anonymity that buried a man's life under the accumulated experience of a race or century.

Loneliness was not merely the lack of friends but a sense of isolation from other men and the stream of life. It was a state that came from within, not from without. It was a reality as well as a condition to Thomas Wolfe. "O Lost!" rang through his books like an anthem and everything he did was in part an attempt to overcome this loneliness. As his perspective grew, Wolfe came to believe that it was possible at least to understand this loneliness. He did not feel alienated; he was alone because all men were alone. He could not join the cultists and faddists of his day; he must meet and master this challenge, not flee from it.

This sense of loss and loneliness in the midst of a rich and varied life was heightened for Wolfe by a belief in chance and fate in human affairs. He often wrote and spoke of "the secret weavings of dark chance that thread our million lives into strange purposes that we do not know." [30] He knew of "the huge and nameless death that waits around the corner for all men, to break their backs and shatter instantly the blind and pitiful illusions of their hope." [31] He was obsessed by the fear that he would not finish his work. Much of this was the posing of youth, the frantic desire to deny shadows by affirming them. Yet there was truth in his words, and the belief in chance and darkness is in all his fiction.

As he mellowed and pursued his design, this feeling underwent a change. He came to believe that though chance operated in men's lives it was possible to live fruitfully within that chance; to rise, in a sense, above the darkness. "I am beginning to learn pity for human weakness—I have a compassion for all of the poor blind fumbling Creatures that inhabit this earth," he wrote his mother while working on his first book, "a compassion I did not have at twenty . . . People are driven by avarice, meanness, ungenerous living for themselves and all about them, but somehow I don't feel the loathing for it I once did . . ." [32]

He mixed his pessimism with pity, or at least with a deeper understanding of human conduct. Though he never abandoned his determinism, he finally admitted that pessimism was no more valid than optimism. "No—what one comes to realize is that there is a reasonable hope that one may cherish in life, that makes it well worth living—and that the childish pessimist who denies this is as lying and dishonest a rogue as the cheap ready-made optimist and that, indeed, of the two brands of rascals, the merchant who deals in Pollyanna optimism is a better man than he whose stock in trade is snivelling, drivelling Pollyanna pessimism." [33] Like

Stephen Crane, he believed that there were moments of heroism when a man might rise above life and see it all.

Wolfe could not belie his country origins, and worship of the earth as a symbol of both time and good ran through his work. Along with other writers of his time, notably Willa Cather, but with a more mystical perception, he believed that the earth was the repository of virtues because of its timelessness. He often spoke of "the eternal silent waiting earth that does not change." [34] The earth was stable, unchanging, virtuous, the source of life; it was home. As he elaborated his work and developed his ideal that America was the land of the future and therefore the home for which he searched, he transferred this whole concept to his native land. "You may ask what all this has to do with America— it is true it has to do with the whole universe—but it is as true of the enormous and lonely land that we inhabit as any land I know of, and more so, it seems to me." [35]

But the country did not fascinate him in the same way as the city. "Men have their visions from afar and in a lonely place, and the great vision of this earth and all her power and glory has ever had the city at its end." [36] He was the country boy held captive by the city's daily pageant. He was intrigued by New York, "that enfabled rock of life we call the city," [37] trying to catch in webs of memory all the faces, events, colors, and sounds of city life. "He heard, far off, the deep and beelike murmur of its million-footed life, and the mystery of the earth and time was in that sound," he wrote of the city in *The Web and the Rock*. "The city flashed before him like a glorious jewel, blazing with countless rich and brilliant facets of a life so good, so bountiful, so strangely and constantly beautiful and interesting, that it seemed intolerable that he should miss a moment of it." [38]

He denied the stereotyped picture of city life. "The big wicked city that one hears so much about is also a very busy and hard working place," he once wrote. "It would be ironic, wouldn't it, if one eventually discovered that he had come here to keep out of mischief." [39] More perhaps than any other writer of his generation, Wolfe was spellbound by city life and tried to discover its secrets and what made it meaningful.

142 WRITERS IN TRANSITION

Much of this fascination derived from his own rural origins; inevitably the strangeness of the city drew him. But the causes of the fascination lay deeper than mere curiosity and lack of sophistication. The city was, in fact, the focus of life; its variety gave it more meaning, more choice from which to draw the central stuff of life. It was also a place of loneliness. In the midst of so much life, man was yet unknown; this irony attracted Wolfe most. If man was alone in his childhood in the country and alone in his youth in the city, what could he do to humanize life? How could he move beyond himself into others? Wolfe had come not to study the city but the people in it, and concluded that the city was in essence not so different from the country in the demands it made on people. "Is not a man, then, taller than a tower? Is not the mystery in an atom of tired flesh greater than all these soaring lights?" [40]

He enjoyed the freedom of life in the city; it is not without significance that he worked in New York and only returned home rarely. Yet the city could not resolve his conflicts. "He brought to it the heart, the eye, the vision of the everlasting stranger, who had walked its stones, and breathed its air, and, as a stranger, looked into its million dark and driven faces, and who could never make the city's life his own." [41] It came in the end to the old question: could Thomas Wolfe go home? For all its beauty and vitality, the city was rootless, lacking the stability that he thought was home.

Wolfe knew the city's inequalities. As his social sense sharpened late in life, he saw more and more of the human hardship in New York, worsened by the Great Depression. "It was a world that seemed to have gone insane with its own excesses," he wrote of the rich and unheeding city of that time, "a world of criminal privilege that flouted itself with an inhuman arrogance in the very face of a great city where half the population lived in filth and squalor, and where two-thirds were still so bitterly uncertain of their daily living that they had to thrust, to snarl, to curse, to cheat, contrive, and get the better of their fellows like a race of mongrel dogs." [42]

Unable to resolve the conflicts in his life in the city any more than in the country, Wolfe slowly realized that his quest for home was a personal, inner search. Between 1920 and 1936, Wolfe passed from revolt to discovery, from revolt against the surface manifestations of life to discovery that the important facet of life is the hidden face that no man shows the world.

While writing his first novel, between 1920 and 1926, he attacked the culture and money craze that flourished around him. Like other literary spokesmen of discontent, he disdained the world's standards, and believed that he was lost to the mass of humanity. But this sense of loss was not that of the Lost Generation. It was more profound, for he perceived a great truth: loneliness is not a product of society but of men. In even the best of worlds the artist and sensitive man suffers isolation.

His quest was too personal to entrust to a group or movement. "I do not feel that I belong to a Lost Generation, and I have never felt so. Indeed, I doubt very much the existence of a Lost Generation, except insofar as every generation, groping, must be lost." [43] His travel impressed upon him the fact that literary expatriates had little to offer: ". . . when we fled from our own country and sought refuge abroad [we were] not really looking for a place to work, but looking for a place to escape from work . . ." [44] He did not feel that Europe had much to offer America. While he greatly admired much of the Old World's culture, he saw that decadence lay beneath the surface. Interested in change as well as chance, he could not accept a static way of life; the very fact that the Old World was old obscured much of its charm to him. "Tradition, which saves what is good and great in Europe, also saves what is poor, so that one wades through miles of junk to come to a great thing." [45]

Wolfe's travels in Europe impressed upon him something that seemed to elude his fellows; he believed, as Hart Crane did, that the past was dead and that what it offered was valid only if it could be used to build the future. The country of that future was America. "I tell you we have got to live in our own country and be what we are, and that no one who has ever known and felt America can find living in Europe as interesting or beautiful." [46]

His anguish and loneliness impressed upon Wolfe the central

fact of every great artists' work: art does not depend on time or circumstance, but upon insights into the materials of life. For Wolfe those materials would always be his secret America. Real work elsewhere was impossible, for he could not do without the color and vitality of his native land. For others France might be a mecca; for him she was a museum. With his second novel, *Of Time and the River,* he began to treat in earnest the America that occupied the rest of his work and which he believed was the hope of the future.

Wolfe's criticisms of American civilization were more profound than the superficial commentaries of many contemporaries, for he saw that something essentially good lay beneath the gilt surface that Sinclair Lewis and others so readily attacked. "I am a citizen of the most powerful and interesting nation of modern times—and I wish to God I knew how to make something of it . . ." he wrote.[47] Wolfe detested the Babbitts and materialism. But he also believed that these were merely surface scars on a healthy body. He had no patience with those who called for a different culture. "Instead of whining that we have no traditions, or that we must learn by keeping constantly in touch with European models, or by keeping away from them, we should get busy telling some of the stories about America that have never been told." [48]

In more ways than one, he knew whereof he spoke. "I had found out during these years that the way to discover one's own country was to leave it," he wrote in *The Story of a Novel,* "that the way to find America was to find it in one's heart, one's memory, and one's spirit, and in a foreign land." [49]

What was this America to which he turned, and why did she hold him so? Much of his interest came from his own family background. Coming from rural origins, he was conscious of the power of the land itself. He had traveled through America, taking in her variety and endless richness of life. He believed that men were freer here than in Europe, for he lived long enough to see firsthand the spread of fascism in Europe. In America men were less fettered by tradition and rules, were more vital and honest; they were more free to explore life's channels than men in an older civilization.

America's youth and untouched vigor formed the foundation of his belief in her future. "America was young, America was still the New World of mankind's hopes, America was not like this old and worn-out Europe which seethed and festered with a thousand deep and uncorrected ancient maladies. America was still resilient, still responsive to a cure—if only—if only—if only —men could somehow cease to be afraid of truth." [50] He believed that America had one great advantage over Europe: if there were wrongs and evils here, America could begin anew. "There were stronger, deeper tides and currents running in America than any which these glamorous lives tonight had ever plumbed or even dreamed of," he wrote in *You Can't Go Home Again.* "Those were the depths that he would like to sound." [51]

His America was many things: the land itself, its sense of time-lessness, its richness, its people, its cities. It was a land of paradox, despair, and hope; it was like other lands, but with the great difference that it was young. It had possibilities of unity and new development that no other nation commanded. In a sense, Thomas Wolfe was America. The tortures of youth and development were America's too, and he believed that those problems would be answered in America for the benefit of all mankind.

The Great Depression, during which Wolfe wrote most of his novels, was a profound event to him as to the rest of his generation, for he saw America at the crossroads. The collapse of the tinsel world of 1929 was all the more graphic to him for his provincial origins and romantic view of life. Never really a part of the city's glittering whirl, never identified except as an observer with the wealth of the 1920's, he saw the human drama of the depression from the double angle of both participant and analyst.

He condemned "the half-life of wealth and fashion that had grown like a parasite upon the sound body of America." [52] As he saw the effects of the depression on the lives around him, he believed more and more that the tragedy might have its usefulness, for it at least would force his countrymen to examine their values. "As men, as Americans, we can no longer cringe away and lie. Are we not all warmed by the same sun, frozen by the same cold, shone on by the same lights of time and terror here in America?

Yes, and if we do not look and see it, we shall all be damned together." [53]

Under these conditions, his social sense sharpened. But as the crisis deepened, he declined, as in the 1920's, to identify himself with the cause of any special group. He felt bitterly that many classes of people had been cruelly hurt by the depression, but he believed that all men needed help, not merely the workers or the Negroes or the Jews. "But really isn't this just another way of saying that every great man or any good man is on the side of life, and although I am myself the son of a working man, I go so far as to say that an artist's interest, first and always, has got to be in life itself, and not in a special kind of life. His devotion, his compassion, his talent has got to be used for man and for the enrichment of man's estate, and not for just one class or sect of men," [54] he wrote his one-time schoolteacher, Margaret Roberts, in 1936.

He saw the depression as a great national crisis, a crisis of culture as well as economics. It was more than a pitiful succession of personal tragedies. He saw in it a great national tragedy; the sum of a nation's faults. It was, in fact, a kind of passage between the old and the new. "You have lived through one kind of world," he wrote his mother in 1931, "you may live to see the beginning of another one." [55]

Wolfe privately believed that the old capitalistic system had come to an end, though he disliked reformers and their panaceas. The emergency turned his social sense upward instead of downward. Had he lived, realizing as he did that he personally had come to the end of the first phase of his writing, he might have lent his pen to the cause of social change. On the other hand, his preoccupation with the meaning of life itself may well have kept him from involvement in current problems.

In any event, the crisis failed to solidify his determinism. He believed in the blind play of chance, in the inexorable action of the past upon every man, but he did not succumb to rigid determinism. Where the Great Depression seemed to others to prove the theory of economic determinism, it said something else to Wolfe. He could not believe that a nation so rich and vital would fail to meet this challenge. With wisdom and direction it would emerge cleaner and stronger. He felt that the depression and its attendant misery might well act as a purifying flame.

In the end, it was a question of affirmation. He could move forward to new discoveries, or he could rest on his laurels. The answer was never in doubt; he had come, true to his American origins, to accept growth and change as the only constant values in life. "And the essence of all faith, it seems to me, for such a man as I, the essence of religion for people of my belief, is that man's life can be, and will be, better, that man's greatest enemies, in the forms in which they now exist—the forms we see on every hand of fear, hatred, slavery, cruelty, poverty, and need—can be conquered and destroyed." [56]

He had said at the beginning of his quest that he would go home again, and in the end he did come home. He had sought, he insisted, a father; this father became for him the force that unified life. Not merely the father of the flesh, but the father that overrode time and chance, the father that was security and continuity, "the image of a strength and wisdom external to [man's] need and superior to his hunger, to which the belief and power of his own life can be united." [57]

In seeking to go home again, Wolfe did not so much seek the fancied security of former times as the innocence of childhood itself. As all sensitive men do, he came to see that such innocence cannot be recaptured; in that sense he could never go home again. From this he saw a larger truth: life does not lie in innocence but in experience. The Great Depression and his final realization of America's potential were crucial to him in this light. "But I am grieving for the dead no longer: I know that you can't go home again, but I know also that our home, yours and mine, and every mother's son of us, is in the future, and I believe in and trust in life, and think that it is valuable, as life is valuable, and must be won and saved, and to that end I am now willing to devote all the energy, talent, faith and hope that in me are." [58] Wolfe had spent his youth seeking some knowledge and power external to himself which would solve his problems and explain his world, and he came in the end to the larger and truer realization that only he who accepts life and prepares to meet it can grow and understand as an individual.

It was a noble vision. If the challenge of the time was hard, it could bring forth the strength needed to meet it. Wolfe's answer was no compound of sentiment and wishful thinking; he had seen too much of life for that. From his work and observation he distilled a single message: man (therefore life) is eternal. Nothing could destroy either, nor could man deny his responsibility to meet life. Like Walt Whitman and Hart Crane before him, he believed that the creative artist could and should lead in the march of progress.

Out of all his struggle he fashioned his myth of America. He had seen the Old World and believed it lost; the New World would save humanity. As though he sensed death at his elbow, Wolfe left a testament to his belief in man and his America. "I believe that we are lost here in America, but I believe we shall be found . . . I think the life which we have fashioned in America, and which has fashioned us . . . was self-destructive in its nature, and must be destroyed. I think these forms are dying, and must die, just as I know that America and the people in it are deathless, undiscovered, and immortal, and must live." Frequently bitter at his own faults, anguished by the world around him, he did not abandon his dreams of the future. "I think the true discovery of America is before us. I think the true fulfillment of our spirit, of our people, of our mighty and immortal land, is yet to come. I think the true discovery of our own democracy is still before us. And I think that all these things are certain as the morning, as inevitable as the noon." [59]

He developed a kind of stoicism, which was the basis of the "divine myth" which he said was the secret of his work. Man's triumph would not come through any childish belief in progress but through suffering. Struggle was the price of life, for it separated the good from the bad. "Man was born to live, to suffer, and to die, and what befalls him is a tragic lot," his hero wrote to a fictional editor in his last novel. "There is no denying this in the final end. But we must, dear Fox, deny it all along the way." [60] Years before he had said: "If you would know what that faith is, distilled, my play tries to express my passionate belief in all myth, in the necessity of defending and living not for truth, but for divine falsehood." [61] That divine myth was the father, home, the life and the nation he had sought; it came to be life, the thing that stood outside lives and gave them meaning.

As a hungry and impatient youth, Thomas Wolfe had craved fame and success; as a weary and tortured man he knew that success and found it bitter. "I wanted fame—and I have had for the most part shame and agony," [62] he wrote in 1935. In 1938 he stood on the threshold of a new phase of writing; his broadened perspective and greater powers were now at the service of his country and her future. In that year, at the age of thirty-seven, he journeyed west before beginning new work, and contracted pneumonia. Convalescence did not cure the illness and on September 15, 1938, he died at the Johns Hopkins Hospital in Baltimore of a brain infection. Asheville, which had provided so much material for his work, was his final resting place.

Critical opinion of Wolfe in his own time was sharply divided between those who felt, like Bernard DeVoto, that genius was not enough and that Wolfe violated so many literary rules that his novels would never be more than an outpouring of questions and torments. Others saw in him the first true genius and fresh creative talent in American letters in decades; they swept aside as irrelevant the complaints about his form. They prized instead his message. Certainly, the amount of his writing is formidable, running to thirty-five hundred pages of fine print, with fully as much, if not more, pruned from his original drafts. Of his novels, *Look Homeward, Angel* is the most finished. As a tale of his childhood it has unity and boundaries; one's childhood does end. For power of expression, few books in recent American letters can match *Look Homeward, Angel*'s presentation. Perhaps no other novelist has given so full and graphic a picture of family life. For the rest, much of his work is obscure, overloaded with detail, covered like the forest floor with such a wealth of growth that the earth is hidden. If judged as individual novels, the flaws are too obvious to ignore. But he insisted that he only wrote one novel, a story printed as four novels and two volumes of short stories, and his work is better judged in that light.

It is not difficult to trace the influences upon Thomas Wolfe's writing. By his own admission he owed much to Joyce and D. H. Lawrence and many other innovators. His naturalism, his American angle of vision are not new. But like the work of Stephen Crane, his work remains unique. His style may be partly derivative, but the content is his own. The lyrical beauty of the writing, the compelling quality of the characterizations, the insight into the human situation set the work of Thomas Wolfe apart from contemporary currents.

It is easier to criticize than to appreciate Wolfe; to see in his often tedious prose the wanderings of a confused and adolescent mind; to mistake his vigor for mere confusion; to mistake his lack of balance for lack of message. Yet over all his faults as a writer looms the mass of his inspiration, the moving quality of his insight into man's loneliness and isolation. Few writers have had his courage in baring their inmost thoughts. Few have tried so hard to explain the workings of the mind. Few have gone so far to help others understand their lives. If he did indeed fall short as a craftsman, it does not detract from the greatness of his effort.

The reader who persists will find much inspiration in the work of Thomas Wolfe. The neglect now surrounding his writing may change and he may become what he so longed to be at his death, the spokesman of a new and vital America. He told his own generation what he tells a later one: not that the road is easy, but that there is a road; not that meaning in life is assured, but that it is possible.

None of his work came to Thomas Wolfe without soul searching and agony of spirit. It may be that much of his work will fade, but his vision will surely last and he would appreciate that. As he said in his final work, he heard something in the night saying:

To lose the earth you know, for greater knowing; to lose the life you have, for greater life; to leave the friends you love, for greater loving; to find a land more kind than home, more large than earth— Whereon the pillars of this earth are founded, toward which the conscience of the world is tending—a wind is rising, and the rivers flow.[63]

Whatever his vision might have meant to others, he knew its secret meaning to himself. And he would always be on that dark river's flow.

Notes

STEPHEN CRANE: THE IRONIC HERO

1. See the photograph of Crane in Lillian Gilkes, *Cora Crane* (Bloomington, Ind.), 102.
2. John Berryman, *Stephen Crane* (New York, 1950), 15.
3. to John Northern Hilliard (Summer, 1893), in *Stephen Crane: An Omnibus*, R. W. Stallman, ed. (New York, 1952), 595-596.
4. Corwin K. Linson, *My Stephen Crane* (Syracuse, 1958), 31.
5. to Nellie Crouse (January, 1896), in *Stephen Crane's Love Letters to Nellie Crouse*, Edwin Cady and Lester G. Wells, eds. (Syracuse, 1954), 43.
6. *Maggie*, in *The Work of Stephen Crane*, Wilson Follett, ed. (New York, 1925), X, 151.
7. Thomas Beer, *Stephen Crane* (New York, 1923), 96.
8. *Stephen Crane: An Omnibus*, 594-595.
9. *Ibid.*
10. *Maggie*, in *Work*, X, 151.
11. *Ibid.*, 156.
12. to Miss Catherine Harris (November 12, 1896), in *Stephen Crane: An Omnibus*, 655-656.
13. to Mrs. Armstrong (April 2, 1893), *Ibid.*, 593.
14. *The Red Badge of Courage*, in *Work*, I, 29.
15. *Ibid.*, 87.
16. *Ibid.*, 86.
17. *Ibid.*, 51.
18. *Ibid.*, 147.
19. *Ibid.*, 150.
20. "The Open Boat," in *Work*, XII, 29, 47-48, 56.
21. to Nellie Crouse (January 12, 1896), in *Stephen Crane's Love Letters to Nellie Crouse*, 35.
22. Beer, 205-206.
23. to Editor: *Leslie's Weekly* (November, 1895), in *Stephen Crane: An Omnibus*, 628.
24. to John Northern Hilliard (1897), *Ibid.*, 673.
25. to Lily Brandon Munroe (February 29, 1896), *Ibid.*, 648.
26. to Joseph O'Conner (1898), *Ibid.*, 680.
27. to John Northern Hilliard (1893), *Ibid.*, 596.
28. Berryman, 288.
29. *Maggie*, in *Work*, X, 218.
30. *Work*, VII, x, xiii.

31. *Work*, I, 160.
32. "A Mystery of Heroism," in *Work*, II, 102.
33. "War Memories," in *Work*, IX, 212.
34. *Ibid.*, 238.
35. *Ibid.*, 201.
36. *Ibid.*, 219.
37. "A Man—and Some Others," in *Work*, XII, 75.
38. *Work*, III, 121.
39. *The Red Badge of Courage*, in *Work*, I, 70.
40. "The Open Boat," in *Work*, XII, 51.
41. "George's Mother," in *Work*, X, 49.
42. to Nellie Crouse (January, 1896), in *Stephen Crane's Love Letters to Nellie Crouse*, 44.
43. to Wallace McHarg (April, 1896), in *Stephen Crane: An Omnibus*, 650.
44. Berryman, 225.
45. to John Northern Hilliard (1897), in *Stephen Crane: An Omnibus*, 674.
46. to James Gibbon Huneker (1897), *Ibid.*, 674-675.
47. Berryman, 25.
48. to Nellie Crouse (January 12, 1896), in *Stephen Crane's Love Letters to Nellie Crouse*, 35.
49. to Nellie Crouse (August 31, 1895), *Ibid.*, 30.

EDITH WHARTON: THE NOVELIST OF MANNERS AND MORALS

1. Edith Wharton, *A Backward Glance* (New York, 1934), 1-4.
2. *Ibid.*, 73.
3. Edith Wharton, *The Age of Innocence* (New York, 1920), 221.
4. *A Backward Glance*, 28.
5. *Ibid.*, 57.
6. Edith Wharton, *The Fruit of the Tree* (New York, 1907), 31.
7. Edith Wharton, *The House of Mirth* (New York, 1905), 347.
8. *Ibid.*, 87-88.
9. Edith Wharton, *The Valley of Decision* (New York, 1902), 150.
10. *The Age of Innocence*, 145.
11. *A Backward Glance*, 22.
12. *Ibid.*, 44.
13. Edith Wharton, *The Custom of the Country* (New York, 1913), 541.
14. *Ibid.*, 19.
15. *The Fruit of the Tree*, 280.
16. Percy Lubbock, *Portrait of Edith Wharton* (New York, 1947), 9.
17. Edith Wharton, *The Writing of Fiction* (New York, 1925), 3.

18. *Ibid.*, 36.
19. *Ibid.*, 18.
20. *Ibid.*, 13-14.
21. Edith Wharton, *Ethan Frome* (New York, 1911), 36.
22. *The Age of Innocence*, 324.
23. *Ibid.*, 268.
24. Edith Wharton, *The Reef* (New York, 1914), 334.
25. *The Writing of Fiction*, 7.
26. *The Valley of Decision*, 583.
27. *The Fruit of the Tree*, 624.
28. *The Writing of Fiction*, 138.
29. *Ibid.*, 28, 171.
30. Edith Wharton, *French Ways and Their Meaning* (New York, 1919), 65.
31. *The Fruit of the Tree*, 96.
32. *Ibid.*, 555.
33. *French Ways and Their Meaning*, 95.
34. *The Fruit of the Tree*, 624.
35. *The Valley of Decision*, 622-623.
36. *A Backward Glance*, 379.
37. *French Ways and Their Meaning*, 31.
38. *The Valley of Decision*, 640.
39. *The Custom of the Country*, 513, 545.
40. *The Writing of Fiction*, 156.
41. *The Age of Innocence*, 242.
42. Lubbock, 150-151.
43. *The Writing of Fiction*, 66.
44. *Ibid.*
45. *French Ways and Their Meaning*, v.
46. Lubbock, 166.
47. *Ibid.*, 192.
48. *A Backward Glance*, 379.

ELLEN GLASGOW: THE QUALITIES OF ENDURANCE

1. to Bessie Zaban Jones (February 7, 1934), in *The Letters of Ellen Glasgow*, Blair Rouse, ed. (New York, 1958), 150.
2. Ellen Glasgow, *The Woman Within* (New York, 1954), 41.
3. *Ibid.*, 30.
4. to Walter Hines Page (November 22, 1897), in *Letters*, 25.
5. to Walter Hines Page (May 12, 1900), *Ibid.*, 32.
6. Ellen Glasgow, *A Certain Measure* (New York, 1943), 104.
7. *Ibid.*, 15.
8. *Ibid.*, 14.
9. *Ibid.*, 30.

10. *The Woman Within*, 125.
11. Ellen Glasgow, *Virginia*, Old Dominion ed. (New York, 1929), 145.
12. to Joseph Hergesheimer (January 7, 1924), in *Letters*, 70.
13. Ellen Glasgow, *The Battleground*, Old Dominion ed. (New York, 1937), 247.
14. Ellen Glasgow, *The Romance of a Plain Man* (New York, 1909), 106-107.
15. *The Battleground*, 384-385.
16. *Virginia*, 13.
17. *Virginia*, 65; *The Battleground*, 227.
18. *A Certain Measure*, 12.
19. to Frank Morley (December 7, 1943), in *Letters*, 340.
20. Ellen Glasgow, *Vein of Iron* (New York, 1935), 461, 248.
21. *The Romance of a Plain Man*, 204.
22. *Ibid.*, 202-203.
23. *A Certain Measure*, 114.
24. *Ibid.*, 119.
25. *The Battleground*, 301-302.
26. to Arthur Graham Glasgow (October 11, 1919), in *Letters*, 65.
27. Ellen Glasgow, *Barren Ground*, Old Dominion ed. (New York, 1937), 524-525.
28. Ellen Glasgow, *The Deliverance*, Old Dominion ed. (New York, 1937), 128.
29. *A Certain Measure*, 153.
30. *Barren Ground*, 128.
31. *The Deliverance*, 91.
32. *Barren Ground*, 273.
33. *Vein of Iron*, 294.
34. *Barren Ground*, 484.
35. Ellen Glasgow, *Vein of Iron* (New York, 1935), 421.
36. to John Chamberlain (December 2, 1935), in *Letters*, 201.
37. Ellen Glasgow, *The Miller of Old Church*, Old Dominion ed. (New York, 1933), 335.
38. *Barren Ground*, 525.
39. *Ibid.*, 235.
40. *A Certain Measure*, 158-159.
41. to Bessie Zaban Jones (February 7, 1934), in *Letters*, 151.
42. *Vein of Iron*, 201.
43. to Walter Hines Page (May 12, 1900), in *Letters*, 32.
44. to Allen Tate (July 4, 1933), *Ibid.*, 140.
45. *A Certain Measure*, 67.
46. *Barren Ground*, viii.
47. *The Woman Within*, 128.
48. *Ibid.*

49. *A Certain Measure,* 118.
50. *The Woman Within,* 195.
51. *A Certain Measure,* 46.
52. to Van Wyck Brooks (August 23, 1941), in *Letters,* 288.

WILLA CATHER: THE ARTIST'S QUEST

1. Edith Lewis, *Willa Cather Living* (New York, 1953), 175.
2. Quoted in E. K. Brown, *Willa Cather* (New York, 1953), 3.
3. Willa Cather, *O Pioneers!* (New York, 1913), 301.
4. Lewis, 32.
5. Willa Cather, *Death Comes for the Archbishop* (New York, 1927), 261.
6. Willa Cather, *My Antonia* (New York, 1918), 262.
7. Quoted in Brown, 50.
8. Willa Cather, *On Writing* (New York, 1949), 58, 93; *Not Under Forty* (New York, 1936), 49-50.
9. Quoted in Brown, 66.
10. *Not Under Forty,* 48.
11. *On Writing,* 19.
12. *Ibid.,* 84.
13. Willa Cather, *The Song of the Lark,* rev. ed. (New York, 1937), 571.
14. Willa Cather, *One of Ours* (New York, 1922), 406.
15. *O Pioneers!,* 119.
16. *Ibid.,* 308.
17. Willa Cather, "Neighbour Rosicky," in *Obscure Destinies* (New York, 1932), 40.
18. Willa Cather, *Lucy Gayheart* (New York, 1935), 78.
19. Lewis, 119-120.
20. *Ibid.,* 57.
21. *My Antonia,* 328.
22. *The Song of the Lark,* 95.
23. *Ibid.,* vii.
24. Lewis, xvii.
25. *O Pioneers!,* 255; *One of Ours,* 207; *Lucy Gayheart,* 220.
26. Willa Cather, *The Professor's House* (New York, 1925), 221.
27. *One of Ours,* 102-103.
28. *Not Under Forty,* 74.
29. *On Writing,* 25.
30. *Ibid.,* 70.
31. *Not Under Forty,* prefatory note.
32. *The Professor's House,* 67-69.
33. *One of Ours,* 43.
34. *Not Under Forty,* 99.

35. Willa Cather, "Nebraska: The End of the First Cycle," *The Nation*, 117 (September 5, 1923), 238.
36. Quoted in Brown, 227.
37. *The Song of the Lark*, 277.
38. *O Pioneers!*, 123.
39. "Neighbour Rosicky," in *Obscure Destinies*, 31.
40. *Death Comes for the Archbishop*, 95.
41. *On Writing*, 5.
42. *Death Comes for the Archbishop*, 34.
43. *Ibid.*, 292.
44. *Ibid.*, 234.
45. *Ibid.*, 278.
46. Quoted in Brown, 69.
47. Lewis, 184.
48. *Death Comes for the Archbishop*, 291.
49. *On Writing*, 103-104.

SHERWOOD ANDERSON: THE SEARCH FOR UNITY

1. See Irving Howe, *Sherwood Anderson* (New York, 1951).
2. Sherwood Anderson, *Poor White* (New York, 1920), 129.
3. Sherwood Anderson, *Windy McPherson's Son* (New York, 1916), 139.
4. Sherwood Anderson, *Marching Men* (New York, 1917), 216-217.
5. *Ibid.*, 149.
6. to Norman Holmes Pearson (September 13, 1937), in *The Letters of Sherwood Anderson*, Howard Mumford Jones and Walter B. Rideout, eds. (Boston, 1953), 387.
7. Sherwood Anderson, *Many Marriages* (New York, 1923), 90.
8. *Sherwood Anderson's Memoirs* (New York, 1941), 279.
9. to Charles Bockler (1930), in *Letters*, 202.
10. to John Anderson (April, 1927), *Ibid.*, 72.
11. to Paul Rosenfeld (March 10, 1921), *Ibid.*, 72.
12. to Norman Holmes Pearson (September 13, 1937), *Ibid.*, 287.
13. *Marching Men*, 65-66.
14. Anderson later discovered to his chagrin that there was in fact a Winesburg, Ohio, but he had never intended to localize the actions in the book.
15. to Paul Rosenfeld (October 24, 1921), in *Letters*, 80.
16. Sherwood Anderson, *Winesburg, Ohio*, Compass Books ed. (New York, 1960), 36.
17. *Sherwood Anderson's Notebook* (New York, 1926), 183.
18. Sherwood Anderson, *Beyond Desire* (New York, 1933), 291.
19. *Winesburg, Ohio*, 234.
20. to Van Wyck Brooks (December, 1919), in *Letters*, 53.
21. *Memoirs*, 315.

22. to Waldo Frank (November 7, 1917), in *Letters*, 23.
23. *Sherwood Anderson's Notebook*, 167.
24. Sherwood Anderson, *Perhaps Women* (New York, 1931), 57-58.
25. *Memoirs*, 389.
26. *Perhaps Women*, 112.
27. to David Karsner (December 22, 1924), in *Letters*, 135.
28. *Sherwood Anderson's Notebook*, 153.
29. *Perhaps Women*, 41-42.
30. *Ibid.*, 57.
31. to Charles Bockler (December 13, 1930), in *Letters*, 310.
32. *Sherwood Anderson's Notebook*, 197.
33. to Trigant Burrow (October 12, 1921), in *Letters*, 75.
34. to Roger Sergel (April 15, 1937), *Ibid.*, 377.
35. *Perhaps Women*, 123.
36. *Beyond Desire*, 50.
37. *Ibid.*, 52.
38. *Perhaps Women*, 57.
39. *Ibid.*, 48.
40. *Sherwood Anderson's Notebook*, 126.
41. to John Anderson (April, 1927), in *Letters*, 167.
42. *Sherwood Anderson's Notebook*, 21.
43. *Ibid.*, 83.
44. to Burton Emmett (May 8, 1938), in *Letters*, 287.
45. to Karl Anderson (August, 1922), *Ibid.*, 89.
46. to Jerome Blum (April 25, 1924), *Ibid.*, 124.
47. to Frank Fuller (1936), *Ibid.*, 341-342.
48. to Theodore Dreiser (December 22, 1931), *Ibid.*, 256.
49. *Sherwood Anderson's Notebook*, 147-148.
50. to George Freitag (August 27, 1938), in *Letters*, 407.
51. *Memoirs*, 504.

HART CRANE: SPOKESMAN OF VISION

1. See Philip Horton, *Hart Crane* (New York, 1937), *passim*.
2. All quotations from Crane's poetry are from *The Collected Poems of Hart Crane*, Black and Gold ed. (New York, 1933).
3. to William Wright (May 14, 1919), in *Letters of Hart Crane 1916-1932*, Brom Weber, ed. (New York, 1952), 17.
4. to His Grandmother (February 10, 1916), *Ibid.*, 4.
5. to Gorham Munson (December 13, 1919), *Ibid.*, 27.
6. to His Father (January 5, 1917), *Ibid.*, 5.
7. to Gorham Munson (November 23, 1920), *Ibid.*, 48.
8. to Charmion Wiegant (May 6, 1922), *Ibid.*, 86.
9. to Gorham Munson (January 15, 1920), *Ibid.*, 31.
10. to Waldo Frank (June 20, 1926), *Ibid.*, 260.

11. to Gorham Munson (October 1, 1920), *Ibid.*, 44.
12. to *id.* (November 20, 1922), *Ibid.*, 105.
13. to *id.* (January 5, 1923), *Ibid.*, 114-115.
14. to Allen Tate (May 16, 1922), *Ibid.*, 89.
15. to Selden Rodman (May 22, 1930), *Ibid.*, 351.
16. to Gorham Munson (April 27, 1928), *Ibid.*, 323.
17. to Morton Zabel (June 20, 1931), *Ibid.*, 374.
18. to Allen Tate (July 13, 1930), *Ibid.*, 353.
19. Hart Crane, "Modern Poetry," in *Revolt in the Arts,* Oliver M. Sayler, ed. (New York, 1930), 297-298.
20. to Allen Tate (July 13, 1930), in *Letters,* 354.
21. to Gorham Munson (February 11, 1921), *Ibid.*, 54.
22. to Allen Tate (March 1, 1924), *Ibid.*, 176.
23. to Gorham Munson (June 18, 1922), *Ibid.*, 92.
24. to *id.* (November 26, 1921), *Ibid.*, 92.
25. to *id.* (January 28, 1921), *Ibid.*, 52.
26. "A Discussion with Hart Crane," *Poetry,* 29 (October, 1926), 34-41.
27. to William Wright (October 17, 1921), in *Letters,* 67.
28. Hart Crane, "Sherwood Anderson," *Double Dealer,* 2 (July, 1921), 42-45.
29. Crane, "Modern Poetry," 295-296.
30. *Ibid.*, 296.
31. *Ibid.*
32. to William Wright (December 24, 1922), in *Letters,* 110.
33. to Eda Lou Walton (November 27, 1931), *Ibid.*, 389.
34. to Isidor Schneider (March 28, 1928), *Ibid.*, 322.
35. Crane, "Modern Poetry," 297.
36. to Allen Tate (July 19, 1922), in *Letters,* 94.
37. to Alfred Steiglitz (August 25, 1923); *Ibid.*, 145.
38. Horton, 132.
39. Cf. Brom Weber, *Hart Crane* (New York, 1948), 326.
40. to Gorham Munson (July 22, 1921), in *Letters,* 62.
41. to *id.* (May 16, 1922), *Ibid.*, 86-87.
42. to Yvor Winters (May 29, 1927), *Ibid.*, 299-300.
43. to Gorham Munson (January 15, 1920), *Ibid.*, 31.
44. to His Mother (November 16, 1924), *Ibid.*, 193.
45. to Charlotte Rychtarik (July 21, 1923), *Ibid.*, 140.
46. to Alfred Steiglitz (July 4, 1923), *Ibid.*, 139.
47. See Crane's comments on Maxwell Bodenheim's definition of poetry and its function in Weber, *Hart Crane,* 405.
48. to Gorham Munson (January 5, 1923), in *Letters,* 115.
49. The present writer has not undertaken an analysis of *The Bridge* except as the poem and its concepts fit in with Crane's larger views. Interested readers may find analyses of the poem in Horton,

Hart Crane, 193-275, and in Weber, Hart Crane, 251-378. Crane's own analysis of the poem can best be found in his letters of appropriate date, and especially in his reports to Otto Kahn in Letters, 240-242, 304-309.

50. Horton, 25.
51. to Waldo Frank (August 19, 1926), in Letters, 272-274.
52. to Otto H. Kahn (September 12, 1927), Ibid., 305.
53. to Waldo Frank (January 18, 1926), Ibid., 232.
54. to Gorham Munson (February 18, 1923), Ibid., 124-125.
55. Collected Poems, xxiii.
56. Ibid., xxv.
57. Ibid., xxvi.
58. D. S. Savage, "The Americanism of Hart Crane," Horizon, 5 (May, 1942), 306.
59. to His Mother (December 22, 1926), in Letters, 280.
60. Weber, Hart Crane, 325-328.
61. to Otto Kahn (September 12, 1927), in Letters, 308.
62. Horton, 269.
63. to Solomon Grunberg (February 8, 1932), in Letters, 396.
64. Collected Poems, xiv.
65. to His Father (January 12, 1924), in Letters, 170.
66. For an excellent assessment of Crane's work, see Horton, 303-319.

THOMAS WOLFE: THE WEB OF MEMORY

1. See Elizabeth Nowell, Thomas Wolfe (New York, 1960), passim.
2. Thomas Wolfe, Look Homeward, Angel (New York, 1929), 108.
3. Ibid., 276-277.
4. Thomas Wolfe, The Story of a Novel (New York, 1936), 4-5.
5. Thomas Wolfe's Letters to His Mother, John Skally Terry, ed. (New York, 1944), 76.
6. to His Mother (May, 1923), Ibid., 49-50.
7. Ibid., 53.
8. Look Homeward, Angel, 391.
9. to Henry and Natalie Volkening (May 14, 1930), in The Letters of Thomas Wolfe, Elizabeth Nowell, ed. (New York, 1956), 227.
10. Thomas Wolfe, You Can't Go Home Again (New York, 1940), 20-21.
11. Thomas Wolfe, Of Time and the River (New York, 1935), 79.
12. to Benjamin Cone (July 27, 1929), in Letters, 193.
13. to Margaret Roberts (August 11, 1929), Ibid., 198.
14. Look Homeward, Angel, 476.
15. Thomas Wolfe, The Web and the Rock (New York, 1939), 140.
16. Of Time and the River, 550-551.

17. *The Story of a Novel,* 21.
18. *Of Time and the River,* 170.
19. *The Web and the Rock,* 262.
20. to Maxwell Perkins (August 29, 1931), in *Letters,* 307.
21. *Look Homeward, Angel,* 1.
22. to His Mother (January 4, 1923), in *Thomas Wolfe's Letters to His Mother,* 42.
23. *The Story of a Novel,* 51-52.
24. *Look Homeward, Angel,* 192.
25. *The Web and the Rock,* 682.
26. *You Can't Go Home Again,* 321.
27. to Julian Meade (February 1, 1934), in *Letters,* 321-322.
28. *Of Time and the River,* 134-135.
29. *You Can't Go Home Again,* 499.
30. *Of Time and the River,* 81.
31. *The Web and the Rock,* 109.
32. to His Mother (September 25, 1926), in *Thomas Wolfe's Letters to His Mother,* 134.
33. to John Hall Wheelock (July 19, 1929), in *Letters,* 185.
34. to *id.* (June 24, 1930), *Ibid.,* 236.
35. to Maxwell Perkins (July 1, 1930), *Ibid.,* 239.
36. *The Web and the Rock,* 585.
37. *The Story of a Novel,* 38.
38. *The Web and the Rock,* 91.
39. to Margaret Roberts (March 7, 1938), in *Letters,* 729.
40. *The Web and the Rock,* 687.
41. *Of Time and the River,* 412-413.
42. *The Web and the Rock,* 401.
43. *You Can't Go Home Again,* 715.
44. *The Story of a Novel,* 29.
45. *Of Time and the River,* 669.
46. to Alfred S. Dashiell (November, 1930), in *Letters,* 273-274.
47. to Aline Bernstein (November 8, 1928), *Ibid.,* 150.
48. *Of Time and the River,* 669-670.
49. *The Story of a Novel,* 30.
50. *You Can't Go Home Again,* 730.
51. *Ibid.,* 321.
52. *Ibid.,* 397.
53. *Ibid.,* 328.
54. to Margaret Roberts (May 20, 1936), in *Letters,* 520.
55. to His Mother (September 21, 1931), in *Thomas Wolfe's Letters to His Mother,* 211-212.
56. *You Can't Go Home Again,* 738.
57. *The Story of a Novel,* 39.
58. to Belinde Jelliffee (February 1, 1938), in *Letters,* 707.

59. *You Can't Go Home Again*, 741.
60. *Ibid.*, 737.
61. to Alice Lewisohn (January, 1926), in *Letters*, 104.
62. to Maxwell Perkins (March 31, 1935), *Ibid.*, 449.
63. *You Can't Go Home Again*, 743.

Suggestions for Further Reading

STEPHEN CRANE

CRANE MADE the biographer's task exceedingly frustrating by writing few letters and by failing to date or save most of those he did write. Fortunately, however, these handicaps have not prevented a handsome and well-edited volume of his correspondence, R. W. Stallman and Lillian Gilkes (eds.), *Stephen Crane: Letters* (New York, 1960). Some of this correspondence had previously appeared, together with some critical appraisal, in R. W. Stallman (ed.), *Stephen Crane: An Omnibus* (New York, 1952). The student would do well to consult this excellent volume. No present biography of Crane is adequate, but the best known is Thomas Beer, *Stephen Crane* (New York, 1923), which is noted for its evocative style and shrewd judgments. The book is marred, however, by a certain flippancy of approach and by errors of fact, not all of which, it should be noted, are Mr. Beer's fault. The most recent biography is John Berryman, *Stephen Crane* (New York, 1950). Though often listless in style, it is accurate and is the product of an excellent critical mind. Lillian Gilkes, *Cora Crane* (Bloomington, Indiana, 1961), is the only biography of Crane's wife. It is of great interest in itself, and also contains much hitherto unused material on Crane. Daniel G. Hoffman, *The Poetry of Stephen Crane* (New York, 1957), is a thorough critical study, though, in the present author's view, Mr. Hoffman sometimes takes Crane's poetry too seriously, especially its potential symbolism. Crane usually wrote his poems hastily, often after betting on the speed of composition with a friend, and it is a moot question how seriously he took them. This does not, of course, deny their importance. Crane's works have been listed in A. W. Williams and Vincent Starrett, *Stephen Crane: A Bibliography* (Glendale, California, 1948).

Crane's work was collected once in a handsome though unannotated edition, Wilson Follett (ed.), *The Work of Stephen Crane*, 12 vols. (New York, 1925). Virtually all of Crane's work of interest to the student and reader appears in this collection. Two valuable memoirs contribute to the Crane literature: Corwin K. Linson, *My Stephen Crane* (Syracuse, 1958), a delightful and perceptive memoir by an artist friend of Crane's youth; and Edwin Cady and Lester G. Wells, (eds.), *Stephen Crane's Love Letters to Nellie Crouse* (Syracuse, 1954). These love letters, preceded by a valuable introduction, are among the most important of Crane's correspondence. While it is sometimes difficult to tell in them when he is serious about his life

165

and work and when he is posturing for a potential sweetheart, they are colorful and vital to the student of his life.

Crane awaits his biographer, and though such a work would be of major importance in American literary biography, the undertaking would be fraught with scholarly peril due to the fragmentary and conflicting sources and myths around the man and his work.

EDITH WHARTON

EDITH WHARTON was among the least demonstrative writers in recent American history. Armored in social convention and personally formidable, she did not invite or welcome the critical or informal examination of the biographer. Her letters have not been collected and few are available except in fragmentary quotations. There is no biography of her. The best source of information about her remains her memoirs, *A Backward Glance* (New York, 1934), which is among the most fascinating of American literary recollections both for what it says and for what it leaves unsaid. Percy Lubbock, *Portrait of Edith Wharton* (New York, 1947), contains a great deal of valuable memoir material, together with analysis by a close friend who himself possessed a fine critical mind.

In recent years Mrs. Wharton's work has attracted critical attention and to date two detailed studies have been produced. Blake Nevius, *Edith Wharton* (Berkeley and Los Angeles, 1955), is a well-written, though incomplete, discussion of her work. Mr. Nevius possesses a sensible critical faculty and has done much to draw attention to Mrs. Wharton's work. He discusses at length the major themes in her work. Mary Jones Lyde, *Edith Wharton: Convention and Morality in the Work of a Novelist* (Norman, Oklahoma, 1959), is a more detailed analysis of Mrs. Wharton's philosophy. Though it is often replete with technical jargon and is not on the whole brightly written, it makes a considerable contribution.

ELLEN GLASGOW

THERE IS no biography of Miss Glasgow, though she was on the whole not secretive about her work. Her letters, which tend to be frank and well written, have been collected in Blair Rouse (ed.), *The Letters of Ellen Glasgow* (New York, 1958). The collection is a balanced and well-edited sampling of her correspondence and is indispensable to the student. Miss Glasgow herself wrote an engaging and often disingenuous memoir, *The Woman Within* (New York, 1954). A judicious reading between the lines suggests a great deal about this fascinating woman's inner life. She also felt obliged to collect her own criticisms of her work, *A Certain Measure* (New York, 1943). This little book should be better known, for it offers a fascinating glimpse of an author's mind at work in assessing her own aims and place in American literature.

She has not attracted critics, though one suspects that her reputation is now on the incline, for she is at last being recognized as more than a regional writer. The one full analysis of her work is of recent date, Frederick P. W. McDowell, *Ellen Glasgow and the Ironic Art of Fiction* (Madison, Wisconsin, 1960). Though Mr. McDowell is a fine technical critic and offers an intensive analysis, the book does not descend into the technical jargon that overgrows so much modern criticism. It is on the whole well written and acute in its observations. Louis D. Rubin, "Miss Ellen," in *No Place on Earth: Ellen Glasgow, James Branch Cabell, and Richmond-in-Virginia* (Austin, Texas, 1959), is a slender but fine work by a major American critic. Readable, penetrating, and surprisingly inclusive despite its brevity, it is an admirable discussion of some of the basic themes in Miss Glasgow's work, and offers an explanation of her sense of isolation, together with an assessment of her importance.

WILLA CATHER

WILLA CATHER can hardly be called the scholar's friend; her will expressly forbids the quotation of any of her correspondence, thus placing all future biographers at an almost impossible disadvantage. This reflects her suspicion of historians and critics, whom she often confused with newspaper reporters, whom she despised in turn. The prohibition extends to all manner of reproduction; her works are not available for use as vehicles for motion pictures, the stage, television, recordings, or radio, a result of her acute distaste for loud radios and her disillusionment on seeing the scenario for one of her works which had been purchased by a Hollywood studio. She was, to say the least, in dead earnest about her work and was very concerned about the manner in which it would be presented to future generations. She was also one of those now old-fashioned people who believed that writers' works should be read, not seen on film.

Nonetheless, E. K. Brown, *Willa Cather* (New York, 1953), published by and written with the assistance of her long-time friend and publisher, Alfred Knopf, is a judicious and thorough study. It tells us about all we can expect to know of her private life, and includes sagacious and sensible analyses of her works. Mr. Brown and other scholars have been helped by Miss Cather herself in two very outspoken and delightful collections of essays, *Not Under Forty* (New York, 1936) and *On Writing* (New York, 1949). Miss Cather was a very determined and outspoken woman, especially on art and good writing, and these attributes of her personality did not diminish with age, as these essays show.

A number of memoirs are also of help to the student. Miss Cather's closest friend and long-time companion, Miss Edith Lewis, wrote a fine brief sketch of her to be used by E. K. Brown, and which was subsequently published by Mr. Knopf as *Willa Cather Living* (New York, 1953). Miss Lewis's book is highly readable, brief, and contains very shrewd and candid analyses of Miss Cather's personality and work. It is in no sense servile flattery, the last thing Willa Cather would have tolerated. Elizabeth Shepley Sargent, *Willa Cather, A Memoir* (Philadelphia, 1953), is also the report of a friend. Much of it is irrelevant, but it also contains many anecdotes and judgments that are of interest and use. It is far more critical of Miss Cather than any other friend's memoir.

The most formidable critical study of her work is John H. Randall, III, *The Landscape and the Looking Glass* (Boston, 1960). Covering all her major work, the book offers a general interpretation of her writing and is written in the best tradition of technical scholarship. The present writer feels that it inclines too much toward a symbolic interpretation of her work and misses the point of her writing in some instances by insisting that she was alienated from her world and unfulfilled in her private life. It is, nonetheless, basic to the critic. David Daiches, *Willa Cather: A Critical Introduction* (Ithaca, New York, 1951), is an earlier appreciation of her work which began a revival of critical interest. It is neither all-inclusive nor technical, but has much to recommend it. Josephine Jessup, *The Faith of Our Feminists* (New York, 1950), offers a brief essay on Miss Cather, and compares her work with that of Ellen Glasgow and Edith Wharton.

SHERWOOD ANDERSON

THERE IS no adequate biography of Sherwood Anderson, and thus one of the most human, genial, and attractive modern American writers still awaits his biographer. His letters, a delight to read and often revealing, have been collected in a well-annotated edition by Howard Mumford Jones and Walter B. Rideout (eds.), *The Letters of Sherwood Anderson* (Boston, 1953). The letters are quite frank and are the starting point for any study of Anderson's work. His own *Memoirs* (New York, 1941), written shortly before his death, are fascinating, presenting as they do not only a wealth of information on his life, but also on the eras and areas in which he had lived. Unfortunately, even more the case here than in most memoirs, these are not always accurate in detail, though the general picture they present is true enough. Anderson's memory often played tricks on him and he was given to embellishment of the past. The only biography of him is Irving Howe, *Sherwood Anderson* (New York, 1951), which, while written with stolidity and common sense, is incomplete and misses much of Anderson's warmth and essential humanity. Because of his earthiness and humanity, and the rather small framework in which he worked, Anderson has not attracted technical critics. He was not given to symbolism or jargon. When the accounts of recent American literature are tallied up, however, he will be found far more important than critical opinion now holds.

HART CRANE

UNLIKE OTHER figures in this volume, Hart Crane is the subject of one of the finest biographies done in American literature, Philip Horton, *Hart Crane* (New York, 1937). Long out of print, it has recently been reissued by The Viking Press and should be read by every student of modern American poetry. Written with great compassion and restraint and often in a moving style, it is a model of clarity and common sense. Crane's frank and sometimes verbose letters have been collected by Brom Weber (ed.), *The Letters of Hart Crane 1916-1932* (New York, 1952), and are also of great use to students of modern American poetry. H. D. Rowe, *Hart Crane: A Bibliography* (Denver, 1955), is a convenient list of most recent criticism on Crane. Brom Weber, *Hart Crane* (New York, 1948), is a full-length critical study of Crane's poetry but suffers from a pedestrian style, far too much technical matter, and confusion. It fails to make any full assessment of Crane's total vision as revealed in his work. L. S. Dembo, *Hart Crane's Sanskrit Charge: A Study of The Bridge* (Ithaca, 1960) is a somewhat slow-paced but perceptive study of Crane's total vision and the sources of his work. Crane's poems have been collected as *The Collected Poems of Hart Crane* (New York, 1933). It is distressing to realize that this slender volume is the life work of a major modern poet, and that in his lifetime he probably received less than five hundred dollars for all its contents.

THOMAS WOLFE

OF ALL MEN, Thomas Wolfe should least need a biographer in view of the quantity of his autobiographical writing. This has not deterred scholars, however, who realize that there is really no such thing as critical autobiography. Elizabeth Nowell, *Thomas Wolfe* (New York, 1960), thus answers the need for a full-length life of this major figure. Based on Wolfe's work and correspondence, it is both biographical and critical. The criticism to be leveled against it, oddly enough, is that it fails to reveal much of Wolfe's private life and the sources of his writing.

Wolfe's own letters have been collected by Elizabeth Nowell, editor of *The Letters of Thomas Wolfe* (New York, 1956), a monumental tribute to the man and his work. Like his writings, Wolfe's letters were frank and really an autobiography in themselves. The letters in John Skally Terry (ed.), *Thomas Wolfe's Letters to His Mother* (New York, 1944), are a convenient source for information about his youth and family life. Wolfe's book *The Story of a Novel* (New York, 1935) offers a good glimpse into his method of work and general ideas.

Herbert Muller, *Thomas Wolfe* (Norfolk, Connecticut, 1947), is the only real critical study of Wolfe's work, and despite its brevity is an admirable effort. Louis Rubin, *Thomas Wolfe: The Weather of His Youth* (Baton Rouge, Louisiana, 1953), is another finely written piece of criticism by a major critic of Wolfe's formative period. Richard Walser (ed.), *Thomas Wolfe: Biographical and Critical Selections* (Cambridge, Massachusetts, 1953), presents the work of numerous critics of Wolfe in one book and is a good starting place for any critical work. Oscar Cargill and Thomas Clark Pollock (eds.), *The Correspondence of Thomas Wolfe and Homer Andrew Watt* (New York, 1954), and the same editors' *Thomas Wolfe at Washington Square* (New York, 1954), offer interesting insights. Pamela Johnson, *Hungry Gulliver* (New York, 1948), is a slender but good study by an English critic.

The Wolfe family has furnished many memoirs, which are to a large extent repetitive. Hayden Norwood, *The Marble Man's Wife* (New York, 1947), is a biography-memoir of Wolfe's mother. Mabel Wolfe Wheaton, *Thomas Wolfe and His Family* (New York, 1961), written by his sister, is filled with anecdotes, pictures, and recollections.

AMERICAN CENTURY SERIES

Distinguished paperback books in the fields of literature and history.